OMENSETTER'S LUCK

a novel by
William H. Gass

A SIGNET BOOK

Published by
THE NEW AMERICAN LIBRARY

SIGNET TRADEMARK REG. U.S. PAT. OFF. AND FOREIGN COUNTRIES
REGISTERED TRADEMARK—MARCA REGISTRADA
HECHO EN CHICAGO, U.S.A.

SIGNET BOOKS are published by
The New American Library, Inc.
1301 Avenue of the Americas, New York, New York 10019

PRINTED IN THE UNITED STATES OF AMERICA

OMENSETTER'S LUCK

"*Gass has written a book to set beside the fables of destroyed innocence that are the peculiar triumphs of American fiction. The events he gives us are larger than life and far, far stranger. . . . Those of us who lament the retreat of the novel should welcome this book.*"
　　—Geoffrey A. Wolff, *Washington Post*

"One would be criminally tone-deaf and almost snowblind not to register the sonic and visual brilliance of the language."
　　　　—Paul West, *Book Week*

"*It leaves the deepest mark, demonstrating once again that the novel is both a form of wisdom and a means of attaining it.*"
　　　　—Roger Shattuck,
　　The New York Review of Books

"*Omensetter's Luck* is the work of a totally committed, totally uncompromising and extraordinarily gifted writer."
　　　　—Walker Percy

"*William Gass has a great deal to say. And he says it feverishly with an excitement of words too long absent from the novel. . . . Omensetter's Luck is a stunning book. . . . William Gass hews his words of thunder.*"
　　—Dayton Rommel, *Chicago Daily News*

WILLIAM H. GASS
was born in Fargo, North Dakota, in 1924. He was educated at Kenyon College, Ohio Wesleyan and Cornell, where he received his Ph.D. His stories have appeared in many literary reviews and in *The Best American Short Stories* of 1959, '61 and '62. Mr. Gass is Associate Professor of Philosophy at Purdue University.

Other Outstanding Novels
in SIGNET Editions

UNDER THE VOLCANO *by Malcolm Lowry*
The story of a man's efforts to defeat the sinister forces
within himself. "One of the towering novels of this
century."—*The New York Times*   (#Q2902—95¢)

DEATH ON THE INSTALLMENT PLAN *by Louis-Ferdinand
Céline.* New translation *by Ralph Manheim*
The first complete and unexpurgated English version
of a novel that shocked the literary underground in
Europe and revolutionized contemporary fiction. The
father of black humor fiction, Céline's novel is rich
in characterizations drawn from the French country-
side and the Parisian marketplaces. (#Y3000—$1.25)

YOU CAN'T GO HOME AGAIN *by Thomas Wolfe*
The turbulent years of the depression and the gathering
storm clouds prior to World War II provide the back-
ground for Thomas Wolfe's brilliant last novel, the
story of a sensitive writer trying to see life clearly and
to convey the unvarnished truth.   (#Q3025—95¢)

ISLANDIA *by Austin Tappan Wright*
A young American goes to live in a 20th century
Utopian society where the people are technologically
primitive, but highly sophisticated in their understanding of life's meaning. "One of the most remarkable examples of ingenuity in the history of literary
invention."—Clifton Fadiman   (#Y2870—$1.25)

to, for,
and because of
MARY PAT

The editors of *Accent,* when I most needed it, gave me generously of their friendship. The first two sections of this novel, in somewhat different form, appeared originally in their magazine, and although the magazine has ceased to exist, I like to think that I shall always be writing for it.

I am also grateful to the Purdue Research Foundation for a grant which enabled me to finish this book.

The Triumph of
Israbestis Tott

Now folks today we're going to auction off Missus Pimber's things. I think you all knew Missus Pimber and you know she had some pretty nice things. This is going to be a real fine sale and we have a real fine day for it. It may get hot, though, later on, so we want to keep things moving right along. And now I'm going to begin the sale with the things back here by the barn. You've all had a chance to look at everything so let's bid right out for these fine things and keep things moving right along. The sale is cash as usual and Missus Grady is inside to take care of that. The ladies of the Methodist Church are kindly providing the lunch. You can see their tables across there in Missus Root's lot and I know you'll want to help all these ladies just as they are helping you. It'll be good I know. All right I'm going to begin the sale back here so if you folks will follow me we'll get started.

It was his first excursion. He had tottered about in the yard for several weeks despite the high grass, and for three months he had practiced in his bedroom and in the living room and halls, but he was going to try himself in earnest now. He'd said he'd see the summer under and he had. The grass was burned. There were flecks of yellow in the cotton trees. The weeds were wilted and long in seed. Where were all his friends?

Once he went out in the morning down the street and everyone was up and he knew everyone. He could hear the anvil ring and Mat's mild voice between the ringings singing to the horses. You could shout from one end of town to the other and be heard. And in the morning Mat was like a bell.

Israbestis rubbed his cheek. Who was the man with the gold teeth?

He was out of touch. He used to stop at Mossteller's place. Mossteller was a quiet fellow but he loved to joke. He used to stop in Lloyd Cate's on the way. Lloyd would put his foot up on the stove and say he'd overet himself and swear that it was cold if it was May. He and Lloyd would talk until the train whistled for Gilean. When the whistle blew a second time, Lloyd would take his foot down and they would both go and stand in front of the store and stretch. Well, Lloyd would say, I've got to get at it. Israbestis would shake his head sympathetically and walk off to the station.

People passed impatiently around him. They walked so fast. A crowd was gathering by the barn. Its paint was scaling badly. The roof sagged toward a thorn tree. I caught a kite in there, he said. The main door hung by one hinge. Windows were broken and the darkness jagged. The house, however, was square and firm, beautiful everywhere, without a crack, each brick made by hand and laid by a master. The sound of the crowd grew as he came slowly along. All along the front were tall narrow windows Lucy Pimber showed candles in while it snowed on the carolers.

Sam raised his hand and peered between his missing fingers. Everybody laughed. People inched among the chairs and couches on the lawn or sat in rocking chairs and talked or leaned against divans and talked, shading their eyes with their hands. They handled vases, fingered silver spoons, smoothed hand-quilted quilts. On the shaded porch the women squeezed themselves between card tables set with tilting towers of china cups, bubbled colored glass and painted plates. In the back, by the barn, the men gathered in serious pairs to smoke, heft heavy implements, and think. Under the lamps at a side of the house, young children sat and fussed with the laces of their shoes. Sam Peach yelled, looked at his fingers gone, and spat. Everybody laughed, and he held up between his missing fingers a ball of twine and with his full-fingered hand a fine old saw, a rope, a rubber mat, a can of lime; while in high-backed and formal chairs, beneath the scattered shade of half-dead elms, old ladies and old canes leaned together and nodded jerkily. Too bad, they said. Too bad. Too bad.

Not much of a woman. Mean, thin, and silent. Samantha's friend. He excused himself when bumped.

I saw this house go up, Israbestis said. First on the street.

That so?

I saw the cellar dug and the first brick laid. I was in this house the very day Bob Stout, who built her, fell from the Methodist steeple.

That so?

He fell on the iron fence that used to go around it. Parson Peach, he'd just come then—no, no, it was longer ago than that, Huffley's day it was—Huffley was a builder—took Furber's place—anyway, Huffley had the fence torn down.

That so?

It was funny about the fence because—

Lutie Root? It was her lot across the street. Was that the one her old man got in a swap for a flock of geese? Yes. There was a story. No. That wasn't Lutie Root. She had a harder eye, as hard an eye as her old man had, like translucent rock. She went in the winter. He'd forgot. Hard eye and all, paler and paler till it went out. Who were all these people?

Sam Peach held up a set of jelly molds, a length of screen, an antique drinking cup he claimed was pewter but was not, a box of bolts, a rake, rope in a tangled figure-eight. Sam wiped his face with a spotted cloth he'd knotted to his neck and nodded to the crowd. He exclaimed how hot it was, remarked how hard he worked, in what repair a wooden wringer was. His face was flushed from shouting and the waving of his arms and while he talked he switched from cheek to cheek tobacco with his tongue and when he spat he made a wide and running stain upon the ground. Sam smiled his dark brown teeth. He pointed to a flaw. He threw apart his arms. His nose twitched with harmless honesty. He told what he would use a crooked miter for if he had one, and said how much his missing fingers brought the day he'd knocked them down, and how he'd sold the saw, too, for a dollar more. Everybody laughed and bid. Sam tipped his broad-brimmed hat. He winked, and the friendly lines by his eyes drew in. His wife marked down the sale. They both moved on and with them moved the crowd and everybody's laughter.

I don't know that fellow, Israbestis thought.

I saw this house go up, Israbestis said. First on the street.

Oh?

They built things those days—

The summer had been hot. The ground was hard. The drive was dusty. Cars had been driven in the drive and dust raised. The dust had settled on the grass by the drive and turned it gray. Children had written their names on the tops of dressers. Wasn't anybody going to shake his hand?

Quite a sale, Israbestis said.

Lot of junk.

Oh no, not—

He thought he knew the fellow with the black cheroot. God if he didn't look like Hog Bellman. Israbestis felt his stomach tumble. Gas. Italians, he'd heard, had bought it. It was such a big house. Somehow he forgot there were Italians. In those days there weren't many. Sometimes they came to repair the railroad. Or were they Mexicans? Sicilians? Did it make a difference? It always seemed so far away for Italians. There were Italians of course. More and more. And now in this house that used to blaze with lights.

You seen Miss Elsie Todd?

Who?

Maybe McCormick or Fayfield? They used to come in a lot.

Hog Bellman. A high white hat on him. My god. Hunting in the marshes in the time of high water. Mat making them be quiet. Not a bird but the rush of water. Hog Bellman. My god. There's the chief. Good.

You get around pretty good, Israbestis said.

I get around fine. I come to all of them. I never miss a one. Rain or shine. I never miss. Don't see anybody much any more. Don't see you much, Tott, been sick?

Been fine. Just fine.

Wops got this place. Going to tear it down. I had no truck with them. Troublemakers. They'd come to town nights and make trouble. I got on to them quick enough. When I was chief I kept things peaceful and the jail full. See the papers?

But Bob Stout built this house.

I remember the time they was fixing the bridge down to Windham. A clutch of them was down there—cheap labor and all and I always said they was cheap too, like Mexicans—and there was a clutch of them big ones. They was big and burnt like niggers from working in the sun. Some of them even was niggers I guess. Yes. We never had any niggers in this town till now.

There was Flack.

Who?

Jefferson Flack.

Soon as the sun came down they was at it. Came in here by the wagonload.

I was here—I lived here then.

You was? Of course you was. Well they used to come in piled up like logs on them wagons and when they let the tailgate down it was like letting a load of logs loose.

They would jump out of the wagons as soon as they got to the edge of town. There was one who—

All at once they would pour out. Har! They was big ones!

Big ones, Israbestis thought. There was only one big one. He and his huge hee-haw. Who was it always called poor Brackett Omensetter that—the huge hee-haw? Sometimes the walls in Israbestis' room closed at their corners like a book and would not let him remember. Now the sun drove his eyes down. There was nothing to see at his feet. It could have been Jethro Furber, but it wasn't. Hee-haw.

You don't look up to snuff Tott. Been sick?

Not a day.

Seen Cate?

Ah—no. He's still . . . ?

Saw him at the farm. Too bad. Too bad. He's real bad. Pretty old you know. Pretty old. Shakes bad. Shook the whole time I was there. Terrible. Won't last long. I had a bitch did that as soon she whelped. Her jaw bobbled and her teeth clacked—constant . . .

Dull old fool, Israbestis thought, he's got no flair. I know these stories. Most of them are mine, my mouth gave each of them its shape, but I've no teeth to chew my long sweet youth again. A terse man years ago and sheriff after Curt Chamlay had angered his badge in the snowy weeds, the fellow never drew a breath in his old age, but watered everyone he knew with words, haphazardly, like Israbestis did himself, he was afraid. Long? sweet? The heat . . . it was the heat. They had come to the train to meet the Reverend Jethro Furber: Samantha, Henry, Lucy Pimber, both Spinks, Gladys Chamlay, others, Rosa Knox and Valient Hatstat. There had been quarrels over that, oh god, such resourceful bickering. Well he didn't sweat as much now as he had then, that was one thing. The steam from the engine had seemed to issue from the ground. Neat, he remembered thinking as Furber stepped down, and then the Reverend's arm reached out and bit him. Howdju. He supposed he flinched. Neat. Neat, stiff, pressed, black, burning. The Reverend grabbed at Henry, Henry mumbling. The wheels of the engine creaked, steam threatened the cars, and they all retreated awkwardly toward the station, Furber bowing briskly. He's tiny, he's just *tiny*, Samantha whispered, and their new minister suddenly ran into the station where, through the window, they saw him climbing the stairs.

. . . well you was never married was you? Har. Well you got a pension I hear, and that house. Us men die before our women usually. You don't have to worry about that. There's

Samantha though, ain't there? Well you got that pension and that house.

Yes.

Lloyd's got the shakes.

They would sit in the boat and fish in the river. The trees hung over and shaded the sides. They would drift in and out of the shade, eddying with the river, watching the cork float, their broad hats tilted, shading their eyes. It would be pleasantly cool in the shady places where the roots of the willows and the beeches came mossy to the riverside, and the water was black by the boat. They would get caught up in a curl of the river, the water still and black by the boat, until Lloyd would reach up and pull on a limb and the boat would coast out into the sun again where the water sparkled and slapped gently against the hull. It was warm and comfortable and there weren't many fish, but just slow and easy drifting down the checkered river.

Careful Lacy. He'd nearly forgot. Ford and Jasper and Willie Amsterdam. Most people didn't know about that. Careful must have been sixty then. He fought Morgan's men. The fire was a great kite flying to the river. Careful Lacy. He'd nearly forgot. Had an ass like an ape.

Like fishing, said Israbestis Tott.

Some.

Fishing's fun.

I like sledding better.

Sledding's fun too.

You're pretty old. How old are you?

Pretty old.

I bet. What do you do now you're so old.

I was postmaster once.

Not really.

I was. I was postmaster for this whole town. I had the job all by myself. I did it all.

You ain't postmaster now.

No. I was once. I used to be.

My dad says I'm the busiest he ever saw.

I bet you are. What do you do?

I live in a tree.

What kind of a tree?

A high tree. It goes way up into the air and you can see clean to Columbus.

That's a good way.

Oh it's awful high. A thousand feet. Well, good-bye.

The boy had vaulted a bench. It had Henry Pimber's buttocks on it. Israbestis considered; shook his head. The sun, too . . . no shade anywhere. He could have told that boy

14

the story of the man who went to pieces, he'd have liked that; or the story of the high and iron fence. He'd begin it, gently, and then the boy would say:

Why'd they want a fence, though, anyway?

And then he'd say:

It was the kind of fence that a good stick would make a good loud noise on if you was to run it along.

Oh.

That was the kind of fence they wanted—a high iron one with tall sharp pickets close together that would ring loud and handsome with a stick. But not everyone wanted a fence just like that.

Why not?

Well some thought it would be nice to have a fence with deers in it or trees like the one that used to be around Whittacker's, the undertaker's.

I don't think much of that.

I never did either, Israbestis thought. I never did. And boys were all like that. Pop. Well. Even my own ears are weary.

There were rows of straights and rockers, kitchen and parlor chairs, both painted and upholstered, rows of empty old embraces. Everybody wants it new, he said. Then he saw where he could sit: on the slope of the cellar door. She put up a lot of vegetables and fruit and things, Mrs. Pimber did. Every year. Now for myself, I'd want a house that had a little more than my weak poozly tracks all through it. I'd want some corners other folks had warmed. I'd sit in my chair in the quiet by the window, and watch the purpling air, the lazy hats and horses, and I'd think back on . . . well, the seasons of families, the passage of blood through the house, just like, you know, it passes through me while I'm standing here. I'm not too old for that. He should probably have apologized for his teeth. The man's sleeves were too long, they needed an elastic. There were good days, though, days when he remembered mostly drugstores. A bee flew by his face. Omensetter was a wide and happy man. Fact. At least he had that straight. And in the mornings Mat was like a bell. But Mat had finally faded like a sound. Okay, okay, just let me ease . . . myself . . . The sun slid from his back, and it was like swimming for a moment—that moment of cool green coasting when you've jumped. He closed his eyes, but the lids flamed. Furber never listened either. He declaimed. Tott sighed. Swimming took away your weight. Was that the reason he loved the smell of drugstores, and all those drawers? It was Omensetter's luck. Likely. To lose the heaviness of life. That Furber fellow, for instance, was

15

nothing but bones, and even those you could have wrapped in a hankie. Yet he weighed a ton. Didn't he, by george! a ton.

Now folks we've got four fine beds here and we're going to sell them all. Kids, don't bounce on the beds. These are fine beds and the springs and mattresses all come with them. You can feel what shape they're in. It's first rate. Here's your chance to get a real good bed. Say can everybody hear me? There's too much talking, ladies, please. All right, fine. We might as well start right here and go right down the line. This here's solid cherry, and isn't she a beauty! There, just feel that mattress. Looks like new. Lot of use in them yet. Of course if you don't want to use the springs and mattress that is on it, you don't have to. You can put anything on it you want to. Look at that wood. Well now what'll you say to start for this cherry bedstead and this fine mattress and good springs. Who'll say twenty-five?

Gaiety was continuous.

Don't talk to dirty old men.

Henry Pimber had lain with lockjaw in that bed, and the Reverend Jethro Furber had planted prayers around it like a hedge, and later Israbestis had followed him downstairs, the minister cursing Nature, Man, and God, at every step.

Israbestis moved his feet with effort. He was tired and stiff. He made his way slowly to the back of the house through the crowd flung out now like a ragged shirt and cupped some water from an outside tap, rinsing the dust from his mouth. He spat and watched his spit ball up in the dirt under burned-out marigolds. At the frayed edge of the crowd the chief was gesturing to a man whom Israbestis didn't know. The chief held out his badge. The man craned to see Sam Peach. The chief touched the man's arm. The man moved away, turning his side, craning to see Sam Peach. The chief's badge gleamed. Israbestis counted balls of spit and made, with difficulty, three. His dark room now seemed cool and restfully confining. You could imagine maps in the wallpaper. The roses had faded into vague shells of pink. Only a few silver lines along the vanished stems and in the veins of leaves, indistinct patches of the palest green, remained—the faint suggestion of mysterious geography. A grease spot was a marsh, a mountain or a treasure. Israbestis went boating down a crack on cool days, under the tree boughts, bending his head. He fished in a chip of plaster. The perch rose to the bait and were golden in the sunwater. Specks stood for cities; pencil marks were bridges; stains and shutter patterns laid out fields of wheat and oats and corn. In the shadow of a corner the crack issued into a great sea.

There was a tear in the paper that looked exactly like a railway and another that signified a range of hills. Some tiny drops of ink formed a chain of lakes. A darker decorative strip of Grecian pediments and interlacing ivy at the ceiling's edge kept the tribes of God and Magog from invasion. Once he had passed through it to the ceiling but it made him dizzy and afraid. Shadows moved quixotically over the whole wall, usually from left to right in tall thin bands, and sank behind a bureau or below the bed or disappeared suddenly in a corner.

Lying there staring at the wall in the partial darkness hour on hour, the pain rising as periodically as high water and leaving only a slight backwash of relief when it receded, Israbestis lamented bitterly his lack of education. He sent himself on journeys with an effort that brought sweat to his brow and moistened his palms and the back of his ears. He took ship down the faint crack rivers. He cut his way through matted, tortuous jungles designated by the pale leaves. He trudged across vast blanks of desert and drank thirstily at muddy holes. The days that he was in the wall he thought of himself primarily as a sailor. He conjured up bright images of sail, green swells on the reaches of the ocean, the brown slabs of river mouths and the awesome blue chop and the trailing spray of troubled weather. Climbing the shrouds, the springs of the bed squeaking like a rolling deck and hull and like the tackle in the block, he would sight a dark cloud puffing from the horizon. Funneling up, it would run at the ship and Israbestis would hitch himself on his elbow, waving his other arm free of the clothes, and shout, "Look out, she's coming on, look out, look out," for he knew no nautical terms and nothing of seamanly action. Pain would storm at his eyes. Sweat would drip from his nose. "She's a blower, captain, aye, she's a roller, captain," Israbestis would cry. "The worst I've seen in these seas." The hiss of his words was like the spray from the bow. Israbestis screamed in order to be heard above the wind in the rigging that was howling in the shrouds and through the ports of the ship. Then all of a sudden it would be gone. He would watch the paling cloud and the dimpled water disappear before he fell, for a moment, asleep.

In this way he visited the ports of the world. He was a Chinese, a Hindoo, a sheik; he rode upon wild Asian horses and on the back of elephants in India, while on camels he crossed the African wastes; but the farther he traveled, the more bizarre and remarkable his adventures, the less satisfying was his life in the wall. More and more his fancy had to supply his vision with its objects, had to make up even the course and color of the sun, the feel of the ground, so different everywhere, and above all, the smells that inhabited the corners of the earth. He was conscious, always, of the inadequacy of his details, the vagueness of his pictures, the falsehood in all his implicit etceteras, because he knew nothing, had studied nothing, had traveled nowhere. Consequently he was never fully in the wall, he was partly clenched in the bedclothes, clawing at the skin of his legs and biting his arms. He was only partly bowed by rain or sand or sleet, crouched before the attack of lions or wild tribesmen, swimming for his life. The pain struck without obstruction then, and he closed like a spider on it.

On better days he left the wall although he always began in it. Gently closing his lids to allow an eyelash of light, he would push off from the bank and coast by the torn hills, poling the grease-spot marsh, and by the time he had baited his hook and dropped his line in the plaster chip he was in the history of his life, out of the wall, in the old slow world. He sat by Lloyd Cate's stove or he leaned back on a bench on Lloyd Cate's porch in finer weather. He took his early morning walk through the town, the anvil singing out, and he went to the depot three times a day for the mail. He would stop at Mosssteller's to talk or at the bakery, passing the time in the pleasantest way with news of people, conditions of the land or crops, predictions of the weather. All his friends were clear in his imaginings. He knew them by their dress, by the mannerisms of their walk, by their characteristic tilts and gestures. His dreams were not embarrassed by clichés, but in each he always knew the precise feel of the air, what manner of birds were singing, the position of the sun, the kind of cloud, the form of emotion in himself and others, and every felicity of life. As his friends approached he called out gaily to them. "Hi there, Pete. 'Morning, Michael, Billy. Well if it ain't Claude Spink, by god, and Nichol Ames." They came to visit in his illness. Hog Bellman. Bullet in his back. Careful Lacy. Pants undone, silly grin on his face. Bob Stout with nails in his mouth. Samantha. Sister. Like a rod in watered silk. Tale after tale he told, each many times over, getting them right or trying to, amazed at what he forgot and what he remembered. There was a secret in every one and he tried to discover it. When the Hen Woods burned, for instance, the way he told it you could taste the ashes in Careful Lacy's mouth. Indecision was put as plain as a cow in a field. Luke Ford. Ben Jasper. Willie Amsterdam. And then May Cobb. Of course he hadn't, but he knew what it was like to be the man who'd had her. God. Not pretty. Not round in the rump or full in the bust, either, but god! Every line of her

18

was essential. He put that plain too. He made it seem as if the juices of the body would all squeeze out. He often saw her up to her elbows in cream. Her twisted mouth. May I have more punch she asked politely. Damn loud band.

Careful Lacy was riding the back roads; the fire was a cloud. He knew the secret to that. He walked through the whole of his storied past, greeting everyone: Kick Skelton, Eliza Martin, May Cobb. He kissed the pits of her neck. There was Brackett Omensetter, Lucy Pimber, Lemon Hank. And all the dogs. And all the cats and cattle. Hog Bellman with a knife. Swine and sheep. Madame DuPont Neff, from Paris, and her udders. Something French. But best of all May Cobb and the blades of her shoulders. His eyes would open sometimes and Israbestis would climb like a well young man from his bed and walk down the echoing halls. He would go all over the house, in a fever, putting his hands to furniture and geegaws until his hands were black. Sometimes he climbed to the attic and felt the relics. Other times he went to the barn in back or to the basement. But always he would weary at last and drop to the floor on his knees, wherever he was, weeping noisily. It was then that he would have his worst attacks.

Now folks we've got this china here. You all know what Missus Pimber did with paints. A lot of you I know been waiting just for this. It's plenty hot so we'll get right along. We got here a decorated—this a toothbrush holder, Grace?—a hand-painted toothbrush holder my wife says. It's china, and it's signed by Missus Pimber with her name. See there? Now everybody'll want this and so what'll it be, what? All right a dollar, a dollar I have to start, one dollar, so I have one, one, who'll say two, two, I have two over there, right off, and everybody wants it, now do I hear three, that's three thank you now four and who says four, four, and who says fifty then, fifty. I have three and who says fifty, three twenty-five—look, that's not much to ask for a hand-painted toothbrush holder—once more and you're out. Three twenty-five? twenty-five? Three, then, it's three to that lady over there thank you. Now we have here a fine china bowl, also hand painted, and it's a dilly. Hold it up there George so the folks can see it. That's a honey, ain't it, hay? What are them, birds? That's signed by Missus Pimber, too, right there. Hold it higher George so the folks can see it. Oh say now what'll it be to begin? See them birds? Ain't they pretty? What am I bid? Lots of mashed potatoes go in that, boys. So, so, so now, let's begin, and what'll you give for this hand-painted bowl?

Longlegs, like a small smooth pebble walking, crossed a

brick and stopped on a line of mortar. If he walks another row I'll get him, Israbestis thought, but the spider ran up three and sat, waving a thread-thin leg. Israbestis put the shadow of his hand over the spider. It rubbed its feet together. From the withered end of a marigold another spider swayed on a strip of silk. This one was small and black with yellow spots. Ants milled by the wall, chasing one another back and forth. Israbestis wiped his brow and leaned against the house. He could feel the blood beating in his stomach. Don't talk to dirty old men.

Pardon me. Maybe you can tell me how old that cradle is. The one by the churn there—there by the tree.

The young man's shadow darkened Israbestis' spider. It ran swiftly up two courses and halted in the sun. Israbestis followed the young man's finger and shook his head. I'll have to see, he said, though I most likely know it.

Don't take any trouble. I just thought you might know.

I watched this house go up. First on the street.

Really?

I saw the cellar dug and the first brick laid. As a matter of fact I was in this house the very day Bob Stout, who built her, fell from that steeple over there.

Really?

Quite a builder Bob was. You can see. Look at that brick. All hand made. He fell right on the iron fence that used to go around it. It was Saturday. Between Good Friday and Easter.

The Methodist? My wife and I go there.

Really? Well, that's the one—the one he fell from. Before that the Redeemer's church stood there. Or very near . . . very nearabouts.

Bending over the cradle was a young woman, plainly pregnant, who pushed at it with a cautious finger, her head swaying slightly as it rocked.

It's awful cute, she said.

Israbestis felt his stomach tumble. Gas, he decided. Israbestis knew the cradle of course, but how had Lucy Pimber got it? He struggled to recover himself.

That—that was Brackett Omensetter's cradle, Israbestis said. Missus Pimber—the woman of this house—never had any children herself.

And Israbestis continued to talk while he wondered. Had it lain in this house all these years? And what could it mean to her? how had she got it?

How old would you say, the young man said.

Pretty old. I guess it's pretty old. I don't know how long it was that Omensetter'd had it when he wagoned over. That was ... that was '90. Thereabouts.

But the Reverend Jethro Furber filled Tott's skin and clothing. He stood by the cradle, as dark as a corner, reciting—jingles. Tott's head hurt; there was pressure against the inside of his eyes. The child had died. But the child had survived.

He had a craftsman's hands—Omensetter had. He likely made it. Hands quick as cats. And there were two girls—he had two daughters when he came. Let's see. It must be ... The older one was nine. Wasn't she? Nine. Make it 1880 maybe.

Do you remember that?

Not well, Israbestis thought. Not well. Not well. Why? The child had survived and they had gone down river. But if the child had survived, they'd have taken the cradle with them.

I remember Omensetter coming, Israbestis managed. Everybody who lived here then remembers that.

What is it made of—pine?

Yes. Pine.

But the Reverend Jethro Furber fluttered in his clothes. It was hot, now, as winter. The steep sun was snowing. And holding his stomach, Jethro Furber began singing a song for Samantha:

> a greedy young spinster
> ate, live, a lobster
> and now every winter
> when she sits dinner
> as a kind of remonster
> he pinches her inner

This, Israbestis remembered. This, he heard clearly.

It's awful cute.

I don't think it'll go for much. Maybe we can get it. Come on. Hon?

I don't imagine anyone who remembers it will bid, Israbestis said.

Why not? It's sweet.

Too old, he thought. Too dead. Too shocked. Omensetter must have left the cradle behind—left it in the Perkins house—and sometime, closing up or renting out, Lucy Pimber found it there. And never said a word. These years.

It's a long story, Israbestis was saying, a long story. This is Brackett Omensetter's cradle. It's not a name that means anything to you, I imagine, but there are a few of us left, like old leaves, I guess—Israbestis cackled desperately—who were here when Omensetter drove his wagon into town. Nothing's ever happened like it. Not here. Nothing ever will, is my guess. Omensetter, now—he was—

Hon?

Too old, he thought. Too dead. Too shocked. The way he'd told it always, it was luck.

It had been a wet spring, you know, Israbestis continued—well, wetter than most you'd want to call wet—and the road from Windham to Gilean was all mud and running ruts and deep brown holes. There was hardly a day it didn't rain, but the day Brackett Omensetter drove over was as warm and clear as this. He had everything he owned piled up in the wagon with this cradle tied to the top of it, and nothing covered. That was the kind of fellow Brackett Omensetter was. He knew it wasn't going to rain again. He counted on his luck.

Don't mind my teeth, my mouth is—

Sam Peach came suddenly and people spilled around him. Israbestis was pushed from behind. Sam was talking in a loud voice and pointing to the churn. He moved the handle up and down. Israbestis struggled against the crowd. There were strange legs against his. He pushed to the edge, his stomach turning. Sam laughed uproariously. The crowd roared. The laughter fell on him like blows. A tall farmer clapped his hands and howled. Peach was selling the cradle. To perish with the owner, that was wise.

Israbestis rested under an elm that was dying of disease. Was that Mabel Fox? Mabel Fox's head was larger and her ears were a fox's ears. When he was a kid, and Mabel was a little girl, the boys used to say: do you know Mabel Fox? and then laugh raucously. They used to chant: Mabel Fox has ears like a fox; put her head in a box and let's throw rocks. That couldn't be Mabel Fox. Her head was too small. What had become of Mabel, he wondered. Put her head in a box. Dead likely—too. He stared at the ground until his vision blurred. Do you know Mabel Fox? He saw a blade of dry grass, suddenly, as something strange, not grass at all. It was like looking at a word until it melted. Mabel Fox has ears like a fox. The world seemed to dwindle in his vision of the blade. Then he reached down and snapped it off. Let's throw rocks. He held it for a moment on the tips of his fingers. It lifted, halted in the air, dropped between his feet. He studied its eaten edge, its blunted point. He carefully set his heel on one dead end.

Furber-like behavior. Tott laughed explosively, in pain.

There was the story of the man who went to pieces, and there was the story of the high and iron fence. There was the saga of Uncle Simon, the Hen Woods burning, and the hunt for Hog Bellman. He had them all. Hours, weeks, months—a life—they'd cost him. Were they all as wrong as the one about the cradle? Well, he'd said he'd see the summer under, and he had . . . a small success. He'd see . . . It was on the morning of the sixth of April . . . on the morning of the sixth . . . Dickie Frankmann found two of his Tamworth hogs with their throats cut. That made, between Huff and Staub and Gustin, eight in six days, and Ernie said Hog Bellman, mad as a man can be, had done it. Curtis Chamlay rode out to Frankmann's as he'd ridden out to Huff's and out to Staub's and Gustin's. Frankmann riding by him, standing in the stirrups too much. He looked at the carcasses and blood. There wasn't a print though the sty was mud and Chamlay's weight forced water to the edges of his boots. So far it's only Tamworths, Dickie Frankmann said, and there ain't many of them. What has a ghost got against English pigs?

The shoes in front of his were like his own. Black and cracked like his, they laced with hooks and went above the ankles. Soiled white cotton socks oozed out of the shoes and piled up into limp and shiny gray serge pants. The pants were dotted with grease spots. Dirt was caked in the wrinkles, the fly misbuttoned. Suspenders of yellow webbing and brown leather held the pants to a shrunken chest where a frayed, collarless, formal shirt bunched under them and under flowered blue elastic bands. Don't you hear good anymore, the chief shouted. A car backed roughly out the drive. The chief retreated, fanning the air. Israbestis blew the dust from his nostrils, but it lodged in his broken teeth and filmed his shoes. Israbestis rubbed the stubble on his chin. He sank to his back with a weary groan.

How big of a cat have you ever saw, the boy asked.

Well now I've seen some pretty big, said Israbestis Tott.

How big?

Oh let's see. There was Mossteller's cat—huge with yellow eyes—he was near twelve when he died and the size of a dog.

How big of a dog? As big as a pony?

Don't be silly. No cat's as big as that. I swear, though, Skelton's cat might of grown up to it, give him time and rats enough, where he hunted by the station. It was alive. At night stars were scattered in between the shed crates, all by twos, a mean red. Why I remember if you rattled a stone in there, there'd be a scuttering like leaves blown down a road by a strong wind. Skelton's cat would snarl at you for spoiling his stalk, and you'd see his eyes beam up sudden from on top of a box where he sat, lashing his tail, I figure, to the beating of his heart.

You can't hear that.

Of course you can't. I didn't say so. But cats have got the hunter's heart. If you knew how to, minding it ain't easy, not to be picked up like a marble and pocketed to home, you can hear them beat at dusk, just at the time when you can see through their swallowing eyes, if you look hard and straight in at them as they grow fat for the evening, and see backwards down their tight cat strings to their very hunger.

Honest?

You just listen. It ain't easy. Quieter than paws is all their inner talking; just the same, their hearts are speaking to the grass and to the falling dew and to the stone.

What do they say?

Nothing you can put in words. But you've seen cats and how they get low in the grass and put their eyes on what they're after. Have you seen them with their mouths aquiver and not a sound coming out? They want the whole world to be still while they move.

So the rat won't run?

Yes, certainly—so the rat won't run. So the bird won't fly either. So the longlegged hopper will brush his teeth and the goldfish float close to the claw water.

How old was Skelton's cat when he was near to a dog's weight?

Mossteller's cat?

Skelton's cat.

He was about the age I was then.

How old was that?

Fourteen maybe.

That ain't very old. Mine's twenty-nine.

Really? That old?

Well twenty-nine or thirty-three.

That's as old as I ever heard of.

I knew it.

But he lived too long and got too fat.

What happened to him?

There's a story in that.

I knew it.

I know you knew it.

Tell me the story, then. I like cats—soft ones anyway, that don't scratch.

Here was no soft cat, boy. No sir. Leather fur he had, and as for scratching, why he could leave his mark on brick as easy, well, as a rake makes ruts in the spring dirt.

Boy. I knew it.

I know you did.

Please—tell me the story then, if he had leather for his fur—boy. I like that. I like stories about Kick Skelton.

Did I tell you about Kick Skelton? He's the man who went to pieces.

Sure you did.

No I didn't.

Yes you did—did his cat go hunting with him like his dog did?

Just wait. Like I said, Kick's cat lived by the station. He lived around it in the spring and fall and summer like birds live around their nests. I suppose like rats around trash too, because they did. Maybe Kick's cat didn't live by the station at all. Maybe, because the dump was near, and the rats came to live around it, Kick's cat came to live around the rats, and the station just happened to be there. I was never sure about that. Anyway, he did, though he was no particular place ever, when you looked. But it was all his and he was never far. If something happened strange: if two things different noised together, or if someone laughed a way he hadn't heard before, or squeaked new boots or made a funny motion, like Able Hugo who used to leap straight in the air sometimes, just for the fun of it; whenever anything happened the least from the usual, for he was terrible against that, he'd be to see—and all the trains. When a train was late he'd sit in the bed and stare down the track and lash his tail until the whistle sounded. Still he'd sit there until the train came down on him and at the last second, as slow and lazy as you please, he'd turn his back and walk away.

Golly.

In the winter he often slept inside the station. He knew to an inch how far from the stove to sleep. He knew where everybody spat and where we stamped the snow from our boots, shaking the floor, and where the wind came pouring, snowflakes with it, rattling the paper spills we kept in the woodbox. He knew where a live ash from a pipe might land or a whittler's shavings, and he'd figured the fall and roll, I'm sure, of every checker to the corner when the board was spilled, as it often was if Jenkins played. Jenkins. Now there was a fellow . . . However . . . Kick's cat knew everything about the station. He knew where most of the light fell, and the talk, and where the smoke went. He knew even, I bet, how many flakes would blow to the stove when Kick came in. He balled up on a piece of canvas under a bench and covered his nose with a paw. He sighed and sucked in his sleep sometimes, and sometimes he snored.

Not really.

It's a fact. If we had time I could show you where he'd scratched some bricks like I said he could.

Honest?

Course.

Not really.

Ever watch a cat stretch? Cats know how to live.

I know it.

Cats beat us at it bad. Now Brackett Omensetter, though—

I know it. Did he stay there all the time—in the station I mean? Kick's cat?

He didn't sleep there often enough so you could say he lived there, for he was sometimes out in the worst of the weather. In the middle of the winter I'd find his tracks in strange places, and in the winter most he kept his habits secret. I'll tell you about that later.

Did Kick's cat have a name?

A name?

Yes, a name. Like Isaac, maybe, or Brineydeep.

Gracious. Brineydeep?

If I had a cat I'd name him Brineydeep or Isabel.

I thought you said you had a cat.

I just said that. If I had a cat he'd be as big as a pony and have a long tail. Did Kick's cat have a long tail? Mine would, and when he did, I'd call him Whiskers instead of Brineydeep probably.

I don't follow that.

What was Kick's cat's name? Molly's turtle's Sam, which is dying.

His name was Kick's cat.

If he didn't have a name you couldn't find him. I know a kid got his name erased and he went away forever. Nearly forever. Longer than that even. You go bango, you know, bango!

What happened to him?

He went away invisible so no one could see him.

No one at all?

Only trees. Things like that.

Who told you so?

A man. Bango! You go bango!

A monkey.

Maybe a monkey. Say. What was Kick's cat's name?

Kick's cat.

Just that?

Just that.

Why?

Because that's whose cat he was.

26

I bet he knew everything about trains and stations.
He knew everything about trains and stations.
I bet he knew when trains got to Chicago Illinois.
He knew when trains did anything.
I bet he was fierce as anything, like a turkey.
Turkeys aren't very fierce.
I hate turkeys. They gobble at you.
Well Kick's cat was fiercer than that.
I bet. I bet he could fly.
Of course he couldn't.
He could.
No.
At night. At night he could.
Say, who knows about this cat, boy, you or me?
Tell me how he knew about trains and stations.
You going to listen or talk?
I want it to be a long story.
It is a long story.
Put everything in it.
I always put everything in it.
Is it good and long? Good stories are long.
Well, they ought to be, anyway. So, let's see: Kick's cat knew everything about trains and stations. He could gallop up a rail like it was a walk and skip across the tracks without moving a cinder in the bed. He perched on spouts and dropped sudden on unloaded crates to claw and sniff out the city wood. When a train was in he would march through the cars, his tail fluffed up and curled over his back, rubbing against the passengers and purring the only time he purred, with a deep bass purr, like a tractor's. The passengers would give him things to eat: peanuts and crackers and candies and fruit and sometimes the centers of sandwiches. Kick's cat hated bread. I'll have to tell you about that. It came from the time some fool boys locked him in the washroom when the train was leaving. Their names were Frank and Ned and Harry and they were fool boys playing at bandits. I call that story the story of Kick's cat's fierce revenge, or sometimes I call it the story of the boys who played at bandits. It depends on which end I come at.

Boy.

Anyway, Kick's cat hated bread. He would lick it clean if it was minced ham, but afterward he'd hook the slice with a claw and toss it down the car. He ate the inside of a lot of sandwiches, come to think of it.

Cats hate fruit.

Not Kick's cat. He was no ordinary cat, haven't I been telling you that?

I hate bread.

You don't hate bread.

I do.

You don't.

Kick's cat hated milk.

He loved milk. He doted on it. He drank three gallons and a pint a day.

He didn't.

Maybe more than that. I couldn't say.

Honest?

That's a way cats have. They've got to love milk and fish and chase mice and rats and birds. Otherwise they ain't cats. It's what they call a law of nature.

I hate ice cream.

No you don't. But that reminds me of old Doc Orcutt.

Bah on doctors.

Ah but Orcutt was special. He had a beautiful beard.

Bah on beards. Was that really his name?

Orcutt? Sure was. And you can bet he heard about it. But he could tell wonderful jokes on himself. Lord. There was the time, well, it's the story I call the story of the cut-rate tonsillectomy.

I don't want to hear about it.

It's funny.

If it's tonsils it's not funny.

Ice cream put me in mind of it. Think of it that way.

My cat hates milk.

You don't have a cat and if you did he wouldn't hate milk, but if he hated milk he'd be a beaver and bite you in half like a log.

Kick's cat then.

Well. He was big and tawny. He had a face as round as a barrel and great wide circle eyes.

Cheese. I got to go. That's my ma. She'll be awful mad if she sees me.

But what about Kick's cat?

I got to go.

But I haven't come to the story. You don't know about the rat either. You see there was a particularly big gray rat, as big as a boot maybe, maybe bigger, and that rat wasn't afraid of anything.

Boy. But I got to. I got to go.

But the rat. It was the rat that bit Kick's nose. Remember? It was the challenge to the fight.

Bye.

He'd arrange a fight between Kick's cat and the boot-big rat...a chase and a fight...between cars, in the walls ... whisker to whisker ... it would last all night. You should have heard the way the wind passed between his paws. Arrange ... So I'll arrange ... Well, he seemed a nice boy, one of those our nowadays have lost. Too young for the story of May Cobb. And how would he learn his history now? Imagine growing up in a world where only generals and geniuses, empires and companies, had histories, not your own town or grandfather, house or Samantha—none of the things you'd loved. No, I didn't finish about Bob Stout. Boy—your own leaves are keeping your eyes from the trunk. I could arrange for pirates. Fire at the Hen Woods. Uncle Simon, the ancient bony sycamore, burning and breaking my heart. I could arrange that. But the boy was gone, wrapped round by his mother. Yet I remember everything. Kick's cat. Droplets of cream along his jaws. Omensetter swinging his arms in a dance. Surely they should be of use. No. An odd lot. He couldn't even auction them off. Still—suppose they were sold? Could he bear to live through that sweet weather again, through that purple sky and lingering haze, the long clouds losing the sun, the twilight deepening the roads and lying in the tracks till dawn? Or so it seemed then—when his flesh was young.

The churn was sold. The cradle. He didn't see who got it. All the tools were gone. The rope. The canned goods. Even empty soda bottles dull with dust. Sam Peach had cleaned the back and swept one side. Sofas. Chairs. The row of ladies was empty. It was the heat. The sky had a vacant blue. Was that fellow the son of Parson Peach? Could that be? First Pike. Let's see. Then Meldon, Rush, and Furber. In the Redeemer's. Huffley after that, and Peach. Oh he was out of touch. Well there was no resemblance. Lamps. Satin shades and tassels. Now plates and coffee mills and cups. The crowd was with him in the front. It seemed smaller. More painted plates by Lucy Pimber. Pepper mills. Goblets of cranberry glass. Cut crystal bowls. Linen. Rugs. Sheets. Towels. Quilts. Rags that were old clothes. To perish with the owner. That was wise. Samantha. Sister. She would sell his bones. What would his bones bring?

Israbestis rose with effort. To climb a tree so high you could see Columbus from it—what a wonder. It was Omensetter's luck. Not a story, an illness. He'd never live its telling. Henry Pimber died of Omensetter's luck, too, one way or other, everybody said. The boy had died at that—the infant. How lucky was he? anybody?

If you ask me that minister is mad. Will you shush? In that garden, bless me, back and forth, back and forth, all he does is walk.

Well, I told old Harris if you use your heart like that, you'll stop, Doc Orcutt said, but if you don't it'll just plug up—you're just as dead and there's no effort in it. The doctor slapped his thigh.

Tott—you've shut your house. In effect, you've shut your house. You can't forget, and you don't dare remember.

I remember who said bless me. In that garden, bless me . . . Yes. The darkie. Funny . . . Omensetter was dark, he was brown, a deep brown like pot roast gravy. Israbestis chuckled. Then Furber was dark in his cloth, small and dark, though very pale of skin . . . oh, very . . . very pale . . . a moon out, somebody said, where the stars had been.

The tap when he reached it was warm. He searched the bricks, aware of his sweat. His eyes went over every pit and crater. He saw his spit crusted flat in the dust and spat again on top of it a cottony spit. He pushed aside the stems of marigolds and inspected all their rusty petals. The pungent scent cleared his nose. He hunted patiently through their leaves. There, beside his foot on the walk, stilting on its thread-thin legs, the pebble stood. Israbestis bent down and it suddenly fled. He pursued it down the walk with his thumb, jabbing. It nearly escaped his reach, which would have been too bad, for they were alone in the world, but he put his thumb down and the longlegs went out like rays around it. Then slowly they curled up. Bango, you go bango, Israbestis said, feeling the cement warm his thumb.

What are you doing mister, killing spiders, a little girl said. Yes. Killing spiders, Israbestis whispered, getting up.

Good. I hate spiders. They crawl you up.

Yes.

They're nasty.

Yes. Nasty, said Israbestis Tott.

The Love and Sorrow of Henry Pimber

⌐ 1

Brackett Omensetter was a wide and happy man. He could whistle like the cardinal whistles in the deep snow, or whirr like the shy 'white rising from its cover, or be the lark a-chuckle at the sky. He knew the earth. He put his hands in water. He smelled the clean fir smell. He listened to the bees. And he laughed his deep, loud, wide and happy laugh whenever he could—which was often, long, and joyfully.

He said to his wife when it is spring we'll go to Gilean on the Ohio. That is a fine place for the boy you're making. The air is clear.

Therefore, when the snow sank quietly away into the creeks; therefore, when the rivers had their bellies brown and urgent; when the wind went hungry about the bare-limbed trees and clouds were streamers; then Omensetter said the time is coming and we must be ready.

They washed their wagon. They ironed their Sunday things. They braided the hair of their daughters. They did everything that didn't matter. It made them feel good.

They brushed the dog. They piled the firewood left from winter neatly. They pinched each other a good deal on the behind. Everything that didn't matter and made them feel good, they did.

It rained a week. Then Omensetter said it seems that we are ready, shall we go?

They piled their belongings on the back of the wagon. They heaped them up, one on top of the other: flaming tufted comforts and tattercrossed quilts, plump bags of clothing and sacks of shoes and sewing and a linen tablecloth with stains that were always hidden by the plates; two ladderbacks, a stool and a Boston rocker, a bench of quite hard and eloquent oak, and a drop-leaf table whose top was carved into faces and initials by no one they ever knew; jars, a framed view of the Connecticut River, rubber boots; and in boxes: wooden spoons and pans and stove lids and pothandle holders and pots, tin silverware and nickel-plated medallions and a toothpick, somewhere, thinly tinted gold with a delicate chain, a mezzotint of St. Francis feeding squirrels, some tools for shaping leather, two pewter goblets and thirteen jelly glasses, seven books (three of which were about birds by the Reverend Stanley Cody); a collection in tobacco tins of toy rings and rice-bead necklaces, amber-colored stones and tiny china figurines and stamped-out metal dogs and cats and horses and two lead hussars in tall hats and bent guns whose red paint had all but worn away; ten and twenty penny nails, dolls made from sewn chains of stuffed cloth, small dishes and large crocks, a paper cockade, four flat spiders dead a long time and saved under a stone in the hearth; a saw, a hammer, square, a sledge, other things that were called dolls but were more like pressed grass or pine cones or strangely shaped sticks or queer rocks; any kind of shell whatever—turtle's, robin's, snail's; and not in boxes: a tight bucket and an unassembled plow, a spade, a shovel and an ax, a churn, a wooden tub and washboard, and a great white ironstone basin and a great white ironstone pitcher and a great white enamel pot with a chipped lid that was terribly cold in the morning; a shotgun and some harness and a spinning wheel, a compass in a leather case that always pointed to the west of south, and arrows for the unborn boy to shoot at falling leaves and sparrows in the fall. They piled them up, one on top of the other, until there was a tower in the wagon. On the top they lashed the cradle. The tower teetered when the wagon rolled. They said maybe everything will fall into the road but they really didn't think so, and they didn't trouble to cover anything. Of course the rain would stop, they said, and it did. Omensetter hitched the horse to the wagon. He hopped up with a great flourish and addressed the world with his arms. Everyone enjoyed that. Omensetter's wife swung up too. She rested her arm on his leg and she squeezed his knee. Omensetter's daughters whooped up the back. They snuggled under quilts. They made a house in the tower. Everyone said a prayer for the snowman dead a week. Then Omensetter chucked, the dog barked, and they set out for Gilean on the Ohio where the air was clear and good for boys. They left behind them, where they'd kissed and talked, water dripping lightly from the eaves of their last and happy home.

There were still a few people in Gilean when Brackett Omensetter came. It had been dry, for a change, all day. George Hatstat's rig was mired down on the South Road even though the South Road drained into the river, and Curtis Chamlay had turned his wagon back from the western hill that afternoon, being a stubborn man, three hours after he started slipping on its yellow sides. That meant the hill should be impassable since the other slope was generally worse. Consequently everyone was thoroughly amazed to see Omensetter's wagon come sliding down and draw its tilting peak of furniture and tools and clothing into town behind a single wretched horse. They looked at the unprotected quilts, the boxes and the stilting poles, the muddy dog, the high-lashed swaying cradle with bewildered wonder, for all day, in the distance, choked gray clouds had dropped their water in the forests, and even as they watched the wagon coming, away above the western hill, sunshine shining from it, there was a clearly defined acre of rain.

Pausing only to ask directions, Omensetter drove rapidly to the blacksmith's shop, bawling out his name before the wagon had fully stopped and announcing his occupation in an enormous raw voice as he vaulted down, his heels sinking so deeply in the soft ground it held him a moment, lurching, while he rubbed his nose on his upper arm and Matthew Watson emerged from the doorway blinking and shaking his apron. Omensetter rushed to the forge and bent over it eagerly, praising the beauty and the warmth of the fire. He teetered as he pummeled a leg that he said was tingling, his face flushed by the coals and his shadow fluttering. Mat inquired his business. Omensetter groaned and yawned, stretching with an effort that made him tremble. Then with a quiet exclamation he moved by Mat and took a piece of leather from the bench; wound it around his fingers like a coil of hair; let it straighten slowly. He held it gently in his huge brown hands, rubbing it with his thumb as he talked. He spoke in a dreamy monotonous voice whose flow he broke from time to time by peering closely at the edges of the strip he held or by bringing it sharply down against his thigh, smiling at the sound of the crack. He was very good, he said. He would start tomorrow. There was no one in the town brought up on leather, and Mat had far too much to do. That was certainly right, he thought. Mat would see how he was needed. His thumb moved rhythmically. His words were happy and assured, and if Mat's doubts were any obstacle, they calmly flowed around them. I shall work out very well and you can easily afford me. Before Omensetter left, Mat gave him the name and address of his friend, Henry Pimber, who had a house which might be rented since it was empty and dissolving and sat like a frog on the edge of the river.

Henry Pimber smiled at Omensetter's muddy clothes, at the girls leaning over the side of the wagon, laughing; at the running, barking dog, the placid, remote wife; though he was conscious mainly of his own wife, quiet in the kitchen now, endeavoring to hear. Sheets of water still glittered in the road; the sky muttered; yet the wagon stood uncovered, belongings piled into a tower; and Henry felt amazement move his shoulders. Three flies walked brazenly on the screen between them. Omensetter was cross-hatched by the wires. To Henry he seemed fat and he spoke with hands which were thick and deeply tanned. His belt was tight though he wore suspenders. His dark hair fell across his face and he'd tracked mud on the porch, but his voice was musical and sweet as water, his moist lips smiled around his words, his eyes glimmered from the surface of his speech. He said he was working for Watson, mending harness and helping out. Henry noticed several squares of screen clogged with paint. There was a tear in the fellow's sleeve, and his nails had yellowed. Clay eased to the porch from his boots. Henry's wife was in the parlor then, tiptoeing. She held her skirts. He said his name was Brackett Omensetter and he came from out near Windham. He was honest, he said. Flies already, Pimber thought, and the swatter in the barn. But they were something to fix his eyes on and momentarily he was grateful. Then his vision slipped beyond the screen and he received the terrible wound of the man's smile. His weakness surprised him and he leaned heavily against the door. He had a horse, Omensetter said. He had a dog, a wagon, a pregnant wife and little girls. They needed a place to stay. Not large or fancy. A room for the girls. Land enough to vegetable a little and hay the horse. Henry listened for his wife and shook his head. The screen was no protection—futile diagrams of air. He shifted his weight and the clogged squares blotched Omensetter's cheek. There was mud to his thighs. It hung on the wagon's wheels and caked the belly of the dog. His teeth weren't really clean. Henry realized that heavy-jawed and solemn as Matthew Watson was, as slow and cautious, as full of dreams of geese as he was, continually making the sound of a shotgun in his head, Omensetter had nevertheless instantly overpowered him, set his fears at rest, met his doubts, and replaced his customary suspiciousness with an almost heedless trust; yet to have sent Omensetter to see him this way was strangely out of character too, for Watson knew perfectly well that the ancient Perkins house which Pimber had so recently inherited was very near the river and a yearly

34

casualty of flood. The paint was peeling and the porch would soon be split by weeds. Henry sighed and flicked the screen. He had overpowered even Matthew. Matthew—who listened only to the high honk of the geese and his own hammer, and whose sight had been nearly burned out by the forge.

He had a place, Henry finally said. It was down the South Road near the river, but he hadn't thought of renting it on such notice, at such a time of year. There were difficulties ... Omensetter opened out his arms and Pimber, trembling, laughed. There, you see; we'll care for it and keep it well in life. Pimber clenched his fists upon the curious phrase. His wife was in the crook of the door, holding her skirts, breathing carefully. It's down the South Road, though, he said, and near to the river. We all love the water, Omensetter said. Lucy and I are good for houses and we will promptly pay.

Who knew what sort of boots? Five narrow boards between his feet. Three flies regaining the screen. The shadows of clouds on the panes of water. His wife gently rustling. And the stout man is talking, his hands undulating. A button on his shirt is broken. Under his arms there are stains. His stubby fingers clutch the air as though to detain it. Lis-sen. Lis-sen. The dog runs under the wagon. We have wives of the same name, Henry finds himself saying.

There, you see, Omensetter said, as if his words included explanation.

Pimber laughed again. It's down the South Road, I'll get the key. As he moved away he heard her knuckles snap. Behind him she stood stiff and motionless as a stick, he knew. She wouldn't like the mud on her porch either. He said the days of the week. After the habit of his father. He said the months of the year. Then he went the back way for his horse and prepared to hear about his crimes at dinner. Five boards between his boots. Mud on every step. A half a button missing. How many down? His face was broken when he laughed. Sweetly merciful God, Henry wondered, sweetly merciful God, what has struck me?

Omensetter left the wagon out all night, and the next morning he took his horse down the South Road and pulled Hatstat's rig out of the mud where three horses had skidded, kicked, and floundered the day before. Then he went to work as he'd said he would, bringing Hatstat's carriage on to town while his wife, daughters, and the dog moved in the wagon things and cleaned the house. Henry rose at dawn. His wife was scathing. Wrapped in the bedclothes she confronted him like a ghost. He dawdled along the road to the Perkins house until he heard the children shouting. He tried to help and thus to handle everything he could: he peeked in boxes on the sly and sat in chairs and backed apologetically from room to room ahead of brooms and mops and mop-thrown water, observing and remembering, until, obedient to some overwhelming impulse, astonished and bewildered by it though it filled him with the sweetest pleasure, he secretly thrust one of their tin spoons into his mouth. But this action ultimately frightened him, especially the delight he took in it, and he soon apologized once more for being in the way, and left.

Hatstat thanked Omensetter graciously, and he and Olus Knox, who, with his horse, had helped Hatstat the day before and got mud rubbed through his clothes and lumped up in his crotch, said nice things to people afterward of Omensetter's luck and thought, at the same time, of flood.

Rain fell a week and the river rose, water moving against water, a thin sheet of earth and air between the meeting rise and fall. The rain beat steadily on the river. The South Road drained. Clay banks slid quietly away, pools grew; runnels became streams, streams torrents. Planks laid across the street sank from sight. Everyone wore hip boots who had them. Everyone worried for the south.

You didn't tell him about the river, did you, she would suddenly say. Whenever Henry was at home now his wife quietly followed him and in a venomous low voice struck with the question. She waited for the middle of an action like filling his pipe or settling himself to read, often when he had no thought that she was near, while shaving or buttoning his pants. You didn't tell him about the water, did you? How are you going to feel when the river's up and you're down there in a boat, getting him out? Or don't you intend to? Is it dangerous there when the river floods? Mightn't you drown?

I might, I might. Would it please you?

I'd have no husband then to shame me . . . You didn't tell him about the river, did you?

He knows, he said; but his wife would offer him a sweet and gentle smile and sadly turn away. He would try to read or strop his blade—continue whatever it was she'd broken into—but she would suddenly be back again.

Mightn't he?

Before he could direct an answer she'd have passed into another room.

He saw the waterline on the house, you mean? That's how he knows?

Lucy, I told him it was down the South Road.

She laughed.

He knows the South Road, does he? Isn't he from

36

Windham? So you told him it was down the South Road. Did he see the line on the house or the moss on the trees?

Oh for god's sake stop.

Those wretched things he had piled in his wagon will be afloat.

No they won't.

He didn't seem to care, though, did he, if they got wet or not. Doesn't strike me as a good sign of a responsible tenant. You'd want to know that kind more than a minute, I should think, what with mud on his boots and clothes and a wagon full of trash wide open to the weather.

Lucy, please.

Them and that baby in her . . . the land so low.

Shut up.

When he rose from his chair or put down his pipe or slammed the strap against the wall, then she would go, but not before she'd asked how much he'd got for it.

The rain stopped but the river rose anyway. It crossed the South Road with a rush. It filled woods. It drowned ponds. It carried away fences. Receding from its mark, it left silt sticking to the sides of trees. It flung skeins of slime over bushes. It took more than it gave. Olus Knox reported that the water came within thirty yards of Omensetter's side yard fence, and it seemed to Henry that more rain had fallen than had in years, yet in the past the Perkins house had always borne the stain of flood high on its peeling sides. Things are running for Omensetter, he said to Curtis Chamlay with what he hoped was a knowing smile. Curtis said apparently, and that was that.

⌒ 2

Henry Pimber became convinced that Brackett Omensetter was a foolish, dirty, careless man.

First Omensetter ran a splinter in his thumb and with amusement watched it swell. The swelling grew alarmingly and Mat and Henry begged him to see Doc Orcutt about it. Omensetter merely stuffed the thumb in his mouth and puffed his cheeks behind the plug. Then one morning, with Omensetter holding close, Mat's hammer slipped. Pus flew nearly across the shop. Omensetter measured the distance it shot and smiled with pride, washing the wound in the barrel without a word.

He stored his pay in a sock which hung from his bench, went about oblivious of either time or weather, habitually permitted things which he'd collected like a schoolboy to slip through holes in his trousers. He kept worms under saucers, stones in cans, poked the dirt all the time with twigs, and fed squirrels navy beans and sometimes noodles from his hands. Broken tools bemused him; he often ate lunch with his eyes shut; and, needless to say, he laughed a lot. He let his hair grow; he only intermittently shaved; who knew if he washed; and when he went to pee, he simply let his pants drop.

Then Omensetter bought some chickens from Olus Knox, among them one old hen whose age, as Knox told Henry after, he thought his buyer hadn't noticed. The next morning the hen was gone while the rest ran fearfully and flew in hops. At first they thought she was lost somewhere in the house, but the girls soon found her. They were diving, Omensetter said, hiding under the lifting fog, bending low to see beneath it the supernatural world and one another's bare legs stalking giants. The hen lay dead by the open well and the dog crouched growling at its lip. Henry had come to collect the rent because his wife insisted that he go in person—face to face is safer, she said—and Omensetter showed him the eyes of the fox reflect the moon. The girls swung in graceful turns around the hole, their dresses palely visible. His eyes are like emeralds, they said. They are green emeralds and yellow gold. That's because they're borrowed from the fire at the center of the earth and they see like signals through the dark. Then Omensetter told them of foxes' eyes: how they burn the bark from trees, put spells on dogs, blind hens, and melt the coldest snow. To Henry, kneeling gingerly upon a rotten board, they were dim points of red, and his heart contracted at the sight of their malice.

How do you plan to get him out, he asked, rising in front of Omensetter's chest.

You can see how bad the well wanted him. He'll have to stay where he's been put. That's the way it happened and maybe the well will tire of him and toss him out.

Henry tried to laugh. Kneeling had made him dizzy and a button was missing from Omensetter's coat. Our fox is in our well, our fox is in our well, our well was empty belly, now our fox is in our well, the girls sang, whirling more rapidly.

Be careful there, he said, those boards are rotten and one's missing. The cover should have been repaired.

It was his well really, and he fell silent when he remembered it. Then he tried a cautious, apologetic smile. It might be the fox that had been stealing Knox's chickens, he thought. That would be like Omensetter's luck, certainly—for the fox to seize the bitterest hen, gag on her as he fled, and then fall stupidly through the ground. What an awful thing: to have the earth open to swallow you almost the moment you took the hen in your jaws. And to die in a tube. Henry found he couldn't make a fist. At best, the fox must be badly bruised, terribly cramped, his nose pressed into the damp well wall. By this time his coat would be matted and his tail fouled, and his darkness would extend to the arriving stars. A dog would bloody his paws and break his teeth against the sides and then wear out his body with repeated leaping. By morning—hunger, and the line of the sun dipping along the wall, the fetid smells—bitter exhaustion of spirit. No wonder he burned with malice.

You know what those eyes are? They're a giant's eyes.

The girls squealed.

Sure—that hole goes through to the land of the giants.

Omensetter struck Henry heavily on the back.

As a boy Henry hadn't been able to carry a bucket brimming from the well; he couldn't spade or hoe with strength or plow; he couldn't saw or wield a beaverish ax. He stumbled when he ran; when he jumped, he slipped; and when he balanced on a log, he fell. He hated hunting. His nose bled. He danced, though he could never learn to fish. He didn't ride, disliked to swim; he sulked. He was last up hills, stayed home on hikes, was always "it." His sisters loved to tease, his brothers to bully him. And now he couldn't even make a fist.

Honestly—what are you going to do?

Omensetter swung happily about the well with the girls, their bodies casting a faint shadow on the yellowish grass.

Naa-thing, they sang, naa-thing.

Omensetter must feel the cruelty of his mood, Henry thought, or was he also free of that? Shed of his guilty skin, who wouldn't dance?

Of course you can't do that, he said; you'll have to get him out. He'll starve down there.

He'll have to stay where the hen has put him, Omensetter said firmly. Spring will float him to the top.

That poor animal?—you can't do that. It's dangerous besides.

But Henry thought how he would fare if the earth spoke of his crimes. Suppose the instant you uttered a cutting word, your cheek bled.

Anyway, you'll have to board it up . . . the girls, he said.

Suppose your tongue split when you lied.

This well, it's in a manner of speaking . . . mine. I totally forgot—the existence of . . .

He sighed. Murder would also be suicide.

I'll help you close it up, he said.

Oh they enjoy it, Omensetter said. They'd cry if I covered it.

The girls pulled gaily at their father's arms. He began to whirl like a ribboned pole.

How long . . . do you think . . . that giant's eyes . . . will last?

Henry held unsteadily to a sapling.

You could shoot him, I guess. You have a gun.

The well wants him . . . maybe he'll get out . . . hooh . . . it's getting dark, girls . . . no . . . whoosh . . . stop.

I'll do it then, Henry said, and he imagined the shot leaping from the barrels of his gun to rush at the fox.

Lamps lit in the house. Henry measured the walls of his sky while he drifted away to the buggy. It wasn't dippered yet, but soon there'd be nothing to aim by, for darkness would silence the fox's eyes. The grass had begun to glisten. Animals felt pain, he understood, but never sorrow. That seemed right. Henry could crush a finger, still the wound might be a war in a distant country for all the concern he could let it cause him, he lived so fearfully; but such a creature as the fox filled up the edges of its body like a lake the shot would dapple as it entered. You could startle an animal, but never surprise. The buggy's seats were slick, the dew heavy. He thought he should have a cloth somewhere, a piece of toweling. There were bats overhead. Yes, here's where he had it. Henry began to dry a place for himself. Fluttering like leaves, the bats flew securely. And would the stars be startled, looking up, to find the fox out burning in their early skies?

There you are, you've been reasonably careful, you've kept your butt dry.

Henry spoke crossly and the carriage began to bounce him.

So the well went through to the land of the giants. Why not? Should he turn away from that—that callousness and that romance—to Mrs. Henry Pimber's firm prim mouth? her festive unlatching hands?

Omensetter's a natural-born politician, Olus Knox had said; he's what they call the magnetic kind. How inadequate that image was, Henry thought, when he could draw the heart right out of your side. Jethro Furber had been dramatic, as usual, painfully pinching his hands together. That man, he declared, lives like a cat asleep in a chair. Mat smiled gently: a view full of charity, he said; but Tott was laughing at the sight of Furber actually holding the pieces of himself together while he tried to condemn Omensetter's simply harmony and ease, as Henry guessed, with such a tranquil image. Yet how could Omensetter bear that terrible pair of eyes? Of—of course, Furber stuttered. A cat's a pretty thing, of course. How pretty a man? Is it attractive in a man to sleep away his life? take a cow's care? refuse a sparrow of responsibility? Tott shrugged. The cat's an unmitigated egotist, a slothful beast, slave to its pleasure. No need to preach, Tott said, nettled; cats were his idols. I've seen him, Furber swiveled to catch each eye, I've seen him—wading. The memory made Henry grin, slowing the buggy. Wading? He pictured Jethro standing in a puddle, trousers rolled. Tott claimed afterward that Furber filled a chair like a leaky bag of potatoes. No—no—an unsteady stack of packages, a teetery tower, an uncertain clutch—yes —a chair full of perilous parcels—or—in sum: a bunch of unbundling bundles. And sleep? sleep? Sleep is like Siam—he's never been there. It was true, Henry thought, they were utter opposites. Furber's body was a box he lived in; his arms and legs propelled and fended for him like a cripple's crutches and a blind man's cane; while Omensetter's hands, for instance, had the same expression as his face; held out his nature to you like an offering of fruit; and added themselves to what they touched, enlarging them, as rivers meet and magnify their streams. Wading. Amused, Henry formed the word again, and allowed himself to watch the woods fill in. Pasting kites, Furber'd said. Rolling hoops. Hollering in the street. Fur-burr (Henry answered now as he should have then), Fur-burr, you're just an old lady . . . yes—a lacy old lady. But the evening had filled in Furber too, and his fierce puritan intensity. For that, Henry was grateful. He knew he'd never get used to the hot dark white-faced little man, always and seldom the same, who claimed one Sunday that the Lord had made him small and had given him his suit of pulpit clothing so he could represent to everyone the hollow inside of their bodies. No, hardly a lacy old lady. We're all niggers here—within, he'd shouted. You have a stomach cramp, he'd said, doubling, knotting his arms about his knees—then I'm its shadow. Once I was eight feet tall, he'd exclaimed, but God made me small for this purpose. What sort of talk was that? . . . blackened body-hollows. Jesus, Henry thought, like the well's column. Suppose he'd fallen there himself?

> Ding dong bell,
> Pimber's down our well.

Henry tried to urge his horse into a run, but on the badly rutted road, in the poor light, it refused. He cursed a moment, and gave up.

> Who pushed him in?
> Little Henry Pim.

Omensetter was no better than an animal himself. That was right. And Henry wondered what it was he loved, since he thought he knew what he hated.

> Who'll pull him out?
> Nobody's about.

What Omensetter did he did so simply that it seemed a miracle. It eased from him, his life did, like the smooth broad crayon line of the man who drew your cartoon at the fair. He had an ease impossible to imitate, for the moment you were aware, the instant you tried . . .

> What a naughty thing was that,
> To catch our little Pimber at,
> Who never did him any harm,
> But . . .

Or did he move so easily because, despite his size, he wasn't fat inside; he hadn't packed the past around his bones, or put his soul in suet. Henry had seen the engravings—of the skeletons' dance. It was, however, a *dance* . . . and if you had to die to dance . . . ? What were the chances of the fox? The fox, he felt, had never seen his past disposed of like a fall of water. He had never measured off his day in moments: another—another—another. But now, thrown down so deeply in himself, into the darkness of the well, surprised by pain and hunger, might he not revert to an earlier condition, regain capacities which formerly were useless to him, pass from animal to Henry, become human in his prison, X his days, count, wait, listen for another—another—another—another?

When he reached home his wife immediately asked him if he had the rent and how much was it, but he passed through the house in a daze, wild and frantic, and went off again with his gun without answering, so she had to yell after him—what fool thing are you up to now?—but she would see, he thought, bitterly observing that she hadn't thought of him as off to murder or to hunt but only as a fool bent on his foolishness; and in the back of Omensetter's house, not bothering anyone, he shot the fox out with both barrels. The shot screamed on the well sides and one pellet flew up and struck him on the arm so hard through his jacket that it stuck; but he, with great effort, since the cool stars watched, paid no mind to his wound, hearing the fox thrash and go still. Furthermore I'll board it up tomorrow, he thought.

Driving home slowly, his joy draining away and leaving him fearful and cold, Henry remembered how, as a boy, he had waited at the top of the cellar stairs for his father to emerge, and how, when his father's waist was level with his eyes, without a motive or any kind of feeling that he recognized, he had struck him a terrible blow in the stomach, driving the air from his father's lungs and forcing him to bend abruptly, dropping his startled face near. Henry's mouth had filled with saliva; the base of his tongue had tingled; he had taken breath. Yet thank God he had run, weeping instead. Saliva washed over his teeth as he fled. He remembered, too, the sound of apples falling slowly on the stairs. His legs had been the first of him to be appalled. They had fallen apart like sticks.

Killing the fox had given him the same fierce heedless kind of joy, and now he leaned back in the buggy, careless of the reins, weak, waiting his punishment. Indeed he did feel strange. He had sensed his past too vividly. His head rolled with the road. He knew, of course, it was Omensetter he had struck at. He took no care with their life, that man. Luck like his did not come naturally. It had to be deserved. Anger began very faintly to stir in him again, and he was able to steady his head. But the night had blackened, the moon and stars were now under clouds, the world around him had been erased. He sank wearily in his clothes and let his head wag loosely in the circle of his collar.

Upon the beach Henry Pimber rested, passing five white carefully gathered stones from hand to hand. He could not see his face where it had fallen in the water. Omensetter's darkened house stood in his head amid clipped grass. Cold dew struck him and the sound of water in the dusk, soft and distant, like slow steps that reach through sleep, possessed him. The man was more than a model. He was a dream you might enter. From the well, in such a dream, you could easily swing two brimming buckets. In such water an image of the strength of your arms would fly up like the lark to its singing. Such birds, in such a dream, would speed with the speed of your spirit through its body where, in imitation of the air, flesh has turned itself to meadow. The pebbles fell, one by one, to the sand. Henry struggled with the urge to turn his head. Instead he bent and picked the pebbles up. The moon appeared. The pebbles were the softest pearls—like sweetest teeth. And Lucy's lamp went through his house and climbed the stairs. He flung the stones. They circled out, taking the light. One sank in the water's edge; one clicked on a greater stone; one found the sand; another brushed the marsh weeds. The last lay at his feet like a dead moth. He drove home slowly for a clouding moon.

Henry loved to tell of everything he saw when he passed Omensetter's house, though he was cowardly and quiet about the fox, and neither he nor his listeners ever thought how strange it was they took such interest in the smallest things their newest neighbor did, for Omensetter cast an interest like a shade. It was as though one could, by knowing when his beans went in or when he cut his firewood for washing, hoed, or simply walked a morning in the oak and maple woods like a tree among the trees himself, learn his secret, whatever his secret was, since it must somehow be the sum of these small things all grown together, for as Doctor Orcutt was so fond of pointing out, every measle was a sign of the disease, or as Mat Watson said, every turn of wind or rift of cloud was a parcel of the acreage of weather.

Henry asked him how he knew it was a boy, for girls, he said, were also known to kick, and Edna Hoxie, thin enough, she said, to crawl inside and pull a fat one out, stopped by to offer up her service for the time. But Omensetter said he knew. He said that birthing would be easy for a boy who'd learned to crawl already. Don't be disappointed, Brackett; Olus Knox has three, Henry said. Each time his wife conceived he hoped like you, and he has three. He finds it hard without a boy, with three who'll trade his name away when now she's past her time. It could be just the same with you. I hope not... but it could be just the same. You shouldn't count too much on what comes out of her this fall or figure from how hard the baby kicks or from how high it rides. Still Omensetter laughed. He said he knew. He'd read the signs.

At first the wound was merely sore and then the arm was stiff. Get Doctor Orcutt for the love of God, Henry said, and slunk to bed. There the stiffness spread into the neck. Lucy learned in Gilean that Orcutt was with Decius Clark at the bottom of the county. When Watson and Omensetter arrived, Henry had ceased to speak and his face grew tight as they watched. A shotgun wound? Then slippery elm, I think, Mat said. Lucy wept, running from room to room with balls of cloth in her arms. The lips drew back from the teeth, the eyelids flattened. Opium, I think, Mat said. The body bent.

The room should be dark, I think, Mat said. Lucy stumbled up and down the stairs and the jaws at last completely locked. She was drawn in by the wheeze and when Omensetter asked her suddenly: have you any beets? the rags rolled out of her arms. The Reverend Jethro Furber, his twisted figure like a knotted string, was murmuring, immure him, cure him or immure him—some such thing—if he were really in the corner like a clothes tree, was he? was it Watson where the walls were willowing? Matthew drew off Lucy to another room. How easily he saw them. Godhead hid from him His holy farse. Immure him, Fermy murmuring, cure him or immure him. Through the withering wall he watched her try to kiss him when he helped her on the bed; tear wildly at her clothes. All I lack is a little luck and I'll lick that lock, who said? Mat then tiptoed to the bellowing hall and shut himself in its largest closet. Around him linens, towels, and female things were shelved.

Omensetter made a poultice of mashed raw red beet and bound it to the wound with rags and to the palms of the hands. Henry felt his sight fail as his lips yawned and air strenuously pushed itself between his teeth. Mat observed them from the doorway, apparently calm; but there seemed to be a button broken on his shirt and a tear in his sleeve. Then his body melted. It's up to Henry and the lockjaw now, Omensetter said; it's just between them. I'll stay, Mat said, he needs some company. But Furber hung like a drapery demonstrating him, his hollow—all could see it, billowing thinly, the wall gauze, and God's laws flickering. Omensetter's hands were stained with beet. He doesn't care, he said, his body also dwindling. You loosened her clothing, good, Henry heard Omensetter say as his footsteps faded on the stairs, now she's asleep. Mat held to Henry's hand while Henry whistled steadily like steam.

Orcutt came by evening, tore the poultice off the wound, gave opium and aconite, forced lobelia and capsicum into the mouth, stared at the bandaged palms but did not touch the wrappings, waited for vomiting. Watson said to Henry afterward that in his opinion the jaw had already begun to soften, and he was not surprised when the vomiting began. I'd have sworn it was hopeless, Doctor Orcutt said. The Reverend Jethro Furber came to pray and the jaw was loose by morning. Edna Hoxie, midwife, brazen, asked Omensetter for the recipe and bragged to everyone how easily she'd got it.

That Omensetter had a secret no one doubted now. Gossip was continuous, opinion split, the atmosphere political. One would have thought it France. Henry's own salvation was the central thing, and Henry was frequently vexed to the point of tears, weak as he still was, by the constant queries, the noisy quarrels, the wild conjectures of his friends. Nothing escaped them: chance was reperceived as calculation, distant possibilities were carried briskly into likelihood, the flimsiest hypotheses spun into woolens for a tapestry, and each conclusion was communicated to the town like a disease. At first consigned by nearly everyone to God and so to the faith of Reverend Furber, though always by a smaller group to Science and hence to the skill of Doctor Orcutt, the cure —except for a scattered few who insisted upon the will and constitution of Henry himself—was now almost universally awarded to the beet root poultice and the luck of Brackett Omensetter. But what did this amount to? This credited the cure to . . . what? Edna Hoxie had an increase of trade, though Maggie Scanlon—unwedded, large—scoffed at the question. Don't he always get what he wants, she said. He's happy, ain't he, the sonofabitch. I wish to god I was.

For Henry his illness was a joy and agony that still went on. Whole days it rained continually and water spilled out of dry containers. He would sit in the sun with a blanket on his knees and feel the rain come down on the stiff summer leaves and fly from the dusty spouts. He begged the fox's pardon constantly, as weak and palsied in his chair, as loose from his will, as he'd been during the first days of his recovery. His arm would dart out, seizing a flood of light in its fist. Well, he'd exclaim in surprise, it still seems to be raining. Lucy would shriek at him, the sun drum on his chest. His eye entered everything like a needle even yet—penetrated, looped, and then emerged—and he hung these pictures on a string like beads around his neck. For hours he fingered the air obscenely, and when he moved, he felt they clicked. He would say to his wife: here's your vulva, it's next to the nose of the beagle; or he'd say: here's your blood, dark as wet bark; or he'd say: here are the stools your bowels are shaping; on and on, until she struck him.

Cruelty brought no relief, as sight did not, and yet he sometimes thought his pain might simply be the pain of his shedding, since it often seemed that he was sloughing like a snake the skins of all his seasons; his white fats and red flesh were lost in a luminous wash. Sunshine lapped at him, rose over him, and soon there were pieces of him drifting off—his head like a hat, legs like logs. Then gently he toweled his bones until they shone. They made a fair tree; they weren't so bad. Henry hadn't been prepared for anyone like Omensetter. He'd been content to believe that he would always live with usual men in a usual world; but he'd lived with himself all these years like a stranger—and with everybody else. So on these shining armatures he fancied that he shaped a fine new unstreaked clay through which life lifted eagerly like moisture warming toward its heat. There was no mistaking Omensetter's likeness; Henry was newborn in that waltzing body now; he had joined it as you join a river swimming; surely Lucy must have seen . . . but he didn't mind if she had. Perceptions no longer pierced his eyes—his needles returning; instead, he poured out giddily.

In this mood Henry could remember piling up a mountain in the wagon: the quilts and comforts, the toys, the tools and the utensils—tasting their metals in his mouth. Clouds were living in the river; Gilean was resting by it, the air so clear. There was every house out honest and every barn banked proper to the weather. The trees were beautiful and bare, and the tracks of the wagons glistened. On the way they'd sung *Rose Aylmer*. Then sometimes they counted birds. There were rings in the pools of water by the road and the air was clean as it is after rain. He thought it would be healthy for the boy to live by the river, to catch fish and keep frogs, to grow up with good excitement.

But his wife would come and jar him loose. Age had beautifully lined her jaw. Her knuckles were huge. She rattled tins and silverware in drawers.

Where have you got to now? what are you thinking?

Nothing.

Nothing? You should see your face. Nothing!

Nothing.

It's fatty. You should see your face. It's fatty.

No.

What do you go to the shop for? You can scarcely walk yet you're always off down there, and in this weather when it's hot. What do you talk about? Does Tott tell stories? Or is the Furber preaching at you, trying to fish your soul out like the last pickle? Oh, I know what's happened. You've gone to the devil. That's what's happened.

No.

It's fatty.

He would sit so quietly within the shadows behind the forge that visitors scarcely noticed he was there. It was like the effect of his illness, for after a period of pain and confusion he thought his eyes had cleared and he had watched from his bed as if from out of the world. It had been as he imagined it was like to be invisible. Your eyes were open. People looked into them but they didn't think you saw. They were less than a mirror, no more than a painting of eyes. The sickness was nothing. Many times he had struggled to say that he could hear. Being stretched to pieces was nothing. Many times he'd tried to shout I can see, I can see you—hissing instead. Fighting for breath was nothing. Burning was nothing. Locked in a shrinking boot of flesh, hour after hour he remembered Jethro Furber's prayers.

The child of Decius Clark, said Doctor Orcutt through his beard, is very bad. A bee stung him six weeks come Tuesday on the neck. You never saw a bigger swelling.

The doctor's fingers formed an egg.

Clark used to be a potter. Quit. He's farming now—or trying to. Not much account. I won't collect.

Orcutt aimed his spit.

Let's see that finger Matthew smashed.

You're a bastard, Truxton, Watson said.

You took on so, I thought I'd see. Well, Brackett? No charge for curiosity. The nail grow back? Mat told me that he knocked it clean away—is that a fact?

Omensetter held his hand out silently.

Orcutt grinned.

Mat's took up surgery, I see. Might drive me square from business.

He turned the thumb.

A scar of great bravery, the doctor said. What do you charge?

Mat shook his head helplessly.

Well, it always happens, cut like that.

Orcutt dropped the hand. The arm fell muscleless.

A sledge ain't a very thoughtful knife. The next time you get stung like that you see me right straight off and maybe you won't grow up such a swelling.

I hit him accidental, Mat exclaimed.

All round you're mighty lucky, mister, Orcutt said.

Then he asked Hatstat how the fishing was.

Rotten, Hatstat said.

Always is, this time of year, the doctor said.

They should be up.

Ah, George, they never is, you want them to. Ain't that right, Brackett?

It isn't cool enough, said Tott.

Mat rattled through his tools.

It was stifling in the shop, and fiercely hot by the forge.

Well he's a friendly sort, Clark is, said Doctor Orcutt, spitting. Not much account. I won't collect. But friendly. His wife is taking on about the boy but Clark is calm, I will say that. He's calm. How's your infection, Henry? It all gone? Ain't you out a little early like a winter robin?

It's been weeks, Henry mumbled, backing deeply in the shop.

Home remedy—by god, it's killed an awful lot, Henry. Could have lost that arm, you know. Fix your horseshoe game permanent. Does Brackett play?

We won't let him, said Israbestis Tott.

Too bad, I'd like to see that.

Juice oozed from the doctor's mouth. He spat a running stain.

Everyone fell silent.

The child of Decius Clark is very bad, said Doctor Orcutt once again, but Decius is a friendly sort, and calm.

...Then there was Israbestis Tott entertaining him with tunes: jigs, trots, polkas—Henry thought his mind would break. Then there was Matthew Watson, who sat by his bedside with his huge hands in his lap like a pair of frogs; there were endless files of whispering women; there was Jethro Furber in the costume of a witch, threatening the divine with spells; there was Lucy, lovely as a treetop in the door's grain, Furber as a drape, Mat a lamp, Tott a shriek, Furber both frogs, Orcutt their leaps...

A hen's first egg is always female.

Orcutt burned his spit.

Mares who've seen the stallion late have colts. Scientific fact.

Luther Hawkins tested the blade of his knife with his thumb, then sighted along it and winked at the tip.

Ain't it the month, he said. The women get the odd ones.

Orcutt shook his head.

All thought a while in silence. The iron was a pale rose.

I read a Swiss professor . . . hell . . . what was his name? . . . Thury. That's it, Thury. He says the same Danielson—downstate—has tried it. Works with cows. Works fine. Fact.

Orcutt showed his teeth.

But I couldn't say, you move the problem on from cows to ladies.

Henry giggled against his will.

It's out of my experience, Watson said, and George Hatstat laughed like a whistling train.

Orcutt hitched about and peered at Henry through the dark.

How's Lucy these days, Henry? Bearing up?

Watson put tongs on the iron.

Orcutt rolled his chew. His lips gleamed.

She ought to get out more.

Wars, Watson said.

He began hammering.

Wars, he shouted, more boys . . . replace dead ones.

Sparks flew in arcs and showers to the floor.

Doctor Orcutt wiped his mouth and stared at Henry through the rain of sparks.

The bar—reluctant—bent.

The doctor leaned back, tilting his chair. He gazed solemnly at the ceiling where a spider dropped itself by jerks from a beam.

Omensetter threaded a needle.

There was a lull in the hammering through which Henry's ears sang.

In passing, Lloyd Cate waved.

Each man looked morose and thoughtful.

Tott patted his pockets, hunting his harmonica.

Finally Orcutt said: lucky to be alive by god—in a low but outraged voice.

The hammering began again. The cool iron jumped.

Luther Hawkins moved the blade of his knife with caution, rolling back a sliver like a piece of skin. Hatstat followed him intently, while Omensetter stabbed a piece of leather with his needle.

Orcutt straightened; spat heavily at the dropping spider. The spit bore it off. At this the doctor slapped his knee and stood.

Authorities I've read . . . honest scientific minds, remember, gentlemen . . . claim males are made in special weather . . . they result from special postures . . . or depend upon the testicle that's emptied. Honest scientific minds. It's quite a problem for them. Some screw for science only in the afternoon, while others keep their faith with evening—here Orcutt chuckled—it's a matter of light, I understand, but which makes which I can't remember.

He hefted his bag.

You rest easy Henry, hey? No lifting. No climbing. No spading. That sort of thing.

Beneath his beard, Orcutt loosened his collar.

Or it's the length of the dick—how far it throws the seed.

The doctor carefully dusted his trousers.

Whew-ee.

Thus he remained a moment.

All that's manure, he said. Manure.

Then he strode away.

Henry watched the forge until it burned his eyes.

Later Curtis Chamlay looked in to ask if anyone intended fishing in the morning, and Luther Hawkins, admiring the point on his stick, carrying on the conversation in his head, chuckled.

Dogs don't care, he said. It's a fact.

George Hatstat said: know what Blender said that Edna Hoxie told his wife? douche with milk if you want a girl.

And all she does is douche with the Dutchman.

Hawkins picked dirt from a crack.

That fat Dutchman—how does he get on?

Take it easy, Chamlay said, laughing. Tott's ears are burning.

Why should they, Hawkins said. You listen at that preacher like he does, his ears hears every word there is.

That Dutchman, Chamlay said. I'll bet his cock is curly.

Pig's cock, Hawkins said.

Blenker isn't Dutch, Tott said.

Shit.

Hoxie says boys swell the right teat more.

Ah shit.

No, honest, Curt.

Hatstat clutched his chest.

Girls make special aches in the left side. That's what she said.

She's full of shit.

In the dust Hawkins began a drawing of the Dutchman mounting.

It's meat that does it, Chamlay said. Beef. It's got some chemical.

The bar began to glow again.

Hawkins scratched his drawing out.

I saw one in a bottle at a fair, he said. A little thing, you know. Pink and purply—whatever color. It was pickled . . . wrinkled . . . real pale and upside down in the stuff . . . looked like a pig . . . but dead . . . jesus.

Mat hefted his hammer impatiently.

Hawkins drew a mason jar.

It depends on what she eats, Chamlay insisted.

Then Hatstat made a disrespectful noise.

Come on Omensetter, what do you think? is it going to be a boy?

If she lolls about and stuffs on candy, Chamlay said, she gets a sugar baby—

Naw—shit.

You've got boys, George, right? But Rosa Knox? When Rosa's pregnant all she eats is sugar buns. Ask Splendid Turner if she don't.

Luther Hawkins nodded.

Fact, he said. A scientific fact . . . I wonder what that little Perkins devil filled Maggie Scanlon's belly with.

That Perkins, Chamlay said. I know him. I'll bet it wasn't cock.

You think that belly's growing up from spit, Curt, George said.

What a bitch, said Hawkins. She'll give birth to dogs.

Mat's hammer rang the metal.

Afterward, when Mat had hushed his iron in the rain barrel, they discussed fishing for a long time. Olus Knox had come and he was always eloquent about it. Everyone, that is, but Omensetter did, who sewed on silently, a look of intense bewilderment on his face.

4

I couldn't sleep. Did you notice how restless I was and wound in the sheets? The weather must be changing. I'm always restless then.

She filled her cheeks with air.

Henry ignored his wife's voice; dipped his hand in the wind. The leaves were learning of the cold. He turned his palm, allowing the wind to pass between his fingers. Cool as hill water it seemed to flow from the pale clouds. This is how it feels, he thought, to run through the cup of Omensetter's hands. Time goes coolly through the funnel of his fingers —click, click, click—like water over stones. When he had lately felt the wind he seldom had another feeling; yet there were moments, as if in dream, when he could plunge his hand into the air and feel the stream at the lip of Being, and the hesitating water. There was a bather at the precipice with breasts as great as God's, nippled as the berry bush, bright as frost. Corn golden hair was gathered to His thighs. Not in my image. Nothing like me. But in the dream that disabled him, he was afloat on the brink, poised above the incredible gulf like a bird, while each minute frightened him by passing over. With his hands on his ears he could feel them falling. Below lay an empty plain where the bright stream dried. It then became a road that thinned to a rail in the cold horizon. He heard the roar of a miracle coming, a long beak looking for snakes.

A soft plop. The air rushed out.

It's going to rain, you can see that.

Henry withdrew his hand.

The rent is due. I'll walk.

Walk. Walk. He'll walk too. You'll pass.

Likely, he said, fetching his coat.

Is walking what the doctor ordered? Whoo. Our room was stuffy as a tomb last night. Didn't you feel it? I don't want him here heaven knows, that beast. He's like an animal. Breathes like an animal. Awf. Smells like an animal. Heaven knows I don't want him here.

That's why I'm going. He won't come.

Oh no it's not. He'll come. He'll come along. You want to meet him out of sight of me, that's all. You should stay right here and rest. He's just a beast, a beast. And with her big lately he's been a while without her—unless he never paid any mind to her pain.

Lucy, please.

Now they've had that boy it'll be a bit before he'll dare to come at her again, I'd think. Imagine that fat creature sprawled on top of you. I'll bet there's fur on him there like a tom cat's.

For Christ's sake.

Oh pooh, don't be a prude.

She plunged her spoon into a bowl.

I wonder how poor Matthew can afford him, she said in a quieter voice. He can't make as much as his rent, I'm certain of that.

I wish to god—

Salt. Wasn't it last time I left out the salt? You remember. They were flat. You complained all evening and it was wretchedly hot.

Sometimes she made Henry think of steam—of something dangerously vaporous and white—but she stood at the counter now as stiff and metallic as the spoon whose edge she wore around and around in the bowl that she pressed into her stomach.

Well he works hard and I'm sure he's worth what he's getting . . . You're down there most of the day since your sickness.

Omensetter saved my life. You hate him for it.

Oh for sweet sakes, Hen, you know you always denied it. You never said he saved your life before. That sort of magic? You only want to rile me.

She suddenly turned to him with a weak sad face.

I've a lot to complain of myself, Hennie, not just about salt, Hennie—a lot to complain of. You know . . . our . . . and, oh you oughtn't to do me this way, Hen.

Her face grew hard again.

Well. Wasn't that what you said? It was Doctor Orcutt, I thought, you gave your gratefuls to. Hoosh. My arm tires easy. In this kitchen. You should have seen him in this kitchen—my personal place. Chopping beets. These counters aren't my height. Well they weren't made for me but for your mother of course. He stained the wood in them badly, you can see it—there—there—

No, those—

See—over there—and here—and there—there—ah the dirty beast.

She released the spoon and put her palm on the counter; began patting the wood.

Your mother, now, could stir a day and never sigh more than her usual.

Well he works. He's handy.

Oh I'm sure Matthew never regrets him. He *is* handy.

She set the bowl down with a jar.

Though what an easy fool he is to dance the tune for both of you.

Mat pays him properly, and after all, he's grown.

Hoo. He's huge. Takes care of his children on that, does he? And his wife too? She must be mighty saving. What is he owing you?

He pays, he pays.

Lalee. Of course he pays. He's what, if I weren't such a well-raised lady, I would call a poor stupid bastard—a poor stupid bastard.

Well, Lucy that's one thing—you *are* a lady.

She looked at him sharply.

More than you're a decent man, she said.

Then she began to cry and turned from the counter to blow her nose.

Doctor Orcutt, thought Henry. I hate him. His teeth slide in his beard and his eyes cross.

Come out of the door. Are you hearing me? Henry? When he was here he stared at me like an owl.

You should comb your hair.

It was indecent—how he stared. Stared. He's just an animal. Hairy as a bear. His head turns the whole way around.

I'm going.

Go then. Go. You'll pass in the woods, the two of you. I know. You'll pass. Must you be walking there? You're catching cold again. I saw you shiver.

No.

Like an old dog going everywhere there is a patch of sun to sit and shiver in. No one ever comes to see us. People used to—Gladys, Rosa, Mat. No one now since you were sick. He always takes the wood path. Why?

It saves time.

Time? Oh dear. Time. The animal. Smell him. There's no time to him. There's only himself. Like a cow whose bowels are moving. Heavens—time. What do you want from him? You'll never get it, whatever it is. He cares for no one, don't you know that? Not even you, Henry. Oh look what you're doing—letting the wind in. Shut the door.

The path took Henry Pimber past the slag across the meadow creek where his only hornbeam hardened slowly in the southern shadow of the ridge and the trees of the separating wood began in rows as the lean road in his dream began, narrowing to nothing in the blank horizon, for train rails narrow behind anybody's journey; and he named them as he passed them: elm, oak, hazel, larch and chestnut tree, as though he might have been the fallen Adam passing them and calling out their soft familiar names, as though familiar names might make some friends for him by being spoken to the unfamiliar and unfriendly world which he was told had been his paradise. In God's name, when was that? When had that been? For he had hated every day he'd lived. Ash, birch, maple. Every day he thought would last forever, and the night forever, and the dawn drag eternally another long and empty day to light forever; yet they sped away, the day, the night clicked past as he walked by the creek by the hornbeam tree, the elders, sorrels, cedars and the fir; for as he named them, sounding their soft names in his lonely skull, the fire of fall was on them, and he named the days he'd lost. It was still sorrowful to die. Eternity, for them, had ended. And he would fall, when it came his time, like an unseen leaf, the bud that was the glory of his birth forgot before remembered. He named the aspen, beech, and willow, and he said aloud the locust when he saw it leafless like a battlefield. In God's name, when was that? When had that been?

Omensetter was in his large coat today. Pieces appeared between the trees. Then tousled hair. Round hot face: determined, splotched. Pebbly teeth. His arm was lifted in a wave. This disappeared. His hand sprang out of a limb. Henry began to trot. Omensetter crossed a small glade, his feet hidden by bushes. A branch leaped in front of Henry and split his vision at its waist. His pulse grew noisy in his ears. We must take care, he thought, everything is against us.

The elder's pods won't hang through winter I'm afraid, Omensetter said. The moss is thick and the caterpillar's fur is deep.

I thought I'd walk your way, Henry said, for exercise.

Omensetter laughed. His teeth were bleached.

It wasn't for the rent, I knew you'd be along with that . . . And how's the boy?

The boy is fine. We have him sleeping south to catch the sun.

What have you named him, I haven't heard.

Amos.

Omensetter lingered on the word.

I've an uncle of that name who's rich.

He chuckled.

Lovely, Henry said. Amos Omensetter. Yes. Lovely. And the girls?

The girls?

How are they?

They're fine, and Lucy's fine. The dog is fine too. So am I.

Good, said Henry. Fine.

The aspen's leaves, he saw, were yellow early. Omensetter held money in his hand. There was a spatter of red in the maples. There the money was and there the end was. It would settle in his hand and be good-bye. Omensetter would present his back and wave. The white oaks, still green, would swallow him, the sound already gone he walked so softly in the forest. Henry bent and picked an acorn up. If there were any other way. He filled his hand with acorns, flipped them idly. Omensetter's fist hid the money and Henry was grateful for that, but he saw he had trimmed his nails, and Henry felt terribly wronged. He tried to search Omensetter's face for a deeper sign but they seemed to be standing in a cloud of gnats. Henry waved his hand in front of his eyes.

I'm glad to hear that Amos does so well, he finally said.

It would never do, he thought, to ask if he would live there free.

I want to see how far the turning's gone. Let's climb the hill, it isn't far.

Omensetter held aside a pin oak's limbs and Henry followed him.

A leaf would now and then detach itself and sail into the valley. Henry tried to speak but Omensetter led. The wind flowed around him as around a rock, and Henry didn't feel his voice was strong enough to salmon such a current. He watched a broad leaf break away and dip while the woods sank below them like a receding wave. They stopped for a moment on the bare hillside and Omensetter pointed to the flare his wife's wash made behind the trees.

Orcutt says she shouldn't do such work, Omensetter shouted, so I've taken to hanging it myself.

He lifted his shoulders expressively.

I can't get the girls to.

Then Henry realized that he could see through that massive green and changing tide as if to bottom.

It was since his sickness . . . Everything began with—since his sickness. Once to petrify and die had been his wish; simply to petrify had been his fear; but he had been a stone with eyes and seen as a stone sees: the world as the world is really, without the least prejudice of heart or artifice of mind, and he had come into such truth as only a stone can stand. He yearned to be hard and cold again and have no feeling, for since his sickness he'd been preyed upon by dreams, sleeping and waking; and by sudden rushes of unnaturally sharp, inhuman vision in which all things were dazzling, glorious, and terrifying. He saw then, he thought, as Omensetter saw, except for painful beauty. If there were just a way to frighten off the pain.

The path was steep. His head was nearly level with Omensetter's marching feet—his softly polished shoes. Henry felt abandoned. The blasted fellow understood his luck. He knew. The wind blew strongly and streams of tears protected Henry's eyes.

Perhaps it was the height, perhaps the wind, perhaps he was catching cold after all, but Henry felt his senses blur and merge, then focus again. Something was trying to come up—Omensetter was shouting that the frost was finicky— something was leaping against the sides of his skull. Ah—god—the fox, Henry thought, knuckling his eyes. He'd had the hen in his mouth, life in his teeth, saliva running. Feathers foamed over his nose. And then the earth had groaned. Just a moment ago. He'd never nailed the well shut, though now when he closed his teeth it all latched. Some went early, said Omensetter's shout. The leaves were minnowing. Had he thought they were playing at Adam and Eve? three children and a dog? PARADISE BY RIVERSIDE. Perhaps by Springwater Picturesquely Overrun. Exorbitantly leased from Mr. Henry God, a lesser demon, with insufficient spunk to make a Christ. No. Not Omensetter. He'd always seemed inhuman as a tree. The rest—who visited—were human. They made him sick inside his sickness. There was Mrs. Henry Pimber, her untidy hair, dull eyes, her fallen breasts and shoulders exclaiming grief and guilt at his demise, while every gesture was a figure in a tableau of desire; there was the Reverend Jethro Furber, a blackening flame, and Mrs. Valient Hatstat, rings spotted on her fingers, a small white scar like an unwiped white of egg lying in the corner of her mouth; there was Doctor Truxton Orcutt of the rotting teeth and juice-stained beard, who looked like a house with a rusting eave; there was Mrs. Rosa Knox, sofa-fleshed and fountain-spoken, with an intermittent titter that shook her breasts, and also Israbestis Tott, together beggar, hurdy-gurdy, cup, chain, monkey; and there was Mrs. Gladys Chamlay, the scratched rod, nose like a jungle-bird's, teeth like a beast's; Miss Samantha Tott, so tall she had to stoop in the sun she thought; and all those others, with their husbands or their brothers, invisible, behind them, making sounds to celebrate the death of tea-weak Henry Pimber; while Mr. Matthew Watson, neither praying, speaking, crying, or exclaiming, uncomfortable in a corner, surreptitiously scratched a rash through his trousers.

They haven't turned . . . in earnest yet, Omensetter said.

Not Adam but inhuman. Was that why he loved him, Henry wondered. It wasn't for his life—a curse, god knew; it wasn't for the beet-root poultice. It lay somewhere in the chance of being new . . . of living lucky, and of losing Henry Pimber. He had always crammed humanity in everything. Even the air felt guilty. Once he would have seen each tree along this slope boned humanly and branched with feeling like the black bile tree, the locust, despondent even at the summit of the highest summer. How convenient it had been to find his friends and enemies embarked in tame slow trunks, in this or that bent tree, their aspirations safely in high branches and their fires podded into quiet seed. He could pat their bodies with his hands and carve his name and make up animal emotions for them no fruit could contradict. It was always easier to love great trees than people. Such trees were honest. Their deaths showed.

Come on Henry—what the hell—let's get where we can see.

They were silver in the spring. They were still new green like the river. The sun came to them. The wind turned them. And a dark deep glossy green grew on by the head of summer. It was like the green he sometimes saw when the sun was right and the wind had died cover a stone that was lightly under water. There was hedge green and ivy, slick as slippery elm and cool as myrtle. There was slime green pale with yellow; some that was like moss or grass beneath a rock or the inside of a shuck of corn. There was every shade of green in the world. There was more than the rivers had, more than any meadow.

The wind rushed over the brow of the hill, billowing Henry's coat and flattening Omensetter's hair. Behind them, in the valley, the leaves were quiet as if at the hilltop they had sponged the wind. Here the rush covered their ears. Omensetter shouted something. Henry's toes curled in his shoes to catch the ground. He sidled awkwardly, his coat lashing his legs until his body seemed to sing like wire.

. . . the notch.

Henry ledged after him. His coat ballooned. Somehow, in this mad place, he was losing everything. Omensetter vanished. The ground seemed to fall away. He hadn't known the sea had holes but how else did you drown? Then he saw Omensetter's bushy head and he dropped into the notch where the wind roared above them like Niagara Falls.

Henry sat on a rock and pulled his coat round him.

You don't like it, Omensetter said.

Oh no, it's fine.

They had to shout.

The cold stone pressed against him.

Lovely view, they said.

It was a terrifying wind.

I come often, Omensetter said. A boat's out. I wonder whose.

Henry shrugged and held on. He thought of the wild beauty of the trees, his own affection for them, his romantic sentiments, his wretched illness with its lying clarity.

Will you climb here in the winter?

Omensetter made a face.

Too cold. Freeze. Don't you love the noise?

No, Henry thought, I don't love the noise; the wind will wash my wits out.

But in the winter, he reflected, when the sun was in the west, the leafless trees would print the snow. Chamlay's snake fence would lace his south fields. Every bush would blossom, each twig sharply thrown, and every paltry post embark for consciousness as huge. The wind might blow here constantly, it would alter nothing; but this was the season of change, Henry's coat billowed out from him, and Omensetter's countenance escaped into the valley. An immense weariness took hold of Henry now, though the sun in the notch was warming. Of course—he'd been a fool—Omensetter lived by *not* observing—by joining himself to what he knew. Necessity flew birds as easily as the wind drove these leaves, and they never felt the curvature which drew the arc of their pursuit. Nor would a fox cry beauty before he chewed.

Remember? . . . remember coming, Henry shouted finally, pointing to the western hill.

Omensetter put his head up in the stream where the wind blew away his words.

Ah . . . uddy. . . . raid it would ray . . .

You were afraid?

. . . ott?

Were you afraid of getting wet?

Ah . . . ur.

You saved my life.

. . . ott?

I said are you happy in Gilean?

. . . ur.

Omensetter left the notch abruptly, and started down. Obedient, Henry followed, and saw between them and the sun a broad-winged hawk like a leaf on the flooding air. The sailor of the wind is loose, he thought; my life is lost down this dead hill. He had raised his arms and now he let them fall. I'm dreadfully sick . . . stupidly sick. A scientific fact. Quiet giggles shook him. And I've scarcely been alive. Henry Winslow Pimber. Now dead of weak will and dishonest weather. Some such disease. How would that look carved on my stone? He stumbled. ". . . for sweet sakes, Hennie, you'll never have a stone . . ." I shall be my own stone, then, my dear, my own dumb memorial, just as all along I've been my death and burial, my own dry well—hole, wall, and darkness. I ought to be exposed upon a mountain where the birds can pick my body, for no one could put himself on purpose in this clay. Besides, anyone who's lived so slow and stupidly as I have ought to spend his death up high. His mouth filled. Poor, foolish, stupid bastard, foolish fellow . . . foolish words . . . But I'd have made a worthier Omensetter—all new fat, wild hair, and furry testicles like a tiger's. Henry spat. A scientific fact. The saliva drifted against his coat. And when I arrived in my wagon like a careless western hero, clouds would be swimming in the river. Rain would fall beyond us in the forest, the Ohio like a bright hair ribbon . . . Gilean—a dream. Lalee. Naa-thing. Lalee.

I have to sit somewhere.

Oh no, keep up. We'll go on down.

Lucky was he? Was he, Henry wondered—with his polished shoes and all his new concerns.

The river disappeared beneath the trees.

They walked by the creek by the hornbeam tree—Omensetter, his hand in his greatcoat pocket where the rent was, his back indifferent as a wall—by elm and oak and maple, in the bowl that turned by the riverside, toward Henry Pimber's house where Henry followed, by the aspen, by the suede green sassafras, the beech. The silver morning grass was golden and resilient now. The slate was clean, the sandstones rich as brown sugar, and the red clay, softer after sunshine, moist, kept their feet to the slate, the sugar rocks, and the rough, resilient grass.

I've got to rest, Henry said.

The log was stripped of bark and bleached. It lay by the creek like a prehistoric bone.

Oh say, you've been sick, that's right. That hill is sort of steep. How are you feeling now—good? . . . fine, that's good.

Omensetter took money from his pocket.

We'll have to move when we can find a place. It's a little wet there for the boy—you understand—it's a little low near the river. Well . . . You've been kind.

The money emptied into Henry's hand.

I'd better see to Lucy now, Omensetter said.

He swayed rhythmically a moment like a bear.

Lucy will be fine.

Sure—still, she must be watched—the boy . . .

Omensetter waved. Limbs divided up his back.

Good-bye.

So, Henry thought, well . . . he's going to leave the fox where he has fallen. Anyway, that's that. Yes. That. Because it was impossible to speak in a wind. And there was only weather in it, after all. Weather. Leaves. Pollen, he'd been told, from infinite plants. Dust, too, of course. And the grains that carry cooking, bloom, and pine tree to the nose. Seeds naturally. Flies. Birds' song and the growl of bees. Himself—Pimber—rushing along. Yesterday it was the long night rain that fell, misplaced, through morning. Tomorrow? Tomorrow might be calm.

All right. I'll hide high up. I'll do that. Anyway, why speak in a wind? Didn't I wait for a wind to say: you saved my life?

> Ding dong bell,
> Pimber's down our well.

Didn't I wait until a wind could blow away my lie?

> Who never did him any harm,
> But wound his soul through a sleeve
> of arm.

Just the same I thought the way you walked through town, Henry was whispering just barely aloud, carrying your back as easy and as careless as you would a towel, newly come from swimming always, barely dry you always seemed, you were a sign. Remember that first evening when you came? You were a stranger, bare to heaven really, and your soul dwelled in your tongue when you spoke to me, as if I were a friend and not a stranger, as if I were an ear of your own. You had mud beneath your arms, mud sliding down the sides of your boots, thick stormy hair, dirty nails, a button missing. The clouds were glowing, a rich warm rose, and I watched them sail till dark when I came home. It seemed to me that you were like those clouds, as natural and beautiful. You knew the secret—how to be.

Henry cleared his throat. And had he simply been mistaken? Or had Omensetter been persuaded of his luck so thoroughly that now he guarded it like gold, and feared being thieved? Henry wrapped his arms like a kerchief round his head. Omensetter had been robbed already. Everybody but the preacher stole from him. Furber merely hated. But what I took was hope—a dream—fool's gold—quarrel—tooth-some hen, Henry said. How weary he was, and sorry ... sorry for everything. He was sorry about the rent, about the house, the damp, the open well, the river. He was sorry for Omensetter, sorry for Lucy, sorry for the children, sorry for Lucy again. He was sorry for himself. Tears pooled in his eyes.

Just the same, Henry said, I thought you measured us by your inhuman measure like the trees, and we were busy ants in hills or well-hived bees whose love was to pursue the queen and bring on death. When you put my hands in bandages and beets I thought I understood. There was no shade between us ever but the shade I'd drawn. You were the same to human or inhuman eye.

Henry slid from the log and hushed his whispering. He pushed at low shrubs until he couldn't see the sycamores. It was thick in this part of the woods. He parted the branches with his arms. Brackett Omensetter before he left had hid behind his face and made his back a wall. The man had been a miracle. He had, Henry spoke out angrily. A miracle. Not to be believed. And now he took defense against the world like everybody else. No miracle, a man, with a man's mask and a man's wall. Henry chuckled, unfastening the belt of his coat. He tugged at it. It would be strong. His pooled tears ran. If Brackett Omensetter had ever had the secret of how to live, he hadn't known it. Now the difference was—he knew. Everyone at last had managed to tell him, and now like everybody else he was wondering what it was. Like everybody else. Henry wiped his eyes. Don't look for Henry here, my dear, he's gone. He's full of foolishness, and off to kill a fox. But I'll not die as low as he did, for I could ornament a tree like the leaves of a maple. No. It should be tall. A white oak maybe, with its wide lobes. There was beauty in the pun: leave-taking. Though it wouldn't be an easy climb for a man who'd been so sick so recently. Still the sun would reach him early there and stay the day, the wind blow pleasantly. It ought to seem like leaping to the sea. He went by cherry and by black gum trees calling their names aloud. He was the Adam who remembered them. Tears nevertheless began again. How sorry for it all he felt. How sorry for Omensetter. How sorry for Henry.

The Reverend Jethro
Furber's Change of Heart

~~ 1

Rough dogs, barking, splashed into the river chasing sticks.
Coats and ties had been hung in the trees and men were
hurling stones at soda bottles or skimming pieces of slate and
loudly counting the skips. He picked out squealing children
and the laughter of the women. If there hadn't been a wall he
would have seen them scuffling on the edge of the water. The
land fell and the trees parted so that seated where he was the
Ohio might have made his eyes blink, but the wall was eight
feet high and wound in its vines like a bottle of claret. The
bench was damp and cold, shadowed all morning by the
elms, and he slid his Bible under him. It was a poor garden,
given over to ground ivy and plants that preferred deep
shade, for the sun reached it only at the top of the day when
it found an opening between the crowns of the trees and the
head and body of the church. Absently, he felt the pores of
the cement. The shadows of the elm leaves passed gently
over the vines and grasses. In winter one could see quite
easily through the gate at the end of the garden to the river
lying placidly in its ice—leaden, grave, immortal. He had
never learned when the key had been lost but the lock was
rusted now and the double gates were bound. By spring,
when the ivy leafed and thickly curtained the pickets, his
blindfold was complete. Nevertheless he could see the sand
rising in little puffs and the brilliant water striking the shore.
It wasn't true, but Jethro Furber felt he had spent his life
here. Certainly he had brought to the garden the little order
it had, laying the walk with his own hands and clearing the
graves of weeds and creepers, carefully scrubbing the
markers. The rough cold bench was as familiar to him as his

skin, and the garden, with its secret design and its holy significance, was like himself. He smiled as he considered it (he had considered often), for the body of any symbol was absurd, as ridiculous as Christ's body was, so lank and ribby. And those crudely fashioned timbers thrust clumsily in the earth were foolish. The crucifixion was so far from love. How far was he from what he meant? . . . pale, pinch-faced little man in Negro-colored clothing, the nail-eyed reverend, Jethro Furber, fourth in this church and a liar; how far was he from the conscience of his people? That Scanlon girl was turning around, blooming her pink skirt, and The Noisy One was calling to his dog. He saw the hair of The Noisy One tossing like a girl's; his stones were shattering the water. Furber had told them what was due the Sabbath; he had thrown his voice on its knees before them shamefully; he had warned and threatened; he had rounded his words with brass and blown through them strongly like a choir of trumpets. But what use was it to preach? Futile. Futile. He could not face them down again. That, too, was futile. In three corners of the garden there were graves, crookedly laid, where the no longer living persons of his predecessors had been put away, and there was still an empty corner left for him to lie futile and forgotten in. All was proper and correct. Even the clichés of the preacher were correct: the no longer listening ears, the no longer swelling lungs, the no longer laughing teeth or dancing hair, the no longer bitterly envenomed prick. He struck his thigh, half rose, then settled slowly back again. Omensetter's stones dipped and flew and lit like gulls upon the water. Furber rubbed his teeth together so they squeaked, then shivered at the sound. Soon the sun will reach the bench, he thought, and the leaves will whiten. He would wait where he was. He would have to. Certainly he would not go out again.

He had his rehearsals here. Slowly, his head bowed, the Bible held firmly against his chest, he would circle the garden. His eyes would sweep over the ground near his feet, over the bruised leaves and bared roots, the grass stubble and the mud that oozed between stones. Lilies of the valley grew thickly near the wall where trails of crumbled mortar, smears of river damp and moss, were visible under the vines. Violets, chickweed and the buckhorn plantain flourished. There was privet still alive from a feeble attempt before his time to divide the garden with hedges, and a rose which the wind burned to the ground every winter sprawled over a rotting willow stump, its canes nearly leafless from disease, struggling to bloom. Chafers would feed upon the buds, yet he would stay his hand, verifying, once again, the destructive course of nature. Orange yellow when it flowered, it was a climber, and he thought he recognized its fragrance. A neighbor of his mother grew it, or she had ... like a dream of gold along her fence—*Rêve d'or* ... and golden honeysuckle up the trellis of her porch, with strident morning glories too and clematis as purple as the robe of a king; and there were pearl-white lily trumpets, forsythia and lilacs like so many fountains, four o'clocks and bleeding heart, begonias spilling out of baskets swung from chains, straw flowers, daisies, pink hydrangeas that she sometimes fertilized with nails to make them blue, weedy magenta phlox and columbine, verbena, floppy red petunias, bachelor buttons, zinnias, round transparent pennyroyal to dry and press between the psalms, rose geraniums in pots along the rails, gentians, pinks, sweet peas, nasturtiums of the clearest orange ... he peered at all this thick sweet beauty through the pickets, frightened somewhat, for they kept a dog, and at the rough sweet lawn, so cool and moist, the walk around it edged with snowy ageratum and violet alyssum, pansies pink as lips, stonecrop squeezing between the bricks, while in the beds behind them there were sky-blue asters on hooping stems, pale and methodical, as perfect as if they had been grown by spiders; and hidden by high grass and goldenrod and stock he would watch the woman, Mrs. Kermit Hazen— Maisie was it? did she live beyond her operation? Fidel was the dog—stretching her garish yellow print across her rump and show the roll of her stockings when she bent to cut the stems and pile the flowers in her dusty apron. Tears would form in his eyes, running the figures of the flowers and the woman together, and he would press the fence slats cruelly into his cheeks. She'd have planted marigolds nearby and through the fence he would reach one, uprooting it roughly and rubbing his face with its pungent leaves before he went into the house and gave his cheek to his aunt to kiss so she would sneeze.

As he walked he meditated on some passage of scripture or some thought he'd found in St. Jerome or Augustine, trying to penetrate and reformulate it. Finally words would begin to rise, his throat would move, he would begin to mutter and his fingers drum on the book. Although he had taken the same steps many times—indeed he had minutely organized them and given each a symbolic character—and though his downward glance seemed vacant and his posture affected, he did not miss the movements of life at his feet. Indeed he fed his soul on these sensations and there they mingled with his thoughts on equal terms, for Jethro Furber felt that Nature was the word of God as certainly as scripture was—his task, therefore, to watch and listen, to interpret and bear witness. We should all be watchmen, and we should pray that God will open our eyes to evil and burn our hearts to admonish the ungodly. Think, he often said, how the demons howl. Their voices are rough and crude; they live in fire; they scream; they sever their words as their heads are severed; but is not the justice of it sweet? In the same way the worst of this world signifies the best of the other. While saying this his voice would rise, his hands flutter, his eyelids squeeze rapturously together.

Rancorous ivy. On the other side of the wall, at the edge of the river, the sand burned. The river lay afire. Kingfishers fell like spots across the eyes and laughter was yellow. Every Sunday Omensetter strolled by the river with his wife, his daughters, and his dog. They came by wagon, spoke to people who were off to church, and while Furber preached, they sprawled in the gravel and trailed their feet in the water. Lucy Omensetter lay her swollen body on a flat rock. Furber felt the sun lapping at her ears. It was like a rising blush, and his hands trembled when he held them out to make the bars of the cross. May the Lord bless you and keep you . . . He closed his eyes, drifting off. They would see how moved he was, how intense and sincere he was. Cause His light to shine upon you . . . . He would find the footprints of the dog and the imprint of their bodies. All the days of your life. . . . The brazen parade of her infected person. Watchman. Rainbows like rings of oil around her. Watchman. Shouldn't we be? I spy you, Fatty, behind the tree. He wanted to rub the memory from his eyes. Glittering. Beads of water stood on her skin and drop fled into drop until they broke and ran, the streaks finally fading. Her navel was inside out—sweet spot where Zeus had tied her. She was so white and glistening, so . . . pale, though darker about the eyes, the nipples dark. Open us to evil. He made a slit in his lids. Burn our hearts. Shawls of sunlight spilled over the back of the pews. Nay-ked-nessss. The droplets gathered at the point of her elbow and hung there, the sac swelling until it fell and spattered on her foot. Nay . . . nay. To enclose her like the water of the creek had closed her. Nay . . . Proper body for a lover. Joy to be a stone. Please, the peep-watch is over. Please hurry now. Hurry. Get out of my church.

Though surely not now. With the baby scarcely born she should be home beside it; yet she likely had it cradled in her arm where it would root for her teats in the loose open folds of her dress. Always blue or yellow for some reason, it was lacy around the throat and fell like a golden fountain from her chin. Joy to be a thread. Lord. And all the other mothers, even all the men, smiled, wishing her breasts were their own. Dee dum dee dum. How'd it gone? While his mother lay sleeping, Big Jack had come creeping... Guilty of nessss. Um... some, something to tipple from her mountainous nipple. Cover her nay... No, that wasn't right. Shaymmm. He had mixed the days. So far apart. Years apart. Yet alike. Yet the same. The sky was the same clear blue. There'd been the same sweet breeze—everything as crisp as lettuce. Not years, of course. Seasons. Exactly two. And they were scuffling and shouting down there beyond him, out of his reach.

The rolling brilliant blue and yellow balls, the stiff white wickets, the dark sweet grass lay beyond the fence, and a large man in a white shirt, his coat on the grass, was kneeling, squinting along the handle of his mallet, while a girl in white slippers, puffs of rabbity fuzz at the toes and heels, in a gauzy dress as green as the grass was, as cool, turned very slowly about and swung her mallet in a slow circle; and Mrs. Kermit Hazen was there too, her feet well spaced, leaning forward a little and using her mallet like a cane, speaking rapidly to the man as he sighted until brushing his knees, he straightened up and pointed the grass-stained nose of his mallet at her, making her teeter with laughter; then, taking his stroke, the beautiful bright ball rolled down a gentle slope through the wicket and struck the yellow with a resonant clack. There was also a ferret-faced boy in a black suit and white collar who kept clearing his throat and spitting and who was supposed to be playing though he didn't know how but only rubbed his stomach and complained of an ache.

Futile... Oh my deliberately driven heels clattered on the shale and I held the Bible like a black stone tightly to my chest, pressing the buttons of my coat against me, and I said is this a Sunday thing and does the service come so easy off that you can laugh and shout within the hearing of the steeple? His heart replied to the pressure of the buttons, thundering. The congregation had come by the riverside, going home, while Omensetter was throwing sticks for the dog, shattering images in the water, when a sudden gust blew the ragged straw he always wore on Sunday into the Ohio where the current swept it quickly out of reach. It was studded with fish hooks and sat on the crown of his head like an untidy nest. As if it were a stick, his yellow dog pursued it. There was consequently great excitement and the betting and the bowling of the laughter rose to Furber with such a ring of vulgar, brazen joy that he rushed in anger from his garden, as pale-eyed and black as he could make himself, and flew down among them to stalk stiff-legged like a jackdaw, clacking futilely.

Initially, between the trees, he caught sight of whirling, jumping bodies. Heya-heya-heya. Someone climbing. Rocks pitched after a board; and on the river, tilting patches of reflection. Heya-fulla-heya-heya. Boys were sliding down the bank on their buttocks, roughing the scaly sand. They sailed a can lid on the water where at first it turned, floating, then sank, burning like a mirror. Hiyah-smilah. Hee-mee? Coltch. Skirts rose slowly, slowly subsided. A parasol flew open with a snap. Or-rawk. Gah. Houf. Half buried in the shingle, a deep red brick was then awash. Yo-yo giggy. Teetoo. Sheek? Num! Lissa-lissa. A willow leaned out, trailing its leaves in the water. Someone was hiding under the canopy. A stream of sand poured down the Cate girl's back. Though she wriggled suggestively, hand to her mouth, she had no points to her chest, and Furber decided she still had a glabrous cleft. Ze-e-e-p. A ribbon went up, revolving, and fell over a branch. Sweeping the beach with a broom of leaves was a flimsy little girl in pale green organdy frock, very stiff and frilly, very city. He couldn't place her. Whar? Bally. Karck! karck! karck! Some were crying for the hat; some were shouting for the river; others favored the dog. But no one was really prepared to bet against Omensetter. Furber knew they were pretending that.

The current caught the hat, spinning it round and round on its crown. The dog, his nose cresting the water, swam faster, and the crowd's excitement grew. Children ran frantically about. The women tried to restrain them and restrain their husbands who were slapping their knees, waving their own hats, and calling out encouragement to hat, dog, and river. Arthur was clearly gaining and there was cheering for him. Omensetter smiled. He had the wide moist mouth he bragged his son would have. The hat leaped ahead then, finding its place in the blood of the river. Arthur lunged, and the hat bobbed. There was more cheering. The fever was rising. The hat sped away, a speck in the plaster light. Omensetter yelled come back above the shouting and his girls yelled too, come back, come back. His wife sat placidly, her hands folded on her belly.

This is the church. This is the steeple. Look inside and see all the people.

The testaments against his heart, he kept a firm grip on

himself. Trailing kerchiefs, violet and green, pale hands like iris out of sleeves, the young girls were turning. That night he would dream of maidenly garments. He smelled sachets of lavender. People began shading their eyes and leaning forward. Omensetter was yelling come back. Arr-thurr! His brick-red neck was netted with thin lines. Piercingly, his daughters yelled come back, severing their words. Their bare feet were clenching pebbles and water ran down their legs. People shouted kum-baack! heyheyhey kum-baack! Children ceased running and scuffling. A few took hold of their mothers' hands. One of the Hatstat boys was standing on his head and his brothers were clapping. Kangaroo, Furber thought. Kangaroo, he almost shouted. Why in the world should I want to do that? Yazebo heenie, yazebo! The dog was tired when he turned. He was deeper in the water and his nose dipped once or twice. Higher on the bank, Furber saw the hat go on. He felt it spinning on its crown, the hooks in its band hanging down in the water to the nose and teeth of fishes. The dog had failed, and the hat that Furber had so often seen and hated, Sundays, on that thick unwholesome head was finally gone. He regretted that he had not flipped it from those popping eyes himself, and sailed it off. Now he felt no elation for what the wind had done. The dog bobbed and thrashed. If Omensetter swam for the dog, would he take off his trousers? Lord save us from that. Light streamed from the water a⁻ᵈ ʰ ᶜ passed his hand wearily over his eyes. The river was a streak of red on his lids. A jay was calling. He devoutly hoped the dog would drown.

It was a mistake to have come here. The women had red hands and peasant bodies—legs as thick as trees. Not that it mattered. He'd forsaken all that. Furber stirred, deliberately and painfully kicking his ankles. The book was uncomfortable. Not nearly wide enough, it was biting his thighs. He slid to the bench and immediately felt the damp through his trousers. The Cate girl, for instance, or May Cobb. What would happen to them? They'd grow dugs and hair like any woman. May Cobb already had. Blond doubtless, downy, curling under, perhaps a hint of red, of reddish . . . it was one of the laws of God. They'd carry their new mouths about with them for a few months—always moist, a bit inflamed. The farm boys would finger their breasts with less skill, certainly, than they milked the cows, preferring the unbuttoned flies of their friends. Their thick stubby fingers were like chewed on school pencils, rows of dents like rings around them, the paint broken and scaling, yellow mostly, why was that? . . . they had dirty, bitten, discolored nails; their hands were rough already; they had stupid hands; they had stumbling, bad-hearted hands; clumsily pawing hands, clumsily unhooking hands, poking, pulling, parting, jerking, why? . . . to insert a cold wet nose? ah, the dog with damp fur! say, chuck chuck Charlie, a smart slap on the butt and bottom's up old girl, that's love . . . mmmn pet the love dog, Dickie, nnnm? Eeee, goody geedge! Then to marry and settle down. How fares the thumb, boy? well? Aye, merry, 'tis the sign of the penis. With the women, look you, observe the ear. The parts appear and come together. So obesity and malice. So grumbling and nagging. So gossip, envy, spite, and avarice. Slowly settling into. So feminine weakness. Heartless piety. Savage morals. They come together. No more goody geedge. Ruthless, lifelong revenge. Zrr. Grease in a cold pan. Stay off from gingerly lobed and delicately whorled ones. Thus appear the parts. Mind your uncle, boy, who knows. And the men then. Lewd speech and slovenly habits. And the peasant's suspicion, his cruelty and rancor, his anger, drunkenness, pig-headed ignorance and bestiality. Inevitable they should be parts. Hoolyhoohoo. All in the normal course of nature. And they were saying we had evolved. What did it mean? But, he said in a voice that was clearly audible, I protest this world of unilluminated cocks. He caught the sense of his own words—so absurd—and his body began to shake—half in laughter, half in despair.

It would nearly always end like this—with an outburst of speech. He would come to the bench and sit quietly a while, his arms tightly folded and his feet clenched; but after a time he would be impelled to jump up hugging his book, his lips moving as he began to pace, intently examining the ground. Before long the rhythm of his walk would alter, and while his free arm gestured grandly, a series of expressions, each eloquent of feeling, would pass rapidly across his face. Finally some real emotion would cause his eyes to smart, eventually to water, and his mutterings would swell and sprout and put out leaves, taking their place in an oratory that was personal, ornate, and violent. Sometimes he would go directly to a corner of the garden where the gravestones of what it amused him to call his ancestors were placed, and there he would nonchalantly rest his foot upon a marker and in a low, meditative voice, with only an edge of surprise and wonder to it, like Hamlet's at the grave of Yorick, exercise his art upon a multitude of sacred topics . . . the pews packed, the fans and hankies still, the feet still as he bore them on from thought to thought, as safely by their perils as a hare through a thorn bush.

Futile love, Horatio, futile love. My hand droops from its wrist. No lily better. Yet there's a finger stiffly thrust. Mark

it. And the nail shine. *How long had they loved one
another . . . my smile's like a floating leaf . . . this flesh on the
bones of Eve, our lovely mother, and death in the fruit of the
tree?* The delicate wires of my hand, the delicate wrist-hinge,
the sharp cuff, the willow limbs . . . *How long had she lain all
trouble full, so lankly haunched, disconsolate, the yearning in
her, the apple burning? Or did she squat with reverently
mingled hands beneath its branches while it bloomed, to
wait . . . oh la, patiently . . . her soul like a mollusk?* My
trunk is bending and my forelock's sliding. *She knew what she
wanted.* I ought to be holding something while I talk, a
fragment of our Universal Mother, something not too
foolish, something common nonetheless and simple although
richly emblematic. A piece of Palestine perhaps. I laugh, my
teeth appearing. And the moon. Well the rose is too common
and the phallus too foolish. Are you there, in the tinkler,
Mother, just as much? Nevermind. My hands will serve. Fine
threads throughout bind the tubes. *See her in there, in my
palmist's body; see her, how she know? Picture her, your
parent, Horatio, your initial mother, wandering in the garden, far from her spouse: thin, hairless, hard, slat-limbed
. . . a child . . . everywhere angular and skimped on,
scarcely papped . . . a smooth-loined boy. But hollow, my
friend, oh so hollow. Listen. There's wind bottled in her. And
what did the serpent promise—to be like a god, to know
good and evil—what was that? It was the apple Eve ate of. It
was the apple, the fruit, the fullness, she wanted.* Rub up the
lamp, lad. Let's have jokes and poetry. Let progeny appear.
That's one for Tott if he could grasp it.

> Nell ate lettuce,
> and on its leaves
> Bel sat thinking
> of enemies.

> Nell ate Forcas,
> and on her tongue
> hell fell burning
> for Christendom.

> Nell ate Satan,
> and in her lust
> well was growing
> an incubus.

> Nell ate me,
> and up her sleeves
> fell fall turning
> with all its leaves.

For an incubus, too tame. Incubus:

> It ate Nell,
> and from its bum
> shit fell forming
> Babylon.

Chuckling, I slide my next lines up the slippery sleeve. Inky the coils of the darkness up there. Hear her, hear? There's only a rush in the listener's ear. *It was for that she disobeyed. What did she know or care about gods or good or evil, when growing was her concern? Suppose she had been warned not to cross a certain line, or not to sit unmaidenly, or not to pick her nose, or not to yell in the park—would she have disobeyed? For knowledge, for good and evil, would Eve have set her will against her Father's? Ah, Horatio, you and I know women. Not for that. But she'd have eaten the apple anyway—to be the mother of all living. And how perfectly the sign was chosen, think of it, Horatio. Pendent from a crown of leaves, this globe, so firm and smooth and red without, so soursweet and white within, holds at its core, like tears, its seeds. Oh it is very moving, Horatio. It makes me weep like an aunt at a wedding . . . or an uncle at a wake . . . which? . . . am I aunt or uncle, man or mother, Horatio? . . . it's too riddling.*

Dressed in black hose and a loose white doublet, he was smiling gently, his eyes were shining, he looked directly at Horatio, with deep intent, prepared to go back over his speech to improve it, change its meaning if need be, anything, so that it might be eloquent. *Flesh*, he might begin, *flesh is male and female in one fabric, interlaced like fingers, good Horatio, and death's their double shadow; therefore there are four of them together in this wedding bed.* Straighten smiling; on tiptoe turn. Sweet my dancing clothes, sweet blossoms on my dancing branch, my arm unrolls. *Bone cell, skin cell, gristle cell, blood cell . . . bone . . . bone . . .* rap against the wall like a stave. *Yet since flesh is partly canine—mark the tongue, Horatio, the abundance of saliva, the lowered snout, the panting breath—we must add a fifth. Bone . . . oh love this glove of flesh contains—the mother of the world. What kind of dog do you imagine serves this purpose best, one that nicely fits the hollow of the lap and has soft hair, do you vote for that? Finally, because death has a fat bald stubby nigger slave with neither genitals nor fingers, we must count to six . . . in one love bundle all enwrapped . . . and you will admit, Horatio, that only a god could have contrived such a tangle.* Outside the bedroom door the wedding party beats on pans.

Be fruitful. Wasn't He a merry joker, the Old Man?

Sometimes while he walked he would break into wild half-whispered words instead, and turn with open arms to the walls and leaves, his gaze fixed ecstatically on heaven, adopting the posture of saints he'd seen in prints. *I am the Francis of this place. I feed these vines and they grow tame for love of me.* Or unable to stomach his own acting, he would turn to mockery. *Oh give us a dramatic speech.* And often he would oblige, charming himself with his rhetoric like a snake playing the flute.

What is the holiest thing in God's world?

Hands lift to his eyes as they did each Sunday when he spoke from his sacred stump.

Everything is God's—hearts, stars, and carrots, dry sticks and infinite spaces—hah? We start with that. What shows His limitless glory?

The private parts? More dainty japery. Pun of God. And what do we say to that? Bla-a-a-a-a-

He bends near the twigs of a bush and stares at them fiercely. Have you heard we compete, you and I, like Jacob and angel? You're entangling my air. Laughing coarsely, he snatches the head from a flower.

The good man? His mouth pulls apart at the corners. *Gah.* He leans weakly against the wall. *The loveliest river?* His eyes light, his thumbs plug his ears, his fingers waggle. *The sun when it burns in the heart of a cloud?* He skips . . . la, la, la . . . his eyes turn up in despair. *No. No. Oh no no no. There's no reach for Him in these; there's no extension of Him here. Why He would soften with such exercise; grow short of breath and weak.* Wobbling, he bends his knees, cane feeling the flagstones. *Are we more amazed when the strong man lifts his leg than when he lifts the chair he stands on? Whoo-ee. Impressed? Indeed.*

A swift kick has swithened the spirit of love. So stiffly military, a statue unstuck, he speaks.

Consider then that He is present most in what seems fartherest from Him.

Youthfully to the bench soars, torches around him, vibrating arms: *oh this is His greatest triumph—to turn dung into a monument.*

Ah well, too bad. I've given the game away.

Um? I have? Pity.

Hiccoughs.

So then it is the Devil, of course, the sly old snake, who is holiest . . . think of that. He fell, he was The Fall itself, the suicidal star; but he fell at the end of a fine elastic. It is the cord through which he even yet is fed and thrives. Obvious

*when you think about it. Eh? Nonsense. Obvious. She-e-e
. . . cluck, cluck, cluck . . . Try to think. Try. Quack, quack,
quack . . . Satan shows God's power best. Oh you're cows.
Browse then, damn you. Wallow. Drink. Moo-oo-oo . . . How
well He wears the tragic mask; how splendid perfect
goodness is in such a role! Was God not Pontius Pilate? And
everybody else? He was the nails, the spear, the thorns, the
soldiers asleep. For christ's sake, how can you disbelieve it?
It's yes now, is it? That's better. Yes. A brilliant performance, you agree? Yes. Oh yes. Listen. It's HE in that red
clothing. Hah. Good day. It's He. It's old St. Nick, the jolly
redman. Now then—applaud. Applaud. Pigs. Pee-e-eegs!*

You and I—you, master builder, spinner of threads, you
and I, like Jacob and angel, we—fight. The spider floats on a
bit of web. Furber follows grimly; raises his foot.

*Nevertheless pigs. Oh yes. Evil is His chiefest work. Take
some delight in it. Do. Do do do. He might well have set
aside one of the six days of creation for it. Man, woman,
fawning dog, nigger, gnome and worm, then rest. Which day
would it have been? Gnomesday? Manday or Wormsday? Or
did it rain, keeping Him in, pruning the masculine crotch?
Dogsday? Well no matter. Applause is due Him. You ought
to stand and cheer Him, hats in hand . . . Ah, there He is, at
the top of the tent, in pink tights and carrying a striped
umbrella. Nononono nets! I hope you're on to this. It is His
chiefest work. Oh you'll feel it; you'll get a taste of it. But
listen. To have put Himself safely, entirely, in even that . . .
there my dears, there . . . there is glory!*

*But wait. The devil is a clever fellow surely. He hides
himself, eh? Good. Where? Where's he hid? Find his face in
the picture. He'll have lit on the sweet cream like a fly in a
dairy. Why there he is, tree-twigged and woolly-swaddled,
outspread to rise, grimace on his geezer . . . oh ho! in the butt
and body of the best . . . ah ha! in the goody's soulskin shoes,
a comical surprise, who'd ever figure . . . Flack? Goody's got
gah-lory in his gut, Flack; that's what goody's got, gah-lory.*

Flack? Where are you, Flack? Help me up.

The colored man would come without a word and help
Furber to his feet wherever he had fallen and lead him,
palsied and weak, to his room to rest.

The Lord succeed my pink borders.

Yes sir. I hope so. Yes indeed.

He had gotten his days confused. The air had done it.
From where he sat there were easily visible hips on the rose.
That little girl had been from Cleveland, a guest of
Chamlay's. He hadn't seen her since. Her bloomers had been
green too, a matching shade, flowering beneath her skirt . . .

sweet and cool. Who'd made the broom? His legs filled with energy. Kangaroo! The opening curtain found him to the left of the stage poised on his right toe in the posture of Mercury. Slowly he folded his limbs and sank to his haunches . . . Up! Without warning he was soaring, turning, wingspreading; then he was rising again, going up and up, wheeling, floating . . . Fish in the skywater, a glint of gold as he passed through the limbs of the seatrees, deeply voyaging, even to the purple shadows along the bottom where he lay on his side to wait for seamice, small luminous shrimps, and butterflies. Wasn't that the shadow of the hat, the hooks hanging? Or was it a moon in a green sky? There's the line come down, a homemade spinner, Knox's surely, a little rusty, the sinker's already clouding an inch of the bottom. What's he using, grubs? Fly maggots maybe. Nothing heaves with life like they do. Two or three are forked on the hook like peas. Is it channel cat he's after? Is that where I'm lying. Um. His spinner's dancing. Catches the eye. Revolving white haunches. What if I bit? The moment the mouth surrounds the grub, the throat will endeavor to swallow. Saliva will skid the grub along; the hook will be carried down. Ah but the angler—that's the mark of his boat passing . . . see the streaks and bubbles of the dipping oars?—retracts his line. The hook pulls free of the grub and lodges its point on the roof of the mouth or in the side of the cheek or at the root of the tongue. Then it's up . . . turning, spinning . . . up . . . and you're out and it's all over. Sweet world of air, another element.

And this is the garden. Constraint in her voice, a certain thickness, harshness, was it scorn? She wouldn't let the little colored man help her and now she struggled with the latch, pushing at the door with her bony shoulder. She knew Gilean society for what it was. You couldn't be much if you were sent to such a place, especially if you were no longer young. She was right. It was only too clear he'd been banished. The door yielded suddenly and she staggered through it with an embarrassed cry. In the church it had been pleasantly cool and dark, even his room had seemed restful, but the light in the garden was painful; the air was hot and smelled of dust. They had fastened walls of stone to a wooden box. This is your suite, she had said disdainfully. The church itself had a certain crude charm; he wouldn't mind it. What was it called—Pike's Peak? She was saying that Reverend Rush had little interest in gardening. There was a smudge on her arm now and if she would only move a bit he might edge by. The Chamlay woman had referred to *Mister* Rush, over and over, very determinedly. Quite correct, of course, but in the sticks they ought to say "Reverend." He was always so busy, poor man, so busy, even in his last days . . . Professionally sad face. Then sour, hard Mrs. Pimber, with a twitch. Pretty once. A distrubing woman, somehow. Was it the way she walked or the stretch of her lips? Mumbling, mumbling, the Flack fellow shuffling—what sort was he? She'd just begun mumbling. Yes, her mumbling was new. Self-conscious? She had a permanent stoop; walked with slightly bent knees; crick in her neck. Her brother was nothing like her size though he had her lumpy nose. God if *he* wasn't a fatuous ass. That joke at luncheon about putting him out to pastorage. What was she saying? . . . you can see. He stared grimly at the garden. ". . . when the dew was still on the row-zezz . . ." We can't afford to pay someone to keep it up, though Flack does dig about in it from time to time, don't you Flack? Yes ma'am, now and then. She was a little belligerent about the money, he thought; she was warning him maybe; and to the darkie she was threatening. Yes. He was complaining he was old. No one had thought to donate the labor, of course; that's how things were done in the church, for christ's sake, didn't they know? That rear pew's got a little rickety, Mr. Knox. Chuckle. I'm afraid it'll collapse in the middle of the offertory music. Touch his shoulder. Please, not a rheumatic complainer, anything else; a liar, a peeper, a thief. At lunch, who seemed interested in money? Mrs. Pimber? Mrs. Pimber. Important to know. They were suspicious of him, he could see, held his fork properly for one thing. Stingy farmers, stinking of cows. Oh it would be dreary here—a wilderness, a desert. Well St. Jerome had thrived in one . . . and drawn the women to him. The walk was overgrown with creepers and covered with dry green leaves. It would have to be relayed. There was a sundial but the gnomon was missing. A pagan object, he said, pointing. She smiled. Endless mouth. He wondered if the children teased her much as a girl. Not so long ago really. A maidenhead like a bass drum. They might have called her Bones. There's quite a lot . . . of Samantha Tott. Oat weed. Jimson. Nettle. The trail of a garter snake in the dust, or a rope. Crabgrass and dandelion. At least there was a wall. Plantain. Ah Miss Tott, you're lagging. This might be difficult for her, after all. Here was St. Francis as a bird bath, missing an arm, with a dented nose. St. Francis, for christ's sake—in this Protestant yard. Watch the thorns, he said, you'll snag your dress. He'd bet a rhino couldn't puncture it. An improperly cut stump next. Couldn't they do anything right? He dug into it with his toe. Alive with ants. Wasn't a muscle jumping at the hinge of her jaw? How her brother did jabber—lazy looking young fool. Pike's Peak. And that Lutheran language. He was the one. Perhaps the pastor would appreciate another cup? Pastor has a lump of gas as large as a penny balloon lodged in his lower intestine. He would like to fart but he doesn't dare to. Cowardly pastor. That Chamlay woman had unfriendly eyes, and Mrs. Knox, Rosa was it? didn't keep her bust up. He'd wade over there. In the corner bronze chrysanthemums were blooming. The unseasonable heat had made them ratty. Nearby there were patches of bare ground thickly layered with dust. He chuckled. This is where you put them when they're all used up? That was cruel. Is this Mister Rush, he said, looking down. She was coloring. The blood's up for Mister Rush. Rest his soul. If he'd worn a hat—what a chance. Anyway he bowed his head. Bad form, no hat. Some sort of symbol. The dead ground in Gilean didn't look like this. This was a pauper's pocket. He had half a mind to say so. There was a hankie in her hand he hadn't seen. Up her sleeve? The dust. Dab at her nose. Made of putty. Samantha Totty . . . grew her nose . . . in her potty . . . like a rose. He indicated the flowers. In his honor? That was cruel too. Did he have his hat on when they slid him under? The weeds do get about, don't they? Oh me oh my I'd like to cry and wash the evil from my eye. You'd never guess that all of this was dug in June. Or did he die in July? Last through the fourth? Miracle of growth. Lid twitch. Dust again. Talking through her hankie. Not very proud . . . discouraging . . . lack of action . . . years of service . . . loved him though . . . a fine inscription on the stone . . . You might point out that the church never moved him up. Left him to rot in this hole in Ohio. What was his weakness? Little girls with creamy underclothes? It was a tradition to be hung here despite the churchly laws. Forever for their sins. Gilean. End of the line. Get off. The Negro man was blowing his nose. He did it delicately and Furber was surprised. She did have good brown eyes. But wore a bracelet. The others are over there? and there? I suppose we might as well go. ". . . the son of God dis-cloh-oh-zezz . . ." That damn tune was haunting him. "Oh He walked with me, and He talked with me, and He told me I was His oh-n-ne . . ." Out that gate? No?

Two years of living in this garden like a toad. They didn't weed it for me, or clip the hedges, or mow, or reset the walk. I failed at that too. Didn't I touch OK's shoulder nicely, pitty-pat the back of C. Chamlay? Whose knee did I fail to squeeze? And now The Noisy One. Futile . . . futile. They're no longer listening. The breeze seems gentler where he walks.

Where he stands the sun seems warmer. The ground grows easy for his feet. Useless for me . . . hopeless.

Furber had recognized, almost at once, the drunken spirit of the man, so Indian-skinned and wild. The knowledge had run through him like a fire. It had been raining again, and blowing. He'd darted into Watson's shop, shutting his umbrella. Behind it a man like a range of hills. But he'd been greeted simply with a smile. Mat had said: Mister Furber, this is Backett Omensetter, just come on to here from Windham. Backett, Mister Furber preaches in our church. Both of Omensetter's hands had reached for his, enclosing it warmly. His own had seemed terribly pale and damp, wrongly inside of the other's, like a worm in fruit. He'd withdrawn it in panic, and pleading urgent business, he had fled. He'd strode about the church in sodden coat and trousers, gesturing with his umbrella. Oh this is no ordinary magician! Then anger and chagrin had overwhelmed him. Mister Furber preaches in our church. He had beaten his fists against the wall until he felt he'd broken them. Mister Furber preaches in our church. When they ached he shouted at them: well, well, do you enjoy this? what have you both deserved?

If I played the banjo . . . How's the fishing Olus? oats nicely? hay? ain't it hot though, ain't it rainy, ain't it cold? The wife? thin whiny Marjorie for instance? sour Susan? Pat the fat? curdled Carol? bitch Clariss? Has Constance come into her awfuls yet? and it don't scare her? god it did mine—put the terror to her. How's your old bald ma, Willie Amsterdam? And that indian she's got living with her? Boylee, your balls has gone soft, that's all. Borers? hoppers? rust? Ever try tobacco? way up here? shit, Ames, you're in for a surprise. Pork's a poor price again. Well screw those dirty assed pigs. A hog's as mean as hell, boy. I mean it. They don't come any meaner. A mean hog's real mean, all right. That's no lie, let me tell you. Mean. Yeeee. And hailstones as big as your fist a-slamming into the ground whop. Yar? Judas the Profiting Priest. Here's Al. That dog's got a tongue on her, don't care what she licks. Kekekekekekekeke . . . Oh Lord we pray you not to forget your good servants here in Gilean. They're good faithful servants, Lord. I've been here all the time, watching, watching, watching, like a toad in the high grass . . . God oh merciful God . . . and they're good faithful servants, you bet they are, and they need rain, they need rain bad. Preachers is just people, ain't that right Curtis? Catholics are cannibals—they eat their own. Babies—god, boy, do they have babies. Say, how they hanging?

Like Judas Priest. Here's Luke. It's damn good manure, I'll say that. Best shit in the world. Get any geese? Connie's got a bloody bunny; she'll not lay for love or money; Patrick thinks that's awful funny; he has neither dough nor dummy. Rum a dum dum, rum a dum. Say Luther, how come you to break that wagon's wheel? ran over a stone, Turner, why? you ran over a stone, Luther? didn't you see it? naw, Turner, naw, the kid had it hid in his fist. Rum a dum dum, rum a dum. Pastor astor faster faster, has a cock he cannot master, crows so loud he always haster, pastor astor faster faster. Rum a dum dum, rum a dum. The god damn government. Listen he could hit a man harder than anybody I ever seen, even if he was a nigger. Whop. I mean really. Blam. Heemeny heemeny ho ho ho, I took my wife to the carnival show. What did she see there, heemeny hee? She saw a cunt on a male monkey. What did she think of it, heemeny ho? Well what she thought of it, I don't know, since she's left me for the carnival show. Rum a dum dum, rum a dum. What's your flavor? I love orange. Only thing keeps me sober is you can't pitch horseshoes drunk. Chamlay can. Alfalfa? barley? timothy? rye? Sing us another song soon, sing-a-ling, sing us another song soon. Flax corn clover. The god damn government. Ding dong bell, pussy's not so well. Billy Butter has a lover, whom he's taken to the clover; roll me over, Billy Butter, and I'll leave my home and mother. How they hanging? Like Absalom—by the hairs. I love cher-rie. Here's Fred. If you think grasshoppers is bad in Ohio . . . Say, what fun do monks have, Lloyd? Why I don't know, Boylee, what fun do monks have? Nun, Lloyd, nun. Whoo-oo-ee. The little ones, the little green ones, when they move through the grass you'd think it was raining. Wheat's wet. That's all I think about. Wheat. I sleep awful. I love lickerass. Well say now Boylee, what fun do nuns have? Gol-lee, I don't know, Lloyd, what fun do nuns have? Nun, Boylee, nun. Whoo-oo-ee. Off Sandy Point there's a hole in the shape of a horse's collar and they're all in there, the hundreds of them, and some days you can see them, golden, lying in quiet bunches like pieces of sun. Do you know Mable Fox? All the same I've heard them convent cemeteries is full of bastards. No lie? They use hairpins. Never wash. Cannibals. Knew a cat did that—ate her own. Naw? Billy Butter has a lover; without no hands he lies above her, fucking lightly as a plover, first his sister, then her mother. Here's Ben. There ain't no law in the Redeemer's church against a good fuck, is there Furber? Why of course not, Luther, only it's got to be your wife, and beyond five inches it's a sin to enjoy it. By christ you're a good sport, Furb. By christ you are. Pat. Hey boys, ain't Furb a good sport? Squeeze. By christ. You can play at our picnic. Rum a dum. Rum a dum. Rum a dum dum.

Furber had come in the late fall following that enormous summer, now famous, in which the temperature had hung in the high nineties along the river for weeks, parching the fields, drying and destroying; weeks which had, unmindful of the calendar, fallen undiminished into October so that the leaves shriveled before they fell and fell while green, the river level fell, exposing flat stretches of mud and bottom weed, the Siren Rocks were seen for the first time in twenty years, quite round and disappointingly small, and an unmoving cover of dust lay thickly everywhere, on fields, trees, buildings, on the river itself which crawled beneath it blindly like a mole. In October the Hen Woods burned, towers of flame—burning willows, sycamores and beeches—toppling into the river and causing smoke and steam to cover the lower bend like a fog. Young Israbestis Tott, to the shame of his sister, ran wildly up and down the bank opposite the fire, throwing himself to the ground in a fit of despair when a silvery, fine-limbed sycamore the rivermen called Uncle Simon, long a landmark on its part of the river and said to be nearly one hundred and thirty feet tall, finally burst into flames and spilled its branches on the water. Normally shy and awkward, Henry Pimber had embraced him manfully. In October, too, the Reverend Jethro Furber, comparing himself to a dry wind, preached his greeting sermon on a threatening text from Jeremiah. He wondered why it was that God was laying waste the land, and he found the answer in the sinful Gilean souls he scarcely knew. "Because the ground is chapt, for there was no rain in the earth, the plowmen were ashamed, they covered their heads . . ." But I didn't have to *know* them, I knew them already, he always said when he tasted the bitterness of that disastrous day again; but this excuse had ceased to serve him. He simply found it on his lips as automatically as he found the formulas of worship, and the bitterness remained.

The church was still, wrapped in layers of heat. Particles of dust blinked as they sank past the gray windows. Missus, what's her name? Simpson? not Simpson, of course not, Simpson's a widow woman . . . Spink, god; Simpson . . . Sampson? . . . Stinson? no, Simpson . . . Simpson's the Cleveland woman's name, the doctor's wife, this one doesn't limp at least though she looks like a bundle of rags . . . Mrs. Spink, although she'd finished playing, still hovered nervously over the keys. . . . thinks she should play something else and that's why I'm waiting . . . Cool, black, immaculate, himself silent, he surveyed his congregation. . . . but I'm waiting for effect, madam, dramatic effect, and I wish you wouldn't hover; relax . . . Gray shoes, gray floor, dry splintery wood, gray windows, creaking benches, dry coughs, gray female faces. The women, expressionless, were fanning themselves, and the men were mopping their brows and running large spotted bandanas under the backs of their collars. From time to time one of the women would lean over and yank on a child's arm, straightening it in its seat. Missus Stimson? has it a *p*? she also called me doctor, that's why I thought . . . no . . . Kinsman . . . where in the world did I get Stimpson, I don't know any Stimpsons . . . she married a surgeon who carved her knee for nothing, nine times she said . . . yes it's certainly Kinsman, where did Simpson come from? . . . had two children, both abnormal . . . funny . . . Kinsman, Kinsman . . . my creative years are passing, doctor, don't you think? face in hankie, reddish nose tip, trace of tears . . . And *doctor*—that was more like it. Stiff, harsh, unmoving, in the continuing silence, he counted them, examining their faces, achieving domination and command by staring, as one did over dogs. First face: fat and puffy, pale from the heat, flickering behind its fan, eyes opaque, ah, the tongue is darting like a snake's, tick, tick, tick, a strand of gray hair flopping, tick flop, tock flip, tongue again, tick tick. In front a line of shoes well disciplined, each flat on the floor, all dusty, one, two, five, seven, ten, that's five to the left of the aisle, and on the right, four, six in the second row and the same left, the weak bench empty, I figured that, then four, why that little bitch is crimping pages in her hymnal, then four more, she couldn't have been any older when her husband fell out of the window and broke his back . . . didn't paralysis set in? people wondered did he fall or was he pushed? quick, I'd better begin, six, eight, I've drawn them as tight as I dare . . . just a bit . . . a boot in each shoe, dirty too, the dust has surely sifted in, dry crinkled skin, gnarled yellowy nails, think of those toes when you preach . . . and underneath the blood about its business. He steadied the Bible stand and spoke the first words of his text. Mrs. Spink began to play. They stopped together and Furber glared at her. Why don't you teach piano, Mrs. Simpson, you play the organ so well, I'm sure you could manage. Averting her eyes, Mrs. Spink began again, gathering strength as she went along until the notes were jostling one another and the piano whined. Does she think I've forgotten my lines? Furber made a helpless gesture and some of the congregation stood. What was the number? one twenty-two? Up-down, undecided, half-up-down. Like weather images in clocks. We'll sing number one forty-four. Shit, that wasn't it. They're standing; their toes are bending; their toes are rubbing the ends of their all-in-line shoes. Ah, thank God, here it is. One fifty-seven please. "We rise to praise the living God." Great christ, was that right?

He could have set fire to it, the garden was dry enough, and burned it clean—privet, vines, and weeds; but he waited in his rooms through the winter instead, weeping and dreaming. The congregation dwindled; it was the high snows, they said, and then it was the spring rains, and then the planting, and the unseasonable heat and strong winds, and then they no longer troubled to lie, they just stayed away; and Furber climbed slowly to the pulpit, and Mrs. Spink played and some sang, and then he spoke to a crack in a window, and crawled down after like a drunkard from a tree. He knew complaints were being made about him, but why had they sent him from Cleveland if not for this—to be a lash to Gilean, Gilean to be a rod to him?

And then by god he got them all back. But that was before The Noisy One and The Noisy One's nesting hat and dog. Now it was touch and go again. Bark. Oh yes, bark away. They were a family of apocalyptic beasts.

It was the fore-edge of summer when he started work in the garden. The work was idly begun, in a desperate moment, and continued obsessively, like a madman picking imaginary lint from his sleeve. He cleared the graves of weeds so their mounds were defined; tore the vines from the stones, scrubbing their faces; and then read the labels aloud as well as he could, beginning with Pike's, for Pike was the first and demanded the honor.

> Rev A dy Pike
> when his churc
> was a cabin
> die o his love
> 18 9

The other inscriptions were stupid and dull, lines of sweet memorial cant, but this one never failed to lighten his spirit. Andrew Pike had been the first to preach along this stretch of the river, and among the dead in the garden, he had the only ghost who mattered. Stories were told about him still, by Tott and Mosteller mainly, by Lloyd Cate sometimes, by Watson rarely; they were vague, confused tales, anguished and full of disaster, passionate as the legend on his monument; and Furber began coming to Pike's corner often—to redecipher the lines and ponder them. The Reverend Andrew Pike, when this church was a cabin, died of his love, eighteen nine. He was surely only his skeleton now, wrapped up in the earth like bones in butcher's paper. Furber wondered what it was he'd struck—grub or worm most likely, hardly fly. It was strange the stone didn't call him brother. Perhaps Brother Pike would appreciate another cup. Cookie? Missus Hatstat made them. Her first name's Valient. Tott says she was named for her stays. Poor Pike must have bitten hard. The stone seemed to say so. Anyway he's altered; Pike's fisher now. There's the shadow of his boat, floating quietly in the corner, bulging the water. And here's his line come down, a little curly. Furber bent over and tore off a tip of ivy. This is Brother Pike who preaches in our church. He has the voice of an indian, Backett, you ought to like him. Howls when he feels the need. We're proud of him. Those are the scalps of twenty devils at his belt. Just give him into Omensetter's hands, then we'll see who the darkie is. Have another brownie, they've nuts all through them, I put in plenty. Thanky kindly, Missus Spink, but if I do I'll surely sink. Second face: thin and polished, nose like a pick, brows like woolly caterpillars, pale bluish lip, eyes closely ringed like the first years of a tree or like pebbles newly fallen in a pond or like . . . ah, he has the low blood . . . cold feet, undoubtedly, all year round. Mister Pimber, isn't it? husband of the money one? in truth she has an iron haunch and thigh. Let's see, who was it? Grave Pythagoras . . . who ate the gold his converts gave him. Nine plus sixteen equals twenty-five. And turned base flesh into a gold hypotenuse. The pastor haster. It's them beans. "But he that is of a cheerful heart hath a continual feast." On whom, oh jackal's muzzle? On his cheerful heart, kite's beak. Bag of gas in the ass. Pike baked bears he had throttled with his toes. Indeedy, we compete. Try to remember please that plants, in warm Christian friendship and full cherry-leaved cooperation contrary to the vicious allegations of that damned Englishman, purify and replenish the air. Lies, lies. They soak up light and exude shadow. Enter Tott talking. Hand claps. Lovely. What you've done. Don't you think, Samantha? This garden has been positively—refurberished. Want to wrestle? Care to share a joint of cougar Pike has squeezed the life from with his knees? Giants in those days; now ghosts, now you and me.

Furber rose and began to walk, rubbing his buttocks. The hour was passing. Then they'd draw their wagon off.

The others—Meldon, Rush—bragged of the number of their years. Thirty-five in this church unchanged since its

84

building; then Rush, exceeding even Meldon's strength of jaw with forty-one . . . forty-one years in the wilderness . . . and never a lion. Ordinarily they moved their ministers around—a very irregular proceeding, this interminable tenure. Always conscious of what he stood for, what he meant and ought to mean, Furber roughed the dark cloth of his coat with his fingernails and paced off the flagstones carefully. Dusk had fallen. Several fireflies, by glowing together, had haloed the head of the chip-nosed saint. He had smiled in his grief. In the half-light, the stone was faintly showing . . . it was Andrew Pike in his ghosting curtain . . . and he remembered leaning toward him drunkenly to say, ah Pike, breathe your spirit into me. Six years had failed to dim that memory. Six? It *was* six, surely? Somehow it seemed an eternity . . . the moment of his birth. He'd sat there several hours in a kind of stupor, rousing to weep and to bite his hands, occasionally to press his forehead painfully against the ground, sincerely miserable yet vaguely conscious, too, that Flack, his nigger soul and shadow, might be watching. This intensified his performance and greatly increased its range. He was boisterous, then silent; he cursed and begged; he confessed and threatened. He crumpled to a ball, like paper. He marched, cheering: heyheyhey. He snickered while he wept, and joked while he prayed. Spitting, he offered up his soul. Vain, he was humble. Proud, he was ashamed. I sign my petition, he cried, carried quite away, with my thirty million names. And I am lonely among my voices, these voices roaring in me. At last his strength began to fail him; he wearied of it all, and finally caring for nothing, went half to sleep. Through his head, to the tunes of children's songs, his pitiful beliefs, his little sentences of wisdom, danced foolishly as he dozed, the meters they were forced to skip to reducing them to a vulgar gibberish. He tried to rally his thoughts and form them in unassailable squares, but not a line would hold, they broke ahead of any shooting, and the Logos wandered disloyally off, alone, rudely hiccoughing and chewing on pieces of raw potato, looking surly and dangerous. No book but Nature is the word of God. Logos. No ghost. Whirled. Screech. Hisssst.

> Willie the whiny,
> his nose nice and shiny,
> will die, die, die;
>
> as Millie the silly,
> her belly so hilly,
> will die, die, die;

and Minnie the bunny,
whose buttocks are yummy,
will die, die, die;

so Lily the beauty,
her bust absolutely
high, high, high,

must just as fully
fall willy nilly,
and die, die, die.

Once before, but in an entirely different manner, he had
received a revelation. He was eleven, still a sexless child,
weak even then, with signs of palsy and an affinity for fear so
pronounced that he had driven his parents nearly out of their
wits with it. At that time he sought out terror as though it
were a sweetly scented flower. Black and white, bowlegged
with a blind eye, Mrs. Kermit Hazen's bulldog would rush
across the lawn from his customary place beneath a bush to
snap at Furber's shadow where it fell between the picket.
All too often they found Jethro lying unconscious there, and
then his mother and father would embrace one another,
weeping, wondering what in the world they were going to do
with their child and why he had been taken with these
strange demented ways, so cruel and unnatural. They denied
him every book they had not carefully examined themselves,
just as they forbade him the Hazen's fence and later the stone
quarry and the bluffs beyond town, and finally all farmyards
because of the geese and railroad stations because of the
engines, then funerals, cemeteries, zoos, and circuses, cellars,
closets, attics, deep woods and vacant houses, athletic
contests, fires, rallies and revival meetings—indeed any form
of public excitement—and they tried to shelter him from the
noise and violence of storms too, as well as from every other
remarkable exertion of nature; but none of these prohibitions
proved of any use for he wantonly disobeyed them, and his
father's threats, his mother's hysterical seizures, their hours of
mourning and commiseration, since they were things he
greatly feared, he sought as eagerly as he sought the bulldog,
or accounts of cannibals in books, or the dizziness which
always overcame him in high places.

To forbid him the Bible was unthinkable, and since it was
a book he might be safely seen with, Jethro Furber's
knowledge of it was complete at an early age. He read how
they stoned a man for gathering sticks on the sabbath. It was
easy to imagine himself in a circle of stones and implacable
faces—the faces the worst—for had he not been stung by

pebbles and knocked down by a clod of dirt and beaten, too, by his companions? Third face: small and dainty, nearly smooth, the features barely pinched out on the surface like the decorations of a cookie...tremulous smile...tiny jaw that jiggles. When he fell, the sticks he had gathered were somehow scattered all around him. The people then shared out his clothes and other belongings, and his family drove the memory of him from its mind as he'd been driven from the village. His wife, too, forgot him, even the touch of his hand. Why not? a hand's a hand. Was he a hero? Standing disdainfully in their midst, did he say: come now, who shall be the first? And then: well thrown, good Korah, son of Izhar, playmate of my youth, friend in my manhood, neighbor and love. Or did he run till a rock broke his knee? Perhaps he beseeched them. Perhaps he fell at their feet and they dropped a boulder on his skull. No, here we are: he begins by begging. The stones come anyway and they sting. Why the amazement? A fair trade—stones for sticks. He never believed they would throw at *him*. Good friends, my kinsmen. But he must protect his face. He huddles, making himself small. The stones begin to hurt and now he's running. Ah, the fun's begun. Go faster. Faster. Hurrah.

Hero? Unlikely. Anyway—to whom? Once you're dead there's no difference, the kites aren't fastidious.

He read how Korah, son of Izhar, son of Kohath, son of Levi, was swallowed by the earth with all his followers, while fire consumed two hundred fifty more. He read how Lot's daughters lay with their drunken father; how the Lord destroyed Sodom and brought the flood. He read how the Lord smote the firstborn of the Egyptians, and how, at the behest of Moses, the sons of Levi slew three thousand of their brothers, and later every male of the Midians, and their male children, and also all of their women who had slept with men, keeping only the young virgins for themselves. He read how Israel, at the order of Joshua, slew all but a harlot in Jericho, and how Joshua hung five kings from five trees before destroying their cities, and how a certain Levite, whose concubine was ravished in his stead by men in Gibeah (for they were pederasts and would have preferred him), afterward divided her in twelve parts like a pie and sent a piece to each of the tribes of Israel that they might make war on Benjamin. He read how Saul and his sons and his armor-bearer and all his men died on the same day, and how Uzzah was stricken for touching the ark when the oxen faltered, and how Ammon ravished the sister of Absalom so that Absalom had his brother slain, and then how Absalom stole the loyalty of the people from his father who was king, and to vex his father lay with his father's whores, and at last led the people away. He read how finally Absalom was defeated, and how he fled on an ass and was caught in the branches of a tree where Joab, his father's captain, bled his heart for the dogs with darts. He read how Joab spilled the bowels of Amasa on the ground and received the head of Sheba which was thrown from the walls of his town to turn away the wrath of King David. He read how the Lord put a plague upon Israel, His anger consuming seventy thousand, and how Amasa was revenged, for Solomon had Joab slain, and how much in love Solomon was with foreign women so that the Lord took ten of the tribes of Israel from him and gave them to Jeroboam, whom, however, He later cursed with a terrible curse, causing his son to die.

These and many others. He saw Absalom alive in the oak and the head of Sheba falling from the wall and Joab's sword entering Amasa. He heard the Lord curse Jeroboam through the mouth of His prophet Ahijah: the dog shall eat those of the house of Jeroboam who die in the city, and the birds shall eat those of his house who die in the country, and all of his house shall be consumed as a dry cake of dung is consumed in the fire. He imagined the men of King David at the foot of the wall, the head of Sheba looping over, and Joab running to catch it before it smashed on the rocks, spoiling its features, for the king liked to have the heads of his enemies brought into his presence since he hoped to find the meaning of their death in the final arrangement of their faces. Here is the head of a foolish man. Why does he smile so wisely? Fourth face: small moustache and triangular chin, nervously winking eyes . . . something in them? ah, he's chewing on his tongue . . . wink tick chew tock, wink wink. You've waited too long, now what's her name's begun, de dum de dum de dum de dum: we rise to praise the living God. Oh no indeedy. Incorrect. The third stone, reddish, small, flat with rounded edges and a glacial nick—the first two having fallen grievously short—was thrown by a ferrety boy in a sailor suit. It skipped twice before turning toward its target, then twice more, quickly, striking the giant between the eyes so that he fell with a groan, shaking the earth. There was generous applause and considerable shouting. A pillar of dust rose from beneath the body, two thousand sneezing. With the clangor of arms the armies collided. Yar. Yar. Yar.

He saw Absalom alive in the oak. The locusts flew up in a cloud and the servants of King David saw them rising and knew where Absalom was. While Joab pierced his heart and ten men struck him, his mule was grazing. Absalom said, ah my father's friend has come, my kinsman; but Joab did not speak, affixing the darts. The head of Absalom then was like the head of Sheba tossed from the wall top and like Amasa's who was murdered on the highway; it was like the head of the Levite's concubine sent as a message to Judah; it was the head of Goliath and the other stone man; it was like the head of Saul and the five kings Joshua had hung in the trees; it was like the heads of thousands brought one by one into his dreams and held by their hair as the oak had held Absalom, all those whom war and plague and treachery had slain, each in the griff of a warrior, and all the heads were smiling in the same way . . . wisely . . . and Furber heard King David muttering, why are they smiling? what is the meaning? for head after head, even those with sad eyes or poor teeth, those who met death weeping, were smiling. Everyone stood in a group near the tree, even Jethro, who was shortest. Abner, wearing the ringlet of leaves, had already hid. Ruth, the fat girl, began the chant.

hingle-dy
dingle-dy
this is so sing-a-ly
if we go single-ly
we'll find the crown

Then they all ran, Jethro screaming, bringing his parents running from the house. In the tent with the king there were people on benches, wailing. The king said: shall I cut this child in two? Just so. Someone was playing the piano and everyone rose to sing. Oh I do believe you Lord, I do. Jethro ran to the front, saying: I have seen Absalom alive in the oak. From there his father dragged him, squalling. Never again. No more religious circuses, you understand? Not even a psalm-singing acrobat? A little introductory music please. Ladies and Gentlemen. Let me call your Attention to the Top of the Tent: the Lord of Hosts! all the way from Egypt! floating! in Thin Air! and without Nets! without any Support! of Any Kind! No one Else in the World is Capable of such a Feast! Dum diddy dum dum, dum daaaa. But it was the stoned man he saw most. When they began throwing he ran to a small hill. Flies drank his sweat. It was only a game called king of the mountain. A stone came out of the sun and struck him just back of the ear. Death in every direction. He staggered drunkenly down the slope into their arms.

ringlet
ringlet
where's our kinglet
king has run away

Furber did not stay long with the later books. He was
disappointed with them. Of *Revelation* he was even a little
disdainful. What this saint had dreamed of, Moses and
Joshua had done. His book was filled with the wind of
trumpets and the insubstantial wings of angels, and while
there were cataclysms of all kinds which the emperor's
prisoner promised would destroy a fifth or a fourth or a third
of the earth, his threats were like those Jethro himself had
sometimes shouted from his yard at the bullying fat girl with
whom he often played and who had showed him, as Rome he
supposed had showed John, her private parts; and in
consequence no one whose foot would raise real dust in the
road was deprived of his bowels by the sword; for Furber
had already read how King David had numbered Israel,
angering the Lord, and how the Lord had offered him a
punishment for his people: either three years of famine,
three months of flight before their foes, or three days of
pestilence brought by an angel, and how King David had
wisely chosen the latter, saying: let us fall into the hands of
the Lord, for His mercy is great; but let us not fall into the
hands of man; so Furber felt, even as a boy, that if the Lord
really wished to bring the world to a terrible end, He would
not toss earth and heaven together or bring forth fire from
the ground or roll up the sea like a scroll, but simply
withdraw Himself so that the whole earth and the heavens
beyond the earth would settle quietly into the hands of
man.

I have seen Absalom alive in the oak; I have seen his neck
between the branches; locusts flew from his hair. Then a
servant of David saw him also and ran to tell Joab. Oh
prevent it . . . prevent it! But Joab has come in his gown of
blood to bare the breast of Absalom, while Absalom
watches, and find his heart. I have never seen the Lord God.
But I have seen Absalom alive in the tree.

Jethro was a priest of Midian, father-in-law to Moses, and
a wise adviser. Furber, too, determined to live for the
church. But at first it was only the wild times and his own
terror that attracted him: the immense stretch of the
opposing hosts and the harsh cries of battle, the plagues and
the engulfing sea, the cloud and the pillar of fire. Then one
morning, his eyes still aching from an unpleasant sleep, he
came into the parlor where the Bible lay open on a table

before a window, its pages turning in the morning breeze, and glancing idly down he saw these words of St. Paul which seemed to leap from the page to strike him: "For the invisible things of him from the creation of the world are clearly seen, being understood by the things that are made, even his eternal power and Godhead." And his heart stopped. There was an immense silence inside him. It was a silence like that which overtook the world while it slept. "They are without excuse." All night he'd been in the tent of David, before the rows of benches and the clapping people. Heads had been brought in, and David, peering at each closely, had asked him again and again: what do you see? why is he smiling? what is the meaning? The head of Goliath. Laughing, David had thrust his finger in its mouth. You're a fish past biting, old friend. Saul. Tears had soaked Saul's beard though he was smiling. David assaulted the head with his spear. How long has this been happening? Saul—dead—is weeping. And no one dared to tell me. The head of Sheba, caught by Joab's running awkwardly, and Joab's own, and many more of David's captains, smiling. What is the meaning? The page curled and blew over. Furber had cried out: yes, that's so; while pans slid noisily in the kitchen. To Jethro they were trumpets. Even now, as he remembered it, his flesh prickled. That terrible night of heads. There was a plague among the people in the tent. They began to groan and fall forward on their faces. David said: let us sing a song of my own composition.

red
red
maidenhead
Janet's no longer a boy-oh

A man and a woman opened the flap. Jethro rose, shouting angrily: that woman is a woman of Midian. Who plays the harlot with this daughter of Moab, bringing this plague of heads upon us? And he took up David's spear, for David was weeping—Absalom's head was swinging by its hair—and rushed down the aisle to spit the man and woman on it beautifully—bravo. David praised him, saying: you have turned back the wrath of God from the people of Israel. Then a strange head was brought in, a head without features, smiling, without cheeks or lips or chin, and Furber said: who is this? what is the meaning? and David answered: this is the head of Jethro, a priest of Midian, once father-in-law to Moses, and a wise adviser.

His mother came from the kitchen where she was peeling cucumbers. What is the matter, Jethro, she said. This too, he thought, is a sign, even the smell of cucumber, and I must try to understand it. At the end of his dream, while he'd sat paralyzed beside King David, another head had been brought. This is the head of Solomon, your son, a voice said to David. King David rose slowly, his weapons falling from him. But I die before Solomon, he said. Shall I cut this child in two, said Solomon's head. I die before Solomon, David said, his garments falling from him. Tell me I'm not smiling. Tell me. I can't hear you, he shouted, his body falling from him. Tell me I'm not smiling not smiling not smiling . . . But his head wore a smile as sweet and mild and rosy as the heads, for example, of Saul and Amasa, as the heads, for instance, of Goliath and Joab, or as the head of the foolish Sheba which Joab caught so awkwardly just in time. Jethro gave his mother a reassuring peck and asked for breakfast: sugared peaches in cream, fresh milk, sweet rolls with sweet butter, whole strawberry jam.

You'd have loved my mother, Pike. Happy? Proud?

Visiting ladies in elaborate Sunday hats shaded my face from the sun that came streaming through the parlor windows in the summer afternoons. Mother hugs me. He's decided, she says, and they—the ladies with smoothed cosmetic faces—smile and sigh. So young. And mother would always misunderstand them. But not too young to decide, she'd insist. Maybe Aunt Janet would come away from the fishbowl. She hoped the fish would nibble at her finger. She said she thought it would tickle. If she did stop it was always to ram that finger, dripping, into my ribs. Her wide hat would darken my eyes and I would blink at the things which hung from the brim. So you've chosen Christ, my boy, she would say in a low soft voice, putting her face close to mine so I always saw the powder at the bottom of her wrinkles. That's—she drives the finger into my side—fine. Mother hauls me to her bosom in an overflow of love, denting my nose with one of her buttons. He doesn't say much about it . . . but Janet, I think he's had an experience.

Pike, what if I'd said: yes mother, I've seen the private parts of fatty Ruth? Would my life have changed? Much? Oh I should have spoken out. Shame. Not to praise the parts of fatty Ruth. Ah if I'd had your spirit, Pike, when her skirts were hoisted up. Breathe your spirit into me.

wiggle oh
gigolo
we'll live so bungalow
in my soft down below
until you drown

Pike speaks: ladies love religious little boys.

By god Pike, you're right. I was loved. I was held, pinched, squeezed, encompassed by beads. Then Morton, too, sanctimonious old pimp, shook my hand and gave me a hymnal with a broken spine. What number was it? ninety-two? we rise to praise . . . no, nineteen, no, that's the number of the psalm: "the heavens declare the glory"—but Pike, it's what I learned as a boy from Paul, though I was a long time understanding it. "Day to day uttereth speech." What is the meaning? God spoke that day between the lower lips of fatty Ruth but I missed the meaning of his proposition. Well even Moses was slow witted with the burning bush. I missed the meaning again of Auntie Janet who has just now cocked her thumb and taken aim with her right forefinger blam! hug chest quick—too late it's into the rib just under my arm and the moon is falling near, see the mountains and the craters and the lines of snow and ice. There's a chapped mouse squeaking indistinctly cheeses priced at sss-blam! dime. Cheeses. Holey cheeses. Janet, I believe he's had an experience. Well the boy's high-strung. But he's changed; you've no idea. And so young, dear child. He doesn't shake. He may, again, there's plenty of time.

I should have reminded her, Pike, that Jesus was a God already as a fetus, but I've no spirit, no proper spirit. Christ. No ghost. Whirld. Shreech.

> one a pastor
> two a parson
>
> hot cross bun
>
> three a doctor
> four a brother
>
> bake them done
>
> five a reverend
> six a shepherd
>
> eat each one
>
> seven a preacher
> eight a teacher
>
> we're not done
>
> nine a minister
> ten the sinister
>
> end has come

Listen, Pike, you are a stone ghost now, a trick of the light, and perhaps you know already what I'm trying to say, for you've been through it all and died of love, the best death. My face is muffled in my mother's clothing. Her rhinestones injure me. See: my feet are going. Fish flee the forefinger of my aunt. The sun streams over the geraniums. What has this to do with what I feel, with what I am?

Aunt Janet sits carelessly on the edge of her chair, her hands like fruit that's fallen in her lap. Her gaze is soft and watery. The past has overtaken her, just as you, Pike, have overtaken me. I was nearly twelve, you understand, and I would search her eagerly like a lover. But her grief was all inside her, Pike. She might as well have been of stone or plaster like that sentimental saint. And when in my room I would weep, for I was fond of weeping in those days, I realized my grief had no connection with my tears. Anyone might see how they streamed, but no one could know how they burned. Then I tried the private parts of fatty Ruth on my aunt and mother. Oh I was like the searching prince in Cinderella, hiking every skirt. But they've been badly misnamed. There's nothing really private to those parts which I later heard the boys in seminary call the banks of the river Urine, nor did they have the slipper's size; for although all the girls and ladies wore it, none of them seemed nicely fitted. One day—it was sometime after my "experience," perhaps three weeks or a month, and Janet had come according to her custom to nose our fish and stir them up —after her kiss had smeared cosmetic on my cheek and she had cocked her fist and painfully speared my side, congratulating me because I'd ceased my shaking (a pillow for your mother's head, she said); after she'd lit on the edge of the simple ladder chair she fancied because it was as light and delicate as herself, and had taken breath toward one of her favorite "ticklish topics," since her conversation consisted entirely of prefaces, forewords, and introductions to pink tumescent subjects which she safely never touched; and when she had, following an especially long and devious preamble to what I guessed was the problem of the unwed mother, sunk behind the sea which rose suddenly in her eyes as it always did, I saw her—mind this Pike, are you awake?—I saw her, poised on the edge of her chair as I've said her habit was, let go and slowly topple over. We helped her up at once, of course. She didn't seem hurt or even ill. Slipped off, my mother said, because she has to perch and never minds what she's doing. You may think it's my diseased imagination—it has a beggar's body—I freely admit it—but I see her still, whenever I wish, letting go and falling, her skirts flattening and streaming behind her and then ballooning as she turns in the air. I had penetrated the quality of the act, Pike, and I was dreadfully shaken by my knowledge, though I tried not to show it and got away as soon as I dared. She'd had too much of life, and she'd let go of it at last and left the wire. In my dreams sometimes I see her too, slipping from a window sill or off a windy mountain ledge, her skirts rising about her as she descends and revealing beneath them the private parts of fatty Ruth. On she somersaults until I've lost the sense of heads or tails and she has spun herself into a single, broadly grinning, comic mask.

Pike speaks: that was the face of truth on fatty Ruth.

By god Pike you're right. The head of Medusa, with Medusa's softly whiskered grin. Were you turned to stone by such a sight? Morton, I remember, rubbed my back. Humility, my boy, is also important. The hymnal he gave me was dog-eared at all the customary places and it always fell open at A Mighty Fortress Is Our God. Now there was a man who made a downy pillow. Pike . . . when I stopped trembling and fainting, the ladies wrapped me in their warm arms and cooed in my ears and gently ruffled my hair. Aunt Janet's chair had skidded, tipping when she fell. Both were light but my aunt was voluptuous. I held her like a lover, receiving her soul. It was then I felt my whole interior shudder. It was nothing like the palsy of the body. I have that still. It was a fright of the spirit, a terrible ghost-fear. Hats shaded me. The petals of the potted plants were turning purple. She rose through the circle of my grasp, rubbing herself ecstatically against me. Well why not? I was the vulgar flesh receiver, wasn't I? And wasn't it all over, the harsh press and scruple of life? There ought to be some sweet to console her for the fall. So she thought. But it was her limp spirit I held, as helpless, flung over my arm, as a wrap. This was my first use of the godly eye, Pike, and in the beginning I was no better for it. Beads and cameos and buttons cut me. Morton squeezed my arm, the dirty old butt. In the moment that we lifted her, I saw her estimate the age of the zinnias. Ghostfallen, Pike. You know what that means. She was ghostfallen, yet she troubled to guess how recently my mother's flowers had been cut. Well I'd declared for God, my mother said, and smartly dressed auxiliary ladies came to look at me and whisper about Jesus. A fat lot of good it would have done to insist I hadn't chosen him, I'd chosen the Lord of Hosts, His Tent, Tights, and Trapeze, not the same thing at all; so I refrained. My prematurely wrinkled aunt held out her head. Its lips were spread with love. Now what do you make of that?

Pike speaks: in women revenge takes the form of religion.

By god Pike you're right. And I had mine. Faithfully I went to Brother Morton's services and sat apart, not proudly or disdainfully, but in an absent mind, as if rapt; and I dare say there were eyes that saw wisps of pink cherubic cloud like straw in my hair. I bent my head and printed in his hymnals with a pencil end, which you can bet I kept most carefully concealed, every dirty word or line, every bawdy jingle I could remember or make up on the spot (I had an aptitude, but eleven isn't an accomplished age), while throughout I'd note the pages of the hymns I'd written on, referring the reader to them, or I would advise the devout to

> sing psalm one eleven
> if you would see heaven
> but for a good time
> sing psalm sixty-nine.

Pop pop pop, I'd crack the spines. Oh Pike, my spirit was light then. How heavy it is now. Breathe your spirit into me. I don't know what to believe. My luck has left me. I preach and no one listens. Only the crack in the window widens. Nar. Nar. Nar.

Pike speaks: believe nothing that does not sound well.

By god Pike you have something there. But I have a ringing in my ears, and all those noisy faces. . . . The fifth face is a pig's, its nostrils aimed like eyes, its cheek skin moistly glistening, teeth like pebbles overgrown with moss, they've stood so long in saliva, stiff white hair in rows above the brow. Hardly Circean. Let us have another number, Mrs. Samson, say, The Old Rugged Cross. Isn't it nice here in the yard, the fresh breeze and the white wickets? My boy, to follow Christ is nice, you will enjoy it. Happy? Proud? Asleep? Pike? Don't leave me, I'm lonely. Oh lord you weren't a jew's-harp religionist? you didn't squeeze an accordion? slap your knee? jig? Not Samson, damn it, but my Kinsman, the stoned man, whose corpse is blind. What's happened to the light? Ah, Pike, the flies have failed us. That Mrs. Pimber has a strenuously knuckled hand, it just occurred to me to think so, not like Mrs. Claude . . . um . . . Spink, the fidgety, who is losing her hair but goes bravely anywhere there's music because of her calling. How about a bit of Throw Out the Lifeline, that's rousing. Another muffin? Don't drip butter, the cloth's so white, a beautiful expanse of something clean, and the blue shadows of the silver calm me wonderfully, and don't you feel the coolness of the crystal and the silence of the porcelain? No? Another muffin? coffee? please cream and sugar. See the ghostly spirit spill into the darkness, clouding. Dunk? Only on occasion. Mrs. Chamlay fries the greatest doughnuts; you'll love them, Mr. Furber. There's nothing like country cooking. Well I've always loved what's large. The church must have a sale, a way to get going. For sweethearting charity. Cakes, clothes, and kisses. Prizes of chastity. Ice creams are such fun in July. Think of the long white papered tables under the trees. The cool mouth of watermelon. Pike, Pike! rally! rally to me! Rowdies a rarity although known to happen. Threw stones in the pudding of old Mrs. Jasper. Which was bought by Carl Skelton to sicken his dog. It was quite entertaining. I remember the bowl; it went in her auction. Didn't she have some lovely things, poor dear. A shade of blue not too pleasing for chocolate. Who was it that got it? (Samantha has darkened; her lips are severe.) That fat Mrs. Arthur who moved back to Windham. And not a month here. Pike! A desert, Pike, a wilderness Jerome would not have dwelled in. He'd have gathered up his books and gone to Rome. You lived with Indians—very well—but I've fallen among people. Is there no one who will pity me? Speak and say, oh great recumbency of sky, vast chest and hollow water bottle, would you spit upon your image, eh? Ho, Barlar? Grunn? Petvich? Hooloo? Kishish? Quarckaling? Sull Yully? Nannerbantandan? TuK? Too rooky, won't reply, all tweetered up with ravens, swifts, and fowling hawks. Anyway let's have an answer . . . some bird of omen . . . no ghost . . . shreeeeeee . . .

The moon is falling near. Here are the deserts and the mountains. There I am, the raisin-eyed, cross-legged on a stone. Is that a lion feeding from my lap? My spirit dines on salt and water. I don't suppose you know the desert fathers, Pike, you were never a scholar. Well listen, you've much to learn. A monk who lived in one of those Egyptian monasteries found himself set upon by thoughts of distant places, and the desire to leave the dry hole where he was and visit them began to torment him severely as you might expect, for he was put together in the same way as the rest of us—weak eyes and hairless knees. He told the abbot of his troubles, much as I am telling you of mine, Pike, and the abbot said: go to your cell and give your body in pledge to its walls; let your thoughts roam as they will but forbid your body to stir. So the monk did as his abbot suggested and apparently his desires were quelled. Now do you see how wrong that was? Dear me. Satan had that abbot by the heels. He had them all by the heels, even Macarius and Paul and Anthony. He swung them like a storm through the desert.

Pike speaks: pounding the pipe won't punish the plumber.

By god Pike you're quick. I preached in Cleveland once upon that theme. You can't feel the spirit through the body, it's far too thick and woolly. That monk should have fastened his mind to the wall and let his body go hang. There's a better story, though, about the saintly Arsenius who was willed some property by a kinsman of his, a senator. Pay attention, Pike, you've a good deal to learn. When the magistrate brought him the will, ceremoniously phrased and piously laced as our wills invariably are, he indignantly refused it, sending the magistrate away. I died before he did, Arsenius said, and now he's dead, how can he make me his heir? Yes sir, that was the ticket. He slipped the Devil there, and got scot-free. And so it was I saw the fall of my Aunt Janet from the Shaker chair. She died, poor soul, in the jump. Not however like a saint but like a suicide. What did it matter if her body bloomed for thirty years and her face dried? Age made trenches for her eyes. It might have been the source of some annoyance as the years went by, this sapling body and this withered face, but I think she saw what was coming. You have to peek under the covers, Pike; then by the holy rood of Moses what you see! It was only surfaces, before, that frightened me. I pledged my body to the fence but my love fell beyond it. And when I read of war in Israel, it was the banners and dust in that Egyptian desert that moved me, the misshapen trees in which the kings were hung. All wrong. Then afterward, when the armies moved and the warriors grimaced at one another and shouting struck their swords together, I did not linger among the shields and weapon edges like a coward in the camp, but my eyes rode in with the spear.

Pike speaks: o hemulous blarsh! cole shemly kitch! rah poffomouse twild!

Don't mock me, Pike. After I've furnished you with life, it isn't fair. Besides I'm being bitten by these insects for your sake. What's that? Is someone speaking? I'll ask Samantha Tott to teach a Sunday school—now there's a move—a charming thought that's just this minute come to me. Oh I'm ill, I'm ill, I've chipped my nose, and nothing will restore me. Then make a clean breast, eh? Throw myself, you know, like the bride's bouquet, into their arms. My father prints a paper, Pike. All those words. Ah, I'll heel them home and make myself loved like a stray. A miracle, Pike—life out of ink. Why, it frees me. Feeesh? Who's wise? Who is it who keeps buffohoing me? Is it you Flack, or these bloody fever bees? Well, He's a great comedian—the King of the High Wire, and He's surely made a fool of me. Ill. Ill. I no longer feel, I only remember. Look: He's lost His trousers. Say, fatty Ruth had a face on both her knees. Merciful heaven, He's wearing red-hot BVD's. Cherubic windpuffers, they looked like, wrought of hinge-wrinks by a genius: little mump-cheeked North, cruel smiling West. Thus appear the parts. What a howl by all that's holy. Luff? Who said so? Oh breathe your spirit into me! Pike? Don't leave me. Ill. Ill. Ill. Don't leave. Listen. I'm in your debt for six sentences of wisdom, but seven is the sacred number. Yield another and I'll have no other ghosts before me. Be Lombardy Peter, Pike. Seven metals, seven wonders, seven ages ... That sentence of Paul's—I'd almost forgot how it transformed me when I was nearly twelve and picked up Janet's hair shirt from the floor. Tomorrow I'm going to dig up the sundial and beat the body from that plaster St. Francis.

Pike speaks: the way the world is, you have to look down to see up.

You do by god. The thought turned him topsy-turvy. It seemed to summarize the whole worthless way of the world—if there was one. And versions of it began to flutter wildly through his head. You have to look round to see straight. Good enough. Useful. And the rough places plain. But all that's geometry. But it measures the earth. You have to go slow to catch up. Eat to get thin? no, but fast to grow fat, that was a fine one. Then lose to win? fail to succeed? Risky. Stop to begin. The form made noiseless music—lumly lum lum or lum-lee-lee lum—like fill to empty, every physical extreme. Die to live was a bit old hat. But default to repay. And lie to be honest. He liked the ring of that. Flack! I'm white in order to be black. Sin first and saint later. Cruel to be kind, of course, and the hurt's in the hurter—that's what they say—a lot of blap. That's my name, my nomination: Saint Later. Now then: humble to be proud; poor to be rich. Enslave to make free? That moved naturally. Also multiply to subtract. Dee dee dee. Young Saint Later. A list of them, as old Pythagoras had. Even engenders odd. How would that be? Eight is five and three. There were no middle-aged saints—they were old men or babies. Ah, god—the wise fool. The simpleton sublime. Babe in the woods, roach in the pudding, prince in the pauper, enchanted beauty in the toad. This was the wisdom of the folk and the philosopher alike—the disorder of the lyre, or the drawn-out bow of that sane madman, the holy Heraclitus. The poet Zeno. The logician Keats. Discovery after discovery: the more the mice eat, the fatter the cats. There were tears and laughter, for instance—how they shook and ran together into one gay grief. Dumb eloquence, swift still waters, shallow deeps. Let's see: impenitent remorse, careless anxiety, heedless worry, tense repose. So true of tigers. Then there was the friendly enmity of sun and snow, and the sweet disharmony of every union, the greasy mate of cock and cunt, the cosmic poles, the war that's peace, the stumble that's an everlasting poise and balance, spring and fall, love, strife, health, disease, and the cold duplicity of Number One and all its warm divisions. The sameness that's in difference. The limit that's limitless. The permanence that's change. The distance of the near at home. So—to roam, stay home. Then pursue to be caught, submit to conquer. Method—ancient —of Chinese. To pacify, inflame. Love, hate. Kiss, kill. In, out, up, down, start, stop. Ah . . . from pleasure, pain. Like circumcision of the heart. Judgment and mercy. Sin and grace. It little mattered; everything seemed to Furber to be magically right, and his heart grew fat with satisfaction. Therefore there is good in every evil; one must lower away to raise; seek what's found to mourn its loss; conceive in stone and execute in water; turn profound and obvious, miraculous and commonplace, around; sin to save; destroy in order to create; live in the sun, though underground. Yes. Doubt in order to believe—that was an old one—for thus the square *is* in the circle. O Phaedo, Phaedo. O endless ending. Soul is immortal after all—at last it's proved. Between dead and living there's no difference but the one has whiter bones. Furber rose, the mosquitoes swarming around him, and ran inside.

It *was* six, surely. Counting from the moment when he took a spoon to his melon and looked along the row of faces, lips wrinkling, jaws in gentle motion, all in greeting, it was seven; so six from the night at the stone was correct. Andy Pike didn't put up the church as she stands, of course, Brother Rush did that; some of us think the original location was a little west of where it is now, Mossy and me mainly, I guess—you'll meet Mossteller later, first-rate fellow, he was sorry he couldn't make it—but people around here call it Pike's Peak just the same, on account of the steeple, out of love for his memory, you know, not disrespect . . . Fly near the butter. Mossy and me. Me and Mossy. If I tip my cup I may get a peek at the maker. Would he look like a lichen? Nice shape to the bowls, they're feathery; my fingers show through them. Oh God what must be eaten in Your Name—not counting Yourself. That steeple didn't look any more than elm high to me and just a little shovel-nosed. Now that Brother Pike has rotted out his clothes and ghosts to the let of his halter, he's old Andy to this bung-mouth. I'm to see his grave too. What bores the dead are. I'll bet a bible ribbon it's Pike's Penis to the barn boys. Well, like Sir Thomas Browne, I'm great on resting places. Oh yes reverence really. I saw it from the train. Impressive. A round of watermelon slid from his spoon as he raised it to his lips. Falling, it tumbled from the mound of fruit and slipped over the edge of the glass where his deft spoon pinned it just in time. Silly lie. They probably knew you couldn't see a thing ahead of the hills. Why hadn't he said he'd peeked from the second story of the station? Impossible. They thought he was taking a leak. There was, thank god, salt, but they'd never heard of lemon. Actually, it should have been served over ice with a thin slice of lime. Now the melon was warmish and slippery. Poor season? There wasn't much juice. Too little rain? And the fruit should have been laced with kirsch or drowned in white wine. His name was Tott, remember, something Bester. Telegrapher? ticket-taker? grocery clerk? drygoods maybe, or real estate and insurance. He was some sort of pencil-licker certainly. Local oracle. Village idiot. Town pump.

All kinds of containers sat about the table in sullen disconnection. Some steamed despite the hot day; others enclosed pools of green brine where pickles drowsed like crocodiles; still others held up mounds of melting jellies. Fans of ham and meat loaf lay on platters let to drift among conserves and cheeses, and bowls of candied carrots, scalloped potatoes and baked beans bulged above the cloth, scraping sides, while baskets heaped with rolls were set among trays of cake and tins of pie and sheets of slicing cookie. God curse the covered dish. Curse this peasant Trimalchio beside me. Peasant food was poison. Most of them, all of them maybe, just look at Mrs. Grimmouth, were temperance quacks, the worst kind. Piety of the palate. He remembered St. Jerome's favorite proverb: when an ass eats thistles up, his lips have lettuce like themselves. There was a little embarrassment at the platform when he went so briskly off to pee but really it was all right because he was in a sweat to see the tower of God—the spike that was to spit him. Natural function, ladies, like the menses. By the stools of Jesus, as they used to say at school. Here sir, in this antique metal box, all verdigris, I have several curious relics of Our Saviour. What an awesome beauty swells that notion. Too bad the better sermons can't be preached. Debilitating heat . . . terror of traveling . . . rivers of dust. Would he like to wash before lunch? Of course he just . . . but perhaps the ride . . . Has shaken me up? oh yes PLEASE; beneath the stairs? how clever and amusing, perfectly charming, thank you kindly. Just waste space says Mr. Tott. To wash. Flicker of unease: wash-up. Dirty word. Hee. Sloping ceiling, coffin close. Round silver mirror to examine your teeth. Shakes with a step on the stair. Roses on the sloping ceiling. Silver leaves match the silver mirror. The latest improvements. Height of luxury. Jesus I'm going to have the jerks. Button your pants and practice deep breathing. Not built for bowels, the gas overwhelming. Breathed his last. Dung dead. The body of Our Saviour shat but Our Saviour shat not. Would it be appropriate to say, then, that the body of Our Saviour saw but Our Saviour saw not, swot but swot not, swinked but . . . The bowl was deeply stained. Blood of martyrs. "I will wash mine hands in innocency . . ." He covered his eyes; his stomach gurgled; he still heard the train. He'd seen everything through a haze: the stack spitting cinders, the dirt smears dancing, the impatient flies. There was a landscape of flaws in the glass, footprints of fingers, and he found himself traveling along them, ticking each off carefully as though they were squares composing the perilous wandering path of a children's game. It wound over blue-gray wastes and sticky rivers. The mirror bleary, the roses grinning, he shook as though riding. Dust on the sills, boot marks in the aisles, the car close and still, the heat profound . . . a passage to Hell—here, under the rose-smiling slope and the shoe-creaking stair, in company with the sound of water and the oppressive smell of his urine, loud and orange; while the mirror jiggled his image and he bent above the basin Proposing to Purify Himself in Preparation for a Feast of Love; he began to understand the nature of his destination and the extent of his punishment. So far there were significant absentees: the husband of the ledge-chested lady, for instance, and the husband of the woman with the fatuous first name—neither was present. Undoubtedly they scorned him; they hated his appointment, his having been so hastily thrust upon them, so immoderately squeezed between the rails of their objections; and he was cityish too, quite plainly, sour and runty, with a handshake far from hearty, even, one might say, unmanly (better that a preacher stutter); and he had a noticeable general shiver, though these seizures seemed infrequent; and he was pale, truly pale, like one whom caves have shaded . . . yes, overall he gave the impression of something unwholesome and hidden; he was the same species as the spider, bat or beetle, companions who—a class which . . . —or they scorned Tott, they might, he was a determined gabbler, who knew what else? or they were not scorners but the scorned themselves; or rather, being husbands who——no, there was hanky-panky somewhere certainly, and rancor, you could count on it—petty local pride and fancied injuries, little intrigues like snarls of twine. Well his host was pleased with his, ah . . . dear me . . . his divers lavers. Better make no mention that direction. Wit and pedantry were out of place among these dreary villagers. Trees, hills, river . . . yet life was monotonously flat, straight . . . plankish . . . with a dreadful sameness everywhere like dust . . . a climate without any real extremes, deprived of virtue even in its mean . . . though there were trees, the sloping fields, the river, still life was hard, level . . . wood-en . . . inevitable . . . and moments ran on mindlessly like driven cattle, and young men struggled in the net of their friends, relatives, and other connections for a while like dripping fish before wearing out their wills and settling down to live with the rest of the gently poor, their pets, and their obsequious diseases . . . where bitterness grew up on every-thing like ivy. Yet the fact was he wanted their good opinion. Lord, lord, he was a dreadful creature. Why did he mind? They were such small potatoes. How could they nourish him? Furber grasped the chain. "Gather not my soul with sinners, nor my life with bloody men . . ." Bowels up, bladders down. Where had they got their money? another happy conse-quence of papa's passing on? Turreted, scalloped, the clapboards patterned, the roof-tree edged with iron tracery, the house was huge, with wide curving porches and a stained-glass window on the landing; it had been built to be grand. He unsnicked, and stooping grotesquely, emerged. Somebody grasped his newly purified—"In whose hands is mischief . . ." People stood about in the hall, bumping when they moved. Between them, beyond the door, he saw the table, another landscape, harshly white, already cluttered with bowls and goblets. Were there really so many or was he failing to sort them? He smiled and nodded and dropped his jaw like a visor. The ceiling slowly turned. Perhaps there would be blizzards now, tornadoes in the spring, and floods; for he had always perched on the end of the teeter, weighing it down. The air felt like wool. Was it something he'd brought with him from Cleveland? The staircase wrapped itself around the inside of the tower. Of course. They were in the foot of the turret. It had a top like a Prussian's helmet and shone dully in the sun like lead. These people couldn't lift their feet. In the presence of the holy, their voices fell to a murmur, and he could scarcely understand a word. Death, doubtless, did it. Reverence really. That girl had brought it with her. No, she had gotten off a station ahead of him and loosed clouds of stinging Spites which flew from Windham: Old Age, Labor, Sickness, Vice. For prying into the mysteries of women. Passion. Madness. Blind, lying Hope—hemmed in. Click of jewelry, buttons maybe. Rub of clothing. And the sheriffy person he'd met for a moment in Cleveland was missing too. Held at the elbow, he was being steered. Hold on, you don't *touch* the minister. Way up here? at the head? dear me. In the box: fallen air, prostrate winds, unmoving steam. The ladies struggling not to sweat, their hairy parts abead nevertheless. Deep in the tank, deep in the cage—descending. The light is failing. Courage, old friend.

Waiting, his hands resting lightly on the back of his chair, his head alert to tip, what would he say about the food the good Lord of the ladies had provided? *Benedictus benedicat Pro Christum Dominum Jesus Nostrum.* No loaves, no fishes. Just covered dishes. Let thy grace lighten the potatoes but relieve us of the beans. Devil take *them.* No damp cast-upon-water bread either. After all, he was the water in this case. May this food form an image of the twin ends of our lives; may it be as peaceful and resigned on parting as it's noxious and rebellious starting. Is all in order? ready to begin? shall I bow now? I've come home to rolls and biscuits, mom, to hugs of butter and kisses of berry. Stay off foot washing and all blood and body. Cath-all-oh-cizz-zum. Love's no sort of food though hate's a tasty nettle. Love your mother? have another. His hosts intended to sit on either side of him, apparently. His hosts . . . What would the point of it be? How would it be taken? Would it be a cut the town would talk about for years? or was it simply unrestrained conceit? black spite? mere honest gaucherie? Kick your bruvver in his muvver. Envy somewhere. Malice. Greed. That's the way we . . . love our bay-bee. Fit of pique. Rely. The Husband of his Harpist in the Holy House was here, holding on his head and shoulders the head and face of some small mammal Furber couldn't place; heavily cinched about the waist, no bones in his hands; oh yes, there was the fellow with crêpe over his eyes, the one who had the face of a man, as the books of magical secrets say, destined to die by drowning. That made two of them he knew. The Totts were two. Numbering is knowing. Bless these bounteous provisions. In an unctuous bishop's voice. It was Christ's own blood he was blushing. No doubt he'd get the blame for being in between them. Better to cry: I see shit in the soup, turds in the cream; be honest and be out of it—free. Study their faces for a moment. Enjoy the revelation of the word. Yes. Joy. Then smoothly pass the portals and away. But no, god no, flatter like the coward, chew weeds. Moistened by his tongue, his words crossed the burning linen safely. Sparrowing the corner of the table he clenched Samantha's chair, but he heard wingbeats behind him, by god, as the other Tott flew swiftly to seize his. Devil boil his pee. Samantha bent poorly; he bumped the back of her legs. Not an old woman but an old woman. Then it became necessary to rejoin Master Tott. Furber was trembling with maledictions but there was a smile on the greengrocer's face. It was the face of a . . . disciple. Smile matched smile . . . shared flame . . . dead heat. Well for christ's sake are the legs stuck? He grasped the seat and jerked the chair forward. Sunny grin and pleasant murmur. Honey bees. Storm of curses. Reluctant to touch the hot cloth, his hands hid in his lap; the raw melon waited his spoon. My toes are dry though it rains in my heart. That's the tune, all right. My shoes are shined though . . . The fellow was still scraping and squirming. Was he the hallfoot shuffler? Praise be, at last he's comfy. . . . the sole's come apart. Or has it come in holes? where's the rhyme go? Damn. Dum dee. Dum dee. Lord save us, he's clearing his throat. Empty, useless curses. A scalding stream or there's no god. How'd it go? my pants are pressed, my shirt is clean? There's nothing like the old songs, but what's the good if you can't remember them. Mem. Mem. Memory.

Pike, the bearded beaver-skin prophet, scalps of the lost modestly shading his privy members, tiptoed savage-like from vale to glade, hatchet and Bible his only weapons though he held love in his teeth like a dagger, and he brought Jesus to the Indians of the Ohio country so that on Sundays they collected at the cabin Pike had built on the brow of a low hill which quietly sloped to the river close by a clearing where he'd previously set up a cross cut of saplings and a Christ formed of clay, and there the Indians, axes holstered in the earth, their loincloths dragging, knelt to pray by wringing their hands and groaning, eventually receiving a few brightly colored beads before they went away.

Reverence really. He gazed on the steaming plain . . . the smoke of heavy industry: meats, beans, taters . . . O despair. Devil take those seeds. Let them have rebirth in other bodies. Their spirits seek too swift release, all out of season and intemperate. Haunt others. Off. There were some nice pieces spotted here and there, some lovely brown birds on an ironstone pitcher. A breeze in the foliage, their heads erect, perhaps they felt the well water through the glaze. Their beaks were in line and they seemed to be actually in sight of one another. Mrs. Tightsqueeze was eyeing him. What if my thoughts spilled out, madame, what would you do? ah, what if yours did? Her dress held her fiercely braced. A regular full-bellied tumbletit, aren't you? fat of love. Oops . . . ah . . . caught. Is that mustard on the tablecloth? No ma'am, I spilled some thinking. To be a bird at the edge of the pond like these . . . a sweet cool breeze . . . the pebbles would moisten my toes . . . so much at ease. They've twiggy feet, and ironstone birds have no mites in their feathers. Instead I have this windy comedian beside me, and Miss Samantha getting dark. Hell's the tip of an inverted steeple. The lift's descending. Call it Furber's Fiddling Finger. Call it The Gilean Bum Hoist. Here I am and I am innocent. Butt me Billy, Billy Butter, bang me like a windy shutter. What kind of pleasure from her bony lover? Damn, what's her name? Na, na . . . Knox. By covertly scratching her underarm not far from the pit she caused the cantaloupe still on her spoon to roll so severely Furber feared an accident like his own. Someone said how elegant—what was? what?— while Miss Tott, sitting straight as her stoop would let her, dipped her utensil down and then away like the bucket of a ferris wheel, bracelet meanwhile shaking. A salad of canned peas and bits of cheese. Innocence no antidote. That emperor's name? he was a sixth but not the one who preferred the windup metal singing bird. Poisoned himself by bits and by degrees. Furber's gaze slipped by the tip of—how to remember it—Mrs. Knox's nose and leaped her pearly ear and swam into the space behind her. There were dogs on the wall, rusty setters smiling graciously, dead pheasants, several quail, lurching fences. Brought from abroad at conspicuous expense. English country-house and English horses. Furber discovered he hated the British. Was that a chewed on fox? . . . a copse of yellow furze. Oh yes I have various plans for the church. In the event . . . THAT . . . it becomes necessary . . . TO . . . BUT . . . far too soon to say . . . WHAT. Some sort of dry pod mounted on a stick spoke from the distant end. And Tott would never stop. He'd never stop. Never never never. The Chinese water torture. Dribble of reddish fruit juice on the chin of the speckled person . . . now she's dabbing. Young, yet ancient like his sister, he was a button collector already, a museum director, a digger of dry earth, a peeler of print from old paper, feeder upon the past, despoiler of the slain, bugger of corpses. Save oh save. Preserve. Oh redigest. And here's one that fell from the fly of Prince Albert once when bored, uncomfortable, he crossed his legs too closely at a musicale. Note the coat of arms embossed. That milkweed woman was shouting something, seeds were winding from her mouth, heads were turning, all but mine, we are in line like birds, I'm smiling, see, I understand, she nods, she understands, spoons clash, heads swing to me, I'll drop my eyes, dear god, more words and more replies. Somewhere his baby shoes are nailed to a wall, ticket attached. Ask attendant for the story. That fleshy Knox female . . . thoroughly middle-aged, not otherwise so huge, rather rosy-cheeked though it looks like tucks have been taken in her chin . . . the kind of breasts to lay a cock between. Had he seen her husband? was he one of those in Cleveland? local chief? Try one of these, you dirty old man. God I am. Don't say old, though, it smacks of affection. You were wheezing on the station stairs. Ran to see the blue sky sickened by the grime. If I were only a piece of cheese, I could dissolve in her mouth. There it was, smearily between the trees, the teetery tent-top, flying flags. Heartsfallen, I crept down the stairs. Slink now if you like but on the bottom look buoyant. Remember, you've just been relieved. They'd fold nicely over. Rolypoly puddings. Sweet cool cream. Yes, I felt the same when Mrs. Kinsman showed me her knee. Nine operations she said. My Harpist is speaking. Indeed. Indeed. Brazenly she drew up her skirt. But how cowardly are the clergy. Nevertheless I ran my finger down a scar and nearly burst. Does it still hurt? Ah what a liar. Keep your eye on the aerial horses. And the dogs whose mouths have broken open. There goes my plate. It's been terribly hot in Cleveland. Dry. Well we've the lake. And you've the river. Dry. Yes, ma'am. Dry. Like lava. Yes ma'am, indeed. Like lead in the sunlight. Yes indeed. A Prussian helmet's head. Like the river Styx. Oh like . . . O very like . . . they'll find us in our pederastic postures like Pompeii. Somebody called him Henry just now? Who? Millicent? The milkweed virgin? Naming is knowing. I can see from here she's got bad teeth. They've a coon clearing, who's he? Madame, do you know the old tune: Golly Molly Life is Jolly in Your Bawdy House? Her naked knee. Nicest thing about whores would be their willing suspension of taste. Samantha's sizzling sin house. Oh there's always room for improvement. Isn't there though. In all of us? Eh? Oh—room. I said there was room, said room said rrrrrooo . . . . ooooooooo . . . . oommmm. Benches would be pleasant facing the river. Shaded resting places. Comfy-dumfy. With this swelling I'll never dare rise. Kinsman's come over me. Concentrate on the panting setters. There's doubtless a town pig, the Gilean whore, outcast on the outskirts, one who's lost her way, has had hard use, now only narrowly superior to sheep, who might just welcome a regenerating screw. I'll pray for you if you'll lay for me under the green bay tree. My god Furber, you—you're brave.

Resting places. Where, for god's sake, were there resting

places? He hardly knew them, their features dissolved as he looked; yet he knew they were no more at home than he was. There was hair and nose and napkin cloth and painted trim along the stair. He peered through his eyes at the other boys at play, afraid of the cool glass, his incomplete reflection like a boogie watching, or like God, transparent, evanescent, here and there. Good the skull held the head in, the caged chest in safety. He was master of the resting places. How? Where? These pacing cats, these bears, these songless singing birds, these slaty cases . . . If the soul has a body for its grave, graves are no resting places. I am afloat in here. The panes are smeared; there's steam in the air and the litter of voices. They do not touch me. The world cranked by his window. Cinders flew and flags of smoke; the grass was gray; the sun seemed large and orange though it was ʀₒrning; he bobbed lightly in his jar and the shadow of his hand descended on the lap of the thick young lady sitting next to him. There it fluttered gently despite its passion, scratching the smooth cloth of her skirt where a stripe like one upon a peppermint began describing the ample spread of her thighs—thighs which widened beneath her weight, he felt, like puddles of honey. He was sure she'd seen his ghost alight and felt its brushing. With inflated cheeks, wool hair, sewn eyes, she seemed as tranquil as a dove, as pink and plump and smooth besides. Furber flexed his fingers. The head of a rabbit fell asunder. Her eyes were warming, weren't they? Had he seen a slackness in her lips just then? her breathing quicken? Cornering, he watched her chest lift slowly while his hand paled out at her waist. Agony. He began again at the knee . . . thumb, forefinger at a wrinkle, delicately pinched together. There was a storm inside him, gusts of desire, intervals of weakness, rain . . . his hand flew off, then reappeared . . . again . . . He watched it anxiously, each time willing it under until he felt it sink to her skin. A sigh escaped him. Pretty pudcums. She stirred; her legs moved lightly under his fingertips, down tickling, and his undulating flower bird settled in the hollow of her lap. Pet my bunny. Eee, sweet fig. His back was aching. He had brought her to the limit of her nature; he was showing her unventured seas beyond; she wiped her brow with her arm. Seecreeshun—oh my lovey-dolly. His fingers startled, then burrowed toward her privacy. The train lurched and as it whistled she rose clumsily, bumping his leg. His hand fell from the window, ah . . . he squeezed himself, weary. The girl edged up the aisle, hatbox rocking, her buttocks fastened moistly to her dress. A whore at heart for all she is a cow, Furber thought, and as the sun turned he tried to throw his outline under the wheels of the train, but when he peered out all he saw were the shadows of the cars and in them gray oblongs of window, irregularly splotched. Thus the china smutched the cloth. His own plate had escaped him and was passing wildly now from hand to hand. Master of the resting places. Hadn't he this blackened clothing? hadn't he by heart the words for setting out? God cast His shadow over him; he was divine in his darkness; somewhat, like these villagers, an ardent agriculturalist, a specialist in earth. That paten dollie could have saved me? Why not? Put your hand here, reverend, just while we travel, she could have said, and take your rest. Wrong? Aunt Janet had succeeded where he'd failed. It was only luck his image would not leave him. Rest? Peace? There? He'd be a cutout creased by the brilliant rails, cinders would pucker his chest. But she bumped me most unkindly; waddled off. He shuddered; heard the silver clatter. Careful. Care oh care. To sink down rest. Duckie. To touch. These faces all in tatters, words passing, glasses clinking, steam and condensation . . . He drew a line on his goblet. Dewy, cool, a drop hung from the tip. There was no law unproclaiming it. End to his lip then. Off hand. The taste of life. Proof of the labor in the glass. Sad testimonial to love.

Omensetter's luck, they said. Furber thought he could distinguish Omensetter's noises from the rest. What good was a wall that didn't blind and deafen? He could see and hear them as well as if he were on the beach beside them, smoking like a green branch against mosquitoes. Fingering the ivy he touched them more closely than if he held a still attached hank of their hair in his hand. It was a strange method of communication, skipping space and contravening causal laws. He remembered, on those rare occasions when his family entertained in the evenings after his bedtime, how the sounds of their voices would tease and draw him, how the laughter seemed to him so wondrously musical, so richly dipped in something sweet, like jelly in chocolate sometimes, that his mouth filled, and he would creep to the stairhead, straining to make it all out, then smelling them too, their perfume and tobacco, the fragrance of warm cakes and coffee rising with the click of their cups and spoons and their low bubbling speech, and once in a while a word would stand out clearly amid their scraping chairs and rustling garments, bewitching him. How he hated sleep. The world—how did it dare—went on without him while he slept, went on happily—this was proof—for everything he wanted and missed and felt should exist existed just beneath him, as close at hand while out of reach as his own insides, yet tomorrow when he was released and woke and went downstairs the rooms would be stale and unfriendly, a forgotten saucer, maybe, would disgust him, and his parents would be lethargic, cross, and awkward with objects. It had finally occurred to him that he was the figure that altered the sum, just as his presence on the beach so much later had subtracted from everyone's pleasure. So his family and his family's friends were happy because he slept. If he died in the night as he sometimes hoped, thinking to punish them, they would not weep but would pass the hours of his death dipping cookies in their coffee, chuckling, and swirling cream in their frail scalloped cups. Tree, ball, wagon: they were greener, firmer, smoother without him. Hoops, the street: it was intolerable they did not need him, but when he lay in his bed they *were* more completely. Sleep was bearable only if the whole world slept, he'd decided; yes, we must all sleep together, that was just; and these thoughts, the words "sleep together," without his in the least understanding why at the time, had suddenly awakened the monster in him. Then he'd cruelly scraped his ears and listened at the stairhead like a deer. He thought he heard their clothing parting. Certainly they giggled at the flesh they showed. He saw through the barriers of wall and floor the pale tangle of their limbs. Later he understood what people feared in fearing ghosts. Strange forms smoked along the stairs. Shapes moved vaguely in sheets. Holding his throat he'd risen and wobbled to his bed and sought sleep as he'd sought it ever since: as a friend and lover—further: as a medicine and god.

Watchman. What a monstrous liar. He hadn't stopped their games at all. They'd stopped their ears so he made useless noises. Composing sentences he flew down. Kek. Is this a Sunday thing? Ke-kek. Now when he closed his eyes . . . hullabillyhooly . . . what went on? . . . that?

> Creep away, sneak away, leak away—hide.
> There are animals hunting in Furber's inside.
> What will they find there? What will they eat?
> Lungs, liver, the kidneys, and watery meat.

Much later than that lying moment on the stair, in the flower-decked pavilion of his dreams, he'd made love too—to handsome monsters virtuous as witches, their bodies flung full length upon divans, rows of mouths along their limbs beseeching kisses, bald vaginas drawing wind; for he was constantly deceived by sleep. Of course it would not give him peace, and as he'd gradually come to realize it was his own heart he'd heard on the stairs, these visions had entered his

fatty Ruth, or the plump girl on the train whom only his shadow had petted; or any of the thousand simple impulses that hurled themselves helplessly against the walls of his heart: to finger the lobe of a strange ear or sniff on hands and knees a patch of something wet, make bawdy verses up and sing them loudly, leap in the air, chew on the thumb of a leather glove, play soccer in the street ... any sudden gesture of joy or love ... but who could know, when he heard his heart, what the beating was? and who could be expected to understand these gestures, so out of character, so threatening, for weren't they the same moves that went with rage, with lust, with any molesting? well, no matter, it was all a dream, this rapture of touch; you'd taste the knee's rough cover with your tongue; the little girl would squeak and click her eyes; your sweetheart would wet on your hand; yes, words were superior; they maintained a superior control; they touched without your touching; they were at once the bait, the hook, the line, the pole, and the water in between.

He, Olus Knox, Chamlay and Mat were fishing, not getting much, but fishing; trying the rocky point past the big bend, not getting much, but fishing in the very early morning; the boat passing across the long shale crop opposite the clay bank, bringing their bait from the deep to shallow, but with no success but fishing; and he, Olus Knox, Chamlay and Mat had nearly given up hope of fish and had got to that fine point of enjoying, as much as any fish they might have caught, the drops of water clinging to their lines, and the slowly widening rings they made on the surface of the river; when of all things to see floating on the river they saw a large straw hat bobbing on its crown, spinning very slowly, moving very patiently down between the lines toward the boat; and Olus Knox said immediately my god it's Omensetter's hat, but Jethro Furber said immediately oh no it's not, it's not his hat, while the hat drifted to the boat, its brim brushing against the side Chamlay and Mat were fishing from, Jethro Furber and Olus Knox craning to watch it, no one saying a word more or moving to pick it up; and the hat passed under Mat's front line and passed under Chamlay's and rubbed the side of the boat as it passed away around the stern; then Jethro Furber took from Chamlay's tackle box the largest, heaviest sinker he could find and lurching in the boat stood and hurled it into the hat as it went away. Then they drew in their lines and rowed in silence. Jethro Furber scrambled out with the mooring rope and crouched awkwardly on the dock with the rope in his fist thinking of Chamlay's sinker lying in the bottom of the hat and how the brim had curled like a yellow water flower. When the others had gathered their gear and the boat was tied, hearing the child in his voice, yet unable to prevent it, Furber turned to them with an angry face. Wait, he said, trembling all over, wait—just wait.

Thus. Everything so bitterly won, lost. His words had flown like finches. Then the trap of those hands. Why?

It had been raining hard, the wind driving through every protection into his face. He had untented his umbrella, darting for the door. There was the glow of a white shirt . . . not Mat's . . . and a rumpled burlap-colored man. But no one was wearing a white shirt, he remembered. Yet a paleness thatched by shadows from the forge floated before him like a cloud, and there was Mat, reassuringly familiar, his figure fringed by the light of the fire. Had he been able to recover the whole of that scene, even as dull as his senses had been while fleeing the downpour, he'd have found the sign on it somewhere, unmistakably stuck like a poster announcing the Ringlings; but it was all so provokingly vague; he'd been taken unfairly unaware; and there remained with him now only a few scattered impressions—the drifting light, the delicate lattices of shadow and the overwhelming sense of Omensetter's size, of his boundless immensity, with the astonishment which followed on it, and then the sudden inexplicable shame and fear—and even these had an unfortunate habit of mixing with those of later meetings . . . in the open air, in the hot sun, his huge feet shoveling dust, patches of sweat on his shirt like maps of the Great Lakes, the smell of weeds . . . so that sometimes he wondered whether that ghostly presence wasn't simply a flash from the lake or a limestone jut or a maple revolving its leaves employed by that earlier time to enliven it, as if that peculiar brightness were the sign he was hunting, the clown who burst the bright paper ring or the acrobat in silver tights, an hysterical smile painted on his face, who dangled from the trapeze by his knees.

One Sunday, before the service and against his custom, where the people gathered, he went out to Omensetter, Omensetter's dog, his wife and daughters, and he said, the crowd around him listening on, why don't you come to church, you come to town, why not attend the services instead of throwing stones at the water? and Omensetter smiled and said, why if you like, we will; so presently they did. He'd been a fool, a fool—for he lost his fire. Sin sweetened in his mouth. The climate of the pit grew temperate and the great damnation day drew further off. Consequently Furber was convinced that evil dwelled within the pew where Omensetter sat, and he resolved to speak against it. No longer merely a grim phizzed comedian, he saw his arm outstretched to God, his finger pointing like a thorn upon its branch. He saw his open hand before his face, shielding his eyes from horror, his head thrown back and slightly turned away. He heard his voice echo from his mouth as from a well that drew its water from the center of the earth. Behold, oh Lord, your champion here, your fond believer, for Furber felt his body fill with resolution, and he stood in his study to make the gesture. He jerked his head and he arched his back and he raised his arms, and when his eyes lay naked on his face, he shrieked with joy. Yet when he came before the congregation and took his place and book above it, preparing his words for bearing on the subject, shaping his lips for strong sounds, his certainty grew a hesitation, his strength a meekness, and his sounds came down as softly as the gray birds building in the steeple. He listened to himself as to another man. He preached a God, a law, he never knew. He saw the faces of the people widen with surprise and revelation, and he realized that he was already anticipating the moment when he would stand at the church door awaiting Omensetter's laugh, receiving his felicitations as he stood in line—you sure spoke my mind, Reverend Furber, first rate—while his own hand sank in Omensetter's to its wrist, and his heart turned. I am inhabited, I am possessed, he thought. When the opportunity came he broke off and with great effort drew himself into his study where he swore at the walls and damned Flack for a sooty nigger. But the compliment he dreamed he had received from Omensetter, persistent as a fly, pursued him droning, though now the words were mischievously altered so he heard—you sure spoke my mind, Father Furber, first rate—repeated like a chant of such spiritual profundity its significance could not be caught the first time, and this further increased his already intolerable feeling of futility and despair. Yet by god Omensetter was a stupid fellow; he had too large a mouth; he was wrinkled badly about the eyes; fat padded his face; his hair was always flying. His face was just another—the sixth face, that was all—broadly smiling, widely cracked across. The rain had been rebounding when he'd ducked into the shade of Watson's shop and nearly spitted Omensetter on the point of his umbrella. Was the man wet to the skin? No . . . but that was the feeling he gave. Actually . . . what? Tan shirt? open throat? button missing? dry certainly . . . yes, wet to the skin, beaded, draining, flowering in the water like a splash. A curse on the gray light, on the rain that drove him in, on the foolishness that drove him out in it again to run so unbecomingly, so erratically and without heart, while he wrestled with the

115

catch on his umbrella and stumbled through puddles, his dignity drowning in the tub of his trousers, the rain filling his shoes too and crawling down his back like a party of ants so that when he tried to scratch between his shoulders his hat was shaken loose over his forehead and blown beyond a thin wire fence which he at once charged angrily and angrily shook, and it was there, with the wire responding in his fist, that some sense of the impropriety of his performance reached him, its futility struck him, and its folly . . . for he could be as easily observed, he supposed, as his hat could, caught on a stalk of last year's cabbage (indeed he imagined the signs brushed up, jumbles of bright red and blue letters that announced his appearance locally, from Friday to Sunday—he was the darkie on the yellow ground—in his famous role as a cheap buffoon, the small black helpless clown the others drenched with water, tickled with unrolling paper tubes and deprived of trousers, so they might implant their grotesque cardboard shoes on his flamboyantly checkered behind, then to goose to the accompaniment of piercing whistles and terrify with firecrackers and packs of little yapping dogs tricked out in tissue paper skins to look like tigers) . . . its folly was of Egyptian proportions, it nearly brought him to his knees with shame; and he halted himself like an army, folded his umbrella with a great show of composure, and proceeded homeward in a suit of the driest unconcern, head erect, hair knotted, lashes heavy, as if the spring sun were his cover, until, on reaching the churchyard at last, he bolted like a rabbit and threw a tantrum in the vestry, spilling his cuffs and denying the Lord.

Looking back he realized he had unwittingly mimicked Omensetter's habitual manner, for how otherwise would Omensetter have gone home through the rain, if he had wished to, but like one in his natural element, gently at ease, calmly collecting his pleasures. If this was a consequence of simply shaking hands, it made him a kind of deadly infection. I am inhabited, Furber said. Ah god, I am possessed. He would sit in his study for hours, searching his mind for some clue to the nature of the creature, the source of what he grimly called "Omensetter's magic," while from his window he would watch the pigeons wheeling to occupy his eyes. Finally he sought out Omensetter himself when Omensetter was strolling in the fields. Why do you inhabit me, he cried, why do you possess my tongue and turn it from the way it wants to go? Leave me, Omensetter, leave us all. He came abruptly on the man, blurting out his speech before his resolution left him and shouting in his excitement, though the words came just as he'd prepared and frequently rehearsed

116

them. Omensetter halted and turned slowly to face Furber, who must have seemed to have lit like a crow behind him. The fellow's eyes were huge, their gaze steady; his whole body was listening, pointing toward Furber like a beast; yes, like a beast, a cow, exactly: wary, stupid, dumb; yes, as he thought back there was nothing in his manner that could be ascribed to an animal higher, and he had never replied; yet Omensetter had not come to church again, he had returned to skipping stones on the river where the people saw his example and said he was a godless man, while Furber preached against frivolity with heat.

It was truly astonishing the way his stones would leap free of the water and disappear into the glare. Omensetter always chose them carefully. He took their weight in his palm and recorded their edges with his fingers, juggling a number as he walked and tossing the failures down before he curled his index finger around their rims and released them as birds. Furber chose his own stones carefully too. In the beginning, when he had failed so miserably and lost his congregation, he had fallen upon the garden like a besieger and torn away its weeds. You've been in mourning long enough, he declared, enjoying his joke sufficiently he repeated it to Flack who nodded without smiling and responded in his rich contralto: yes, he was a gentle man; a remark which enraged Furber so much that like Moses he flung down the rock he was carrying and shouted: let that be noon and midnight—there; following his words with laughter to cover his confusion.

Now he strode briskly from stone to stone, circling the sixty. How differently we give the semblance of life to the stone, he thought. And it did seem a stone until it skipped from the water . . . effortlessly lifting . . . then skipped again, and skipped, and skipped . . . a marvel of transcending . . . disappearing like the brief rise of the fish, a spirit even, bent on escape, lifting and lifting, then almost out of sight going under, or rather never lifting from that side of things again but embraced by the watery element skipping there, skipping and skipping until it accomplished the bottom. Pike's nothing but a shadow himself, merely a thin dim swimming something alongside the boat, a momentary tangle, a whistle of light. The hat too—passing around them, turning, wetly bobbing—was due, eventually, to absorb too much, to sag, close up and sink. Omensetter threw horseshoes the same way. He sent them aloft and the heart rose with them, wondering if they'd ever come back, they seemed so light. A soft tish . . . and the shoe might slip beneath the surface of the air like the Chinese sage, or painter was it? who disappeared into his picture, except that Omensetter managed this miracle for things, for stones and horeshoes, while doing nothing to untie or lighten himself—no, he heavily and completely remained. Pike died of his love, his stone said. Omensetter's stones did not skip on forever either, though they seemed to take heart, or did they renew their fear? from their encounter with the water; but despite this urging each span was less, like that shortness of breath which grows the greater, the greater effort is required—and plip . . . . plip . . . plipplipplish was their hearts' register and all they were.

Tell me, Mr. Rush, in that uncustomary country, are you comfortable by this time? A child, for all his fright at first, grows used to life too, swells to a fondness even, and sucks on its sweets till they loosen his jaws. Or do you worry whether your bones will be up to the next leap when it will be the end of you again, poor thing . . . oh well, the water will take you on, or the fire, though there'll be new responsibilities as always, new risings required, you'll never escape *those*—but weren't you one, when you lived on air, who badgered the body about spirit? Ghosting's what we've always called for. Be above yourself, that's what we've urged—Pike, you and I—the hanker for the other side. We've no reason to complain, then, if our crotch is cracked by a hurdle. But I wonder—you might know now—is it a lie? What ease instead to melt into the body's arms and be one's own sweet concubine. And Omensetter? Is he, in his fashion, like us? Is it cruel to tease stones so? What's your view now you've splashed under? Whatever he gives them, it lasts only a moment. There's no help for it, they have to come down to a stone's end.

Furber's heels registered loudly on his walk. Not too quick, he moved with the sun; he threw his shadow like the gnomon, his absence warming, his presence cooling, the face of his clock.

Name his name, the missing fellow, so they said, sick so long, who ran from his wife, well almost certainly, hardly surprising, who could stand her? after all these years not to remember, tongue tipped, yet . . . who could stand her? though she had a strange body under those clothes, breasts with buttons, he imagined, stranger soul; it was Henry . . . Henry . . . and she was . . . she was . . . an effect like fallen slag . . . she was . . . there was no such thing as flaccid stone or she'd seem made of it . . . she was . . . no connection to Kinsman, with the crumpled knee and the dainty limp, why do they escape me? oh she's strange, strange, who could stand her? the way her teeth snap, like a toy lock, well that's what he had, a stone jaw, he—Pimber!—and she went to pieces just as though she loved him the night he passed through the valley of the shadow scared to death, that juice-spewing doctor perched beside him like a night-shitting bird, and the god-calling going great guns beneath him, as the Reverend Jethro Furber—ah, 'twas I, in my grave-colored clothing, long a small dear friend of the nearly departed—name his name—in low-pitched swallowy prayers beseeched our gentle God to spare, oh spare, and pled with Him to save, oh save. His Henry, our humbly cherished, that he not be let to cross the limit of the living yet or that he cross quite painlessly if that were the wish of his Father or that he find some comfort among the dead, and merciful rewards, and rest . . . from his wife, one thought, for who could stand her? it would have been no bother to his bones if he had died, they were stiff in their joints already, while through his skin his skull was glowing, nearly safe his teeth were smiling, for he no longer had to stand her, or stand anything, sloughing his sensitive parts; and these, these prayers and these petitions, pathetically strung like beads of kisses round the forehead of a feverish child, *our feverish child,* he had at a critical moment, as though divinely breathed on, in confidential whispers, touchingly described him—I, that is, the Reverend Jethro Furber, he, the sweetly speaking, oh the charlatan melodious . . . name it, name it, name her name . . . just fake, just liar—sprung tears from the eyes of: who first were they? Mrs. Curtis Chamlay, Mrs. George Hatstat, and Mrs. Olus Knox, which were a match for the beads . . . chatoyant . . . like Christ's eyes . . . my soul's eyes . . . and from Mrs. Hesiod Harmon, too, in for the weekend from Bridge, who kept her heart enclosed in heelskin normally, while residing with the Luther Hawkins family still at home, also from Miss Millicent Andrew and Miss Grace Cate and Mrs. Quentin Martin only moved to town a month yet socially as well ancestored as anyone in Gilean, and her daughter Eliza, lovely as lilac, whose hand she held, then Mrs. Emory Root with Lutie on the Sheraton settee, freshly reupholstered in beige wool rep by Mrs. Pimber working evenings till her eyes were sore, and further Mr. and Mrs. Claude Spink, as well as Edna Hoxie, fly that death drew, and Mr. Israbestis Tott, of course, who won the weeping; while later, as the night wore on and the watchmen wearied, ginger cookies Mrs. Chamlay had baked were served with coffee by Miss Samantha Tott, serious throughout and, Furber thought, severe; well there was some sense there, the mumbo jumbo didn't stir her, unless it was the stain of the beets, for it wasn't Henry's life that was the thought of the house but the bandaged hands the doctor wouldn't touch, the red pulse underneath, and the superstition that would catch it if he died, if Orcutt's didn't, since death meant the triumph of the clergy's, they were the masters of the resting places ... and she was ... that other was ... she was ... full, smooth, glistening, white ... while life meant, in this case ... Omensetter's luck ... and it would be just like the Lord to raise up Henry in the circle of the beet's spell ... name her, name her, name her name ... while additional refreshments were offered Misters Knox, Stitt, Hatstat, Mossteller, and Chamlay, who popped in and out looking grave, smelling of spirits and rubbing their faces, for who could stand her? no wonder Henry was going away, the lucky devil; and Furber felt his prayers smoke up to the god of the witches: death is better for you, Henry, better for me too, of course, better for Gilean; defeat him, fight him for us all, wrestle him down like Jacob the angel, perhaps Omensetter will receive the blame, that's worth dying for, Christ's cause; listen, you can't stand her anyway, just think, no more nights and days; listen to me, your spiritual adviser, no more living, what a prize! look, ask Rush, or Meldon ... Pike, yes, ask Pike, he'll speak, he will advise, he's stone himself now, and knows what it means to have relief from feeling ... Henry? remember! it's Omensetter otherwise ... then the dark hollows of his eyes and the woolly eyebrows were menacing, his smile was menacing, the pillow glowing in the pale light was menacing, and Furber heard the whistling of witches or the god of the witches, was it wind through Henry's teeth? but he kept on bravely closing in, his hands sanctimoniously clasped, lips shaping words of love and life and light and Lord—but crying die, shouting die through his whole inside, lungs echoing, liver ringing, belly thundering, die, it's best you die ... but it was as if Henry's body had sunk beneath him, or his bones had risen, for only the bones were showing, luminously shining, ghost lit, and Furber fell back, frightened terribly ... *out of the body, then, as out of a cave covered with stones, He rose alive, a net of thongs and wires His nature now, imperishable, a God* ... and leaving the room to Watson and the watching to Watson, he flew below stairs ... our feverish child, he said, to ooze the tears ... and name the liar ... liar ... name the liar ... loudly ... listen ... Lucy ... it's Lucy ... looo ... seee ... look ... how fat she is and unattractive, her dress hiked above her knee to cross a log, and where am I all this time, where's the watchman? he's waiting God's cruel sign like a weasel in the weeds... oh I leave nothing moving though I breathe with difficulty, my chest heaves ... I've scratched my hands and ankles, haven't I? lying behind those young elderberries and

120

these knuckles of granite . . . Henry, if you'd seen . . . she was . . . she was . . . who'd believe me? I'm the perjuring preacher, only my lies have their ears, yet to touch . . . just to . . . I tell you I saw them bathing in the creek like two cows . . . indescribably smooth and full and shining . . . not a pig's bladder, not a stone the sun's bleached . . . you'd have run away to have a sight of her . . . she snapped in my face like a twig . . . not like a mushroom, either, even fresh and perfectly puffed . . . her son inside her . . . who'd believe me? that she was . . .

He stood uneasily in the door as though an unpleasant thought had caught him by the sleeve. The portentous question still held the air. After a moment he sighed to signify his resignation and turned toward Watson, flinging out his hands to indicate a kind of facing-up was taking place, another kind of defeat. He measured his tone as carefully as a carpenter and struck on his opportunity like a clock. For such a question, a monstrous answer, and he pushed his words by every objection, maneuvering his voice and body eloquently in the small space, bending, turning, shrugging, hissing. . . .

It will be a boy if he says so. If he says so, it will surely be a boy. Sometimes, Matthew, sometimes there's a certainty in things of this kind—from sources of this sort—that's like the certainty that streams from God—*like* the certainty, I say, *like* it, only *like*—for this man's in no way godlike—hardly—but it will be a boy if he says so. As I believe my God, *because* he says. I fancy I'm considered one who strives to tell the truth in everything. Is there only vanity in that?

Listen Matthew, when Omensetter came into the church I could not speak in my usual way. I spoke in his. You heard. Weren't you amazed to hear me speaking in this way and not in mine, my hard and honest way of speaking? Listen Matthew, I spent hours in my room beseeching God. And then I went where he was walking in the new fields, the corn a foot into the summer—let me continue, please!—I put it frankly to him, I asked him why he had possessed my tongue and turned it from the way it wished to go. I said possessed, yes. That was my word. Listen Matthew, and he said: "you would have spoken hard against me"—I admit it, this was so—"and that is why I've taken all your words away. I'll not be talked against." Oh no! Oh no! There was a glow around him, Matthew, as he spoke, and his hair rose straight above his head and his face was flushed and full of the kind of anger I have no knowledge of. Oh no! Oh no! That's what he said. Listen Matthew, he was in the young corn walking and

121

I said leave us Omensetter, leave us all. Oh I accused him. I did. Yes, I said, you are of the dark ways, Omensetter, leave us all. He stopped—wait—he stopped, his hair on end, abush—wait now, wait—he laughed noisily. "I am of the dark ways, preacher," he said. Oh no! Oh no! I fancy I'm considered one who strives to tell the truth in everything. Is there only vanity in that? Then he laughed in that terrible long way. He said: "I am of the dark ways, preacher." Yes, he said: "I walk the dark path." Those were his words. No no, those were his words. They are engraven on me. Listen Matthew, listen, I went home then to our church and prayed to God.

The days were turning back from the frost; it would be warm again in Indian summer. The walk had lost the last traces of dew, his shoes were dry now, the grass no longer glistening though the wall was damp in several places. They were drawing off. He heard the ungreased wheels, the dog barking as it ran beside them, and he felt his anger subside. He ought to visit Mrs. Pimber, perhaps this evening. She'd be nervous, of course, worried, and inclined to pour her heart in his ear. What spiritual work might he recommend? Furber allowed himself to smile as he marked the time. He knew what would be on her mind. She'd groan and sputter. Owf. Ugh. Twenty bushels, half spoiled. Pumping her rocker. This settee. That chair. Jars of watermelon pickles, peach preserves, spiced pears. She'd number spaces in the air and jab at them with her forefinger. Glasses of grape and apple jelly—how many? Blueberries earlier, beans, beets, corn. Now it was pumpkin. More than last year—by precisely how many? Completing her inventory, she'd absently crack her knuckles. Pints of plums and cherries. Quarts of applesauce. Beside the stewed tomatoes, this many of the juice. All under wax and glass. Put up—the favorite phrase—preserved. Left from last year—how many? Then rhubarb and raspberries. Given away—how many? Henry doesn't care for elderberry jelly, he prefers strawberry jam—nevertheless, how many? Save. Conserve. In the stiff dry grass ... through the elder bushes, their berries filling, green, the stream ... Furber waved his thoughts away. Always he fought to keep that image out: he standing, she beside. Lust was not the feeling. Lust was nothing, though in his lust he smelled continually of cheese. Lust was for little girls with scratchy underclothes. Lust was nothing ... nothing. He should try to remember that Omensetter was a man like all men. Just another chest with matted hair. "Every one of them is gone back; they are altogether become filthy; there is none that doeth good, no, not one." She too—Lucy—so bravely named. "Can two walk together except they be agreed?" That was from Amos. Amos. They named the child Amos . . . brazenly . . . Amos Omensetter . . . hurtled from his father's penis like those angels who were spat from the mouth of heaven, bad seed in bitter fruit, to topple through eternity. Out. Like an acrobat through paper. Out. Out altogether. What luck. For the blasphemous thought he struck himself. The garden was stippled with sun let through the elms. There, Furber thought, was the real fruit of life. Involuntarily he stretched out his hand to take the bait. Another gesture. Futile. And sometimes he failed to understand where his satisfaction came from—marching off the minutes on his clock—for he was driving his own life under, too, with every step he took.

> Furber is a sticky pill
> he will make you sick
> he will

Was such spite in him? He sighed. Another gesture. Spite? there was enough. This, though, he would like to have remain: these pieces of shade; was that asking too much? He stopped abruptly but his heart went on, he felt it laboring. He eased his grip on the book and tenderly felt of his chest. At any time, if he wished (and he always did) he could fill his eyes with her. Was this the kind of vision that was sent the desert fathers? Well it was too much, too much for mere mortality—these perverse figures in a painting of the paradise. Ah, Mrs. Pimber. Greetings. I've boiled up six buckets of spying in windows with six cups of sugar and canned three quarts of bachelor love to warm me this winter. That should last nicely if I don't serve it to company, it's calorific. But perhaps Henry really had run away and she did need the clergy's advice and consolation. Chamlay had begun to speak of painful duty—a bad sign. They were worried, yet something kept them off, a fact remarkable enough by itself since ordinarily they'd have had their noses down like dogs. Now it looked as though they had waited as long as they were able. This morning Knox and Chamlay had come to stir him up, to tell him his business by god, and the hope he'd heard in their voices had made him cringe. Curtis had been wrapped in his large coat though the grass was only lightly streaked with rime. While Knox talked, Chamlay peeled dead skin from his lip and flew it from his tongue. Perhaps he should go out. He was, after all, their representative. He wore their colors, bore their powers, exercised their rites.

Consolation for Tott. Yet he had the fear that she would merely pause in her rocking and while humming thoughtfully tilt her face to the ceiling to calculate quart boxes of currants and transform them into jars of jelly. Under the circumstances he doubted his ability to bear it. Was that it really? He might suggest she paint plates, she was fond of decorating chairs.

Curtis, he said, what are you up to? Chamlay looked away through the trees. Someone has to go out there, he said mournfully, she hasn't said a word or been around to see a soul. That's mighty funny, you know that. He wore a fur hat like a hunter's. Thin hot face. Determined. Splotched. Knox on his arm like a cane. Pride, Furber suggested. Pride. Domestic tiff. Protect her feelings. Wait. What she pretends does not exist—for her friends should also not exist, he said. For her friends. Shrewd thrust that missed. Everything missed. Then he saw the badge—damn tinlight—and his heart fell. They repeated their words—in effect, their demands. Nothing else mattered. They repeated them. Opportunity like a hand to be seized and shaken. Theirs. His. Shake. True enough, she had not complained, yet she kept within her house, the shades all drawn, the door locked tight, and Valient Hatstat said she knocked and knocked to no avail. At night, at the back of the house, the curious said they saw a light pass the shaded windows or heard the pump squeak once or twice, the back door bang. A few, more credulous, maintained the barn was sometimes lit, across its upper face, by the same pale and passing lamp. These were boys, entirely, whose fathers fetched them in. Pride. Protect. If she pretends, pretend. The fact is that Henry Pimber has run away—out of Gilean, out of the world maybe—and his wife has gone strange. I didn't know you were a deputy. Shines pretty. Where'd you get it? Something new? Chamlay's arm extends. Fur hat. Whistles his lip skin. Someone had to. Knox is speaking. She won't let you in, but it's proper procedure. Light frosts his glasses. Oh, procedure! He's gone off, there's nothing of him anywhere. Fur at his boot tops. Well it's not that cold. Except inside. Why didn't they go away? If he just thought about it hard enough—go away! Chamlay slaps his gloves. Well it's not that cold. Warm really. Except inside. Shamed and weak, Furber settled to the bench, the sun was cool. Up and down. Slap. Boot gleam. Slap. Coat fur. Slap. Hat fur. Slap. Go away. Badge glitter. A decision of the town board requesting authority from the county seat. Knox frosted eyes. Once taking tea with Rosa Knox he'd had the same feeling. There were three little girls . . . running . . . and she'd said: don't chew your shoes.

Over and over. Slap. It's madness. He has Pimber under his coat. Henry's not been right since his sickness. And so quiet. He used to sit like a ghost in a corner of Mat's shop. Now ... he's gone. Like a ghost. Go away. Yes yes yes yes. Go away. His wife was ill then too. Slap. Not quite right in her mind remember. There, in the dark room, emerging from the froth of sheets, Henry's eyes as hard and shiny as a teddy bear's were fixed on him whichever way he moved. Knox nod. Official frosted glass. Please. What is she doing out there? what is she up to? what in heaven is going on? what has happened? what? Thump. Boot ends. What what what. Olus Knox said ask her. Yes yes yes. Why not? why doesn't someone? why why why. Because of the jars in rows, the potatoes in bins, the apples in barrels, the crocks of pickles and sauerkraut, the drying onions ... Don't be absurd. Because of the gourds . . . Don't be a fool. Interview. The local cause. The sun *was* cool. And she was like an after-image still, a scar of light, a sailor's deep tattoo. She stepped from a pool of underclothing. Oh Anthony had it easy! Because he'd seen the other Lucy mother-naked (buck-naked, Pike, I guess you'd say), yet who'd believe him? I'm afraid the Reverend Furber's not right in his head. It wasn't lust that tumbled him. Lust was nothing . . . for schoolboys really. It had been—perception. His rage rose, filling him. These interviews! these damnable suggestions! He would like to have beaten Brother Chamlay flat as a footed apple. Listen. Then they kissed like needles. And he has a member, gentlemen, you might envy. It looked ... infinite. Beneath it . . . a heap of thunderous cloud. It had risen with her rubbing as they shambled in the water. By its measure it might have been the massive ram and hammer of the gods. You could see it would beget men children only. Well, Egypt was easy on Jerome. And lucky for Macarius he was not with me. Is sin what I saw? is that what burned my eyes and left its brutal image in them? Then—listen—then, so full herself, she spilled his seed, and they both laughed like gulls. Furber slammed the Bible on the bench. No, he said aloud, rising. This is a matter for theology, not for feeling. His anger made him tremble. Nevertheless he straightened and turned to address a host of cherubim, speaking in level measured tones: *early in their paradisal life the Lord God blessed His man and womankind and said be fruitful, multiply. But how could man beget unless his flesh would rise and what was there in innocence to move the simplest muscle in a gesture of desire? Were men to love unmindful, below the beasts, like flowers? It is impossible to know, of course. That moment has passed for all time. Yet watching Omensetter I sometimes think I'm*

125

trembling on the lip of understanding it. It's then I think I recognize the nature of his magic. For whatever Omensetter does he does without desire in the ordinary sense, with a kind of abandon, a stony mindlessness that makes me always think of Eden. The thought is blasphemous, I realize. And this of course is the clue, for more than any man I've ever known, Omensetter seems beyond the reach of God. He's truly out of touch. Furber paced a moment with his arms symbolically flexed. *Sin's nothing but exile. It occurs when God withdraws. Should exile seem so blessed and free?* He strode forward vigorously. *Should everything seem fine beyond the fence, while we . . . Listen to me, listen,* he cried, coming to a stop and holding out his hands, *we know that men are evil, don't we? Don't we? Oh god haven't we observed it often? haven't we bruised our eyes and stunned our hearts to discover the hardness of that truth? Yet Omensetter doesn't seem to be. He does not seem. Seem. Is this correct, this—seem? Oh you're cows! Is this the feeling? I require an answer not a hiccough. Nannerbantan? TuK? Well he does. He does, doesn't he? Well? Well? And what? And what shall we conclude from all of this then?*

We must conclude he is the worst.

He is the worst.

Therefore.

2

Twilight was moving through the woods upon the fields when the Reverend Jethro Furber, pebbles in his shoes, sand pushing between his toes, limped down the River Road to Henry Pimber's house. Trees divided the pale sheet of water on his left, while on his right loomed a bank of darkness like a battlement. The air was quiet, there was cloud, and all the sounds that human silence sharpens were, unearthly, stopped. The house seemed a deep extension of the trees, and Furber began to wonder what fool conceit or cowardice had driven him. He decided it was both: there was cowardice in his coming at all; there was conceit, certainly, in the melodrama of the moment he had chosen. Now and then the moon appeared and bleached a path across the road. He heard a horse, and far away, perhaps in town, a lonely bark. The pebbles pressed against the bottoms of his feet. It had been a delicious pair of pains at first but now it made him wobble awkwardly. Madame, the clergy has come to call: give greeting. He looked about. The long lane was silent. The Holy Spirit has no better emissary: loose loud hurrahs. His mouth twisted sourly as he heard himself. Furber turned past the forsythia, wading in a trench of shade to penetrate the darkness that lay beyond the lilacs, and soon he reached the steps where he could see the neighborly gift of Mrs. Gladys Chamlay glimmering quietly in the moonlight and groaning from neglect. Though its shining is silent, there's speech in the spoiling. Furber considered whether this expression was worth recording and decided against it. He raised the napkin covering the picnic basket and in the moonlight ants splashed like pepper past his feet. Leaning shame against fear, he removed one shoe at last, and in the moonlight emptied it of sand and stones, roughly dusting his sock. Since the leather had a tendency to wad, he shoved his foot back through the shoe's high neck with difficulty. He then drew from the other an easing stream. Both feet comfortably shod again, he tromped noisily across the porch and pounded on the door, startling a bird which rose angrily from its bush. Twice he called her name, then waited, feeling absurd. The aches in his feet were subsiding. He felt he ought to stop and tie his shoes, but he had compunctions about kneeling. In the morning he'd have more than a bruise. Attempting to listen, he went carefully down the steps and quickly toward the back of the house. In that moment the resting branches turned their leaves. Brilliantly, the still grass glittered. He found the side door locked, the rear door bolted. The cellar door seemed hooked. Ineffectually, he tugged and hauled at windows, beginning to wheeze. His heels were rising in his shoes, the laces slapping. Nor could he tolerate the funk he was in. Were there goblins in the gumtrees, ghosts in the cupboards? He had no fear of spirits surely—of brooming witches, of gnomes, elves, sprites. Bear in mind: hate finds nothing hard. He ought to make a note of that. Nevertheless he could not ignore the figure he was cutting. Distraught, he wandered aimlessly about until he stumbled on a stick which, when he discovered what it was, he seized in a fury, attacking the house. By prying with it, he made a window squeak. Next he balanced a rock on a box and stood on these, the better to shove and heave. Yes indeed, he was an accomplished comedian and entrancing equilibrist, favorite of queens. At last he was able to squeeze inside. Something fell as he entered. Whatever it was, it did not break, but rolled slowly across the floor: a-runk, a-runk, a-runk. He couldn't remember how the furniture was arranged or where in the house he was. The children who had spied on her, as he'd been told, claimed she roamed the building with a lamp, but the place was cold, the air unstirred, the darkness unrelieved. He sneezed—curtain across his face. Now where are you, Lucy, he yelled, ashamed of the quaver in his voice. But he might come on her corpse. Swimming in the dark, he might bump it with his nose, or his foot might crush its fingers. Then Henry's head might moon, his fierce eyes stare, the covers close about his neck like foam, and Furber would hear his own voice singing die in a relentless monotone—die die die. He turned back to the window, terrified, bumping a chair which slid on the unrugged floor. Above him, on what he later decided were the back stairs, a figure appeared wrapped in gauze, holding a faintly burning lamp. Sagging. Furber uttered an uncourageous groan. Backett, is that you, Lucy Pimber said in a whisper.

It was, no one could doubt it, a great stroke of luck, and the sense of her words brought him to his feet in a moment. It is I, the Reverend Jethro Furber, he formally announced. She fled up the stairs. The pale light danced as he stumbled after her. Don't be frightened. Don't be frightened. She extinguished the lamp and he thought he would never find her. Before he did, the whole business had gotten thoroughly on his nerves, his old illness had returned, and even his bones shook. He cradled the rail in his arms. He was blind—a buzzing in his eyes. Despite the grotesqueness of the wish, a part of him wanted to be mistaken for the huge hide-wetter who was so marvelously fitted and so universally desired. Another part didn't care at all about that, but would have been immensely gratified to have her fall beneath him, opening easily, whoever she thought he was. So what if her breasts were like pancakes. Nor was that all he wanted, for he was in a thousand careening pieces like a shattered army. However, when at last he dragged Lucy from the linen closet and obtained the lamp—she was a torn and dirty spirit, certainly, for she'd fouled her clothes—he was nearly sickened by the smell of her, it was so strong and fecal. He possessed the lamp but had no way to light it, and while he stood stupidly considering this, she flew through the darkness again, whining weirdly like a bat. In pursuit, Furber fell on the stairs, smashing the mantle. Rattled, he shouted threats. You're to tell no one I fell, you hear, smell-belly, he roared. You're loony, you hear me? You're loony Lucy. He was beginning to see quite well now, and he found her hunched under the table in the kitchen mewing and spitting like a cat. Twisting a great knot in her nightdress, he pulled her out, saying experimentally, "I am Backett Omensetter," in a deep bass voice. When he heard her chuckle he struck out blindly, hitting her several times on the head and shoulders. These blows rendered her docile, and though exhausted by his own emotions, he was able to restore her to the care of her friends without further difficulty or exertion.

Not many days after, at the Hatstat's where Lucy had been taken to recover, he was even able to offer her a good deal of excellent advice concerning the management of her life in the future. He was aware, at the time, of his stiffness, of the extreme correctness of his deportment all in all; but Lucy Pimber, though she seemed as large-eyed as an owl and nearly as watchful, listened to his lengthy and somewhat elaborate monologue, despite the cold remoteness of its tone and the unflinching directness of its message, with a steady, calm, and sober mien throughout, for which Furber, more than once in the weeks that followed, gave grateful thanks to ghosts, elves, sprites, gnomes, witches—all of the disloyal angels, each of the fallen gods.

 3

It was an afternoon of weak sun, the hour was late, and Mat appeared slowly on the end of the street. Outside his shop, as lightly as a water bird, Jethro Furber waited, and so observed reluctance enter the blacksmith's knees. It's lovely to be loved, he thought bitterly, rising to tiptoe and pulling the collar of his coat around his neck. Love . . . hate . . . what did it matter which it was? He was ready for either. His plans were made. His speeches had been well rehearsed. He had his courage and his anger up, his makeup straight, his costume fresh, its creases squeezed so ardently they gave him edges like a knife. Furthermore, he knew his man. That was a terrible thing—to know your man; terrible, that is, for the man known, if it was true. And in this case, it *was* true. He did know. He *knew*. Mat's imagination would undo him.

There was coming toward him now, its body pondering, its temples glowering, a beast, burthenous with shadow. Furber winked. Mat's shoulders were too heavy for his back. Frowns pinched his eyes. Undo—and a totter of limbs, a clatter of bones in collections. Oh he was always such a weighty man.

"Yet His burthen is light." But Mat dragged his shadow like a sled and fragments of dancehall song pierced Furber's head.

> Imagine my distress
> if you undo my dress.
> for if you do,
> oh me! undo—
> for if you do,
> oh my! untie—
> then I'm undone,
> I must confess;
> I'll simply die
> without my dress.

He felt strangely adrift again. A shadow flew under his feet. It was curious—this floating. Better watch it. Hair lapped Mat's ears.

> So if you do,
> oh me! undo—
> so if you do,
> oh my! untie—

Mat was habitually heavy-hearted, morosely kind, distinctly dull in that sense, slow and gloomy; his center of gravity seemed to Furber near his knees.

> consider that my dress
> fits tight across my chest;
> has hooks and eyes,
> and bows and ties,
> has pins and clips
> clear to my hips,

Furber had withdrawn from his skin but he was still cold. Unhappy hands, fallen out of pockets, fluttered in greeting. Greeting? The sky fled without moving. Mat came slowly on.

> and is difficult to press
> so very difficult to press.

Yet somewhere in that ponderous person lived a lively fancy ... yes—as a mouse might nest in a bear or a bird in a beaver. Thus Mat was curious, though a dreadful prude, and if he would gossip only when he felt obliged, he was frequent and unfailing in the discharge of his duties. He was fond of works of popular philosophy which he badly misconstrued, and once he had embarrassed Furber with a gift of some tracts on Eastern mysticism and the occult which he had acquired while a carter in Chicago in his youth.

> If you insist
> that I divest
> the dress that clasps
> me to its breast,
> and guards my honestness,
> and shields my honestness,

Despite Mat's reputation for having what barbers, shaving, call a light touch—a quality unusual, even irrelevant, in smiths—he regularly broke things: chairs, crocks, dishes, cooking pots and tools.

> then whatever you may do
> do to yourself too—

He was proud, in addition, that his thoughts were sometimes deep; that his mind was, on occasion, devious; that he saw through people, or around them, which was often the greater feat; and that he had a flair for finding affinities, however different and bizarre their outward forms (Pimber and Omensetter were a natural pair, he always said) which his friends pronounced both exact and remarkable.

> for that's the golden rule,
> the golden, golden rule—

To Furber, watching Mat's unwilling progress up the street, he represented the perfect pulley, for a gentle tug at one end would move a mountain at the other, or raise an unwilling Lazarus from the dead.

> and when we're finally through,
> this maid shall ask of you,
> that whatever has been done,
> as a gentleman,
> whatever has been done,
> you redo.

First, however, it would be necessary to get in. Furber had been standing for some time motionless, his mind asleep, and now both men leaned toward one another like two sticks thrust weakly in the earth. The street was strangely empty, the store fronts seemed painted on a drop, and Furber had the feeling that they might rise out of sight any moment, the scene change suddenly—and then what? a desert might surround them or a jungle ... hummocks of snow or the restless terrain of ocean. Through his uneasiness he recognized the need for strength and motion, and grasping himself, regained his stature. Normally small and thin, he seemed pulled by his own will through his black coat sleeves and trouser legs and stiff white tube of collar until he was as tall as he thought he ought to be, the total of his body and his shadow so completely cast together that Mat could scarcely have distinguished the separate figures that made the sum.

Ah, Matthew, here you are at last. I feel a chill, he said.

The lengthy *ah*, Mat's name swimming in his breath, the ladybook language, the preacher's tone: the stage. Standing too long, he'd struck a false note; his determination had drained away through his feet. Consequently Watson put his back to Furber's eye. Mat's shirt was stained and the sides of his face were streaked. Matthew, Furber crooned. Matthew, he bellowed. Matthew, Matthew, he chanted, filling his head with the sounds that meant smith, as if these sounds would give him some hold on their object. Didn't a man grow like his name in the long run, and wasn't there a piece of him wedged in it, between the syllables, like meat in a sandwich? How else could you know that the noises fit? It's what finally does those famous people in, his father used to say, wagging a long, plump, finger; every time you're thought of, a part of you gets used. It's slow erosion. Death from simple use. Double U and T. That was his father's life, his father's motto. Wear and wear. And then we're through. It's simply Double U and T. Too much Double U and T. A hole pokes through, he used to say, as through a shoe. And then we're through. Over and over and over he'd say it, wearing the edges of his teeth away. What shall we do? what shall we do? Furber was removed—giddy—all awobble. Another of his father's newspaper truths: where are liquor and tobacco? why, they live in habit's hollow. Over and over and over. If each man were in his syllables somewhere, he could be reached that way. And touched. Over and over. Loved? What did it matter? He could be chewed and swallowed. Jethro, for instance . . . or Matthew. He knew true habit's hollow. Omen—What if Romeo's name were Bob? Or Jethro. What if Jethro's name were—what? a wise adviser, a fluent liar, a slippery spier, a loud woe-crier, a God-denier with his soul on fire—no—what if his name were—what? But you couldn't wear out Romeo. He grew with each repeating. Omensetter. Simpson. Suppose it were Simpson. Or Henry Pimber. Or Olus Knox. A pig wallow—that was habit's hollow. Stitt. Tott. Chamlay. I've your name here, bucko, with my spit around it—how do you like that? Hatstat. Flack. Cox. Hawkins. Cobb. Well there might be something in it. Still another of his father's newspaper truths:

132

thou shalt not take the name of the Lord they God in vain. Were there one, He should have slain ... Had there been, He would have ... My will be done. And thrust the lightning home. Suppose God's name was Simpson. Suppose, all this time, through all this hoot and hollering, He was Simpson. Unhearing. That would explain ... everything. Hey there, Simpson! Hey hey! Not opportune. My name's not Jethro Furber. You've the wrong man once again. It's Joe Pete Andy. It's Philly Kinsman. What would that be like to be? Kinsman. Any. To slip away to a new life. And so be safe from Double U and T. Ah. There was Backett Omensetter, then. He'd worn that man to a shadow, if this was true; his name could only call a ghost.

> Silly Billie
> has a belly
> big as Marge
> and large as Nellie.

Matthew Omensetter. The two of them were twins of a kind, Furber saw that now; they possessed a terrible similarity, and he felt further weakened.

> ... the treasures that she carried
> were mostly deeply buried ...

To be Philly Kinsman ... to swim in a river of trees ... the sun asleep on the grass, in the weeds ... oh god, he was going to die and never—

> ... the belle of the Spanish Main ...

Matthew Omensetter. Both were large-bodied gentlemen, always moist like river clay, darkening their shirts with designs as they worked, speaking in streaks and splotches.

> I shall never marry
> a maid who is a fairy;
> she'd be too military,
> and I've no taste for war,
> or ..... or .....,
> for I've no taste for war.

Both were clay-skinned, too, their deep tans yellowy; and they had thick tropical hair that fell untidily over their foreheads, though Mat's was oftener cut and not so coarse —that was the difference.

133

And I shall never tarry
with a girl who's lost her cherry;
of her virtue I'd be wary,
despite my taste for whores,
ors . . . . . ors . . . . . ,
despite my taste for whores.

Besides there was a looseness about Omensetter's fleshy parts, not exactly unpleasant, he had to admit, not puffy or like skin that's bubbled from the bone as paper does sometimes from plaster, but rather as if the muscles were at ease there, children asleep in their comforts—

"What do you want?" Is that it? Is it thus he addresses his minister? with a *you*. While I cry: ah, ah Matthew, ah . . . while I cry: ah, the gospel author's name, *that* name, you, instead, say: "what do you want?" Well, he would not answer. He'd topple silence on them like the temple. He would not answer to a *you*.

Simple Samson went to the fair,
all of the Philistine people were there.

I want—I want to be Philly Kinsman. Orcut Cate. Mossteller. Jenkins. Amsterdam. He recognized the wickedness and strength of the temptation, but he was sometimes overcome by the incredible sweetness of life, the warmth, the softness of his imaginary women, their skin so white and luminous with comfort.

But a wise apothecary
bid me once be chary
of girls who tipple sherry
and sleep the day indoors,
ors . . . . . ors . . . . . ,
and sleep the day indoors.

In order to survive the silence he would have to think of darkly distant and dissimilar things: the Antarctic, camels, Bogota. Mat's thumbs were hooked to the tops of his trousers, so Furber tried to turn his thoughts to the wood thrush, then to Sardanapalus the king. The blacksmith's belly was large for all his laboring and it was puffing faintly beneath the cloth.

Her nipples bright as berries,
my maiden's great mammaries,
will yield milk like the dairy's,
till I've no taste for more,
or . . . . . or . . . . . ,
till I've no taste for more.

The silence was a cross, but Furber resolved to share it, and he saw with pleasure that Mat had begun shifting his weight, leg to leg, like a bear. It was God's work, God's good work, Furber thought; he'd stand like this forever if necessary, like a holy image, though his church denied him images—well damn them and their dreary doctrines for that—all right then, like a mute accusing witness, an everlasting reminder . . .

> And down where she is hairy,
> I'll cage my wild canary,
> a songbird legendary,
> till it can sing no more,
> or . . . . . or . . . . . ,
> till it can sing no more.

Mat's left hand flew to his face and clawed it roughly, then fell to his side with a slap. His right still clung to his pants like a bat to a rafter. Bogota . . . Bogota, Colombia.

It would be futile to say: as a man, I don't matter. I don't. I don't matter. But remember what I mean, for the body of every symbol is absurd. Tell me: how did Jesus pee? Who will preach on this point? Who will address himself to this question? Did He? Oh yea, Sisters and Brothers, He did. He peed the same as you do. Certainly the same, Brothers. Fully as well, too. Yea, fully as often. A pale straw-yellow stream. It's more likely He was circumcised than He was wispy bearded, weakly blond, girl whiskerless, a boy at twenty though a man at ten, a carpenter each inch a king. He was, in sum, an ordinary Son of God, the average kind, in all ways pious, meek, contentious, thin. Food wedged in His teeth, for instance; His skin blistered. Empty, His belly rumbled; stones cut His feet. Consider a moment the chemistry of The Last Supper. And when hung on the cross, between the thieves, He felt no differently the kiss of His nails than they did theirs. I can assure you of that much. Happy to do so, Sisters; happy . . . so happy, Brothers. So much, too, you're this God's equal. He made His wind like anyone. His buttocks coughed, and I can imagine He was tempted, relieving Himself, to spatter the spider who'd bit Him. His body made Him humble, yet He was piss proud. What sense to say He had one otherwise? What sense? But futile. Yea, Brothers —bombaddybast. They've scrubbed Him, drained His fluids, wiped up His colors, ironed out His creases. Beautiful Jesus—the embalmer's pride.

And Furber then, to pass the time, thought salt, thought dill, thought vinegar. At least he should look at me, he should have the courage. Myrrh. Myrrh. Watson drew air harshly through his nose. If he spits . . . But Furber could not take the risk.

I want to speak to you about a matter, he said, briskly folding up his arms.

It's late.

I know it's late. There's time.

Is there? It's late. I've got a lot to do.

There's time enough, all the same.

I've got to wash and eat. I've had a heavy day.

There's time, I say.

Well what then? about what?

But Furber secured his chest in his arms. Do not answer questions. He wrote "rudeness" on one side of a line. There was Ptolemy, Seleucus, Perdiccas, Gonatus, Cassander—all kings, and Furber cast his eyes down the empty street. They weren't real, they were echoes of buildings. It was as though the morning had been so exhilaratingly cool and clear and sunny that the boards had shouted away their substance, and now, from those earlier hours, only these images had been reflected to the afternoon.

I think I'd better wash. I've got a lot to do.

Got. You've got.

Mat swung about and stared at Furber, blood coloring his face.

Well, he said in a moment, squinting, I really have.

He paused to tilt.

What was it you wanted?

Yes, blink, Furber thought. You've never seen me before. I'm new, a stranger, and my dark clothes dazzle. Mat's tone had altered—that was something. Furber warned himself to move cautiously, not to carry matters too far. This was a contest he didn't dare lose, and his man was restless, uneasy and restless, anxious, worn, not just physically, but spiritually strained, worn and anxious in his heart. Yet he'd have to go far to win, fantastically far, and his confidence was gone. It had disappeared the moment it was called on, despite his careful preparations. Doubt made his voice weak and Mat did not respond to Omensetter's name. Ashamed, Furber repeated it, but Watson did not answer. His head wagged and the tail of his shirt fluttered. How much—the question flew in Furber's ear—how much was Watson paying Omensetter for his help? Could he afford such a man? It might be a matter worth pursuing. But I want to be Philly Kinsman. Furber allowed himself a sigh. There'd be loyalty to be undone, rectitude, Mat's sense of Omensetter's use, his antagonism (and now that this had shown itself so plainly, it proved to be so much greater than he'd guessed—but why? why?), and how many buttons more? . . . faith? trust? belief? each less, each easier, that, too, was something; then plenty of straightout foolishness and ignorance, he could be sure of that. Not so simple, either, to free him from the mulewood he was made of. It was well Mat was weary, it would be will against will. Centipedes, he sang without conviction—waiting. Aphids, slugs. Then Eglon came—a Moab king. Jeroboam. Nadab. Baasha. Elah. Zimri. Omri. Ahab. "And Eglon was a very fat man." He was surrendering again.

It's treacherous weather. Don't you feel a chill?

The forge is banked.

Mat's voice remained weary and dispirited, scarcely polite.

Let's stand beside it, Matthew. I'll be warm enough.

A double-edged dagger of cubit length was well devised and gartered cunningly to the thigh of Ehud the assassin, deliverer of Israel. When Ehud was privately with Eglon in his summer parlor, bringing as he said a message to the king from God, he drew the dagger from its nest and with his left hand, for he was an utterly left-handed man, buried it beyond the haft in the king's belly, a belly so enormously fat that it was not possible to draw the dagger forth again, and it had to remain there instead, death's bone driven deeply, while the king's stools spilled on the carpet in the king's surprise. At first no hue and cry was raised, for Ehud fastened the chamber when he fled so that the king lay shut from his servants in his arbor as though (as they thought) he were answering to a call of nature. Such was the joke God made of Eglon then, and thus was Israel delivered that time.

The doors, yielding slowly to the pressure of Watson's shoulder, squealed. Then Mat was shouting above the noise.

O . . . Omensetter didn't come to work . . . he didn't come to work today . . . he's sick . . . I say he's sick . . . his daughter came to tell me . . . came to say he's sick . . . he's sick she said.

Oh?

Furber gathered to the forge. Coals lit the bottom of his chin. As the door rushed in—scraps of shadow, birding patches. Rehoboam, Abijam, Asa—kings in Judah. All of a sudden Mat appeared willing to communicate—good. He pushed his hands toward the fire. The coals were friendly. It didn't seem at all as if they'd sear you at a touch. He tumbled his hands, scrubbing them roughly. The darkness was a comfort. Dim as a church, at the moment as quiet, the shop

137

seemed a haven, and Furber, yawning and swallowing, smelled straw, then wood and leather, oil and old metal, manure and cooling water. He wanted to sink down and hug the coals to his chest. Flamboyant ... coins of light ... oil, wood, tatters ... fumes from acids, soap, smoke ... the sunlight shattered. He briefly wondered how it felt to Watson—this wild rich place—whether he found any peace in its confusion. It was sad, but churches rarely lived so largely. They were seldom permitted such extravagance of feeling. In fact, they were—at least his was—a sour denial of the human spirit. He caught himself quickly. He'd meant, of course, that they were a sober condemnation of the evil in human nature ... something different. However he was a notorious liar. In this sort of place, Furber could feel life opening out to him, the roof of the heavens rising in the darkness; but it was the darkness, the deep obscurity of the shop that was responsible; it was an illusion of shadow, and he realized with his customary bitterness that whatever his love was he could never show himself honestly to it; he would always undress in the dark. Moving about the forge, he saw that Mat had remained in the doorway, and made out his fingers swimming in the barrel. Furber's impulse was to fly against him like a girl and hammer the blacksmith's chest with his fists.

As you've doubtless guessed, Omensetter is the matter I've come about. It's rather confidential—in my province as a preacher, Furber said, using the word with distaste, but, he thought, with skill.

He'd lost his shadow now, was small, not even thin, leaning over the fire.

Oh?

Indifferent as a stick, Mat rested against the jamb. His rudeness was complete, and though Furber struggled against it, he found that rage had swept him away. There were ancient cities. Think. Palmyra. Nineveh. Corinth. Mat's indifference was a pose. Acre. Tyre. A performance for my performance. Issus. Damascus. Gaza. Rhodes. Now gone. All lost. He's simply afraid. Persepolis. Nor do I appear angry, though I'm burning like this hill of coals. Even the sleeves of my coat are calm. Merv. Nevertheless Furber clapped his hands so sharply and so suddenly, Mat jumped.

I've had inquiries, he said, concerning Omensetter's signs. I meant to ask you before but I saw you weren't receptive.

Oh?

Mat's eyelids drooped; they seemed to close.

What makes you think I'm receptive now?

138

Signs of another kind, Matthew, said Furber, smiling mildly.

Oh?

All those cities, those hollow houses, all those lives, those graves, the graves of hope . . . With a madness like the madness to bury that seizes men, a craze to cover that overcomes all of them, the cities covered themselves with sand and mud, vines, grass, lava, with noisier cities, completer ruins, further graves and further grasses. I am their proper lordship, Furber thought. My credentials make me master of the resting places. That was the way—burial to burial, shame to shame—it had always been since Adam's fig had hidden him, his sex and death together and the same, and surely that was the way it would continue. He—Furber—would be lost in a swallow of persons. The stone in the corner of his garden would not truly speak of him, the great Leviathan would have him, he'd be buried in their bodies—cover after cover coming—for that was the whole of life on the earth, our bodies for a time athwart another's middle, our lives like leaves, generation after generation lifting the level of the land, the aim of each new layer the efficient smother of the last.

Rubbing his chin, Mat alters the closure of his eyes. He also pulls thoughtfully at his nose. Like an actor. Yes. Deep in meditation. Oh yes. But in fact he has the fidgets. May his thoughts be pitch and smoke his wits out.

It seems to me, if I remember rightly, we've—

Been over this before? Yes, in a manner of speaking, we have, but I'm afraid that we must go over it again, though more carefully this time, more thoroughly you know, more thoughtfully.

Oh?

An enormous yawn burst into flower on Mat's face.

So I'm to be the grave of my father and mother. In an agony of embarrassment, Furber covered his mouth. These damnable fancies were the curse of his life. Besides, he merely wished to be Philly Kinsman, an imaginary friend, orphaned for convenience, though no doubt a ducal heir. But they aren't dead yet, they live in the South. He pushed his fingers between his teeth. He'd be their marker, nevertheless; his speech was their inscription. HERE LIES. How could he have known he'd rattle so? MEMENTO. I had a letter last week. Friendly. Complete. The usual sort of news. No concern. No cause. MEMORIAE SACRUM. Scum. Pee bottles. But both are really quite well, and very active in the church. MEMO. With his tongue he'd wet his fingers. MENDACEM MEMOREM ESSE OPORTET. What was

139

passing through Matthew's head? Wind shadows? the language of the dead? Not the specters of his parents, certainly. Well damn them, if I've got to have them, they deserve me. MORS JANUA VITAE. Then the memory of his mother's enclosing arms and fragrant garments overwhelmed him. Flowers bloomed along her like a fence. His eyes were smarting. I've been waiting for Mat, here, too long. It's the shade the weather's taken, and the time of day. MEMORIA IN AETERNA. I've lost my nerve. My god, I don't think of them once in a month, and here I'm bundled in blue and fluffy flannel like a child in a crib. He started to chuckle but coughed instead. You'll be the death of me, she'd often said; what am I going to do with you? what will you turn into? what will you be? Spittle flew through his father's teeth. All right, all right, die down, die down, but you'll find no rest in me. MORS OMNIA SOLVIT. A lie.

Furber groaned, securing Mat's attention, and then he said: perhaps you remember the occasion—

I remember it.

—but you seem to have forgotten what was said.

I don't remember I said much.

All right—what *I* said. You *do* remember? You haven't forgotten?

No.

But you didn't understand it?

No, I understood it well enough, I think.

You refused to believe it?

No, that wouldn't be exactly right.

Yet you did nothing.

What was there to do?

Watch!

Furber drew back, collecting himself, silent, noting that his rush had not made Watson budge. He hardly needed the forge now. His chill had been followed by a fever. Camels. That was an idea. Camels.

Circumstances compel me, he said; circumstances, you know—circles surrounding—they make it necessary to—these things which lie—which are so circumambient—to take the matter up again. I wasn't clear. Am I clear now? I fear not—no. Alas. Ah, but in a moment. I shall be then. Well . . . these cincturing affairs, eh? they force me, you see, they make me, as a . . . missionary—for apparently I wasn't clear before, and—

Oh you were clear enough.

I was? I'm surprised. I can't believe I was. Constrained as by a cingulum . . . Was I really?

Yes, you were clear enough, though I don't follow now.

140

Look Jethro—please—we're both tired and it's the end of the—

Yes, yes. Agreed. The—

Look—it's a difficult time. It's been a long day. I'm tired. Done in.

A tired body makes a ready mind.

Mat began to protest but Furber cut him off. He had thrust both palms forward, and Mat's veiled eyes had seen them. If one person is the grave of another, he wondered, what part is in the arm, for instance? There could be a correspondence, I suppose, of arm to arm and nose to nose, but what if the deceased is a much larger fellow? And justice would be better served in many cases, I should think, if the head of the dead one were hung down in the buttocks of the other, or if the heart of the corpse could be seen through the eyes—that would tell you something. Camel. Hump where the head is. That's why. Two humps: two heads. The heads of infants—several. Or embracing lovers. A camel's good dry ground and thus to be preferred for lying at any length in. Creatures of that kind will come high, likely, once it's known. On such a chance, though, it would be wise to reserve one now. Of course cash in hand in a case like this is certainly essential. Also you could specify the place the camel, when it dies, should be laid to rest. It's the sort of transmigration which might have pleased Pythagoras had anyone had the wit within his time to think of it.

Clodhopper. Pee bottle.

> My name is Philly Kinsman.
> I am a famous bandsman.
> My fife's my wife,
> but on my life,
> when I uncase my trumpet,
> all the ladies . . .
> (in these parts)
> all the ladies . . .
> (bless their hearts)
> all the ladies hump it.

Hell you say—What was wavering? Darkness spinning like the seed of a maple.

> My name is Philly Kinsman.
> I am a famous bandsman.
> Though my trombone
> gives quite a tone
> whene'er the ladies pump it,

> it's very sore
>> from playing more
> music than
>> it bargained for,
> and *still* the ladies pump it.

Mat sniffed, lifting his arm to his face. Light spread over the floor.

You spent the day hunting Henry, I suppose, Furber said, his voice light and quiet, calm and low, scarcely in motion while he searched Mat's face, alert as an animal for any change. How'd it go? a day of stubby fields, eh? They twist your ankles. I know how that is. It's wearing when it's all for nothing. Weeds and burrs—they're everywhere this time of year and very trying too, as sighting endlessly down rows of corn is, and poking in the little caves along the river—you looked there?—depressing when it's all for nothing; and along the fences, the shocks and hayhills—you investigated them? for nothing? Well your clothes look picked and there's a mean scratch on your chin—has it been stinging? Hawthorn thickets would account for it, I'll bet, and berry tangles—damnable things—and that marsh ground, too; did it wet through your shoes and wash your ankles? a bit chilling, eh? Well a nasty business all around—so very tiring when it's all for nothing. Sure. It makes a long day.

Gay songs and vulgar catches . . . death . . .

You don't think that he's run off then? You're not of that opinion? He was an unraveled man, a doll's sort, thoroughly unticked, unstrung, with no heart for flight, thrown by disease—is that your theory? and his wife all the while a flail, a handful of stones—oh I know, I know, he's a friend still, though he's wrapped himself in fronds to winter over like an ambitious hopeful worm, to see the spring, eh? but as a man he was sunken in spirit like those rowboats you see rotting by the shore, aslope with river water, or like that house he rented Omensetter, gone to moss and weeds and soft besotted boards . . . that's the view you're taking? I *know*—I know your feeling. Hoh. I'm a man of feeling too. Yet what was he but some vegetable that hadn't reached her canning, some parsnip or potato? Oh, and his wife's a friend, I know—I *know*. It's distressing. And you're opposed to everything I'm saying. Trust me, Matthew. *Goodness*. So am I. But people have their fears . . . and Matthew—these fears must be put by.

Mat was speaking. His collar had chafed his neck. His tongue appeared. The lord kinkle it.

You can help me, Mat.

At the friendly note, Mat's right eye rose, his hispidulous cheeks bulged with air: puff pop, he spoke.

You are—I confess it, observe that, I confess it—you are essential to me. I have to have you, Mat.

My frankness has dispossessed him. I'm faced by puzzlement—oh hoo ha—perhaps by fear? Bug beneath the rug. Mat rubs his ear. Tick talk.

Don't mock me, Matthew.

That threw him off. His eyes slid. What to make of it. He'd give anything to get away. Well that's my price. I'm two hours late for the Nones myself. Little doth he realize I am the pope's panjandrum in disguise. His mass is shifting. Watch his feet, oh Furb the foxer, he may be big, but he's no boxer.

Don't you trust me, Matthew?

It's not—it's not a matter of trust.

Ah, isn't it?

Furber threw up his arms and darted toward the rear of the shop.

Darkness seeped from Matthew's mouth and spilled like smoke on either side of Furber. A dream. An idol breathing steam. He was running blind and struck something. Consequently.

Just that, said Furber, dwindling. Fears of Heaven.

Lord love us. Everything above us. Love us.

Furber returned to the forge and flung his arms over it.

Heaven forsaking fears.

Oh all right, all right, what else?

Else? Else? What do you take me for? Isn't that enough?

Oh well now nonsense, Jethro.

Yes indeed, you're quite right, certainly, nonsense.

Furber snapped his fingers sharply.

Nonsense . . . but?

He opened out his hands. He slumped.

The pope's chief panjandrum. A genii. Look at the lion. I . . . I . . . shaken to the roots. Towns begining in C: Columbus, Cleveland, Cincinnati, Chillicothe . . . Come and confess? What was he daring? all this god a'mighty amounting? to my making them up? Jesus. Look at my coat's color—is it not honest?

Ah.

Furber placed his palms against his cheeks.

I get no trust.

Oh look here, don't be silly, I don't distrust you.

Under menacing eyebrows, pebble-smooth nose, over sharpening fingers, Matthew's speech stream burbled.

Just the same, you know you tend to . . . well, you're

143

always sort of making mountains, you know, making mysteries out of molehills, always warning and willying the way you do and carrying on . . .

Towns beginning—towns beginning in—god I can't think of any.

Of course I'm not against that. I'm not objecting. Maybe that's your business and you know your business and you're doing what you're supposed to, but . . . well, after all, what are they anyway?

Towns—towns . . . Where have I nestled that dagger? I shall kiss him now and eat him later. Left or right, it does not matter if I contaminate my sacred hand with this pig's blood.

Who has them—these fears, I mean? You have them, is all, Jethro. That's all. You. You have them.

In his face a handful of coals—could he manage? Scoop them quickly—there!

No place for that here, Matthew. No place and time for that now. But we must bruise the serpent, eh?

He peered queerly past his shoulder.

There aren't any children about. That accounts for it. That's strange. Where are they? They play around here, don't they? every day.

Mat nodded. The door was forcing itself into his back.

Roll hoops?

On one foot, Furber began jumping.

Hopscotch—remember?

Warily, Mat moved in from the door as Furber leaped past.

Ever skip rope? kick the can? how about hide and seek?

He stopped, noisily huff-puffing his cheeks. He had never uttered an untruth in his life. All his lies had been . . . necessary.

Jacks?

He faced toward Watson to demand an answer, but his man was deep in bewilderment now.

Mat made a vague gesture, showing his teeth. Phosphorescent, they lit his lower lip.

Furber was back on both feet. This seemed to reassure Watson, who steadied, so Furber began hopping again.

Since O-men-set-ter . . . more-of-them . . . wouldn't-you-say? he said among bounds.

Camel and kangaroo. You could be sewn in the pouch. To take to the air. The day had seemed so clear there'd been nothing to swim in. Now shadows crisscrossed it like the bodies of divers, and those other bright blue days returned to him, clamoring. He stumbled. Mat leaned forward, saying something Furber couldn't understand.

> My name is Philly Kinsman.
> I am a famous bandsman.
> You ladies may have heard of me.
> I can hold a note
> just like a rope
> that's hanging from a balcony.

Stooping, Furber dropped an imaginary ball, and with remarkable reality swept his hand down for the jacks.

> Creep away, sneak away, leak away—hide.
> There are animals hunting in Furber's inside.

You know, Mat, he said, delighted with his performance, when I was a kid I was never permitted to play with other children. The truth is, the others kept me out.

He smiled: there were no hard feelings.

But I watched them—how I watched them—hour after hour: running, jumping, skipping, swinging, dancing, yelling, hopping, singing... Did you like playing house? Never? School? No? Ships and sailors? I'm surprised. I certainly wanted to—with all my heart. So then I'd imitate them, go through the motions I saw, pretend I was outside running with them, shouting with them, running and shouting and dancing about like one of them, no differently made. Well. The Olden Days. They shouldn't occupy us now. Actually, I played caves and craters. And have there been more, would you say, since Omensetter came? He's such a hand with kites.

Mat struggled with his words. He slapped his thighs.

I suppose. Maybe, he said.

Good. We are agreed at last. I knew we would.

What? What? Agreed about *what?*

Furber smiled.

Agreed, that's all, he said. Agreed.

> My harp is highly rated,
> and my flute is celebrated,
> as for my drum, it's equal fun,
> however it's berated ...

Furber moved to Omensetter's bench and began inspecting it.

My lips are highly rated,
and my fingers celebrated,
as for my tongue, it's equal fun,
however it's rotated . . .

Tannin, he said, makes him seem brown. From oak bark, isn't it? Gall nuts. Well, an illusion. He'll be yellowish, by and by. I've heard it enters poisonously through the fingers.

My balls are quite inflated,
and my ass hole's lubricated,
wherever it's located . . .
as for my prick, it's just as thick,

He shifted a knife.
Don't—
Disturb. No.

Yes, my name is Philly Kinsman,
and I am that famous bandsman,
but silent now my symphony,
My fife, my horn, my timpani;

He held up a length of leather.

they've played their last
for any lass
excepting
            present
                    company.

Breasting the feculent flood . . .
What I want to know, in strictest confidence, Furber said, is have you seen him strangely any time?
He moved a rule.
Have you seen him strangely?
He crossed abruptly to the forge.
Catch your death of cold . . . day like this, he muttered. Now have you seen him strangely any time?
Oh my god . . . well, honestly, Jethro—
Have you seen him strangely is what I asked: burning piles of tiny twigs and new-pulled grasses, say, or singing to himself in numbers, one two seven four or so, back and forth, six or nine, or crooning, you might call it, to some object—rock, a branch, a swatch of cloth—or doing things by evens or by odds, walking in a circle or avoiding certain sights, like that of a goose, a cracked glass, or an empty bowl?

gir-affe!

Furber went on slowly, shyly almost, wagging the meaning of his words away, smiling them off, while his eyes searched along the rafters and the point of his shoe dug at the floor.

You mean *that* kind of sign, Mat said. My god—

Well you might invoke Him, Matthew.

Sweet christ—

Yes. That would be wise. He too. Sweet.

I thought by signs you meant just how he knew the baby'd be a boy.

How did he know? It's a question that will do. How?

Furber floated to tiptoe, his face alight.

cam-el! kang-a-roo!

I don't know. I mean—how *should* I know? He guessed. How should *I* know? He wanted a boy bad. You know how that is. Why ask me? He was lucky, that's all. Omensetter's luck.

Mat made to move outside but Furber didn't stir. He held his hands above the furnace and the faint light lathered his cheeks. Your answer isn't good enough, his posture said, while his eyes and lips said it was everything, and confirmed his fears.

Luck. Is that really your opinion: luck?

The silence of the street was intimidating.

hip-po! cam-el! kang-a-roo!

The buildings were of paper. Now against a bench, Mat stood propped. Damn the fat dackering dunce. Again Furber brought his hands, like boards, together.

hiiii-eeeee-naaa!

Does he make swirls in his hair with his fingers? Does he pull at his ear? Does he turn his head from reflections? Is he frightened of gnats?

Poison was once placed in the glass of a saintly priest, but as the priest blessed the meal, intoning latinly the name of the Father, the glass shattered and the poison flew up like a rainbow. No prot gawd could pull that off—never fear. Rome has a first-rate finagler . . .

baa-boon! monn-goose! gazz-elle!

The questions went on, Furber in the same position as before, the same expression on his face, though now he had a terrible desire to laugh, to shout gir-affe, and then such a sweating fear of doing so that the noise turned in his throat like a mouse he might have suddenly confronted on the stairs. It was proving too easy, too damnably easy. Mat might remain in everybody's eye the permanent and same Good Watson but his soul was sinking through the mire of their filthy private conversation toward the central ice.

lynx!

There's no longer any power in those legs and arms or he would throw me out, Furber thought. He's in to his knees already.

horse loris
civet seal

And the Reverend Jethro Furber, guide for the tour, master of the steeple, spokesman for the dead (they have an eye in me, he'd often said), was going too. Would the ground groan like a rotten plank and send him straight to hell? Or would he go down slowly (bitter foolish image) like a proud ship?

ox fox lynx pig lion
jackal ass giraffe
gir-affe!

His soul scaly . . . furfuraceous scalp . . .

To regain possession of himself, Furber began moving violently about, flapping his arms.

Everything above us . . . love us. Bat.

Mat was bending over, coughing.

That painted paper body—coughing. Frog in your throat? a mouse in mine.

What in the world, was all Mat finally said—something like that.

Yes, yes, you might well say so, Furber said, darting up to him. So I say myself. You may laugh, but so I say myself. You see I emphasize the idiotic in it all, the superstitious—the insane, you could call it if you liked. Go that far. Observe that I don't avoid it. I emphasize it. I *insist* on it.

Mat nodded heavily.

Scalps at his belt by the dangling dozens . . . furry midriff . . . a kind of pubicle possession, Pike . . . soul straps . . . ghost clouts . . .

Yet this is the substance of their fears.

Mat mumbling nonnys . . . Go on—chew your knarry knuckle up.

ass asp, fox!

Quite so. No doubt. But have you seen anything unusual, anything to give them rise, some yeast?

Omensetter's not the same as everybody . . . he's different—

Of course he is. Of course.

Furber smiled in celebration.

ass asp fox—snake!

berarzzz ox!

He's most unusual, our noisy friend, quite different—hair, nose, teeth—quite striking, quite remarkable. Ah well, he's a huge enjoyer. Have you ever seen him eat? He's quite original, as you say—unique. And most strange, too. His comings and goings. Quite unaccountable. His attitudes—queer. His step, had you noticed? is not that of an ordinary man. And so you have seen something then. I knew you had. Naturally. In the course of work, you would. Together so much. Close and close and close about, eh? Then these fears I speak of—they're not without foundation wholly?

They are *un*holy.

Oh ex-cellent. Good. Very good.

Furber mimed applause.

lizz-ard

Fret fret fret, Furber thought, delighted; there were mice in the cloud of his mane.

ox fox lynx snake

catamount and swan

A clever witticism, he said, chuckling. All around Omensetter, like a monstrous halo, the unholy burns.

antelope and swam

centipede and swan

Watson lurched toward Furber, threateningly.

Why do you turn everything . . . Look—Omensetter's fine. He's okay. I like him. His work's good—

His work—

His work, sure. For god's sake, let him be. Make up other mysteries. Look—ah god—look, I've been listening a long time. I'm played out. What have you got against him? What did he ever do to you? He's a simple enough fellow and better than most of us.

Ah, that—

What did he ever do to you? What have you got against

him? He's a bit better and a bit luckier, maybe, than most of us—

Yes, Matthew, the point—

So what's the matter? Where's the problem? And me too, for all of that. What have you got against me? What did I ever do to you? I've had a long day. I'm tired. I've been listening a lot. Furber, I've been a long time listening. I'm worn out and I'm sick about Henry. I'm hungry and I want something to eat. There. That's all there is.

Growing near, the smooth-nosed, bristle-crowded moon of Matthew's face, its lines of weariness and worry, its by george bright green eyes . . . what? smaragdine . . . small yellow in them too? pressing themselves upon him, pressing him back. May you guttle brittle glass, you galligaskins. Guzzle oil or acid, all kinds of iridescent poisons. Yes, you're like your sweet peculiar friend, that fatling Faunus, except about the eyes, and then the nose . . . lord, lord, let's see . . . the nose—the nose is—

Furber nodded, waving Watson off.

You're tired. That's it. You're tired, or you'd see better. Tired feet make tired eyes.

Furber was getting tall again. He backed and the forge light flew against the ceiling.

His work, now—there's his pay, for instance—

His pay?

How can you afford him, Matthew? What do you pay him?

Is that what you want to know? what I pay? is that why you've come here?

I had no idea you had so large—so opulent—a business.

Is what I pay your business?

Ah, now, easy . . . because he's better, isn't he? Yes, and luckier than most, too—just as you say, so—

Shit.

So you say shit to a minister. Shit, eh?

Oh well I'm sorry. Okay. Of course I'm sorry.

You think shit's an ugly word for a man of God to hear. Doubtless you do. Still uglier for him to say. And you'd hide your own shame under it—under shit. Why? Because I asked you what you paid, you threw that word at me. Well Luther could shout shit, if he was a mind to. . . . Shit! So can I. As you hear. I can say it. Shit. . . . Oh I'm acquainted with the major product of our days, Matthew, what we principally manufacture, what we spool out—stand to pool and sit to stool is what they say, don't they?—our—

All right, okay. I'm sorry—but I'm tired, like I said, you know—worried. It slipped.

That's the way it goes. . . .

> No offense unless offended;
> my cruelish words for love intended,
> were with hate intensely blended . . .
> > ha ha
> > > ha ha . . .
> an error pharmaceutical's
> an easy one to make.

Well now. And you're tired. Worried. Of course . . .

> A careless tear is soonest mended,
> so if you'd wound your fond intended,
> mortal blows are recommended . . .
> > ha ha
> > > ha ha
> an error gymnosophical's
> an easy one to make.

Well. And you're the only one who thinks of Henry. I never do. Just you. Your friends. I'm out, well out. There's none of that concern in me. In you. Your friends. . . . Well now what foolishness, Matthew. Sorry to have to say so, but—foolishness. I think of no one else. That's why I'm here. That's why I ask my foolish questions. What do you take me for, I wonder? A peck of foolishness, I suppose. Well don't take conceit from your weariness, please don't take pride. No—no—I mean what I say, and so I mean to say it. . . . You take me lightly. All of you take me lightly. All these years. You. Your friends . . . God!—to be taken lightly. . . . Am I a gossip, eh? an old shawled lady? Does the rocker move my blood? Sorry to say—more foolishness, Matthew. A peck of foolishness. No. I've said I'll have my say, and so I shall. . . . I'm merely meddlesome, that's what you and your friends think. I know. No. I will not listen now. Oh no. . . . You've been out hunting Henry all day—that's where everybody's been—all day—out hunting Henry. It's been an effort of the community like a barn raising or a quilting party or a husking bee. Dear god—what am I going to do with you? And I held you all at ears' length once like so many hares. Well where have you looked? along the river? there's mud on your shoes. In another contingent, then—with Chamlay?—well hip hip hooray—with Knox, too, on his right arm handy like a coil of rope—oh I know, I know—and it was meadows for you, was it? or woods? Dear god—it's futile for me to preach. And to think, once—speech. . . . You never thought to search a single spirit, turn out a single skin, to bring a lung, a bowel, a heart, to view. But I'm a meddler, not the master of this church—one of the ladies, regular in attendance, not so strong as I once was and now strenuous in hearing—only that. And if I tell you someone's swallowed Henry like a hungry animal, like a wild beast, why I'm just preaching, making up my mysteries, and the beast is an image I've drawn in the air. No—I will not listen anymore.... And while you hunted, did you swap stories, by any chance? Did you rest a bit on a warm stone, say, and speak of the old times, and of Henry, and his foolish life and his foolish ways? There was the pleasure of companionship, the walk over the old shooting trails, the air, these late fall days, so moderate, sweet—how often did you chuckle? There—you see? I hope so. I devoutly hope so. My god what must I do to make you see? A slap on the back at parting—the friendly sting of a friendly hand. "Tomorrow, Mat, tomorrow, we'll try again tomorrow." Sure. Better luck tomorrow. It was fun. It was like catching fish. It was like hunting deer. No—you're right. I'll forget it. I wasn't even there. How could I know? .... Already I've forgotten—as I promised. But you should remember that my heart's large too, that it contains my people—my whole congregation ... my dear people. You.

Coals in his eyes ... in his face, a scoopful, the speakbacker. Fair? What does he know of— Speak back. You're just a jocose cusser, ain't you? Joe the josser. Quite a jouker. My life for a knife ...

Fair is mostly made of air. You know that little poem? Fffair.... Well. No matter ... Have you inspected Mrs. Pimber's fruit cellar, Matthew? I expect you'll find him there, heels up, in a stone jar—preserved. Oh yes. Positively Egyptian. Or perhaps she put him up in parts, year after year, as pieces broke off. Who knows how many of each? Easy—mind now—take it easy. Don't misunderstand. We've had enough of that. But it's important that you see them: quarts of feet and fingers over there—a new batch, the caps are clean and shiny—then jams of liver and kidney jellies, brains and lungs like cauliflowers floating halfway up their jars, eyebuds bleached like little onions or, if bloodshot, like baby beets—oh no, I hold my hands up to you—you've got to take the tour, why, it's instructive—brains, did I say?— well such a store: glands and tongues and teeth like white corn, pearly ear lobes and lips in soft pink sauce, crocks of pickled pricks— So, Matthew, now it's your turn to flinch. That's not a word a minister should use. Brother Jethro should not say prick; he should not say peter either, or even think ... Well, to the shaded ladies, Matthew, and dishonest men, I shade my words, but we needn't fear. We've been burned so many times, you and I, our hide's tanned now, dark as my suit and tough as Omensetter's leather. . . . So I'm unfair? It's mostly air but I don't care. You don't know that little poem? But I'm unfair? Unjust, unfair—good god no—*precise*. Exact as plain geometry. Please remember that I always speak in figure, Matthew, through emblem and design, you understand. They enlarge my voice like cupped hands. Once, in Cleveland, I called such purity in speaking, such precision and force of phrase, the measure of spiritual space, the algebra of the inward life. No use to do that here. I'm never so grand now, though I've my plans. But for christ's sake, face up, you know how she is. How often did she geld him, I mean? So many times—so many jars. Or did she want him differently unable? There, in her memory—don't you see it?—like a storing cellar, snapped off as they grew . . . all that growing life.

Though the watched pot wouldn't—now there was a bubble—something stirring, the woolly mammoth moving, his face eclipsing queerly.

You follow me?

Nudgewinkbump, as crude as, nearly. Bim. Am I making myself out? The christmas cookie. Making it clearly? Soon I shall. Have patience though patience is painful. Bam. Winken and Blinken and Nod one night crawled under their underclothes. Bum. Please have patience. Wrathfully bitten christmas cookie, curving according to the mouth. And he bulks bigly still. Ape. Like what did he say I talk? like what? Cock-a-doodle-do? An owl, a cat, a kangaroo? He doesn't understand my anger, my exasperation.

Such phrases as: bottled body fluids—they mean nothing to you? Ah well, you're hard.

My dame has lost her shoes. I see a balloon in the day sky—God's plae face. Smiling. Which comes from going about unlaced. Cinderella's was of glass, a glass slipper. None of them was nicely fitted. Glass lets you know.

Shall I explicate the figure for you, Matthew, as I might a holy parable?

My master's lost his fiddling stick and what's my dame to do? Pour the pebbles out. Face of truth. On fatty Ruth. No withy smithy, not he. A gloomy Goliath. Let's go out Daviding. Whom can we dap into dim death, do you think, with our stoning?

Well. As I say—his—wait—Henry's pulsing stalk—hold up now—Monday through Sunday—contain yourself, let me explain—she—Lucy—snipped as often as it showed itself—*as often, as often*—no, no, easy, wait, dammit, wait I say, be easy!—then she boiled the snippings, when she had enough, bound in upright bunches—wait a moment please, one more moment ... like asparagus in their canning glasses—you're making me shout!—to cool and shelve and count them later, contemplate and ponder—you wouldn't—wouldn't jostle—

Shoved, pushed, well—touched . . . jesus . . . bumped, banged, bimmied by god, brushed ... christ ... so, struck, struck . . . you don't *touch* the minister . . .

Your action's clear enough. You don't relish the explanation though it was important to me to complete it. There's no anger in you, Matthew, except your anger against me. Hardly fair, if fair's up.

I shall pee you like rain on a window. I shall dissolve, disperse ... The Lord shall bless my labor. I shall shit you like shavings ... I shall spread, disperse ... The Lord shall bless my labor.

Here are all the jars for June. His favorite time. Wonderful crop. We had a lot of rain. How thick and straight they are; how sweetly shaped; put up so well, if I may praise myself as openly as bees do, their bravery still swells in them—oh I know—christ—all right. For you I shall desist. I'm done. Still I make a splendid—*all right!* Disgusting if you think so. Unjust if you like. But *intolerabilius nihil est quam femina dives* ... Not so near! I have a horror ... ah, god. I'm cold. ... Well then what's strange about him, Matthew? I come back to our sheep; that should please you. What is it? Mind, it's not for me to say . . .

Thank god he's turning away. Thank god.

It's not for either one of us to judge its meaning.

Owl am I? no, kangaroo he said. Well. Did he? He's still stuttering ... Through his back now I can hardly hear the grunting. Not fox. Not likely. Py-thon. Squeeeeeze. Speech? Eh? What?

Then Furber feared he might dissolve in giggles. Mat was folding up, his pleats were touching: kiss me on the eyes before they close, good-bye, sweet love, I had my hand at hunting in my time and read the dung of moose—pathfinder, man of double-barreled gun. Furber touched Mat's arm.

There, there, he said soothingly, just let me be the judge.

Thunder under the mountain ... owl ox.

Hush.

Furber put his hands over his ears. He rocked back on his heels. Quick quick quick the sand the softening sand the bursting board the bog of dreams.

He knows the future, Matthew, admit that.

Fanfaronade ... goose coot.

Hush.

Furber shook his head.

It's plain and clear, he said. Omensetter's knowledge, not Omensetter's luck.

Listen for a minute just this once—

gibbon hare!

I *am* listening, Matthew.

Look—if you, Chamlay, or Olus Knox, or I, or anyone like that—someone, say, with kids, all girls maybe like Olus has, and like Olus wanting a boy to bear his name on—

Vanity.

Well anyway suppose Knox was expecting another—

His wife's past that.

drill bull
gull snipe

It doesn't matter, does it? Just suppose, can't you?

Sup-po-sit-ion . . . mule, rail.

He's waiting for the kid to come, thinking this time it must be a boy, it just must be a boy, and then he talks and talks and talks about it, he talks to each of us about it, all the time talking and talking to us, and to himself, too, of course, and he listens to the women going on about those signs the way they do sometimes, and to the men, too, who are interested in calves, the way Knox is himself, in colts and calves, and then he starts looking for them because he's so concerned, like I said, so full of the desire to see them, and because he wants to see them, why—he does; and then he thinks, it's true, a boy is coming down to me, a boy is coming out of her, and this goes on, you know, like people do go on, and soon he's just as sure as if he'd crawled inside like Edna Hoxie said she could and looked.

So Edna Hoxie said that.

If Knox went on that way—

Disagreeable woman.

We—we wouldn't think twice about it, I mean if his luck held out and he got the boy he wanted.

Laughter carried Furber off, flushing his cheeks and bringing tears to his eyes. He drew a handkerchief from his coat and covered his face.

No, he said in a muffled voice, because it's—because it's Olus Knox we—wouldn't—but . . .

Furber threw up a supplicating hand and withdrew the handkerchief momentarily from his face.

Be—because it's that fellow O—O—ah . . .

The handkerchief flew back and Furber folded sharply over, shuddering.

Because it's that—that fellow—oh—we do—and—that's the hoe—whole of it, Matthew—you couldn't have put it better.

Unclasped and straight again, he filled his lungs and dabbed at his eyes. Watson's body settled slowly. Hadn't it moved? Blinking, he restored the face and its embarrassment—or was it bewilderment? or anger? or surprise? Who knew? A little simple annoyance? no more? Mat was drifting toward the back of the shop out of sight.

Well I'm warm now, Furber said, still gasping a bit. If I laughed like that—if—as often as Omensetter does, why—hoo—it would kill me, like as not. He's sick, you say?

. . . his daw said.

Which?

Whaa?

Which daughter?

. . . ohlderan.

Who?

. . . older . . .

Yes. What's her name?

Name?

Yes. Did you ever hear him say?

The baby's name is Amos.

I know. Amos. Interesting. But the others? The girls'?

No. I don't know the girls'.

It isn't that you've forgotten?

No. I don't believe I ever knew.

Matthew.

What's—

They don't have any. They haven't any names. They are without names. Doesn't that strike you as strange?

Oh I guess they have names.

What names?

Well I don't know what names.

They haven't any names. Ask him.

I'll ask him.

When will you see him?

When he's feeling better. When he's well.

You won't go out to see him?

He'll be back when he's better.

You won't go out to see him?

I might. I don't know.

Have you ever been out to see him?

No, not yet.

156

Not yet? The dog has a name, had you noticed?

The dog does?

Arthur.

Oh. Yes. I guess I knew that.

When you go, ask him.

I will. I'll ask him. It doesn't matter.

It doesn't matter—not to have a name? Well you're weary, I can see that, so I'll say my leaves. But Matthew, before I go I want to make myself—I want to make my meaning—my intentions, my continuous intention—clear to you. I think you can understand and appreciate my anxiety, my very great worry, my desire to do that—to make myself a crystal in your hand. I want to be really clear, honestly clear—direct, you know. I want to be frank, plain as plain, precise—all that, you know—sincerely straight, eh? since, as you're aware, your aid and, dare I say?—esteem—weigh in the balance. I fear, from what I've said, from what I've had to say—you've made me say it—most of it—you have, you have—well, I'm afraid that you may think that I believe—hah—all that—I mean—oh, about the signs: the looking glass, the large feet, the soft dark skin, the sporting hair, the moist eyes . . . dear me no, believe me, trust me—no; that's to believe in witchery—imagine—witchery—late in our old century—when there is no such thing as witchery, is there? —any longer? no—and it's insulting to God—a sin, I should say, Matthew—it's a sin to believe such a thing. Yet people—good heavens—a year's turn does not change them any, a decade's ending does not change them any, twenty-five, fifty, the use of a hundred or a thousand years—nothing—the same—time does not change them any, and they—well—just as one might expect, they will worship anything that sparkles, take fright at any shadow, sin out of witlessness and love of pleasure, from shame of sloth start into violence against the innocent—oh there's no end—no need to tell you that—no end, no end. So finally you may have your dinner. My apologies for that. A long day. Funny that we know Amos, Arthur, Lucy, Backett—

Brr-ackett.

Oh? Brackett?

Yes.

Really? Well. I'm happy to know. A thing like that. What, by the way, did his daughter say he was sick of?

She didn't say. Or I don't remember.

She didn't say. That must be it. Your friend, after all. If she had said, you would remember. Too bad. At a time when all hands—except mine, I fancy—were badly needed, eh?

unfortunate moment for it. Well illness will. You'd think she might have said. Friend and employer. How did she put it? . . . don't remember . . . upset.

She was upset? Why? Did it seem serious?

No—I—I was upset.

Oh? So you didn't ask.

She didn't say. Not serious.

But not upset herself? Childlike? Gay?

No—not—perhaps, a bit . . . natural.

At having to lie?

What?

That.

You're crazy—

We're where we began. You should go out. To see him. Friendly interest. I'm quite sane. And in the future—*watch*.

Furber gathered his collar together across his neck and stepped out into the street. A din.

Do not judge me harshly, Matthew, he said. I work as I can for God.

Shivering, Furber presumed a breeze. A large pale smiling moon.

gull pelican coot kite

Mind, Matthew, he said, turning toward the doorway and Watson's form looming in it, if you notice anything, remember it. The yeast, you know. But don't worry about me. I'm sound.

loris lemur

He struck his chest. Godhead. Balloon.
Yeast can be killed.

sparrow, sparrow

He went to tiptoe, releasing his collar, about to continue, when Watson drew the doors in with a squeal and hid himself behind them.

a lion cheetah goose, the cat stork jackal plover
toucan giraffe, bat newt fox
finch lynx that skink
cow hog ass ox

4

Here the ladies and the gentlemen were, bumping through the door, lining up in his study. Such brazen cheek. Standing in rows—Furber had difficulty, now, remembering who'd been the spokesman or even if there'd been one since like rubber dolls they'd all squeaked—requesting—nod-bobbing —but not exactly begging, not at all respectful—squeezing in his study—nerve, nerve, nerve—they said, while folding elbow into elbow—ah, the brass—that they required from him a more moderate tone.

Here the ladies were and there the gentlemen, very stiff and embarrassed, entering. They nodded vaguely, smiled wanly, looked elsewhere. The ladies first and then the gentlemen—all catty-cornered. Fast old friends, they scarcely knew one another. They ought to be ashamed, it was shameful work, a shameful business, yet they warmed to it—never a great deal—yet they warmed, they warmed enough. A more moderate tone. They were Greeks, were they? these? this stingy beaked crowd? Dorcases maybe. More like. Well this is an honor, ladies. Sorry I can't ask you to be seated. Quite a pleasure, gentlemen, indeed.

The recollection shattered him. He swirled in his room like a storm of snow, striking the wall without feeling. For the Christmas season, for the joyous time, it was their desire that he should put on flesh and a red coat, cry ho ho ho from the pulpit. There would be snow for Christmas and the light sound of bells, and caroleers would gather at the corners of hospitable houses. How he'd had to struggle to hide his surprise and his dismay. For the birthday of the Christ, these words were in their mouths, these words—now. Wet, red, howling, He arrives in the world. We are ready, oh mewling King, they say, for tables of food and newly molded candles and finely burning fires, for red wool stockings and sweet wine and burned beer.

Jesus—may You remember, though so small a God, Your giant father through this time.

The words popped from their rounded cheeks like half-eaten figs while their small eyes roved up and down searching

for something unwashed on his person, their jaws revolving
slowly on the sounds of moderation Furber turned to hisses
in his own mouth now, and their fat moist palms gesturing at
their ears to hear no evil, begging him to protect the young
at least for the joyous season, season of their Redeemer, their
dear Saviour, their sweet Lord. Well it was not *his* Redeemer; it was not *his* Saviour or *his* Lord. He bit his hand in
helplessness and anger. Had his ministry been to swine and
cattle; had it been to dogs and horses, goats and sheep? Now
it seemed it had—or worse—was still to people: to Missus
Valient Hatstat, rings glittering across her knuckles, her
throat roped with clicking beads; and to Missus Rosa Knox,
her flesh straining to be peeked, her cheeks dimpled, hair in
knots; and to Missus Gladys Chamlay, parrot-eyed, head
cocked, a purple birth smear sloping down her neck; and to
Miss Samantha Tott, the doggerel muse—what did her
children sing?

> Miss Samantha Tott
> if she were straightened out
> would be found to possess
> beneath her dress
> as long a crack
> as the Erie track

... anyhow, a lover of the Psalms; and to all those others,
with their husbands or their brothers, invisible, behind them,
making cautious music for the joyous season, for the season
of the Lord's delivery—augh! I shall be sick, Furber thought,
I'll vomit in a moment, I surely shall—or I shall weep.

His ministry. Out the window the Ohio crept between the
trees and a pale sun softened the snow beneath them. He
could, he thought, have preached in Cleveland to a congregation from brick houses—to beautiful women on wealth and
evil. The rich will pay to have their souls revealed. He could
have had tea in the great houses; drank tea poured from
sculptured silver pots to porcelain cups as light as flowers.
There would have been cloths of linen and plates of cakes
and tiny sandwiches arranged in tiers. He would have sat by
the window in a deep chair with laughter and wit like a light
around him though he was dressed in his deep gown of
disaster. There would be silk falling from full bosoms, silk
shimmering in the firelight and reflected in the windowpane,
and his eyes would fill with the white arms and bare
shoulders of women and his nostrils with the delicate
fragrances of their powders and perfumes as they fluttered
near him whispering. Thirty boys would compose his choir,

each richly arrayed. Stained glass would color all the lights and the air would be fused with singing. Well-robed acolytes would serve him as he raised the silver chalice to his lips and blessed its scented wine. Stately they would bear before him down the aisle the cross of burnished silver with Christ wrought beautifully upon it at the moment of His cry. Worshipers when they entered would display the reverent knee and when he mounted to the pulpit he'd lift his eyes and see the dust-filled traceries of light just beneath the dome while his hands ran on rich woods like olive, teak, and ebony. At each step the voices of the choir would rise and swell until he turned, left hand lightly on the massive book, right hand high toward heaven, when they would marvelously burst to silence.

Intercourse, he could have shouted in that silence—adultery. Piss even? Yes. Piss too. He could have cried piss at the steeple and been applauded during tea. Nevertheless there'd be no use, no sense to it. That's what they payed for, the rich in their rich houses with those deep pile carpets and the drapes of velvet he so vividly imagined. Titillation. The wealthy ladies would come from church excited and while they slept beside their obese husbands dream of the hard distended penis of their coachman hung with jewelry. In the privacy of thought and through the secrecy of image, they would enjoy each sin his preaching had suggested. They would wallow safely in the worst sensations; conceive the most obscene devices; place him, their preacher, in vulgar postures; ravish him on ornate altars or on the floors of pews; urge upon him the caresses of small boys, naked under choir gowns, still moist and warm from baths.

Furber stretched, yawning and rising on his toes. Once these had been his secret fancies too. In former times. In good old bygone days. He remembered rolling on the floor, wrapped in them, in pain, in ecstasy. He'd fled them here and so his ministry was here, here in the wilderness of conscience; this sodden dorp and river midden where he preached each week from a teepee as the Reverend Andrew Pike had doubtless done, shaking a crucifix like a tomahawk, stamping his feet, and in every appropriate way playing missionary to the forsaken and savage Gileans. Let bygones be. No use. He'd fled his childhood here, all those flowers and sweet honey, his fears, the evil smell of ink, the shriek of print . . . no use. The wealthy women he was presently imagining would love as much exhibiting their naked souls as their naked bodies, and Furber was aware that he himself as often in his dreams found a naked soul to be a naked body that he took them now together in one glance. For terror you looked to the teeth. Rage lay in the muscles of the legs and arms, hypocrisy weighed on the lids of the eyes, while other dishonesties rang around the pupils like shoes thrown true to the stake.

The ladies egged him on; in Eve's name, they dared him; so he made love with discreet verbs and light nouns, delicate conjunctions. They begged; they defied him to define ... define everything. They could not be scandalized—impossible, they said. Indecent prepositions such as in, on, up, merely made them smile, and the roundest exclamation broke upon them like a bubble's kiss, a butterfly's. Smooth and creamy adjectives enabled them to lick their lips upon the crudest story. How charmingly you speak, Reverend Furber, how much you've seen of this wicked world, and how alive you are to it, they said. And with Mrs. Kinsman he had gotten to a point where, by speaking indirectly, he could ... well ... say anything. The missionaries, madame, when they reached this remote and isolated place, found the natives given over entirely to the most horrible indecencies, utterly sunk in them ... They ran about naked for one thing. It was quite a task, let me tell you, to win them for Christ. They practiced the most elaborate ritual competitions which they pretended were also highly magical and religious. A man, to reach the inner councils of the king and be a priest, during the moon's dark quarter, had to bring a maiden honestly and safely on through seven tourneys undertaken over seven nights until she felt the seven separate excitements, heights, and swooning conclusions that were considered customary; these blissful moments to be accomplished on a consecrated canvas dais under smoking public lights, and the ravishing fulfillments come to in each of the seven now celebrated ceremonial ways which the earliest tribal sages, no doubt divinely guided, had somehow hit on and in moving rhymes then movingly indited: that is, by posture, speech, eyes, hands, tongue, feet, and finally uninserted member; thus leaving her as much a maiden at the end as she had been in the beginning. When you know further, madame, that the virgin in the contest was always the same—an angular, man-hating hag—alas, completely incorruptible —and that she had been performing in the round arena forty years already when the mission beached its boats upon the island, you will understand no ordinary cozy clip or buss or prance or greasy squeeze could move her. Truly, in that country, the priesthood was a peerless calling, and guaranteed the king should always be advised by the noblest, best and wisest men the little nation could command. As I've said, it was quite a task to win them for Christ, but praise the

Lord and the strength of the Faith, for it was done. Here's how: it occurred immediately to one of the mission, a strapping young cleric named Frederick, that if the Christians could only come up with a champion of their own, one who had outdoughtied all others, they should then have a man near the ear of the king who could claim his skill and vigor from his baptism. Conversion would follow hard upon. To achieve this extraordinary end, young Frederick had a plan. This is how he put it into play . . . And then she had offered up that knee, frightfully scarred, and he had gone so far as to *touch* it. A kiss upon that spot, a healing kiss, and he could have marched along her thigh to bliss—such as bliss is. These words of his—for her they were only the prelude to *Lohengrin,* but for him they were the thing, the actual opera, itself. It was just like a woman to want the performance.

Yet he was like them, the rich ones not the real ones, he, the Reverend—with darkness for his dress. In the theater of his head, in the privacy of Philly Furber's Fancy Foto-Cabinet—what thrilling horrors were enacted, what lascivious scenes encranked. Come to the skull show, honey. Gets no babies out of it, just fun . . . fun thin as tish-ee paper, and all rumply crumply.

The difference as it lies these days, professor, between the Christians and the early Greeks? Christians soap their balls, I think—correct, my boy, quite right—whereas the pagans, it is my opinion, always olive-oiled their penises. Yes, lad, yes, and the reason for that is, you see, that in our modern world, we, with wider horizons, steamships, copra, chemistry . . . There was a time, I believe, when a Christian didn't dare to wash downstairs for fear he'd find some pleasure in it. He didn't care to, either, *i* suspect. His sort was not disposed to water. They drew their substance mostly from the baser, denser, massier elements, and one brief wade and gentle sprinkle was enough for them. Go on, go on, that's shrewd; though Gibbon said it, still it's shrewd. Well all danger of pleasure's past, there's no risk now. The Christians, too, always imitating Jews, though always poorly I'm afraid, though they were always Jews, these Christians were, though fallen I fear, have lately cut the ends of their cocks off with consecrated scissors. I should like to put it to the class, sir: what Greek would countenance disfigurement like that, and encourage such a loss of feeling in a fellow? Only that damn Jew, Antisthenes, perhaps. Certainly not Socrates—with his ambidextrous bat and balls. You'll go far, Furby. You've a head, child. All the lines on those amphora would go wrong, sir—how they'd uglify. Amphorae—all the lines on those ampho*rae*—don't forget one subject while reciting on another. Besides that, Master Furber, *uglify* is a barbaric and ugly word. Besides that there's nothing in Robertson or Hume or Gibbon on this subject, Master Furber, watch your step. The penis in repose, professor, with that little hat of skin, why it's a lovely childlike thing, and each man's gentle babyhood is in it. Nor Voltaire, Macaulay, or Carlyle. Please get on. Nor Michelet. But continue. Nor any of the Germans. I remember reading how on one amphora a satyr is depicted balancing, what?—a cup? bowl? plate? one of these, at any rate, upon the point of his prick. Where are your authorities? Prescott? Parkman? dumb. It's not in Renan, surely? Aren't you forgetting Tacitus is silent, Cornelius Nepos equally, and Thucydides likewise? Xenophon notes nothing, nothing. Even Herodotus, or gossips like Plutarch and the Plinys . . . I'd pay a thousand drachmas to see a trick like that, and sell my soul a thousand times not to feel ashamed attempting it myself.

Oh he was like them, like those laced-up ladies—warm from words. A man, he still chewed the nipple, titillation, and risked no freer, deeper draught. Fearless in speech, he was cowardly in all else . . . ah, to be rich, luxuriant, episcopal . . . well, he'd conquered that by flight. Yet to spread simplicity more deeply than cosmetic. . . . These steaming images, Mrs. Kinsman, these strange wants, we must fight them off. You've been given back to maidenhood. Do not despair. Jerome rejoices—he who praised marriage because it made more virgins—good Jerome, his dog, his lion. The injury to your husband was a gracious act of God.

His first announcement had said that the Reverend Jethro Furber would preach on Godless Ways, a customary theme, and surely disappointing. He thought that considering the circumstances most would think something more pointed was proper, and he knew everyone entertained a picture of Lucy Pimber's disarranged and dirty clothes. Certainly they would hope that he would preach upon that picture; define the character of the disaster; say, in short, what ailed the present time; warn, as pastors had of old, with a trumpet. Godless ways were numberless, and even though his congregation knew his rhetoric could skirt the nature of each sin so skillfully that selfsame skirt was flung above the head and chaste discretion tumbled, how much easier it was to follow the outline of general woes when colored by your neighbor's troubles, and how much easier to take to heart the lessons of man's universal flaws, his little mischiefs, if they were enlivened with local examples and the recital of Gilean names.

Well he'd not fail them, he would name a name, but they would have to wait, for it was in the mind of the Reverend

Jethro Furber to preach a series, and the thought of its simple form filled him with radiant power. His outward movements were in contrast stiff and short like shafts and pistons that run in rapid jerks from steam. His ends and surfaces trembled continually; his tongue darted from his mouth and slid its length to disappear; his dark curly hair seemed tightened into knots and forced flat against his head. Indeed his appearance might have given alarm had he not kept entirely to his study, repulsing every effort to communicate, including those of Jefferson Flack who brought the Reverend Furber's supper and left it by his lunch.

The Reverend Furber's designing figure was a slowly circling hawk, its orbits tightening until with shut-up wings, it dropped. Only the quietness was out of place. In his plan there was no quietness. Rather he would make them like the windings of hell, noisy with flame. He had in mind to preach a series, each one a wind of hell, a circle of the hawk, a coil of snake. He paced the room, his body rocking, shouting at God. Always, too, he fought to keep that one bright image out: he standing, she beside. He fought it furiously. He damned the meadow grass that seemed to lie along his cheek all night and the stream that ran like music through him, his voice growing hoarse, lost in his composing, yet always fighting the cool sweet air, the devilish calm, the loosening that followed him. On his shoulder, sometimes, these sensations seemed. Up his sleeves he found he must pursue them, through his clothing, underarms—air like the first of spring, infinitely promising. Then he would shout, writhing, his hands hunting them like crawling things, clawing through his clothes, striking at space, pounding against his ears until he thought the drums would break. All this until he was exhausted and he fell in pillows, hiding his face. Up again his arm described a circle. He floated out, alight behind his glowing eyes, the hawk, predatory of mice.

He searched eagerly for his texts, reading each one he thought suitable aloud in a voice that shook with emotion. He was silent afterward listening to himself. Then with angry mutters he always shuffled on. When he finally bent the corner of a page and shut the book, it was suddenly, without a reading or a silence after, like the hawk's wings come together. He stacked the Bible in the cupboard with several others that despite their excellent condition were deemed by Reverend Furber to have their potency exhausted. They were only fit to serve as prizes for good behavior and dutiful attendance, now, for feats of memory and recital as Miss Samantha, in each case, decided. He was constantly renewing his supply of power. Some demands dispelled it quickly, and he'd seen, in his trouble with the texts, that this one was running down.

He had in stock, especially for the series, one of splendid size and paper, of multicolored type and softest leather. He reached in the cabinet and touched the top. There, he thought, was force and eloquence; he could feel it swelling against the cover.

He was troubled, however, by the immanence of his success. He met it everywhere. It was in the air like the smell of apples—troubling, sweet. Every day of Henry's disappearance was a day of rejoicing, and as the year drifted slowly toward its winter, Jethro Furber sped to his triumph. Yet his visions had increased—in vividness, in number, in the shamelessness of their delights. He rolled in pubic hair and woke with semen sliding down his leg. Sin and sin and sin again. He knew the names. But no name damned this clean and innocent relief. It seemed, God help him, like the action of successful prayer, the momentary prevenience of grace.

For some time the ferocity of his sermons had increased. He was leading them up . . . up. And he was winning. He knew this to be true despite their disappointment at the general, abstract tenor of his remarks at first, despite their uneasiness at his heat, their mystification, too, since the pitch of his language was steep. So that when the delegates of moderation broke upon his privacy, they broke his confidence and peace. Could he trust his judgment? trust his eyes? for he'd been certain they were fattening on his words. The sense of his success rose from them like a warm wind from a field, bending the hairs in his nose. Had he only felt his own pulsebeat? God—more moderate—a more moderate tone . . . Were they frightened? then of what? of the truth— was it? should that affright them, a simple bugaboo? well for what cause? or worse—were they merely afraid of what he might say, the embarrassment of it, caught in the pews, with no page to thumb for response?

And events, too, with a kind of fatality, had fallen in his favor. Pushed against his will toward Lucy Pimber—who could have imagined the extent of his triumph there? Then summoning all his powers, like an ancient Celtic lord, a German chief, an heroic Greek, he had struck down Watson, driving the light from his eyes so that he toppled into darkness and his bones clattered about him. Henry, moreover, had cleverly escaped the combing net. One could only conclude that everything was changing in favor of Furber, everything was moving to the tune of his wishes, everything was changing . . . What was it he heard? trumpets? tambourines and timbrels? church chimes? balustrades of bells?

Success, the tide turned once again, that's what he sensed, and no mistake. Just as he'd won them in the past by turning out his pockets on the stage, he'd win them again with a great performance—a series of them—an extended run—triumph topping triumph. Bright posters posted over town . . . bells and banners . . . ding-a-ling, ding-a-ling dong. He'd give them Christmas by god; he'd fill their stockings for them; and turn Omensetter into candle tallow.

Well this is an honor, ladies. Quite a pleasure, gentlemen. Can you all fit in?

Why were they whining then? . . . whining, damn them, whining . . .

Because they'd have to give up their hope of living like an animal and return to an honest, conscious, human life. The prospect was hard.

⟋ 5

The Reverend Jethro Furber rose that Sunday to the pulpit with excitement blazing from him. There was a stirring in the church at late arrivals, and the broken hum and stutter of interrupted whispers filled it. He omitted the customary rites and spoke at once.

Our Heavenly Father, we speak within Your Hearing. May we speak with Your Truthful Voice. May we listen to Your Voice in us. May we harken to Your Thunder.

He'd spent a sleepless night. More than once, in complete darkness—it was better for the darkness—he had parted the curtain and shuffled to the stand and recited his piece, saying seven different things, believing each. There was no way to call back the words as they rushed out, he'd never remember them, and he was using, in these private sideshows, all his energy: yet before the pale geometry of the windows and in the presence of his own voice, he felt he had been moved to poetry. His flesh had prickled, tears had formed in his eyes, and he thought that at last he'd opened his heart out honestly. But he'd opened it to no one, really—to an audience of ghosts and churchmice. It was possible, of course, that in some corner, Flack, invisible in such surroundings, nigger like himself, was listening; and one pretended always that God, too, took an interest; but in this case—God, mice, Negro, weeping preacher—they came to nothing. He was exhausted, all nerves, disorganized; yet he meant, nevertheless, to try to fill their ears with fire. It was futile to hope that he could bring these creatures up, yet—yet he meant to try. Now he examined the space he intended to preach to. It lay just above an irregular terrain of heads and extended to the gray crossbeams of the nave with their pale dark ax marks and black spots of iron. Beginning at a point in front of him as far as he could leap, it reached through crisscrossing blades of light to the opposite wall where his melting sight composed the space's outer edge. He could imagine, looking at it, how chaos was before the first word. It was a striped waste, a visibly starless night. Dust, chambered in rods, lazily settled in no direction. Indistinctly he could see the tops of those fleshy cabinets which would compartment hell, while above, spanning the peak, were the long bars of heaven and the perching choirs of love. He thought of his voice passing into it, dust dancing to its tune. There'd be land in the shape of his syllables, a sea singing, sky like an echo, plants in bloom burning with speech, animals with yellow answering eyes, and finally men taking form from the chant of their names and gathering in crowds to enlarge their reply to the laments which had created them.

He didn't dare drop his eyes beyond their hair-capped foreheads. He'd slide off a nose or suffer a chin slip. Skid more than plummet—no posturing could mask it—he'd tip, dump! into shoes at the end. To find and utter the proper words, the *logoi spermatakoi* . . . that was Plato's game, poor John's jest. Pimber was the word these creatures wanted. Pimm-burr. He had at least one better word than that. The magic words, if he could utter them, would free them from every earthly thing. The steeple-tip of wise Plotinus. Alone like a bird. Farewell.

Nevertheless his eyes buzzed in their ears and bit their ankles. One, then two . . . one, two, one two—the usual line of shoes—a pair, a pair, another pair . . . So farewell to faces. For god's sake, Mrs. Spink, be silent. Wait wait wait: screw. Gnawing at his nerves. Do not think of old ties—the desert loves the naked. One last look at faces. God. My God. Nose, cheek, chin, hair foresting the brow, ears at the edges, eyes like wells, the wrinkles running off, the raw lips, flaking skin . . . farewell. Christ, what an improbable design. Screw them down. "What are you doing in the world, brother, you who are more than the universe?" Tight. Tight. First—sweet gentle John: "he that loveth not knoweth not God." Then—

full furious Jerome: "I am prepared to cut a foul-smelling nose." Tight down. Furber's right arm sailed. He watched it in surprise. His voice when it began, was calm and light, smooth and precise.

I've intended for some time to tell you that I understand.

He paused, his eyes closed.

None of us wanted this world to begin with. We were orphaned into it. And we were never fooled. Not fundamentally. We've always known we had no place. I'm not speaking simply of our common Christian view. Anyone, however far from us in custom or in country he otherwise may be, so long as he is human, has a soul, and through that soul can sense, the same as we, his strangeness to the life that he's been sent to.

Confidently, Furber strode through the dark.

How I wept and shrieked, the saintly Greek, Empedocles, has written, when I was born into this world, my grave. And fallen in flesh, all infants howl. Empedocles believed that his soul, for its sins, must pass from body into body as water passes many sieves; that it must live through every form of dying and suffer every kind of end. It was his opinion that he had been a boy already, a girl, a plant in the woods, an eagle hunting in the mountains, and had spent, in the ocean, the glancing life of a fish. All the elements, he says, were united in rejecting him. The air had chased him to the sea, and the sea had spat him out on the earth's edge, and the earth had flung him toward the sun.

We are here—yes—yet we do not belong. This, my friends, is the source of all religious feeling. On this truth everything depends. We are here, yet we do not belong; and though we need comfort and hope and strength to sustain us, anything that draws us nearer to this life and puts us in desire of it is deeply wrong and greatly deceives us.

I ask you now to ask yourselves one simple foolish question—to say: was I born for this?—and I ask you please to face it honestly and answer yea if you can or nay if you must.

For *this*?

You rise in the morning, you stretch, you scratch your chest.

For this?

All night, while you snored, the moon burned as it burned for Jesus or for Caesar.

You wash, you dress.

For this?

At breakfast there are pancakes with dollops of butter and you drip syrup on your vest.

So it's for this?

You lick your lips.

Ah, then it's this.

You slide your pants to your knees and you grunt in the jakes.

It's for this?

Light's leaving a star while you stare at the weeds; centipedes live in the cracks of the floor; and the sun, the Lord says, shines on good and evil equally.

So you were meant for this? You've your eyes, your human consciousness, for this?

Well you're not entirely easy in your mind. The weather's been poor. There are the crops to get in, payments to make on the farm, ailing calves to tend. Friends have promised to help with the haying, but they haven't, and you've got to keep your eldest son somehow away from that bargeman's daughter—a bitch with cow's teats.

The mind's for this?

Wipe yourself now. Hang your pants from your shoulders. There are glaciers growing. But you wish your wife weren't so fat and given to malice, and your thoughts are angry and troubled by this.

This?

Very well—you can complain that I've chosen trivialities in order to embarrass you.

Eat, sleep, love, dress—of course you were born for something better than this.

Furber's eyes drew slowly to a smile. The church sprang into being, unrelated colors first, sparks of light, the world seen from a mountain; the delineations, corridors, retreats . . . solidities and meanings. Marvels, they were, all of them, a moment, before they became what they were. He had got off on the wrong foot. Wrong foot—feet made him laugh. His laughter, which was loud and gay, he closed by coughing. Our life is one long stream of piss, he shouted; were we born for this? Shaking, he sank on his heels. How long had he been a-tiptoe? Fine beginning. Empedocles indeed. Had he said or had he only thought the name? In Gilean. Empedocles. As strange as Jesus. Perhaps he should have them stand and sing, then after the singing start all over. He smiled, showing his palms, but he was stuttering and could not utter a number. He drew his hands behind him where they flew at one another.

I'm not a man of many convictions . . .

No no no jesus. There were people leaving. But he kited

his eyes. In the balconies—choirs. How many? who? one, two . . . He felt the richness of his robes and the weight of his responsibilities. Light rained through the windows.

In the be- In the be-

He signaled Mrs. Spink to play and cushioned his head on the Bible. A desperate gesture, it would crick his neck, but perhaps it would impress them.

Rattle of notes—she'd begun. He must husband his resources. Husband. What a word. For the sense of our flesh is slow—how did it go, the old sing-song of St. Augustine?—even because it is the sense of our flesh. He must gain control. The sense of our flesh is slow. *Tardus est enim sensus carnis, quoniam sensus carnis est* . . . yes, . . . its own measure . . . *ipse est modus eius* . . . oh sufficient enough—claws, balls, prick—for the end it was made for . . . *sufficit ad alius, ad quod factus est* . . . yet insufficient—jaw, cunt, lip—*ad illud autem non sufficit, ut teneat transcurrentia* . . . lovely . . . *transcurrentia ab initio debito usque ad finem debitum.* The sign is in the word. Is Mrs. Spink the signal? The finger's lascivious tip . . . whore's hip . . . *In verbo enim tuo, per quod creantur, ibi audiunt: "hinc et huc usque."* No, no farther . . . abuse, abuse . . . my god.

The number of the noise . . . so numerous . . . numberless numbering . . . numb . . . numb . . . what was the numb . . . ?

There was the faint smell of print and paper. The pages felt cool to his cheek. He cuddled his head in his arms. It would be good to remain here and sleep. But in a moment he would have to straighten and face them He couldn't very well confess then that he had no convictions himself and cared nothing for what they believed, for how they adored confessions. Go home, go home, I have nothing to tell you. *J'adore . . . j'adore* . . . That would nail them in.

Spink'll soon tinkle her tune to a stop
end in a jiffy her jiggery hop

Here—here—look—in this trouser pocket I've greed like a tree toad. But he really wasn't mean or greedy. He wasn't lazy or lustful, ambitious or lordly. He wasn't gluttonous or covetous or swollen with vanity. And where were envy and anger and cruelty in the manner of his life? Wasn't it wonderful how easily the words came. Just lies upon lies on the cooling paper, the faint, faint odor of leather, the darkened heart behind his eyes . . . envy and envy and envy and anger . . . envy and anger and aching desire . . . here—here—I shall raffle off my penis as a prize . . . no, let me tell you what I've heard: tree roots have been known to vessel

171

the grimmest granite—that's virtue versus vice in one brief homily . . . oh go home, go home and strike at one another—each so well deserving . . . I don't know, myself, what to do, where to go . . . I lie in the crack of a book for my comfort . . . it's what the world offers . . . please leave me alone to dream as I fancy. Then bend to your homes. To dream as I fancy: a lady plump and charming, light through lemon leaves, honorable and distinguished wounds. Ah well now, Mrs. Spink, so you've chewed up your sour little hymn. Furber tugged at his shirt sleeves and pressed his coat smooth.

Let me—like children—as though you were children—let me tell you about it again.

Now then—thank you, thank you all, yes, thank you—as you will remember, in the beginning, you remember, God—God—*What had God done?*

God had labored five days when He created man. God had sent His presence through the darkness which was lying softly on the surface of the water fast asleep, there to take part, cleaving night from night to make day. Then God had sent His presence down into the middle of the sea, when the sea was asleep, separating the sweet half and lifting it like a canopy above the rest. And then again He'd sent Himself to the sea to gather it, and He'd caught up the remaining water like fish in a net, so that land appeared where the water had been carried away. Thus He labored till the third day.

It would be wise to remember what it was of living things God made on the third day, for He favored the fruits first. He made all seeds—seeds of tender grass and trees of gracious shade. Then He made the moving sun, the alternating moon and brilliant stars, and He appointed some to regulate the night, and others to design and rule the day. Finally, on the fifth, God fastened life in the water and at the water's edge and in the air—whales and seals and salamanders, darting birds. Then as the sea had formed fish after its own, and the air had fashioned even eagles and wild gulls on the model of the wind, so the earth was let to bring forth animals in the living likeness of itself—cattle and snakes and bears, each and every kind.

As you remember . . . you surely remember . . .

When this was done, and the first five days had passed beneath the earth forever, and when God saw what He had made was good, only then did He consider creating man, who was to have, as the sun had in the brilliant heavens, and as the moon had among the stars, dominion over life.

So He prepared. He formed dust about His own breath like a chrysalis. He prepared—blowing in His fist, making

172

man a hollow vessel and shaping earth about His breath with His own hands. He prepared—pouring His breath like a precious liquid through the nostrils of the human jar. Consequently man had a likeness in him that was great and holy from the first, sacred and terrible. Just as God in the beginning had divided the darkness to make light, stealing on it while it lay asleep, and just as God had taken the sweetness from the sea as it rested to vault the sky, so mankind was also divided in slumber, and the darkness taken, and a portion of the divine breath too, to make a wife.

It was only right that these divided halves should come together, part and come together, so that what had once been mixed might mix again, so that what had once been sundered might be sundered again, just as God had done these things during the six days of His labor. Everlastingly now, the sea yields up its heaven. What was earth, soon enough again, is earth. Men and women mingle, and are lonely after.

Yet there was already enmity between the dark and the darkness, between salt and fresh, the sea and its fishes, the air and its eagles, the unmoving earth and its teeming kinds, man and his woman; for night had lost half of itself to day, as the sea had to the heavens, and the earth to its millions. Man could not endure alone, without a likeness of himself, and some say, though I believe they are mistaken, that Adam beseeched God for his mate. Yet when Eve was lifted from his side and the skin tied at the navel, he was not completely happy. Adam yearned, without knowing why, and felt envy, since beside him now lay man perfected, his poorest part ennobled, glorified.

I defy you to find where in Holy Writ it says he was satisfied.

Adam wished the return of his softer half. He wished to be whole again as he was in the beginning. Alas. The earth also wished him back. The sea wished to swallow the land again, and deep night groaned against the light.

Such is the lesson—listen carefully to it—of this remarkable creation.

Now there was in heaven, as you know, an angel, prince among them, the Prince of Darkness. And he felt his wife drawn painfully from him, out of his holy body, fully half of himself, and given a place of dazzling splendor. How he hated it, and suffered his loss loudly.

Then at the end of the sixth day, after God had created man and driven his beauty from him like a specter; when at the end of the sixth day man's beauty was driven from him as the day had been driven from sleeping night and the sky looped over the slumberous sea and life drawn from the nodding earth, God ordered the whole Host of Heaven to kneel to this wondrous pair, so to signify their admiration of them.

But the Prince of Darkness said, lamenting: my Lord, You made the sun and moon to rule the halves of my former kingdom, and You grew plants to supervise the earth, and then You gave the animals these. Now finally You have made this frail potter's figure, man, to multiply and feed and fatten on the beasts.

But God ordered the whole Host of Heaven to kneel to the images of Himself He had created, so to signify their admiration of them.

But the Prince of Darkness, grieving, said: my Lord, You did not mean the moon to play havoc with the daytime, or the sun to rise for the pale canary or set for the remorseless cat. Therefore it is not fitting that we, immortal lordships, should play the camel to man, who has no proper power or dominion over us.

But God ordered the whole Host of Heaven to kneel, nevertheless, and to indicate thereby their admiration for the Lord, Himself, who had created man, this marvel among even the marvelous.

But the proud Prince of Darkness refused.

It was at the close of the sixth day then that Satan, for disobedience and a broken heart, was dismissed with his companions from the loyal Host of Heaven, and like a burning streak of vapor fell by the sun's face into his element.

Hush...hush...What's next? Like a waterstrider, Furber rode a thin film of sense.

Later God made Eden with its rivers and put Adam and Eve to paradise there, though some say He made Eden earlier, before Eve, as it appears in the Bible. The tree of life grew in the garden, and also the tree of the knowledge of good and evil. It was this latter tree of which God forbade Adam and Eve to eat, but they ate of it all the same, as we know to our sorrow. The finer half fell first—the last and best of all creation—so now she brings forth her children in pain and labor, and serves the poorer portion as her punishment.

God created always by division, taking the lesser part, transforming it into its opposite, and raising it above the rest. So should we change our worst into our best.

Furber snapped his fingers. There was a good one. That was the kind of thing they liked. Should he say it again? But he was losing the thread.

There is everywhere in nature a partiality for the earlier condition, and an instinctive urge to return to it. To succumb to this urge is to succumb to the wish of the Prince of Darkness, whose aim is to defeat, if possible, the purposes of God's creation. We do on occasion forget, fo course, the clay we're made of. We do sometimes deny our animal nature and our origin in the earth. But the heroic life is like the thievery and punishment of Prometheus, both painful and lonely, and we do not pursue it long. For the most part men look upon their humanity as a burden, and call the knowledge of what they are a simple consequence of sin. Men, like all things, resist their essence, and seek the sweet oblivion of the animal—a rest from themselves that's but an easy counterfeit of death . . . Yet when Adam disobeyed, he lit this sun in our heads. Now, like the slowest worm, we sense; but like the mightiest god, we *know*.

Lovely lights and swooping swallows, carpeting the distance . . .

So we do not belong. We're here. Like the hunchback is here in his hump, the crow in his caw. Oh god, we're here. Yet we do not belong.

The eye of the animal opens. Think. He *sees*. What a strange thing seeing is to exist in this world. His eye opens—the ferret's eye, the tiger's eye, opens—and there are in that moment and for the first time . . . *images* . . . Imagine we open the eye of a man. Thought lies on the other side of that thin lid. He sees without blinking. Blind, he still sees—the pitiful creature. Of course. He's the wondrous watchman, isn't he? Watching . . . watching like a weasel in the weeds—

What's skittering?

It's this sun in my head. They are naked and exposed, I said. N-n-nay-kidd.

Where—let's see—yes. Who is honest in the dark?

Prometheus? Empedocles? Holy Jesus. He bent his head and saw print running down the pages. Text. He had a text. Who was still here? Space. Embroidered with light. The print was flowing.

Text. He had a text. Text to keep talking.

Inward—in a word—inwardly—in his innards—large guards, were they?—sourly—shards of heart—of pottery—of clay piercing people—in hollowware—in terror of spirit—to fall so inwardly . . .

"And the voice said, Cry. And he said, What shall I cry? All flesh is grass, and all the goodliness thereof is as the flower of the field:

"The grass withereth, the flower fadeth: but the word of our God shall stand for ever."

... but fall down inwardly ...

You then, the scripture says, are the people. You are the grass. You are the flesh, the grass.

Do you imagine that the grass, by growing, can become the cow?

Was there snickering? ... was there tittering? snickering? Who was out there? Embroidered space.

This life—

This life passes like a day in fertile country all too soon.

Touch the book. Touch the book. His fingers skidded on the pages.

Pews were tipping empty.

We've slid to hell! the boards have broken! Are those the dancing ladies? Behold him with his eyes transported to his buttocks. Better there he may perceive the concourse of the anus.

And the fiend . . . He will appear with apple-rosy cheeks and friendly tousled hair . . . with candid eyes and open-ended speech.

Lead us out of this place, oh Lord, that we may have reason to praise your mercy.

Those who remain . . .

Let us pray.

~ 6

It began to snow as Chamlay and Furber reached the house. The flakes fell slowly out of a close sky, clinging to the tips of the high grass and breaking gently on their faces. It was the middle of the morning but the hushing snow and gray light gave to everything a quality of evening. A daughter let them in. Each hesitated to precede so they squeezed through awkwardly, bumping together. Amos was at the breast and the room was full of the sounds of his feeding. He's out with Arthur, she said, attending to her son, her face expressionless, her voice as cold and aimless as the snow. Furber's gaze fled over the room to hide finally in the bottom of his hat. He saw beyond that the cracked and splintered fir board floor, the wood grain nearly gone under a grime of years that turned the whole floor gray. Chamlay stared brazenly about. Motionless and tense, the brown-eyed daughters, their faces pale and drawn, sat leaning forward in ladder chairs set close together against the wall, touching the lower rungs with feet as tentative as birds', and holding hands. A patched and faded yellow comfort draped over a cradle in the corner. Above hung a landscape containing a river. A table whose top was heavily scarred and carved stood unevenly by the front window, a long bench beside it. Furber took out his watch and looked at the photograph fastened to its lid—a picture of himself and two distant cousins, girls of ten, whose names he'd long ago forgotten. Furber appeared strangely white and plump beside them, and held a smile to his mouth which he had always found beguiling. Now he inspected his cousins again. Only then did the dresses on Omensetter's daughters seem homemade and thin, tight and short on them, too frequently and too furiously washed. Furber sighed and snapped the watch shut. He'd never been a plump one. There was a white ironstone teapot on the table with a wooden spoon beside it and a trail of crumbs. The girls gazed at something out the window but gave no sign they saw. They seemed about to issue into flight. A dented and badly tarnished copper pan sat on the hearth. It was likely English, he thought, and of considerable age. From time to time wood settled, sending sparks up the chimney. At last he turned from the dark stones and put his watch away, smiling at the girls. Another picture hung from string and nearing it he made out St. Francis feeding squirrels. Very nice, Chamlay was saying circling briskly, very nice indeed.

On the way they'd scarcely spoken. Chamlay had wanted Olus Knox to accompany him, but Olus showed no heart for it, and Furber, happening by chance to pass, had come along instead. Chamlay was in a rage. He now suggested that the moment wasn't right; that he'd return another time; but silence received him, and as they shifted in the room they failed to draw an eye. Then Chamlay began to question her in a voice that was soft and deferential. Furber moved in front of the girls, smiling still, about to speak, while their mother rocked on cautiously. The girls' lips were pale and parted slightly over clenched teeth. Furber faltered, then went around them and behind their mother to peer into the hall. Chamlay put his questions again. She didn't know where he'd gone, she said. She didn't know when he would return. Chamlay and Furber drifted protectively together, holding to the brims of their hats. She changed breasts without concern, slowly covering the emptied one, which was surfaced with gooseflesh like a lake in a shower. The older girl, Furber noticed, had an elbow chafed.

You may stay if you like. I don't know how long he'll be. If you decide to, they'll get chairs.

Chamlay's gesture of regret went unobserved.

You don't know why, he said.

She blew on the baby's hair and rubbed his scalp with a moistened finger, settling herself a little, twitching her shoulders. The infant's red cheeks worked. Furber touched Chamlay's sleeve and motioned to the door. She carefully kneaded her breast.

He feels he's got to find Henry.

They moved uncertainly as she looked up.

Chairs, she said.

The girls rose, but both men put out their arms.

No, they said.

The girls' hands were clasped, their gazes steady, their mouths exactly carved. Furber chewed his cheek. The baby loudly smacked his lips and the nipple escaped, standing out long and wet.

Why try, she said, what difference will it make? what good?

Amos fought to find the nipple, puffing, about to cry. Chamlay's face was brightly flushed. He held his hand demurely across his badge and Furber failed to catch his eye.

There's Lucy, for one thing, Chamlay said.

The nipple skidded over the baby's cheek. It caught in the corner of his mouth and then sank in, leaving a trail of milk.

Mother, the older daughter whispered, startling the men.

He means Missus Pimber, her mother said.

Well, there's that then, Chamlay said.

Dead, she said, what good?

She rocked more rapidly.

What's any body good for, emptied out?

The law, you understand, has an interest, said Chamlay firmly.

Less use than a barrel, its bottom stove in, she said.

Chamlay shook his head.

You misunderstand. There may have been some violation in his death.

He paused.

Absence, I should have said—disappearance.

178

He can't be punished now for that, she said, he's dead.

How is it you're so sure, Chamlay said urgently, and her head snapped.

Don't play the fool.

Chamlay cleared his throat while Furber went to the door and put his hand on the knob. The daughters, standing yet, fixed Chamlay and their mother with an intense blank stare like the stare of plaster statuary.

We don't want to get caught in this snow, Furber said.

It was the well, I think, she said in a moment, returning her attention to her son. It was that simple circle in the ground. He sure acted queer about it.

Furber came forward and tugged at Chamlay's shoulder.

We never did him any harm I know of, and when he had the lockjaw, he lived for Brackett's sake, it seemed to me.

She thought a bit.

Then—she shrugged—he killed himself.

She stopped rocking and looked over her shoulder down the hall.

I thought I heard Arthur but it must have been another dog . . . He killed himself. It's hard to believe. What harm had we done him? Living in this house? Do you know?

The baby belched and she patted his back, rocking once more.

Not Arthur I guess. Hours he's been out there at it and what harm had we done him? And to die as he must have, don't you think? in the leaves and all that wind, cold and away from every friend and everything he loved. How could he do it? . . . Are you the sheriff? I didn't know we had one . . . Arthur's bark is harsher . . . And what harm? to anyone? I can't believe it. It runs right over, it runs right over me. I can't stand crawling things, can you? Well it just comes over me like that. Terrible.

She shivered.

You want to wash things like that out of your clothes, off your body—rub them away . . . It turns you cold . . . Well, it's terrible to live, for some, I guess.

She let some spit to her finger and began carefully scrubbing behind the baby's ear.

How does it feel, Amos, she said, chuckling, is it good to suck a soft teat?

She looked up at Chamlay.

He has a powerful draw.

She blew gently on the baby's head.

Well we've all forgotten, I guess . . . big as we've got . . . old. Amos—he just wants to sleep and eat. Henry's in the woods somewhere, somewhere in a field, or rump up under water, maybe, someplace. Amos—the mister says we'll call you Amos. Why, do you suppose?

She laughed.

Mother, the older daughter said, mother, please.

She slowly subsided.

You little muffin, she said, nuzzling him. Then her face was smooth and worn and white again.

The fox died better, she said. I've seen a spoiling mouse that still had dignity—but men . . .

That fox now, Chamlay said. It was funny about that fox. Strange, I mean. You were going to let him starve down there, I hear. Why? What was the point of that? Any fun in it?

Come on, Curtis, Furber said, she doesn't know anything.

After a while, you know, it might have begun to whine and whimper.

You're thinking of a dog, she said. A fox dies quiet.

Well what was so funny about it? That gets me. What was so funny? And now you shrug. Well it's easy for you to shrug, I suppose—what with Omensetter's luck.

Oh we've never had much luck.

Chamlay cackled brutally.

How do you think Lucy Pimber feels—her husband gone, lost, no one knows where—sitting at home while we walk through the woods looking for him—and in places where no living man should be?

She smiled.

When I was twelve I had a rabbit for a whole day.

Mother.

Is he worth all this fuss and march about?

For heaven's sake, he's a human being. He's got more feeling than a fox. You ought to be able to see that.

How hard did you hunt for him when he was still alive?

Chamlay swore and turned away.

The baby's head fell from its breast, curd on its lips, eyes closed.

Open the door for these men, she said.

Chamlay and Furber filed out, immediately putting their hats on their heads and drawing deep shuddering breaths. The door shut behind them with Amos coughing.

The air had a nip now though the snow had ceased and flakes were melting on the ground. The sky seemed, if possible, even nearer. Through the bare trees they could see the calm Ohio. Chamlay stood some moments in the yard, Furber quietly beside him until he took to shivering. Then they rode off. Now and then a crisp breeze felt its way through the woods from the river. They left the path and had gone a little on the road when Chamlay sighed. His face had cooled and the determination of his body eased. He spoke out of deep thought, as though alone. Did you ever see, he began, breaking his question suddenly as Furber turned to study him. No, Furber finally answered when he thought he understood, I never did; though he lied, since he knew one other time he had.

⁓ 7

When Omensetter shook the door with pounding, the Reverend Furber shouted no, and drove his fists together. It was six in the evening, he was in his nightshirt yet, his voice was hoarse, and his eyes were badly puffed. All day he'd thrashed about and wept and yelled at Pike. Now he sat in the dark, mooning dimly, cursing his tears and knotting his bedclothes. The room was cold. The coals in the grate had thick covers of ash, and moisture had frozen on the windows. He'd risen early, in the grip of a dream, and stumbled to the vestry where Flack had begun his sweeping. You've been telling people things about me, he'd said bluntly. The colored man had clung to his broom while Furber cruelly accused him. You know all about me. You've given me away. Moments later, Furber had tried to drown himself in a basin. Of course it was an act, another futile gesture, and he'd flung the basin the length of the hall—carrying it carefully from his room first, so as not to wet his belongings. Back on his bed he hammered the wall, wailing and weeping. It was true that the day had passed quite quickly, yet he didn't think he'd snoozed. He'd been in a genuine delirium, then, and he took some comfort from the momentousness of that conclusion. But he was hardly prepared for the pounding which suddenly assailed him—pounding not his own—from without, not within—repeated, thunderous, imperative. The lummox is here, he thought, and he drove his fists at one another so viciously his knuckles skinned.

I must see you, Omensetter said.

Furber almost laughed.

There's no light, no fire. I'm sitting in the dark.

He needn't have answered. Omensetter had no way of knowing he was there—unless Flack had given him away again. He was immediately ashamed. Flack came by his color honestly. The little Ngero would never have betrayed him. It was inconceivable. He had cared for the church when Rush was its master, and he had suffered without complaint through its terrible plague-time under Furber the Furious, Jethro the Pretender, always serving loyally and with equal love, Furber felt certain, though each day, lately, he had seemed to shrink a little, and to go about his work still more invisibly. During all this time, Furber had actually learned nothing about him; he had never taken the slightest trouble for him or shown the least real interest. The fellow had remained a servant, a Negro, a mystery. And why shouldn't he be a mystery? No one is simple, he was about to say, yet how would he know? What had the watchman seen on his rounds? Surfaces. Scatters. He'd kept everything at a word's length, and it was words he saw when he saw her—tight, and white, and shining; it was words he felt when his anger burned him, when he shook and wailed and struck about wildly. Out of the world he could safely take just the ravelings: the color of the bruise on his toe, for instance, or the isolated croak of a frog which surprises the afternoon, or the vision of an intense green slope where a ball coasts under a wicket. Though mankind was his hobby—so he'd often said—he knew nothing of men. Negro seemed more properly the name of a patent medicine, just as mankind, despite his study, was only a compound joke to him. Furber ached, for a change, from the blow he had struck the friend of his church, but there was no help for it now, and he would not bandage either wound by begging for forgiveness. In one way Gilean was more punished than Egypt, he thought, since Egypt was never visited by a plague of lies.

I have to see you, Omensetter said.

What can I do now, Furber thought, pushing himself to the edge of the bed. I'm not all dressed, he said.

He was worn out, defeated. His head buzzed. His feelings were shredded, and he was shaking badly—out and in. He knew he must look a sight. The last few days he had grown increasingly careless. He had refused to shave. He had howled for Pike and got no answer. Incredulous, he had walked around his clock in the garden. Sunday would come soon. There'd be no sermon. He watched the snow whistle through the gate and sink in the Ohio. Since he was done for in Gilean—done for everywhere in that case—Furber wondered why Omensetter could not leave him alone.

What do you want?

I want to speak to you, but I can't shout through this door.

It's late.

I know it's late. There's time enough, though. It's important.

I haven't had my dinner.

Omensetter rattled the knob.

All his speeches ... his beautiful barriers of words ... He thrust a paper spill through the ashes and the room rolled in its flare. After these sounds, would the door come down? The bolt rattled at Omensetter's urging and Furber's hand shook. Wrinkles appeared in the wallpaper; the walls themselves seemed to waver; corners of the room crumpled; the ceiling swooped; there were bats on his pillow. It took a certain sort to undertake such banging—just the sort of loud muscling oaf he was. If he let him in ... then there he'd *be*, filling the door, huge, breathing heavily, the edges of his fists red, lips wet, body rocking, every bit as real as—as what? the bats on his pillow? the chasm yawning by his bed? the hungry holes in the wall? As the lamp lit, the room grew; its objects steadied. Furber dropped a smoking fragment of paper. He gently mooed and blew upon his fingers. The comedy is finished. The floor was icy.

Coming—take it gently—coming, coming ...

Hoo. Relief and fright at silence. To mortify the flesh, Furber heeled the ash, then sought his slippers. There was no harm done. He needed a nightcap to go with his nightgown. Then he thought he knew how he felt—like someone facing execution.

Coming ...

It was true. He was too exhausted to contain any greater emotion. A night's grief, a night's waiting, and now the warden with his keys. Furber's head ached. Yes, his eyes were surely swollen. Pale, the prisoner from his cot ... The gray wet wall of the garden ... forlorn ivy ... dripping trees ... Then scorn for the hankie blinding. Lift fist forward—defiant to the last. Cry death to truth and long live liars. Bangedy bang.

You *were* in bed.

Omensetter gave him a sheepish grin and slapped snow from his shoulders.

That's what I said.

Then it's good I pounded.

Omensetter's hair was in a desperate tangle. His face was pale from exhaustion and filthy from the woods. Furred with a week's beard, it was deeply creased and there were lines of windburn across the cheeks. His clothing was badly picked and burred, pulled out and twisted on him, and he struck at his body repeatedly with his hands.

Furber retreated to a chair.

I've found him, Omensetter said.

Have a seat, said Furber weakly.

Omensetter advanced, buffeting his ears.

I've found him.

You've—

Right. Boy. Yes I have. Ever seen weather so bad so early?

Henry?

Right. Whew. I haven't been in—I haven't been in to work much—what with hunting him.

He's dead?

Sure.

The nightshirt rose a moment—sat. Now, with God's help, Furber would look at him, flat on, for he was all new; his face no longer suited him, nor did his hands. His nose was inappropriate, his words weren't right. There was that false hailfellow tone, the whapping and bashing . . . new. And Furber began to feel his bones gradually burning with shame.

I see, he said.

Ha ha. Yeah.

Omensetter pulled off his hat.

For Christ's sake, did he chew, Furber wondered. In a moment he would snap his suspenders.

Omensetter turned very slowly around in the room.

Then he . . .

In the woods.

There was a little red in the stubble of his beard, Furber noticed. He was wiping his mouth with a wool rag of hat.

You didn't bring him him in?—bring him back?

At this moment, Furber thought, Henry might be propped like a statue in the vestry—the new-found saint and spirit of the woods.

Boy, you should see.

Omensetter looked dramatically at the ceiling.

I mean—holey oley—he's up high. In a tree. Way up there—a terrible climb.

Heavier in his chair, Furber tried to keep his head clear. Have a seat. He tried to imagine what would have to be gone through, but he could squeeze out only a little, it was too grim: the glints from Knox's glasses afflicted him, there were long sloping woodrows, smoked with frost, furry mittens ice had beaded, shouted curses and intemperate commands, squeaking tree boughs, looping veils of snow; yet even these paltry tatters were shameful—Hawkins whittling a wooden penis—for he was burning; his ears and cheeks were aflame from the past, since Omensetter seemed so different than he was, or otherwise than he had been, as he was altogether slow and sad and shy now, or embarrassed—rueful? worried? scared? god knew. "His watchmen are blind: they are all ignorant, they are all dumb dogs."

You mean he's still there, Furber said finally.

Sure. That's what he wanted. Besides—

But how in heaven—

He hung himself.

But—the question crept through Furber's fingers—why did he have to do it in such a silly—in such a circusy way?

Ha ha. Yeah. Why? Boy.

Omensetter began roaming around the room.

Aunt Janet had teetered, soul in her eyes—he could read. Through this damn back and woody shoulders—nothing . . . christ. "The invisible things of him from the creation of the world are clearly seen." Another lie.

How long has Henry—been up there? Furber asked in a proper mourner's voice.

Omensetter hesitated.

I couldn't say. Some time. I'm not a real good judge.

He fiddled with the lamp, reducing the light.

Who have you told?

Nobody—not even Lucy.

She's still at the Hatstat's.

I mean I haven't been home. I came straight here.

Straight, straight, straight. The crooked, straight. He had to scratch his foot.

You wouldn't think anything so cold could itch, he said, apologizing, but Omensetter wasn't really aware of him. Beside the little table, rubbing the edge, he waited. They could forget the whole business, of course, and let Henry hang there—that would be easiest.

So you want me to break the news?

Furber sighed, restoring the slipper, and thought suddenly of Persepolis and rows of granite lions.

It's my business, I guess, he said.

I hadn't thought about that.

You hadn't? Then in christ's name why did you pick on me? Not because I'm a preacher. Am I so close? convenient? friendly? Look—I'm not the by-your-side sort, you know that. For you, I'm neither person nor parson . . . Well was nobody home in the whole town so you were left with me? Too bad. I'm not home either. I've just gone out. The man you're talking to is Furber's ghost. And I'm not going to crawl up a tree to bump him down either, if that's what you expect—I'm not all that handy.

Look parson, don't you believe me? Omensetter made a gesture of entreaty. I did. Honestly—

Furber groaned with annoyance.

He's hanging from a limb.

From a limb like a leaf, I'm sure, Furber said, jumping up. That's poetry—sweet immortal poetry—it really is. The symbolic clown.

Omensetter rushed to the door. Calm and threatening by turns now, he was like a piece of weather in the room. The curtains seemed to lift a little as he passed.

Sorry, Furber said, promptly sitting. I keep forgetting you're a hero. Have a seat.

Furber carefully measured the air into fish lengths.

Gilean searched, but Omensetter found, he said. Am I correct?

I know I was wrong, Omensetter said, his hand on the knob, but I hadn't figured . . . well I was mistaken, I was wrong . . . Lucy said you wouldn't favor—

Favor? favor what?

Omensetter drifted from the door.

Me.

You?

Yes.

You haven't been home.

No.

But you discussed it with Lucy.

No. We talked about it earlier. What I should do.

Then Jethro Furber wondered whether Omensetter wasn't an actor.

What do you keep in that?

What?

That.

This?

Yes.

Bibles, Furber said, still disconcerted—holy things.

A pretty picture.

My god, he's maneuvering, Furber thought.

We've one of St. Francis feeding squirrels.

I know.

Lucy said that you'd been out. With the sheriff.

Chamlay's no sheriff.

He has a badge.

Badge. That's a story.

He has some authority.

186

Furber let it pass. The gosh-boy business was gone. Omensetter was speaking calmly now, but with almost desperate intensity. And he was absolutely still. It was uncanny.

Well he's way in the woods and high in the air. No wonder they never saw him. Nobody'd think to look straight up.

You did.

No I didn't. It was luck. I just happened to. I got a crick in my neck and was working it out.

Omensetter clasped his hands behind his neck and began to roll his head about wildly.

And now his soul's where it serves him. I can't do anything. Furber was knitting his fingers. The whole thing was absurd. He trapped his tongue behind his teeth. Omensetter doesn't notice my puffy eyes. He doesn't notice anything. Long live the pretty speech. Have a seat.

Omensetter riffled a book.

You haven't seen how high he's hung himself. He picked a white oak. It's huge—a hard climb in the cold. I'd like to borrow this. I read sometimes, though not in the winter. The light isn't well for the eyes.

Furber made a low sound of disgust.

He's wearing that gray wool coat with the wide pockets he used to stuff duck shells in. He has his hands down them now, and he's hanging by the belt so his head tilts to the side some when he spins.

Does he seem well rested?

I couldn't tell.

Oh come on—jesus.

Omensetter stared at him.

He turns, you said.

He turns some.

You don't intend to leave him up there?

Ha ha. Boy. Have you got any books on birds?

You do, then.

Sure. But they won't leave him hanging when I've told them where he is and everything. I was a friend of Henry's, so—you know—in a way I wish they would. He's up there, Mister Furber. Boy. I had a notion not to say a word and leave him be, but I guess I can't.

My feet are cold, Furber said firmly. We need a fire in here. I'm cold all over. Somewhere there's a little scuttle—

They'll never find him without a dog, he's hung so high.

Sometimes it gets slid under this stool.

With the wind taking every scent, it took my Arthur time out of mind, plus my wise crick in the neck besides, although Arthur's got the finest kind of tracker's nose.

Sometimes it gets pushed into the corner there.

Maybe they'd have a little luck like mine with the Bencher hound. I don't know.

Or kicked under the bed. I've got a terrible bruise on my toe.

It's bad weather for it, the wind's in your eyes all the time. You know—a fit of pique.

I notice they've been slow to go to dogs—that Chamlay fellow doesn't like them. I just don't know.

Hog Bellman. They remind him, that's why. Say, I want to show you that toe. The nail's black.

Anyway, they'll never think to look so high. He's hung way up. River or field or floor of the woods is all in the world they'll think of.

Ah, here it is—would you think of that—back of this stack of books.

I'd just as soon keep shut.

Let me just poke this up a bit.

You read all them books?

Hum.

After a while, though, that belt will rot or the limb he's hanging from will break.

I thought as much.

I'm surprised he found a branch as high as that to hold him so far out—enough to be above another tree, a little hackberry it is, covered with those witches' brooms. Henry must have had a real desire to die there. I climb easy and that climb near finished me.

Its smoking some. Too bad I've no kindling. Mustn't put on too much. Maybe he farted and flew up.

Furber felt sorry for him. The forceful ends of Omensetter's fingers had left red lines on his face. The corners of his mouth twitched; he blinked; he examined his coat sleeve. Furber had cranked his head around. Now it turned back to the fire. He couldn't have done any better if he'd hit him with the poker.

When I first saw Henry I thought he was a great horned owl.

Damn this Pennsylvania coal.

Furber was squatting in front of the grate. Omensetter leaned down to touch his shoulder.

One day certain, if I leave him there, that bough or that belt will break and he'll come down through the hackberry, branch by branch, and be mostly in bones at the bottom. Who'll know then, for sure, he hung himself up there— beyond anybody else's doing?

In front of Furber: a landscape of coal and ash and faint

188

smoke. You don't *touch* the minister. His nose needed blowing. What a godforsaken thing this was.

And you've chosen to tell me.

Yes, Omensetter said, I know I have your trust.

The imbecility of this remark was so immense that Furber found it impossible to respond to it. He shook his head and rose. The new coals would not ignite. He held the poker. Maybe he should.

Tell me—what's your idea? Why did Henry turn so strange?

He hung himself a way that suited him.

Oh stop it.

I couldn't safely come to anyone but you.

What a thing to say to me—a man of God.

Omensetter looked at him strangely.

Where have you been, Furber said, now out of control. You're in the wrong farce.

You have to believe me. You know the trouble I'm in. I couldn't safely come to anyone but you. Finding Henry where I did was great luck, but Knox, you know, and Hatstat, and Chamlay—

Yes indeed, Knox, the Hatstats, and Chamlay, said Furber furiously, you're right; and Hawkins, Orcutt, Stitt, and Fyle—not out of jealousy, if you're thinking that— Tott even, Lemon Hank, my Flack and Edna Hoxie, all the wives and Splendid Turner, Cate and Bencher, Alfred Candle, that fool Jess Ivry, oh and Mosstellcr, the dutchman Blenker, Amsterdam, that Scanlon woman, Mat Watson too—

Not Mat.

Not Mat? Oh, you—you fool.

Please.

Please? You ask a please of me?

Furber whistled his wind out and regarded Omensetter steadily a moment before speaking again. Then he spoke very slowly and carefully.

But Mat *especially*, he said. He *especially* will think you throttled Pimber and hauled him up. My guarantee. Oh yes—Lucy Pimber too—no trouble there—everybody—your own wife, maybe—

No, not Mat.

Of course, Mat.

Furber chuckled bitterly and slapped his left hand smartly on his cheek.

Why not Mat? Mat first of all. Where—have—you—been? A friend, eh? Hooey. A friend. Friends all. Hatstat too. Chamlay. There's a friend. All the ladies. All the friendly women. Kindly Knox. Tott, who loves stories. The dear dear

Doctor. Stitt and Hawkins. There's a pair. Everybody. Lovable Lucy. Have you had her? She's eager. And Jethro Furber, that sweethearted cuss. Everybody.

He dropped the poker with a clatter and formed two eloquent fists.

Go away. Go away, you idiot. What are you making me say?

His nightshirt swirled around his knees as he turned and began to pace between the table and the wall.

Come safely, he said. The fool. Come safely to me? The idiot. I'm safety? Where—where have you been? My god. My god. A friend. I've spent my life spreading lies about you. A friend, eh? a friend, a friend—

Okay. It's okay.

You—you know nothing of the life you live in. Sweet christ, what a booby—how can I convey—how—how could you be so—so stupid—so imbecile—live so long—know so little—how? Well, it's too late to learn now.

Arms slack, Furber leaned back into the angle of the walls and stared at the ceiling. At last he let his eyes drop.

Look: if a bird were to rub its beak on a limb, you'd hear it—sure—and if a piece of water were to move an unaccustomed way, you'd feel it—that's right—and if a fox were to steal a hen, you'd see—you'd see it—even in the middle of the night; but, heaven help you, if a friend a friend—god—were to slit your throat with his—his love—hoh, you'd bleed a week to notice it.

Furber tottered weakly across the room. He had achieved a splendid effect. It sickened him. He sank on the bed and threw his head in his hands, yet even that seemed theatrical. He had no knowledge of this man. None. He'd never seen him before. And all he wanted to do was hit him—hit him. When Furber looked up, he was still there—waiting.

Seen many hangings, Omensetter?

—

Do their tongues loll out?

—

Do they turn blue like everybody says, and jerk a lot?

—

How many struggle before the trap's sprung, or do they go out praying or cursing the crowd?

—

Perhaps they're brought drugged with their heads in a sack. What's your opinion?

—

Or were the hangings you attended all at night, of niggers

190

maybe, slapped up from the rump of a horse or just jerked away communally and left to choke.

—

You won't answer. Why not?

Furber beat his knees.

It's not true of Mat, Omensetter said. Don't you believe me? Henry's hung himself in his coat.

No, Furber said. No. Of course I don't believe you. Obviously. God. Believe you. No. You choked him with your great hands as easily as you might lift me up and then you fetched him to the top. No one else could have done it.

Omensetter laughed.

Oh, he said when he had got his breath, the hands—I see—with my great hands—yes.

And he began to laugh again.

By all means—tee hee. Ho ho ho. And so he's dead in some tree and looks like an owl. Well, that's fine. He turns in the wind and gets the sun. Splendid. He made a fine fatuous fool of himself and is now in hell. In a pit of hissing, pissing theologians.

All that matters is you trust me.

What a godforsaken soul I have. Ba—Brackett—what a shit I am.

Will you go to Chamlay?

I can't. I can't do that.

Tell him what I've told you, that's all.

I simply can't.

Say I shall show him where Henry's hanging and help to take him down.

You don't understand. It's impossible.

Explain just how I am—my worry. Convince him that I'm telling the truth. Make clear the height that Henry's hanging—all that—and how sure you are it's suicide.

How sure I am, said Furber wearily.

For me.

For you.

Yes.

You're offering me a king of bargain?

You said it was your business.

There are bargains in business.

Just tell him.

And good business in bargains.

Both of us are tired. I'm sorry—you know—to have bothered—with you so sick, you know—but you can see I had to—you can see how it is. You were quick to wonder yourself when I told you that I'd found him.

Furber let his head wobble on his neck.

We—Lucy and me—the girls—we aren't used to living by the side of people. I guess that's it. Lucy thought the girls ought, well, to meet—you know—though neither Angela or Eleanor seems to care about that—well—perhaps in time you learn how . . .

Furber hugged a pillow in his lap.

I thought the weather would be fine for the boy, too, you know, and the excitement of the river . . . I didn't figure right.

And so there'll be a covenant between us.

We'll be going . . . when Henry's down and buried. That would be right. Are there people living all along the river? If we went south could we find an open piece of woods there?

I'm to convince them, then you'll go, is that it? Where will you be? here?

Oh no. Amos has a cold . . . something. Let them come by, it's on the way. It'll have to be tomorrow—morning would be wisest—an early start. It's supper time now, and dark.

Supper time.

Tomorrow's time enough.

Time enough. It's dark, you say?

I'll sure be grateful.

It's the business of the minister . . . to intercede.

Well—

My Aunt Janet was a different sort of suicide.

Golly. I'm sorry.

Furber put the pillow beside him. Golly. Old Aunt Janet. Who threw herself from a shelf made of wicker. What points had she thought to consider, the pros and cons of death and life? He turned inside and recognized at once the passage of the belly, the traverse of the loins, the navigation of the thigh. Now folks, we've reached, in here, the cathedral of the thorax, a natural cavern. No rare woods here, no perfumed wine, no choirs of boys, but Bael with the head of a man and a spider's body, cat and toad growing out of his neck, commanding forty-six legions of devils; Behemoth, full stomached as Omensetter's wife had been with her skin like shining satin, but otherwise an elephant devouring grass like the oxen, his whole strength in his loins and his virtue fitted in the button of his belly, commanding thrice seven regiments of furies; Astaroth, the ugly angel, vulgarly astride a dragon, leading forty legions; Forcas on a donkey; Marchocias vomiting; Buer in a wheel of hooves revolving; Asmodeus; Theutus; Incubus—demon after demon drawn delightfully by Angelo, who made God's finger like an amorous engine for

192

the Vatican. What he really needed was a year abroad to study painting.

Do you know very well the words of Jeremiah?

Furber rose as he spoke.

Omensetter shook his head.

I used a text of his for the first sermon I preached in this church.

Omensetter smiled politely.

It was hot then.

—

Furber pulled his nightgown about him.

And very dry. We had a terrible fire. Burning trees fell in the river.

—

Furber sighed.

A catastrophe.

—

What was Henry's reason; do you have any idea?

Omensetter shrugged.

He was happy when I saw him last, Omensetter said. We'd been to the hill and he was resting on a log. I don't know. It was a good day.

Furber smiled.

A good day. Well then no reason.

You'll tell Chamlay?

"Take ye heed every one of his neighbor, and trust ye not in any brother." That's Jeremiah.

Gee.

You'll be cold with just a jacket.

You can convince him? You'll have no trouble?

Shapes were crowding toward Furber's eyes. "For death is come up into our windows . . ."

Oh, he said, Chamlay? and he waved his hand airily. That will be easy, never fear; it will be easy for me.

✦ **8**

Eight came by horseback with a wagon, hurrying against a late sun already weakened by its clouds. Chamlay came, and Olus Knox, Jethro Furber, Israbestis Tott, Hawkins with the

Hatstats, George and Menger, then Stitt somehow—all ahead of Milo Bencher's wagon. It was a strong wagon, though small; one that could be jounced over meadows and got between trees. The men could see Omensetter peering through the window when they arrived, wiping back the glass with his hand. As they entered the yard Omensetter rushed from the house to shout—the boy is sick—turning from man to man as he did so, trotting anxiously along. His face was pale, bearded; there were bubbles on his lips which popped when he spoke.

Damn near dark, Chamlay said. We got to move.

The boy is sick—the baby's sick.

Gray and frantic, Omensetter moved from man to man while the dog ran quickly around him.

Was what you said to Furber true?

The horses were nervous. The dog plunged through Omensetter's legs and the horses turned, their hoofs destroying patches of snow.

It's all true, yes. But I thought you'd be here this morning.

Disappointed, Omensetter turned to Furber.

Didn't you—

Hey's it true? what did he say?

Yes, yes, Omensetter shouted, yes, it's true.

We've got no time then; it's no job for the dark.

Going to come hard, Knox said, peering at the sky.

Omensetter wound his fingers in the mane of Chamlay's horse.

Was what you said to Furber true?

Better of been, said Hawkins. I shut the store.

It's going to hit thick. Let's move.

Where's Mat?

Who?

Mat? He didn't come.

Christ, Brackett, come on—you got something to ride?

He's got that horse.

He's got a horse all right.

Will this cart-assed wagon make it, Menger asked.

Come on, can we ride these horses in, or will we have to walk?

Told Furber a lot of cock, I bet—a lot of shit.

Better not of.

Christ, come on—it's going to turn on cold.

The baby's sick.

Omensetter blotted his nose.

Well, you should find him easy if I tell you how, but you

194

can't take your horses in, or any wagon either—not all the way.

The horses tightened about him until the dog barked from between Omensetter's feet. Then the horses shied but the men reined close again, leaning heavily from their saddles.

We've got no time, Chamlay said. We're getting old with this waiting.

It's going to snow—just look at that—we're due. We're going to get it good.

Well, you know that long white log there by the creek, Omensetter said. All right, go straight—

Chamlay interrupted with a meaningless shout of anger and instantly the others were shouting too, leaning close around him yelling until Lucy came running out of the house, the girls behind her weeping brokenly, so that the dog in a frenzy leaped at Hawkins and Hawkins sprawled him with a blow.

He's throwing up again, Brackett—awful—an awful something—he can't breathe.

Omensetter broke out of the circle and ran heavily into the house.

Quickly, in tight aimless patterns, the horses moved. The men rubbed their noses high on their sleeves and watched their streaming mouths. The dog crouched, ears flat, threats shaking in his throat. The horses backed and turned and reared and Stitt cursed when he scraped his leg on Milo Bencher's wagon.

Knox dismounted.

It's nothing to fret about I'm sure, he said. I've seen this often; the least little thing will put them off.

Lucy's way was blocked by the Hatstats' horses and she vainly tried to go around them.

We've other children too, she said, pushing against the horses. I've had kids sick before, but never—Please!

George winked at his brother.

I'll look if you don't mind, Knox said, passing the reins to Tott.

Tell him he's got five minutes, Olus, Luther Hawkins said. Just five.

Knox followed Lucy Omensetter running up the steps, Knox nodding nicely to the girls who seemed intent on the horsemen behind their tears.

Knox came out in a moment—the men were standing by their horses—to ask Chamlay where Orcutt was.

He was at the Amsterdams' this morning, Tott said. Em's bad.

Way over there?

God damn this god damn dog, Hawkins said.

Is the kid real sick?

Stitt said it was just a stall, and Chamlay went in, Knox after him.

We'll never get old Henry down today, Stitt said sadly. I'll have to pull this wagon back to Bencher empty.

Where is Bencher anyway—in bed with his sheep?

Ain't the Reverend been quiet, though. You froze your teeth?

I don't care, by god, it was queer—what this fellow Omensetter told you, Furber, George said. I don't mind saying it gives me the trots.

Menger whistled his breath toward his brother, and everyone watched the stream move between them—boil out, widen, disappear.

Shit.

George rubbed his nose again upon his sleeve.

Hee-hawing bastard.

Henry's not in any tree, Menger said, any more than George is, hey George? any more than me.

Stitt said that they were fools for being there, and Furber sneezed, Tott saying after: bless.

You ever hear a tale like that, Stitt said.

I understand one time, Tott said, that Milo Bencher—

Got stuck in Granny Amsterdam.

Oh shut, will you.

I don't care, I never heard a tale like that.

Ever hear a turd talk?

Hawkins tied his horse.

I know what it'd say—

It'd say plop.

I'd say, let's hang the mother-fucking bastard by the balls, said Hawkins.

Cut it out—the kids.

For now the girls were quiet, their hands tight to the porch rail, their eyes at the horses.

You kids got names, Menger asked—and they ran inside.

Agnes and Emerald.

No kidding?

Finally the men laughed a little and walked up and down in the yard crushing pieces of snow. A horse warmly relieved. Clouds of moisture swirled over its dung.

By the balls, Hawkins said. Forty feet in the air. With a length of barb from a rusted fence.

Then Omensetter and Chamlay appeared with Knox

behind them and Omensetter was saying yes yes in a hoarse voice as they came down the steps—he needs a doctor—while the dog ran up to his boots. Curtis was stern and Olus angry.

Somebody ought to go for Orcutt, Chamlay said.

I said he was sick, said Omensetter dully.

Orcutt was over to the Amsterdams' this morning, Tott said. No telling where he's got to by now.

He was brought in smaller than his sisters . . . but a bawler. He's quiet now, though . . . so—clouded over.

You should have sent for Orcutt long ago, Knox said fiercely.

Maybe, Omensetter mumbled, holding the sides of his jaw. I had to go see Furber first, you know.

Why?

Anyway you've had all day, god damn it.

If Henry's hanging where you say, Knox said, then what's the hurry? My god man, your son is sick—sick serious. What's a lifeless body by him? If he was mine—

Hell, if Henry's where you say—

Do they do a lot of good? doctors? I've always wondered if it wasn't better to let things run along their natural way.

God's will, Furber muttered.

That's been my feeling.

Omensetter smiled weakly and spread his arms.

What a lot of shit, George Hatstat said.

You've let things run too far already.

Knox gestured angrily with his glasses.

You should have gone for Orcutt right away, he said. You didn't—you couldn't—you and your damn fool ideas.

You'll have that child on your conscience, Omensetter, Chamlay said.

Conscience? conscience?

Knox carefully put his glasses on and peered at Omensetter closely.

What have we seen shows he has a conscience?

Hey, Stitt said, did you guys just come out here to drop your pants, or shall we get?

Omensetter went about the yard among the horses and past the men, looking at them dumbly as he passed them like a beast himself, and at the trampled ground between them with such sorrow that his whole face had to twitch when he raised it to their faces to form it for the animal passivity it wore. His eyes were rimmed and seemed so deeply sunken they must have seen continually through shadow, and his formerly full cheeks now had the look of crumpled paper.

His breathing was audible and slow, his movements heavy, remote from any mind.

I can still remember coming, Curtis, Omensetter said quietly at last. Clouds—the river—Gilean by it—the air so clear . . . There was every house out honest and every barn banked proper to the weather . . . The trees were bare, I remember, and as we came down the hill we could see the tracks of the wagons glistening. You could see what your life would be. You know—like the gypsy woman who can take your fortune from your hand. Well I took those tracks to be a promise to me . . . And on the way we'd all been singing. *Rose Alymer.* I heard it sung so strangely once I never forgot it. The words are high and fine beyond my understanding but I like their sound. And we counted kinds of birds . . . I guess you think—well, what does it matter? I don't know . . . I remember there were rings in the pools of water by the road, and I thought how exciting for the boy to live by the river, to catch fish and keep frogs, you know; grow up with good excitement. Now he's gone sick, Curtis, in this low place, and there's no honest snow to cover it or cold to hold it firmly even, and the hill we came by is still a slippery yellow. The boy is going to die, Curtis. I just feel—I'm scared he's going to die. He's dreadful sick, I know. You've seen him, you and Olus know he's going to die. Why—he's barely been alive . . . The boy—the boy, too—he was a promise to me. I hold he was a promise to me. If he dies—well you were all—too—promises. Curtis? Olus? George? Remember? Wasn't there a promise to me? He'll die soon, my son will—soon he'll be dead of this low ground and its dishonest weather. I'll cut that on his stone. If he ever has a stone. I don't think that I can bring myself to put him in this clay. I'll put him on a mountain maybe, where the birds can pick his body. Whoever lives so little and so low as he has should spend his death up high—like Henry's doing.

Chamlay rose on his horse.

In his life he only knew his mother.

Knox rose.

I hold there was a promise—Gilean was.

Menger rose. George rose.

All right—it doesn't matter.

Stitt rose. Tott rose. Hawkins rose.

I hope no one will send for Doctor Orcutt now. He'll not be needed. I've changed my mind.

He's worse, Brackett, Lucy shouted from the porch. Please won't one of you find Doctor Orcutt? Brackett? Please. His tongue—he doesn't breathe—someone—please—there's blood—I think there's blood.

No, Omensetter said, no, and his wife faintly echoed him, astonished, no? our child? Brackett? My son, said Omensetter wearily.

He drew himself together with an effort.

There was a promise to me and it was a lie.

His wife fell weakly against the railing.

What's this, she whispered.

I'll go, missus, Israbestis said; I've a notion where Doc is if he saw Emma Amsterdam this morning.

No, Omensetter cried, rushing at Tott and grasping his arm. Bessie, you know him, you know how his teeth slide in his beard, Omensetter said, leaning close; no, I don't want him.

Lucy groaned.

Mother, one of the daughters called, and the girls' cries drew her in.

Omensetter kept his grip on Israbestis.

Bessie, he said, don't go, don't go, I hate his eyes, they cross. You know his eyes. They're stitched to him.

Tott twisted away.

Have you looked, Omensetter roared, straightening, glaring angrily, waving his arms, his long hair tossing above his brow. Go off and find your friend where he has hung himself. Curtis knows the way now, and can lead. And take your wagon to the white log by the creek. Then you won't have so far to drag his bones.

9

The fire and the lamp made pairs of crossing shadows, one steady and firm, one leaping and vague. Her shadow spotted the wall and disappeared, drawn magically back beneath her chair as she rocked, then darting forth to climb the wall as rapidly again. He found himself marking the height. Incredibly swift, it bent itself up from the floor, passing the picture, the long head reaching a mar in the paper and covering a cluster of leaves while the lengthening finial that followed behind struck a rose. Each time it was the same. Omensetter's shadow dwindled under him and Furber had the impression of something being poured steadily through a hole in the floor. The girls sat mute in ladder chairs, their stiff and strangely twisted figures fastened to the wall like ill-cut paper silhouettes. Another corner was darkened by the cradle where the baby, ominously quiet now, lay dying of a closing throat, an occasional wisp of its breath crossing the room like a little draft of air or brief creak of the house. I shall make a rabbit with my fingers. I shall make a tiger. I shall make a bird. His own thin outline oozed through generous cracks and hung alongside wintering ants and modest spiders between the boards. I shall make a goose. I shall make a bear.

There were foolish men in the woods, death in the trees. What did a body matter? It was such a damp low place, hardly fit to put a spirit in. What did they think they were rescuing?

In seminary they'd been called The Great Hypotheses. The One and The Other. The Spirit and its Enemy. Yes and No. A and B. Truth against The Adversary, Father of Lies. A always won, while B. . . .

If I enumerated all the contents of my soul, he thought; if I made a thorough list of them; if I overlooked nothing; if I counted twice; if I wrote each down carefully with a spit-wet pencil end like Luther's accomplished clerk; would I find an item I could say belonged to me, made me, formed my core and heart? Thus The Other always argued.

If you were to place a lamp before a wall and put your hand in the light that flows between them, you would make a shadow. Purse your fingers properly, the shadow is a duck, while with the thumb thrust up, a horse. Then on mastery of these you may try to make a hawk fly slowly with both hands. End of the lesson. Who was teaching?

Death was only another arrangement. For suppose, and mind it narrowly, that life is simply a shadow bodies cast inside themselves when struck by all those queerly various bits and particles, those pieces, streams of—what?—of science. Death in such a case would be only another arrangement.

He said: the fire needs wood; we must keep the room warm.

Why was it sorrowful, The Great Alternative? No hell afterward, but blessedness. What could be more blessed than to rest in a coil of silence—not to be? He'd meant to preach to that. His whole life, he'd meant to preach, to preach . . . Where was his preaching and his preachment now? Would Henry's body, hanging in its tree, be dreaming? Would it be casting in itself another kind of shadow, a goblin shadow, to be feared?

But no dream could wound as cleverly as the painful edges of perception.

. . . while B persisted like a monstrous suspicion. Yes and No. A and . . .

Did they think he was praying, his head so holy, his hands so discreet in the folds of his priestly clothing? Perhaps his lips were moving. The fire sank under the added log. If there were only something in the room beside it, anything—speech—but not this ache of silence.

You can smooth the bruises from our bodies; You can sweep off the sickness that's infected them. Breathe gently on this infant, that he may one day carry in his lungs the fragrance of Your heart.

Crap.

A and . . . It could very well be. What kind of shadow would strangulation cast? How fares the spirit of the throttled man? The soul was once believed to exit from the mouth and nose and return on the insucked air, but just suppose, the breath cut off, belt grimly crimping in the pipe, that while the soul struggled to escape, the bungling body died? Imagine, then, this messy bit of business quickly buried with the soul still stuck like an animal inside. What sounds would funeral speeches make in a dead ear; what meaning would they carry for a skull? The body swells down there, takes water on, then pops—the spirit's out. But what, by this time, is it? What's the shadow in a swelling corpse? a chorus of shouts? Shut in the earth, it dies each minute, each minute is replaced by the reflection of a new arrangement. So it is with us. So it is with me. So. So. It is so like. Buried in this air, I rot. Moment by moment, I am not the same. And all I desire is to escape—get out. Then notice—look carefully on it—what happens when the body splits. The snow-white wormlings of the flies seethe out. The soul, the immortal principle of life, in its last condition, has come to this—this transmigration.

They *are* rescuing something then: Henry Pimber somewhat rearranged—who knows for worse or better? Get him down and smartly under. Play it safe. You never can tell.

Up and down, yes and no, A and B. She rocked. Suddenly it struck him—added up. It was as though he had been jumped at from the dark. Chilled. The rocker creaked. Its legs rubbed in their sockets. All this time a sound—each time the same—had issued from its motion. Yet he'd never heard it. Where was it when he'd watched the shadow pulsing, her head to the leaves and the finial to the rose, the knurl at its blotting? Now the squeal tore at his nerves. It became difficult to see.

For the boy—shall we pray? How?

He got up slowly, sweat gathering coldly on his chest and under his arms, and began to pace. Soon he would prickle. She was only an ear, not half alive, reduced to one expectation. How alive was he—the great square O? Furber risked his name, sailed it across the current of the squeak. O-men-set-ter. Now his name has entered his ear. In whose porches I poured the poison. It has penetrated to his brain. But? Nothing. Blank. Dead then, to that. Dead by so much. Nevertheless alive in some ways—movable. In stumbling shamble. Rocky-walky. Bear shuff. And in the woods the breath of the men as they climb the trees will be floating from their noses just as always. Unperceived. The spirit. The Holy Spirit.

Is it two falls out of three? God wins the first but the Devil takes the next one. There has not yet been a third to anybody's knowledge.

He had a desire to dance, to whirl while kicking his leg in the air, crying kangaroo. He would whirl and whirl and slowly mount toward the ceiling—whirling. Too bad he'd never made a study of ballet.

He *was* moving—stately—like a sailing ship. He saw the woodwork and the paper sliding. Then spots by. Another instance of it. So life and death were ranges of degree and no more opposite than snow and sleet or pie and pain. Note that. Four and twenty black Flacks. Everything alive. Who was the fellow who first said it? It was a matter, merely, of awake. Awake. Ho! the guard! Ho! the keep! So surely the house, and this, the stomach of the house, and these, the flickers of its feelings. Alarm within. Turn out the watch. So surely these are shadows cast inside. By. Then the bitter rocker. Bitterly alive to scrape sensations through its feet and speak. Arouse within! The treasure of the temple's stolen. So then dead—and then alive. Tick-teek. Tick-teeek. Tick-teeeek. Tick-teeeeek. Everywhere upon him. Soles of his feet, behind the lids of his eyes, beneath the roots of his teeth. Furber sank into the hallway, itching intolerably, and like a hairy spider, every twitch meant victim.

Matthew, I lied. Am I not believed as one who strives to tell the truth in everything? He did not say: I am of the dark ways, preacher. He did not use those foolish words. He was merely stricken by my turns of speech and by my mad religious ways. Oh what a meager adversary after all! I could have preached in Cleveland, Matthew—in Cleveland in great cathedrals, in robes so heavy they would weary my arms. But I was fearful and vain of my righteousness, Matthew, fearful for my soul, and I came to Gilean to flee temptation,

202

to put Satan behind me, as they say on Sunday. More terrible theology. Like Henry's in that. With my adversary, the Red Chief, all the time inside me, perched on my liver, feet crossed, meeting with the rest, making his spiel. What sayeth the psalmist? "He sitteth in ambush with the rich in secret to murder the innocent, his eyes are privily set against the poor. He lieth in wait secretly as a lion in his den; he lieth in wait to catch the poor." Poor Henry. Poor Matthew. Poor Janet. So our worthy Jerome also warns us, whose belly wants to be god in Christ's place. As I recall, it was the crotch in auntie's case. If only he could be like Splendid Turner, he thought, who had a soul like a sponge soaked in greed and fornication which Splendid simply squeezed out when he got contrite. In seminary they used to say that Jesus had an upright Peter, but I always said that swearing by that soft apostle made a limp appeal. Whoo-oo-ee. Purple thistles in dizzy rows. He laid his head against the wall, the paper wall, and shut his eyes. Dead to the thistles, the darkness, the golden wood. Musty, cool—the paper wall. If he had an eye at the end of a line and payed it to the bottom of the river, while he stared with his own pair at the sky, what sort of world would his three eyes put together? My eyes comprise . . . Little pimples of plaster, the weight of his body in his soles, old paper, damp paper, cold tips of finger, cloth cooling at the corners of his shoulders and elbows, vague pale rings against his closed lids . . . Or an eye like an aggie—rolling to the corner. To spin into illness. No, the soul a balloon. It was how much air you got. A French invention. Montpellier was it? Like the town. And then stirring behind him. And voices. He swung around. Heat rises. The soul swells and sails to heaven. Bye baby bunting. No. It is the corpse which obliges. Firm flesh refines itself to fearful fumes by water. Who was the fellow? Goes off like a cannon. The capture of Paris. A French invention. He was alive to the firelight, to the moving rows of thistles. If I kick my feet and whirl, I shall rise to the ceiling. I should have studied dancing, I move so gracefully sometimes. You're quite a sport, Furb; you can play the picnic on our banjo.

Great and mighty God, who has brought us down to the grave as careless children to the sea, bring us back from there, for now we are afraid, for we have seen our own death in the heavy water, in the sand our toes have squeezed the print of our own end . . .

Matthew, listen, believe in the Devil. I know you for a man who merely believes in God. Bad theology and careless observation, Matthew. You can believe me, for I have seen him. He and I are on familiar terms. He has a sharp tongue and strange ideas, like myself. We are friends in fact. Men have no other.

The shadows of the lamp were steady but the fire was like dark lace. Their voices were low and intense and filled with surprise; a continual thread of bewilderment and wonder held their words together. You are letting him die, she said, and it seemed to Furber he was hearing something that had been repeated already with an agonizing regularity, like the squeak of the rocker. Omensetter's protests were driven from him. With every word he seemed to wither and diminish. Soon speech would be beyond his strength.

. . . you are letting him die.

Luce—

You are.

Omensetter swayed rhythmically a moment like a bear.

I am letting him be. I am giving him a chance.

A chance to die, she said in a flat cold bitter voice.

Lucy—

She was wasted too, but like a wire. She had lost the fullness of her pregnancy; her skin was pale and drawn, her bones lay like shadows under it; even her astonishing breasts seemed drained, though with the child not feeding, they should have been swollen painfully.

. . . just letting him.

There's no other way.

She rose from the rocker like an angry gesture.

Where is my husband, she said in a whisper.

Then she slid back to the chair. Tick, it said.

Omensetter squatted by her, reaching out.

She brushed at his hands as though they were bugs in her lap.

Luce—

They have forgotten the children as they have forgotten me, Furber thought. He turned toward the girls, and they froze his heart.

How can I know what to do? Fetch Orcutt? Does a hen give her eggs to a weasel?

Let him die, then.

Her fingers flew in her hair.

You'd take more trouble for a cat, she said.

There's nothing anyone can do.

He may have taken death already just from hearing you.

He mustn't.

Mustn't . . .

We've got to trust my luck.

We've a baby—sick. Isn't that enough? What do people

do when their baby's sick? That's all I want—what anyone would want—what you'd have wanted once—nothing strange or new or put on—just what's ordinary—decent—human. Now I look at you—the way you've been—all set on something I can't understand—so crazy—hunching in your self where I can't feel you—and I think it can't be true—your changes—they just can't be true.

I don't want to change. I'm trying not to.

I thought I knew what I loved.

I want to—I'm trying to do what I've always done—

It's worse—Brackett, will you believe me?—it's worse than losing that poor baby—losing you. But I can't trade the baby for you, can I?

Oh no—no—no trade—

You won't be the same. Is that a trade?

What's this now? I don't want a trade.

What will I do when you're dead too?

Don't talk that way.

This is the son I thought you wanted.

Don't—

We loved each other once. Why don't we feel the same love now—now when we need to? Why must we live in these lonely pieces?

We had it on my luck.

All our life till now is nothing—luck—a raindrop hitting. And our beauty? Brackett, is it a weed, annoying you where it comes up? All our life till now I could live in easy, breathe in easy—swallow easy—loving you. It was as though—as though you'd taken room in me—with that I could be happy. But it was luck, you say, just luck. And when I came to you with my arms before me like a present of flowers? And when I said sweet heart, dear love . . . do you remember? Never a foolish name. Dear heart, I said, dear love—

Omensetter attempted to throw himself in his wife's lap, but the arm of the rocker prevented him and his head slid onto her chest, while he flung one arm awkwardly around her.

For Henry. You are letting him die because of Henry.

No.

And you are killing me.

I love you.

You are killing them.

Lucy—

All of us.

I love you.

For Henry—is this for Henry? Did you love Henry more to kill him sooner?

Omensetter clumsily reached his feet.

Those men—they suspect you, don't they? I could see it. They hate us. Why?

I am no mur-der-er, Omensetter howled, raising his arms like weapons above his head. I am no mur-der-er! Can't you see? Should I tear away my skin? Would you see inside me then, and see how my life ceases when you speak this way to me?

The daughters stirred, beginning to weep, and Omensetter turned, remembering them. Furber extended his arms, but they careened down the hall, blindly striking the walls as they went like bewildered birds. Furber sank, groaning, to his knees.

He had fathered every folly, every sin. No goat knew gluttony like his, no cat had felt his pride, no crow his avarice. He had said the psalm against envy, the psalm against anger, the psalm against sloth and the loss of hope, but they were no defense. He had wanted women. He had imagined them in every posture. He had wanted men. There was no perversity he had not thought to practice with them. Further, he had wanted little girls. He had wanted boys. He had wanted most of all himself. He had stolen. He had blasphemed. He had cheated. He had lied—his single skill. He had been cruel and contemptuous, malicious and willful. He'd lacked courage, piety, loyalty, hope. Without moderation or charity, without relish or enthusiasm, he'd led a wanton, heedless, selfish life. In meanness, in darkness and squalor of spirit, he had passed his time. Faithless he'd professed a faith. Faithlessly, he'd preached. Indeed, he'd labored on the Devil's side as if the Lord Himself had begged it of him, and in the line of duty proved that bigotry needs no beliefs, for on behalf of Heaven he'd been intolerant with dispassion, puritanical for pleasure, and zealous out of boredom. Touch me nor, he'd always cried; do not burden me with love. Even now he made himself a monster, overblew his vices so his charge would lack conviction. Was that not, admittedly, the maneuver of a monster? So often clever. Note how sweetly I pronounce her, musically wig-wag my ringalingling tongue. May I not admire my skill like any harlot? Am I not quite honestly dishonest? So in all his mirrors, fair and square, he threw his errors. All this, of course, God knew. God knew, as he addressed Him—mewling, kneeling—his holy cloth and posture were disguise; that he did not believe. Then what did he deserve? Wasn't it punishment enough that he perpetually disgrace his feelings? Had he sinned so much that innocence should suffer this from him?

It seemed darker, doubtless, than it was. Omensetter moved along the steep beach on all fours like some nocturnal animal. He appeared to be gathering stones. The snowflakes were scattered still, but the wind was stinging. There would be bitter weather before morning. Furber had followed Omensetter from the house, forgetting overshoes and gloves, but gathering his coat, scarf, hat—his priestly rigging—and putting them on as he blundered toward the river. He had no purpose. Perhaps he knew some genuine disgust. Once again, in place of feelings—speeches. On a patch of cleared ground above the beach Omensetter set the stones in piles to form a circle. Several times he returned for more, scuttling past Furber with his head down, his body bent awkwardly, one shoulder jutting forward. There was a faint splash as he stepped in the edge of the river. The pale stones lay in their piles like luminous faces. Then Omensetter stood in the middle, swaying, as dark and vague as any of the trees. The poor fool doesn't know how, Furber thought, he hasn't the least idea. The wind blew the sound of shouting up, and then withdrew it. Furber called to him and Omensetter cried out anxiously:

Furber?

What in god's name are you doing?

Furber—will you pray for the boy?

And this, Furber asked, restraining a gesture useless in the darkness.

What comes next? What do I say?

Furber ran about the circle kicking at the piles. There was a spatter of stones in the water and a rush of others in the weeds.

You'll pray for the boy, won't you, Furber? You've nothing against him—a little boy—a baby—you'll pray for him?

Do you know what your wife believes? She thinks, like any decent man, you've gone for Orcutt.

No. She knows I can't do that.

You call this feeble nonsense trusting to your luck? Is asking me to pray—is that trusting to your luck or just more madness? Neither's the least use. You've got to go for Orcutt, the baby's nearly dead of your confusion. You wouldn't listen to your wife—what are my chances? Well I don't love you, that ought to help. I think you're a monster and you are proving me right . . . I've been right about everything all along . . . if only I had believed myself.

There was more shouting—angry tones.

Listen, Omensetter—it won't be endurable. No—wait now—wait for me. She'll hate you. Don't be a—a jackassed

207

donkey, damn you, you don't want that. It's diphtheria, it's no theological disease. No witches' brew or number you can roll will cure it. You've got to go—there's no luck in this world and no god either . . . You stupid selfish fool, you blind dumb bastard, when you come to—it won't be bearable. To have had what you dreamed you had—and let it go . . . Hey, stop that. Christ. You'll never understand. Orcutt can't cure anyone. He can't do a thing. That's not the point. It's your going for him that counts, not what *he* does; it's how your girls will feel—after—how Agnes and Emerald will respond—

Eleanor . . . and Angela.

And Lucy—how she'll—

Omensetter turned and blundered off down the beach, away from the shouting.

I'll pray, Furber yelled after him, I'll pray . . . for what it's worth, he finished bitterly, knowing that he wouldn't pray at all; real prayer would embarrass him. Really, he knew no more about it than Omensetter did about his stones. Furber retreated up the slope. The snow was falling thickly now and his feet and hands were cold. Apparently he couldn't speak with his hands in his pockets. Even in the dark, they'd been out gesturing, fluttering about like moths.

So it was coming true, and he had played the chorus to his own Cassandra. That was put nice, preacher. Shit. Swearing was also an empty habit. What had he said—made up—that wasn't coming true? Aunt Janet hurls herself from the dizzy height of her ladder-backed Shaker. A pretty thought. A plaything like a horse on wheels. The choir of heaven and furniture of the earth, all those bodies which compose the mighty frame of the world—the snow now, his streaming eyes—were they just words, too, just characters, as he had always pretended? It was coming true. God was coming true, coming slowly to light like a message in lemon. Ah, and what was the message? in yet another lingo? Truth is the father of lies; nothing survives, nothing dies; only the wicked can afford the wise. And shouts through gaps in the wnid. Blasphemers are believers. And there were sermons in stone, as he'd frequently said. Wasn't it what he'd always wanted—God to exist? Deep in the weeds, peering between the pickets, he'd dreamed his revenge . . . They were closing in; there was a wagon creaking. The snow fell on him as on a tree. But he really wanted to embrace the body of the symbol. But the body of every symbol was absurd. But not when the gods were Greek. But they never, never were . . . All the while, He was, and only He has been, and only He has the brass to continue.

Oh for christ's sake, let him walk, it ain't far.

Back—back up.

Back?

Yeah, back, everybody back.

What I want's a drink. I'd sell my soul off.

It wouldn't bring the price of piss-in-your-face.

Ah shut your shit.

I'll tell you one thing—that sonofabitch didn't get up there by himself.

My eye, Furber, I got blood in my eye still.

Back, you guys, will you back?

God damn and christ—it's lots of rocks . . . How's it look now, Curtis, can you see?

By god, no more for me, not another fuckin' inch.

Meng's got diarrhea of the dingus and all his strength's leaked out.

Easy . . . jesus. He keeps sliding over on me. Listen, I ain't staying in this thing if he keeps sliding over on me. You got to keep him from sliding over like that. Sweet christ, he's cold, I tell you, cold, sweet jesus, he is—oh god, my leg—my leg hurts.

If you can feel it, you still got it. If you've still got it, what's your bitch?

Ache your belly out and bust.

You can't go far, Boylee, with that leg of yours, I guess you'll lie there nicely where you are.

I'll tell you one thing, Jethro, he didn't get there on his own—not way up here, he didn't—not on your life . . . All right now, George—push.

Oww. Hey. Owwwww. You bastards. I climbed up there for you damn you dirty bastards, when none of you dirty bastards would. You're all bastards all right, all bastards.

Easy Boylee, we're almost there. Tie your tail on.

Your ass may feel easy, but I tell you the world's been shitting through mine.

He's been dragging his. It don't feel easy, either.

Say, my eye, it hurts awful, Furb, it really does . . . You've no gloves on. What are you doing out here without no gloves on? Hey, Furber's got no gloves on.

Faith's a furry mitten, Furber, ain't it?

You should have heard how they sang, it was so sweet, like choirs: only you can do it, Boylee, they sang; fine work, Boylee, that's the boy, Boylee, climb up that ice-cold tree in the cunt-colored dark and just let down that little hanging man.

Tott's a fine soprano.

Well we missed the road someway.

Missed it—hell, you never even shot at it.

Oh shut your shit.

He came down like a rock. Branches snapped like popcorn, didn't they George?

Stitt didn't care to come down the whole way by himself. Go to hell.

He held up a bit near the bottom.

Go to hell.

Lit on a branch like a bird.

I broke some ribs, I swear I broke some ribs, it hurts to breathe.

What did Henry break, I wonder.

He broke his prick.

Like a rock. Down. Wham pop bang. You should have heard him—thunk.

Look out for that goddamn dog. That goddamn dog—he's somewhere around. I'll poison him with a stick.

Really—honest—thunk.

Here we are. Okay. Here—this'll do. Take his head, Luther. George at the middle. Out of the way, Bessie, damn it, out of the way. Ease him up. Don't bitch. Everybody knows it's cold. I'll do the bitching. Easy, easy, slow . . .

You bastards.

Howl your head off.

Henry'll keep nicely, anyway.

Who'll take care of me?

The church will, George. You're for church. The church is here. The church will care for you.

I sure hope Olus shakes a leg.

Now slide him out. Menger—the door.

Please keep the noise down, gentlemen, Furber said, that child is sick to death, remember—he can barely breathe.

Sweet sweat of jesus, I forgot, Luther Hawkins said, and he stood on the porch holding Stitt by the shoulders and the head, swearing long and deeply and with love.

Furber crawled carefully into the wagon. Henry, he whispered. His stomach ached and his face and ears burned, his head felt light, his hands and feet were numb. Snow was captured in his eyes. Henry? The coat was stiff and hard as stone—soaked with melted snow and rain, then frozen. Omensetter had said he was wearing it, a gray wool with wide pockets. Furber ran his thumb on a twig and withdrew his hand with a cry. There were a number of twigs thrust through the coat like nails and the cloth was torn. Of course—they'd been driven in when he fell. Cautiously his hands felt along the arm to the shoulder, brushing away snow. Are you in there, Henry? We can still be friends. He withdrew his hand again when it touched the belt. The cut end, how deceptively strong it was, cut halfway through and then torn the rest of the way by his weight . . . hence . . . to drop, he thought. Henry's in there, but he's in there differently. Furber placed his hands on Henry's head. Snow lay thickly in the hair. And all the while he'd had the forehead of a man who was destined to be drowned. The face was rough and icy . . . pale moon-shaped face. Unshaven, Furber decided, and then he wondered whether, even after death, it grew. He still had his woolly eyebrows. But cold . . . so cold. You've put on weight, old friend, death's diet suits. It was true that Henry was fuller in the—pecked! Furber recoiled, cracking his elbow against the side of the wagon. Of course. Birds pass. There were shapely limbs and dancing leaves. He slid the length of the wagon and lay there, shivering. He was furious with his disease and cursed it fervently. You're an old man already, Furber. You've been shaken half out of life by the effort of living in it. Ah, that would do to preach. Oh shut your shit. When he lifted his face, the snow struck it smartly, and in the light from the house he saw the flakes driven swiftly on the wind. The light was another kind of shadow, he thought, a shadow for a dry, bright so~. It spilled on the porch, running the snow, and he noticed, looking closely, that within it the darker lights of the fire drifted. Of course no soul is simple, though if that were true, if no soul were, what of Plato's grandest argument? The elemental simples cannot decompose. And why not? Of course they cannot come to pieces, but what is simpler than the shadow of a stick? There, for instance: that tuft of weed struck through the snow like a knife, deviously edged; the soul it casts is blue and sharp, though bent a little toward compassion by a hollow in the crust—a soul like Chamlay's maybe. Is compassion's line in Chamlay anywhere? Perhaps not. But the wind puffs, the shadow mists. The weed bends a little, and the soul of Chamlay pales and widens into Olus Knox. It alters altogether, not in parts. Yet cold . . . so cold. The wind blew viciously and Furber turned his face toward Henry. A simple thing but complex in its cause. Rage warmed him a little. He felt a familiar pressure on his chest and he remembered standing by the river and narrowing his eyes at the sunlight that was so merciless from the water while Arthur swam for Omensetter's hat. Yesterday he should have eaten. Flack! Where was the fellow? He tugged roughly in his anger and folds of clothing parted. Heavenly Father, You may call our soul our best, but this, our body, is our love. He lifted one of Henry's legs and let it fall like wood. How simply is our fondness for it guaranteed: we can't live outside of it, not as we are, not as we wish. So this is someone else's body now. He banged a shoe against the bottom of the wagon. Who? The snow softened the sound. Asleep? No. He was no longer living the life of sleep. It was the snow that was slumbering, coasting through these dreams. What power have You, if You can't continue us, and what cruel nature have You to refuse? The moist soul hangs about the body, too heavy to rise. How cleverly, Henry, you avoided that. Henry, listen, Omensetter was nothing, only another man. Now he is given to despair beyond any of yours. Well there you are—we all despair. Were you listening? Nothing but despair. They are in despair, and you're the one in luck. Say, you should listen. Furber shook the body. Observe how we build our cemeteries by you and shape our bodies like yours. We wish to be so like the dead, we living. But we shiver from the cold in spite of ourselves, and we hate your liberty of lying like a stone enough to envy the birds who pecked your eyes. Most of all, we envy you—that you should open them unfeeling to their bills. My god! my eyes are every minute pained by what they see. I should take strength from being blind, if I were you. Vision is no kindly injury. Furber touched Henry's hands—they're cold as mine—then the ridges of his ears. Well no human speech can reach you now. I envy that too. Furber dangled his feet over the end of the wagon. He thought of Maggie Scanlon, whose legs always hung like cracked sticks, and he swung them to and fro. Why have You made us the saddest animal? He pushed himself off and felt the jar in his bones. He cannot do it, Henry, that is why. He can't continue us. All He can do is try to make us happy that we die. Really, He's a pretty good fellow.

⌐ 10

Here's Furber, finally. Out without a boot on. Fire up, Furber. Your ears look nipped like the end of your nose. Watch for your collar or you'll have water down your back.

Stitt's voice welled from the hall. Don't bring him in here,

I've had enough, I don't want to see him any. And Chamlay said of course not, Boylee, we'll leave him outside, it can't hurt him any. Tott, you look old. Then Chamlay came to the front room unbuttoning his coat. George sat on a ladder chair holding a green polka-dot bandana over his eyes and his head in his hands while Luther and Menger warmed at the fire. They had fed it until it flamed and crackled furiously and now they held out their hands in fists, slowly unfolding their fingers and spreading them slowly into fans, solemnly and slowly revolving, keeping their hands in front of them and rubbing them together carefully when the blaze was at their backs, jigging their feet in a trot, wrinkling up their noses, wiggling their ears and making dreadful faces to loosen the skin. There was a pile of outer clothing in the corner by the woodbox and Curtis threw his fur coat down on top of his hat. Gobbets of snow were melting into slush. The slush fed pools which finally burst and ran in streaks toward the low side of the room, channeled unpredictably by the rough floor. Fixed in her rocker, upright, all her blood in her stomach, dark-eyed and staring, Lucy Omensetter watched. From time to time the baby moved and coughed in its corner and all the men looked toward it with plainly angry faces, George even raising his and withdrawing the bandana. They returned to themselves as soon as they could manage to. Chamlay smoothed his hair. His badge glittered brightly from his left suspender. It threw a brilliant dot above a picture on the wall, and as he brushed his hair with his fingers, the dot danced, and when his body twisted, it fled on the wall across Menger's chest to plunge unharmed into the fire. Menger began sucking noisily through his teeth and putting his hands over his mouth. Ache ache ache, he muttered. Luther pried his boots off on the woodbox. They fell with a heavy possessive thud and Lucy started up with a cry that she stifled with her fingers. What time is it? Two, said Chamlay. They all murmured. Furber walked unsteadily to the middle of the room. Where's the dog, he said. Luther swore in a whisper. I wish we had something to eat. He held a red-stockinged foot to the fire and wiggled its toes. Meng, see them red ones? First grade. Tott entered. Ought to get yourself some. Last like homemade. I wish we had something hot—some coffee maybe. He hopped. New thing, socks like this. Furber followed the boot tracks like a hunter, bobbing his head. George began to groan and sway. Flecks of ice still clung to his collar, flashing like brilliants. Someone come back here, Stitt was saying, I don't like to be alone. Tott sat slowly to the table and Luther spat in the fire. It had been a mistake, he said, because Stitt thought of himself as a hero now, and Stitt was simply a no account bastard. Curtis wondered whether Luther would rather have met all those limbs himself, both going and coming, and .Curtis laughed at his joke without pleasure. He rubbed his eyes and felt tenderly of the lobes of his ears. Menger thought they should have taken Omensetter with them. That was the real mistake, he said. Brackett doesn't seem to be around, Tott said hoarsely, and then looked up in surprise. I'm hoarse, he said. No, George said, he ain't around, is he? No I don't believe he is. I just guess he isn't. No. He ain't. And Chamlay wondered whether he wasn't out tending his crops; it was the middle of the morning. Yeah, he's out, George said. He's fertilizing snow. He's sowing ... Luther beat his belly, indicating hunger. He stared openly at Lucy. He balanced on one foot, arms outstretched. Lucy held herself on the edge of the rocker. She bowed like a doll from the waist, canting her chin and lifting her arms, about to speak, while her eyes, unblinking, leaped from man to man with hardly a turn of her head. Her voice wandered a moment and then sank out of hearing, her eyes teetered fearfully back and forth until, with a sigh, she slipped and her gaze fell¹ between them to the floor where it washed from side to side, repeatedly, like water in the bottom of a boat. Chamlay brushed by Furber, who tottered queerly, and Menger lifted a stick of wood, measuring the fire.

Dear lady, Furber began, gesturing strangely.

Chamlay sat stiffly at the table, drawing bills from his pocket and laying them down with meticulous care: smoothing them out, pressing them flat.

Please us and join your daughters, madam, Furber went on, rolling his eyes and looking wildly around. They are caged like birds in the backyard room.

He clutched his chest dramatically.

We shall make your cares, our cares. What shape shall you have them in? Shall they be bats?

Oh stop it, Furber, will you, Menger said.

Shut my shit, is that it?

Jesus—

Any animal, Furber shouted, and all the men stared at him, astonished. We shall take it quickly to our bosoms though they're bitten eachly—

Okay, Chamlay said, and he continued laying down the bills.

Antelope, gazelle, giraffe—

Okay!

We shall form, Furber made a sweeping gesture, one brotherly and sexless chest, a plain of duty, madam. And we,

216

from the towers, shall, and steeples of our eyes, inform you, madam, surely, on the instant that, should any incident, untoward, or—ah, the money!

Furber rushed to Chamlay's side and peered across his shoulder.

How much, how much, he hissed.

Chamlay swept up the pile and held it out to Lucy.

The rent money, missus, wouldn't you say?

Furber leaned weakly against the table, quiet except for his hands which passed frantically over his body—rubbing his face, picking lightly at his clothing, stretching his collar, plunging from there into pockets, pulling on buttons.

You comprehend the significance of this, I trust, Chamlay went on in his solemn interrogator's voice. It was found in Henry's pocket. All ones. In fact we had to pry his fingers loose. I take it, missus, that he died a short while after getting it. Would that be reasonable, you think?

Furber reached Chamlay with a trembling finger.

Easy, he whispered, but Chamlay shrugged.

Henry had his hand in quite a stubborn fist, he said. Like this money mattered to him.

Like it was a message to us, Luther said.

Furber was instantly white.

No, he said.

Well, what do you say?

Easy, Curtis, she's not herself. This is no time—she's sick with worry—wouldn't you be?—my god, be kind.

Furber spoke to Chamlay's ear, but Chamlay simply waggled his head.

It's important, missus, Chamlay said. The law has an interest, you know, he went on, a faint smile rising.

. . . interest of the law . . . I'd forgot, Lucy murmured, quite to herself.

The law has an interest. We all have an interest . . .

. . . law.

Yes. And why would a person who was about to hang himself hang on so hard to a little money?

Oh yes . . . and this . . . you said something of this, Lucy said vaguely.

Well now we have more information. Now we have Henry, and Henry's money.

Henry . . .

She drew her arms in a tightly protective X across her chest.

George removed his bandana and examined it.

When did Omensetter pay the rent, he said.

In christ's name, gentlemen, another time.

217

You'll have to tell us, missus, you know, and while we're waiting here we've plenty of time.

Time . . . yeah. We've plenty of time.

Christ, yes, time, we've sure got that. We've got no damn horses but we've got time.

Menger finally threw the log.

Someone come on back here, Stitt yelled. The lamp is smoking.

What I want to know is why would Henry hang himself so high, Hawkins said. What would be the point of it?

Funny. I shouldn't be hoarse. It's maybe my tonsils, Tott said. Did Orcutt ever tell you about his cut-rate tonsillectomy?

Hawkins pulled tenderly at his nose.

Say, how's the quality of that poky-dot, George? That was a fine lot. There's no more green in the store. I think that's right. There's no more green.

It's just a spotty snot rag, like any other, George said sourly.

Now we have Henry and Henry's money . . .

Yes . . . you have that.

Oh no it's not. The green? George—on my honor, those were first class.

What would he hang himself at all for, Menger said, blowing his nose in the fire with a crisp snap of his fingers. His life was all right. He had no complaints.

Ah there you are gravely mistaken, Menger, Furber said stepping toward him. The great theological question, gentlemen, he said, turning gently around, is not the existence of evil—no, gentlemen, heaven forbid—the great question concerns, rather, the real presence of good; and the great moral question, gentlemen, he said, still swinging slowly, is not the evidence of freedom, gentlemen—lord love us, we've a lot—but the very possibility of law itself.

What's he saying now?

Shut up, Jethro.

Shut. Shut. Shall I? Shall I shut?

Yes, godammit, shut.

I'm ill . . . ill . . . quite ill.

Jesus.

Why would he go that far in the woods, like he never wanted to be found?

George tenderly covered his eye. Out of the cold, it was swelling badly.

Someone come back here for god's sake.

A simple fracture, it looked like to me, Menger muttered.

218

Chamlay rose and flourished the bills.

Here is the money, missus, he said.

He ran a thumb under his left suspender. The dot flew.

It was in Henry's pocket—this money, here, was. He had his fist real heavy on it when he died. Like Luther says, there was a message in it, a message Henry wanted to send to his friends—at the moment of his death.

Chamlay paused.

Right in the very middle of his dying, you might say. Now Henry—you follow me, missus? you don't seem to be following—Henry was hanging in a tree when we found him, considerable high, far in the woods. He had your rent money in his pocket. You don't deny that's what it is—this money? And his fist was closed tight over it—a sign, I'd say, just like Luther says. Clenched . . . Tight . . . Quite a piece in the woods he was, and high, where no one would think to look, very high, in a tree hard to climb.

Curtis, for the love of god—

You comprehend the significance of this?

Where's Orcutt, Stitt shouted. Where is he? What's keeping him?

Orcutt, Lucy said, rising stiffly, releasing the rocker to spill its shadow up the wall.

She was still holding herself tightly by the shoulders and packing her breasts beneath her arms.

The gentle doctor, said Jethro Furber.

He's coming?

He's been sent for, yes, but he had to be hunted up . . . it's cold and now it's snowing.

Brackett went?

I'm sure he had that thought, he—

Knox went. When Boylee fell. He took our horses too, I hope, what he could gather up, Chamlay said. That was hours ago now. Anyway Knox went and not your husband to my knowledge.

You don't know, Curtis.

Furber spread his hands. They fluttered uncontrollably.

Curtis doesn't know. I talked to him and it was in his mind. I talked to him myself and I could tell. It was surely his intention—

That murdering bastard, Hawkins said.

You detestable jackal, filthy swine!

Furber wobbled across the room and fell on Hawkins who held him away in surprise and then with a laugh pushed him down into the pile of clothing which shifted and gave way under him, rolling him off.

Boy, you've changed the roll on your piano, he said.

Chamlay was angry. George took down his bandana and said: I can't open my eye—see?—it's swollen shut. Menger faced the fire, muttering rapidly. Finally Furber turned up and sat quietly, saliva running from his mouth.

You speak too previous, Luther, nothing's proved, Chamlay said. Like I said, missus, where we found him he was high. He had no reason to hang himself. And he had your rent.

Why don't you ask her where he is, Curt? What the hell, let's find out something.

Wait now, Menger, hold a moment. I'm doing this, and that was coming up.

Chamlay fluttered the money.

Ones, he said. Now what would your opinion—missus—be? I say, and Luther says, it was a sign. What do you think, missus? What would you think if you was us? What do you say?

She fell quietly, uncaught.

Stitt began to shout and George to rock in his chair, cradling his head.

I'm not used to this—it hurts.

I know, Georgie, just relax, Menger said.

I think I heard the back door, Luther said, I think those kids went out. You've boots on, Menger, go and see.

My brother's hurt, Menger said resentfully.

Chamlay put the folded money neatly on the table and placed his hands gingerly over his ears. Furber was carefully gathering her up.

She's too heavy for me, he said, but everyone kept their eyes averted and no one offered to help. Jews tear their clothes up, Furber murmured, struggling. Wise.

He wavered in front of Chamlay.

You know how long it's been since I've eaten?

Chamlay did not reply. He tenderly touched his eyes with the tips of his fingers.

We're well met, madame, Furber said, may I make a lewd suggestion?

Stop babbling, Furber, Hawkins said, you make me sick. A flag-switcher—you sonofabitch.

I am Philly Kinsman, the celebrated bandsman, Furber sang, you fellows may have heard of me.

Help Jethro with her, Luther, will you, Chamlay said, he's unable.

No help from swine, Furber cried, beginning to move. I didn't believe, he whispered to her, I only imagined; I never knew, how was I to know that what I said was true?

Chamlay jerked about and leaned over the table to peer

through the front window, rubbing circles on the glass with his sleeve. Tott had hidden his head in his arms.

Singing, Furber lurched down the hall.

And I've a dick that's like the stick I use to beat the boom-a-lay.

Hawkins laughed.

Nuts—just nuts.

Stitt began obscenities.

Olus Knox and Doctor Orcutt, red-faced and tightly wrapped, burst in, snow swirling around them, snow on their caps and collars, snow in the creases of their mittens, snow up their legs to the thigh.

Well Orcutt, Chamlay said, it's good you're here.

Good, is it, Orcutt said, stamping his feet and shaking himself. I've never been so cold. Everybody best be dead or in that neighborhood.

Knox put Orcutt's case on the table, sniffing and puffing and milling his arms. Snow fell in clouds from both of them.

Orcutt! I'm bled out and broke up and no one comes to sit by me, the bastards. Orcutt! They are no damn good, Orcutt, none of them.

Dear me, that's Boylee, Orcutt said, uncoiling his scarf.

My eye—it's my eye—I ran it on a branch—it's swollen—look.

Well George, morning. And Luther. Meng. Everybody here, hey, waiting. How about coffee?

I'll see if there is some. Menger, hunt them girls. You've boots.

Come on back here, Doc.

Well easy for a moment till I warm, Orcutt shouted. Is that dear Henry's carcass in the snow? Aaah. My noble beard is frozen, look at that. A bad sign. A poor beginning. It's really Henry, eh? Olus told me a liar's story. And so he departed, as our good friend Furber would say, much mourned, but not missed. Whew. And where is Furber? Didn't he come out here with you? Is that him lurking in the hallway? Olus said . . . um . . . and there's the child? Well. No noise from him.

How's old Emma, Doc? I heard that you was out along her some this morning.

Well she's sad, Luther. Not so sick as sad. She's took syphilis from the Sioux. Struck down in the prime of her age.

Luther roared and struck the wall with his fist.

I'd never have trusted that Indian on my place, he finally managed. You could tell he'd have a dirty-feathered shaft.

Well, like they say these days, Luther, the only good Indian's a lead one.

Hawkins roared again and rolled off down the hall. Furber stepped back to let him pass.

Hawkins, come in here, Stitt yelled.

I've lost my glasses.

They're in my case, I think, remember, Olus?

Orcutt stood in front of the fire for a moment, enduring a spasm of shivering.

How is Emma, really, Doc?

She's old, is all, Curt, merely old.

Orcutt kicked off his boots. Then he tugged at his beard, leaning into the fire, combing the beard with his fingers.

Let me toss on another.

The wood fell in the fire with a crash and a shower of sparks flew up the chimney.

Orcutt bent over the cradle, silent a good while. How long, he said quietly. No one answered. How long has this been going on? Dammit.

He knuckled his eyes.

Where are the parents?

He straightened quickly.

Bring me my case, please, Olus, thank you. Diphtheria all right. As early as I've seen it in an infant. And bad, Olus—you were right. Where are the parents?

She fainted and Furber put her somewhere. Omensetter's outside somewhere—gone.

Orcutt hesitated.

What are you saying, Curtis? Somewhere? put her somewhere?

Chamlay shrugged.

In the other bedroom, I suppose.

Orcutt blinked.

Furber's here then. Well.

He bent over the cradle again.

Damn these eyes. The wind like to blown them out. Gone, you say? out, hey? somewhere. So Furber's here though. He'll be needed, like as not. Where'd Omensetter get to?

I don't know. Furber thought he might have gone for you.

Orcutt paused a moment in his manipulations, then went on. The baby squeaked.

A simple infant, he said. Utterly neglected. It's criminal. And all this thumping about in here . . . you lummoxes . . .

He shook his head and slumped with weariness.

Bad, Truxton?

Like I said, Olus.

Any chance at all?

Not really.

Diphtheria . . . it's a terrible thing.

Orcutt sighed.

Men, in my experience, are the worst disease, he said.

Then he slowly bent again to his inspection.

11

Orcutt was not disposed to be pleasant. He ignored the question. He sipped his coffee.

We've business here ourselves, Truxton.

The self-appointed.

Someone has to. It's no pleasure.

Ain't it? Well, you'll not mind if I've no patience for it—fresh out of that. But I can figure what you're up to, you been hitching to it all along. It ain't completely usual in you, Curtis . . . I'll say it ain't good either. That sort of thing can wait, don't pile it up on top of all of this. You must be numb inside and that's a fact.

None of us is numb, we've got our feelings—the whole town has its feelings—and I'm surprised at what you say. My feelings—everybody's—they're just the same—you know that. Why, we *harbored* him. From the time he dragged his horse and bragging wagon into town, he made himself at home here. We took him in. Sure—Henry and Watson mainly—but everybody some. You've got no memory for it? the little time it took and what he's done? So you might say my feelings—all ours here—are just for everybody.

You're doing everybody's feeling for them, hey? Medically, that ain't easy.

Dammit, Truxton, you know what I mean. The problem's plain enough, and so's our duty. You should have heard the way that bastard talked when we came out here.

Duty, hey? Delightful word. The *mons veneris* of morality. So considerately short a noise too, duty is.

Orcutt blew on his coffee.

What a curious thing you are, though, Curtis, to speak of duty here so early on such a snowy morning when everyone is thick-eyed from sitting by the fire all night and tipped down in the mind. Or is that your notion?

What's eating on you?

Curtis—know what a doctor's duty is? He swears to it, you know. He takes a sacred Grecian oath. To do his duty.

Orcutt wiped his mouth.

Well it's two thousand years old—the oath is—but that don't help it any. What can a doctor really do, Curtis—ever think about it? I've been at it a long time now, and I know what I can do. Nothing. I sit around and drink coffee. Pass the time of day. It's a damn silly oath, really—pretentious and silly.

Oh well, Truxton—

Sawed both legs off a boy once that was smashed by a wagon. His mother says to me before I leave— I got his legs in a burlap bag his father kindly lent to me—you must be tired, do have tea. Red hair she had like a forest burning, and deep green eyes. So I did. I had tea. It was good tea, Curtis, most excellent of the green kind, carefully cooked, one of the best cups I ever drank—like this coffee now that Luther has so nicely boiled for me.

Look, really Truxton—jesus—

Only thing bothered was the blasted bag. He give it to me and he says: get them off the place, get them away. I drank my tea with the sack resting on my feet. I don't know what she thought it was, maybe she knew. I just prayed it wouldn't leak onto her rug. It didn't though—a little blood on my socks was all.

For god's sake, Truxton, we've been through enough.

I remember another time when I was holding the hand of a fellow in a coma—nothing to do but sit and look wise while the organs of his body ate on one another—a long night, it was, too, before he died—well, his son was sitting in a chair over by the door—he was maybe fifteen, maybe more—and he and I were the only ones in the room with his pa and his pa's snore—and the whole time, the whole time, mind, the whole time this boy sit there by the door looking down, hunting a picture of his hate in the floor, I don't know, but looking down and muttering over and over just loud enough for me to get it: I hope you die you bastard, die; I hope you die; die die die. Finally, you know, I just up and screams at him—thump thump thump, he'd been going, die die die—I yell to shut up, but he wasn't a person, he was a drip from a pump—thunk thunk thunk—die—that's all—and I had to get up and tilt back that chair and haul his ass out of that room like he was heaped up in a barrow ... singing his little tune.

God. Tell them about the cut-rate tonsil—

The old man died of course, like he'd been told to, and then that crazy fool kid went in the barn and fired a shotgun at his head.

Doc? Hey, it's hurting again.

Let me tell you something funny about poor Boylee— we've lots of time.

Time . . . yeah. We've plenty of time.

Christ, yes, time, we've sure got that. We've got no damn horses but we've got time.

Doc—tell them about the—

Well several years back when the tail of the Hen Woods burned—remember?—Boylee was out there fighting the fire and one of the Dilluth children—they've moved since, remember them?—climbed up a tree to watch the blaze—and it was something to see, too—so anyway, while he was watching he caught his foot in a crotch and got it stuck there. Well, as you can bet, he was howling something fearful as the fire burned down to him. Boylee was there too, running wild around the bottom of the tree and yelling like a fool when I rode up with Watson. Mat climbed up there easy and took him down. It wasn't hard, but Boylee—well, I just figure Boylee was afraid a little. Surprising, ain't it? Real scared, he must have been. It's interesting . . . Of course it wasn't snowing then, the twigs weren't frozen into nails and the bark icy, and of course it was broad day and the boy was a mere fifteen feet up, maybe, if that, and the climb— well—the kid had got there. Funny, ain't it, how things happen. Boylee's been mad at me ever since, just because I was there to see him do his dance, and maybe because I laughed so hard. Course the child was alive too, not shit on and bit up and hung out like Henry Pimber.

So you felt him over.

Ah—morning, Jethro—how's it feel to be awake? Good nap?

You touched his eyes.

Well—no . . . no—did you? I just figured it. A dramatic note.

A lie, in short, that's perfect truth. I can understand that.

Look, Truxton, I've been asking you a natural question. You know it's natural. There's plenty of reason for wondering. What do you think? Could he have?

Oh well—how high was he?

Seventy-five, eighty, wouldn't you say, Luther? Hey—you asleep?

No—christ. I'd say eighty easy.

About seventy's right, Menger said.

That high?

Orcutt thought a while, his nose over his coffee, inhaling the steam, his hands warming themselves at the cup.

That's high. It's more a matter for the preacher, seems to me, he said, nodding at Furber who was sprawled on the coats in the corner like a dead crow. He could have seen clean to Columbus from up there. It's hard to tell what a man will do if he's warmed up to it—Boylee for instance.

Why work so hard to kill yourself, why sweat?

And why so high? Didn't he want to be found?

To get shit on by birds like you said.

He'd have fell out of there some time, what was left of him.

The rain would have run right off him.

Well the wind would have dried him good.

Yeah. And the cold would have come on and held him a long time just in the shape he was. He'd have been well kept and damn near sound till summer.

That coat wouldn't have held him. The belt would have broke.

Well his branch did.

Was Boylee nesting on it?

No, I don't think so. He was on the one below it. He cut Henry loose and then he lost him—a cold load, I bet—and when Henry went he busted Boylee's branch off too.

Well, Orcutt said, I'm sorry I missed that. That must have been something. All my life I'll be sorry I missed it.

That's all right—Tott'll tell you about it till you're sick of it.

What do you suppose he went along for?

Without a single reason I can see to do it—that's what gets me.

He was getting well. He was okay—right, Doc?

Sure. What the hell was the point? He was okay—right?

If he goes to execution in a chariot, and I in a cart or by foot, where is the glorious advantage, Furber quoted.

Orcutt felt of his beard and brushed it with his sleeve, happier now it was soft.

It's hard to figure, he said. That's high. Eighty's high. No ladies here? Ah then I'll chew. I must have a chew here somewhere.

He felt himself.

You know I took that sack away on my mare—she could smell it too, she reared around and fished to beat the devil—and I was maybe a mile on the road when I hear galloping behind me and it's father in a lather. The child is dead, he says, and I say that's too bad—it sure was no surprise—so I say that's too bad—what do you say, anyway, time like that?—and I get ready to give him back his money as I figure that's what he's come for, and well, I don't mind if it makes him feel any better, you know. But he says, holding out his hand in a smart-ass way, give me back the bag. The bag, I say, surprised, why? We want to bury him together, he says back, furious with me for being witless. You wouldn't want us to bury him in pieces, would you, separated like that from himself, he says, horrified. And he snatches the bag and gallops away, holding it out at arm's length, the thing beginning to wet its bottom and to swing and kick about by itself like he had a living chicken in it. Ain't that a funny one? Ah.

Orcutt finally dredged a piece of tobacco from his vest and carefully picked off the lint. With one hand he unclasped his knife and deftly sliced a generous hunk.

Just from the physical side you understand, he said—the other's outside science—my guess would be he wasn't strong enough to do it. Not by half. He'd been greatly sick, poor Henry had, and he was never what you'd call a powerful man, not in body surely, or in spirit either I should say. Not enough strength in him and not enough gumption.

Orcutt began chewing, closing his teeth slowly, and sighing as pleasure took possession of him. He leaned into the wall.

Well wind didn't blow him up there.

Well maybe Windy, Wise, and Noisy did.

With a fireman's carry.

The spirit moved him. Reverend, what do you think?

Henry's out there, why don't you ask him, Doctor? And he's smiling.

Furber sat up in a tumble of clothing.

Luther, please bring him kindly. Thawed, he'll speak. He was as hard as Christmas candy once before, when he was sick, remember? Set him right there nicely—by Chamlay the Beastly Badger, or by Ezra and Bessie, who've crossed their hearts in the table—or there, where Orcutt's leaning so in solemn silence, sunk in his dirty pleasure.

Furber rummaged in the pile.

Henry's eyes are out, but his tongue's in, I think . . . Ink.

He picked at a mitten.

So the Lord says . . . ah . . . I am the Lord, says the Lord; I make all things. I stretch forth the heavens alone. I frustrate the omens of liars. Ha ha. I make diviners mad. I turn wise men backward and their asses inside out, and make their knowledge foolish . . . At last here come the monkeys on the horses.

Hold yourself together, Jethro, don't go to pieces. You have responsibilities here.

Do I go to pieces, Doctor? Here's a riddle: why am I so cold upon your faces? That's most unseemly in a man of my position, eh? . . . No answer. Then I shall keep my own good company.

Draped in hats and scarves and overcoats, Furber struggled to his feet.

Let's see: there'll be A to admire me, he said, ticking A off on the finger of a glove he had drawn only partly on so the finger flopped when he touched it.

Then there'll be B to bless me; C to cherish me; D . . . to undress me; E? to encourage me; F to—fondle . . . fondle . . . what an odd word. As ink. All as in ink. Ink's odd.

Hawkins laughed.

You look a sight.

He sounds a sight.

I shall recite a limerick of my own composition. It's very topical.

He held up an admonitory finger.

There was a young man of De Pauw—

The originality, my churchling smirkers, does not reside in the first line. Pffitt.

There was a young man of De Pauw,
who begot a giraffe with his jaw.
When compelled to admit it,
he said that he did it,
to repeal the Mendelian law.

It don't mean anything to me.

Sit down, Jethro, we've still got business.

But my dears—there's more:

All mankind now started to wonder,
concerning this cosmical blunder.
If giraffes, by this pass,
can be got by an ass,
Who's the papa of lightning and thunder?

Say, Furb, that's pretty good. That's not so bad.

Then cried the Archbishop of London,
we are all quite certainly undone.
What such a jaw can,
an Anglican can,
by belling his balls with a bludgeon.

Whoo-ee, man. Whoo-ee.

> By blowing his balls through a blowgun.

Whoo—
Furber, you're disgusting.
Don't be a pill, Olus. Furb, I didn't know you had it in
you.

> Olus is a sticky pill,
> he will make you sick,
> he will.

Hey—good—he caught you right off, Olus.

> However this fraud from De Pauw,
> who claimed to have broken the law,
> broke down and admitted
> 'twas not his jaw did it,
> but his god father's beastly guffaw.

Hah—
Thank you, your gracious appreciation is applauded.
I'd like to settle some things in my mind, Furber, if you
don't mind, Chamlay said.
A minister? A clown, Tott said. Lots of times we've had
him in our house.
You smut muzzling mutt, Furber shouted.
Sit down, Furber, sit down!
But E's here to empty me—watch—he's wearing pink and
has a passion to enter me. D's here to disparage me—there's
nothing he can say, I'm black inside my clothing, black as
ink. And then C—to chastise me, send me to Gilean, stripe
my back. B to blame, to bully, to bluster, to bitch ... A? A's
last—to admonish me—no, surely more than that—no,
perhaps to administer, nothing comes after.
Hey how do you think up those things?
But draw near here, you sons of the sorceress, the seed of
the adulterer and the whore.
Furb—
You didn't know I knew the table of the elements.
It's quite a trick to make up poems like that.
Oh art is everywhere admired. And A is anger, or anguish,
or ague, or agony ...
Quick a trick.
As in ink.
How do you think up all that?
Stop baiting him, Luther, and let's get on.
The Reverend Andrew Pike's my muse.

What's he saying? who?

Oh it's that preacher, Luther, years ago, who was scalped by the Indians, Tott said.

Bait? Did someone say, bait?

Shut—

The righteous man perishes and no one takes it to heart.

He was quite a ladies'—well, an Indian-maiden man, you might say.

T is for Tott and for tattletale. A greedy young spinster—hear that, Totty?

> a greedy young spinster
> ate, live, a lobster
> and now every winter
> when she sits dinner
> as a kind of remonster
> he pinches her inner.

Sit still, Bessie.

How about it, Doc?

Merciful men are taken away and no one minds.

With Curt there glaring at me? Ah, no thanks. Curt's heavy in his head and I'm heavy in my eyes.

Unfortunately, Olus said, Furber's the one that's light of tongue.

Do something with him, Tott yelled.

Wraps, said Furber, squashing a hat on his head and whirling a muffler around. God is kind ... Hello ... Good day ... The weather's fine ... Good hat. Good coat. Good glove. Oh God is kind. Say, against whom are you sporting yourself, pink pants? against whom are you making a wide pink mouth, and drawing out the tongue? are you not a child of transgression, a seed of falsehood?

Look Doc, Chamlay said, let's try to get on in spite of that.

He gestured.

I intend to get on, he said.

H is for snotspittle.

Jesus. Someone shut him up.

Kind cat. Kind dove. Kind dog. Kind gnat. Oh God is love. You should have listened to me. Then you should have had peace like a river. Henry's having some. He's smiling ... smiling ... Love this. Love that. Love lip. Love lap.

I'm here to settle this Pimber business in my mind, and I'm going to—no matter what.

H is for gorgespew.

Aaah.

Dear sweet kind cow. Dear sweet good goat. Dear black blind bat.

Come off it, Furber. That's enough. Dump all that stuff and settle on it.

Why am I so cold upon your faces? Answer: because I am the master of the resting places.

Is he drunk or something?

He's trying to keep Curt from his questions, Tott said. I know him.

Feed the fire now. Keep each your places. Soften Henry's mouth. His ghost will speak. It's out there now, hanging stiffly in him like a drying onion.

Fetch me my bag, Olus, will you? I don't know where it's got to.

Here's a fur hat for a hunter. Prosper the beetles.

Leave that stuff off, Furber.

A muffler from mother. It's like kitten cover. And body is to spirit as—these gloves to a lover.

I'll see if I can give him something—calm him some—he's had a seizure.

Don't worry about him, he's a toothless little weasel.

T is for truthlessness. T is for tickle my tummy and I'll tickle your testicle. T is for touch me not or for tit for tat.

Let him be, he'll settle. He's all done in.

This Omensetter then—I say we should go out and get him.

Don't fire off hasty, Curtis.

Hasty, hell, I go by natural steps, by god, one at a time.

I'll bet he's lit out. I'll bet that's what he's done. He's lit.

And leave his wife?

It's his neck—why not?

Why not, says Tott. Bessie, will you draw your breath in pain to tell our story? It's Omensetter's neck. And a neck's a neck. It's quite a lot. Why not? Says Tott.

Will you shut up, god damn it, will you?

Oh you *are* hoarse, you're *very* hoarse. I believe you've *caught* something.

Boylee's strong, and Boylee had a time up, Chamlay said, holding out an open hand to Orcutt and folding in a finger. And like you say, Henry had no strength at all, he said, folding in another. So I conclude that Henry didn't get up where we found him by himself. Chamlay formed a threatening fist. What do you say, Doc? Want to bet, he said, fanning his other fingers. Lucy Pimber says the last time she saw Henry, he was off to Omensetter's to collect the rent.

Chamlay bent a finger. That rent was on Henry when we found him. He folded back another. So, he said—they met. Both fists drew angrily together, though Chamlay grinned.

Step by step, eh, Curtis, Doctor Orcutt said.

One more step, by god, and you'll be standing on him.

Give up if you want, George. You was always quick to fold, but I think I'll call him. Ah. Thank you Olus. I've got some sort of pill in here.

To pour in the porches of my ear.

Somewhere . . .

Never mind him.

. . . if I can find it.

We got all these Omensetters here now. Menger got them girls in. I say let's find him, Hawkins said.

I say he's lit.

So you can hunt him, Bessie, like you hunted for Hog Bellman?

What do you know about that?

I've heard you tell it.

Hawkins laughed and said: you ever hear a tale that Tott told honest? He's a glory awful liar.

. . . a liar . . .

You like to talk about the law, Curtis—ah, here it is—but the law won't like it. Here they are. One is all you take now—maybe, in a bit, another. . . . Jethro?

Furber said: then you shall bring forth that man or woman who have committed that wicked thing, you shall bring them forth to the gates, and there you shall stone them with stones until they die.

Will you give off groaning, George, said his brother.

Orcutt might as well have spit in my eye for all the good he done me, George said.

You said you were calling, Curtis said. I've more cards.

Ah, maybe. But you're not all that strong. There's cards you ain't got, for one thing—not yet anyhow. Now the way Henry's hanging—up so high—that's a high card, Curtis, like you say, but whose hand's it sitting in? Boylee's strong, you say. Boylee had a time. Okay. How strong would a man have to be to climb up that tree with a dead man hanging to him somehow? I hope you don't think Henry was alive then?

Why are you playing his hand?

Furber said: at the mouth of two witnesses, or three, shall he that is worthy of death be put to death, but at the mouth of one witness he shall not.

He'd be a dead weight, Curtis, all the way. And then he'd have to be hung out there and tied.

Chamlay slammed his palm down.

232

Jethro—that pill now . . .

We've hearts like the teeth of dogs, said Jethro Furber, crouching in the clothing.

Like I said, there're facts you haven't got yet. Have you looked our Henry over careful? Was he strangled? broke his neck? Hah—maybe he was shot. Or cut his throat with a razor, or died of the drizzles and the trot.

Ah—shit—Doc—

There'll have to be an autopsy—that's what I'm saying.

Listen, Furber said, when I was a little boy and learning letters—A . . . , B . . . , C . . . , love was never taught to me, I couldn't spell it, the O was always missing, or the V, so I wrote love like live, or lure, or late, or law, or liar.

Furber wiped his nose noisily on someone's sleeve.

Look, he said, if it comes to law, I'll testify. I'll tell the truth for the first time.

Get out of them coats, god damn it.

I'll say I lied. I lied and lied. I spread hatred against him— all by lies. I turned myself against him—with my lies. I folded his own heart back against itself, and burned it black with lies. And after my lies, he spelled love: luck.

Get him to swallow that, will you, Doc.

I turned the land against him—planting it with lies. His wife was turned against him; his children turned against him—from my lies. I turned Mat, and all his friends, and all of Gilean, against him—through my lies. I put it in your minds to be against him—all by lies. I turned even God against him—by my lies.

Take Doc's pill, Jethro, said Chamlay gently, you're just not well now. Everybody knows it's not in you to lie, whatever else—

With lots of water now—it's like a square one. You need any help to get to the kitchen?

Menger's asleep, that sonofabitch.

Careful, George, you've both the same ma.

I've a fuckin' eye.

I wish I could sleep. I'm dead, but I'm nervous somehow, Hawkins said.

Well put, Puker—dead but nervous—yes. Henry has a lively twitch.

Hawkins swore.

He'll leave, Furber now said earnestly. He promised me. He'll leave.

All those questions you've been asking, Curt: why would he kill himself? why would he choose the middle of a woods? why would he hang himself so high? why would he hold so tight onto that money? why this? why that? well you can ask those questions new again, if you think Omensetter killed him. There are just as many, and the same ones.

So no one would find him. It's simple, Doc. He just hid the body.

That's right, you're no bait, bodiless . . .

Hey—he's by the baby.

You okay, Furber?

Oaky . . . I am oaky . . . Yes, yes, coming . . .

Anyway, Omensetter found him, Tott said, sitting up. No point to hanging him so high in that case, seems to me.

Throw off suspicion, Curt said.

Didn't throw yours off, did it, Orcutt said.

It threw yours!

Oh, Curt's suspicion's all inside him, Tott said. Past his underwears.

Very good, Bessie. Why you're *grow*ing! There's no end—

Shit.

You say shit to a preacher? shit?

Anyhow, it would have been lots easier to bury him, seems to me, Knox said. Lots of easy places.

That's it, Jethro—in the kitchen—get some water.

In a fish, Furber said. I also know a man who's buried in his brother. And then I know another . . .

Menger's asleep, that sonofabitch.

If the ground was frozen, Curt said, then how easy? if the ground was frozen?

. . . another . . . here's another, I know—his tablet reads:

> Mary was my wife,
> and Mary was my mother,
> merry was my life,
> until I met my brother.

Still, Curt, there are a dozen better places: rocks, brush, river—

> He stole from me my wife,
> he stole from me my mother;
> he stole from me my life,
> lest I should love another.

Bravo, Jethro—not a bad tune, boy.

Not with the ground hard as marble.

But Curt, for god's sake, it wasn't, Olus said. We'd had only a few frosts when Henry disappeared, and the ground was easy.

This pill will spell love literally, and sleep my bittering tongue, but should I swallow?

234

How do we know, though—how do we know that Henry was murdered the moment he disappeared.

Come on, Curt—come on.

Okay—so Omensetter waited with the body. He had Henry hid somewhere—a barn, a basement. Or maybe Henry went away—Cincinnati, Columbus—and then when he came back, Omensetter—

. . . towns beginning in C . . .

Ah, nah. Straws, Curtis. They won't hold you.

Chamlay flatted the table.

Besides, you cut the knot.

Shit on you Tott.

Furber spoke through his hands. They curtained his face.

The river, the boy, they beckoned him to Gilean—and now he's done—love's out between them like a candle. Curt, you weren't here, I was, I sat in a corner like a sensitive chair, like their daughters, dressed thinly in despair. No— come to Gilean, the child, the river, told him—come to Gilean, the capital of human nature. And now he knows. There's no further injury that we can do them—his wife or the girls. They will live on like we live, most likely . . . I knew a woman once who fell from a chair and died. We can't keep them anymore in Gilean—question or try them. That will merely injure those of us who've any feelings left—not them. And Curt, we have a trust—as a capital city—we have a responsibility.

Give it up, Curtis. Furber's right this time. They'll soon be leaving, Orcutt said. After they bury their boy as they'll be needing . . . Omensetter didn't kill Henry, though he may have the child on his conscience. He had no earthly reason.

Reason?

Yes, Orcutt said impatiently, a reason, a reason why.

I've got this fuckin' eye.

Reason, Furber murmured in surprise. He had no earthly reason . . .

Then Furber's body shook with the spasms of uncontrollable laughter, his mouth gaped and his chest heaved as if he were Brackett Omensetter himself in the deep bend of his luck, though not a sound emerged, only the whistle of his breath, and a few tears squeezed from the corners of his eyes. The seizure passed before anyone could raise a hand, and Furber, giving them a frightened look, threw the doctor's pill in his mouth.

Orcutt rose and went to the window.

Come on. The snow's stopped. It's light. Let's see what we can do to clear ourselves away.

12

Jethro Furber's illness lingered into February, a kind of joint pneumonia and madness, Doctor Orcutt said; and Mr. Clifford Huffley helped with Christmas and was even now arranging for Good Friday. He was a large ruddy man with sandy hair and he would preach his ordination sermon on the first March Sunday. Lucky thing to get him, everybody said, a boy so near and squarely put together. He hoped to remodel; perhaps he'd add. There was also talk of a new affiliation. Miss Samantha Tott would have a tea next week, inviting only ladies, and Mr. Huffley, then, would tell them how his father, as a missionary, died in Haiti.

Cancer bleached poor Flack's skin gray. Drunk, the Hatstat brothers had a harmless fight. Then the Bencher hound, to everyone's dismay, dropped through the soft Ohio ice in broad daylight.

The Omensetters had moved down river—children, horse, dog, wife, and wagon—no one knew quite where; and it was Israbestis now, no longer Doctor Orcutt, who claimed it had been Henry's purpose all along, in hanging himself in that tree like a trinket, to throw suspicion on Brackett Omensetter. Nearly everyone agreed that with Chamlay so furious against him, Omensetter had been fortunate indeed to escape the blame. The infant lingered on alive, an outcome altogether outside science, Doctor Orcutt said, and Israbestis swore that Omensetter's luck would be a legend on the river—quite a while, he claimed—perhaps forever.

Mr. Huffley had a busy winter; nevertheless he sat with Reverend Furber often, praying earnestly. Consequently he was at Jethro Furber's elbow, gently steering, when one sunny afternoon, the sick man went out walking. The Reverend Furber's cane poked the crust, and once, when he slipped, he swore like a sailor. Mr. Huffley, smiling vacantly, looked away toward Zion. I wonder what will become of me, Huffley, Furber said; but at once he went on hastily: no, that's silly; what's going to become of me, has become. Mr. Huffley, however, was bracing.

Furber's only visit was to Mrs. Lucy Pimber, also convalescing. She had cut her hair and shorn years. He offered her the money that was found on Henry's body, but she refused to touch it, leaning toward his palm and counting. So that's what he was getting for the place, she said, at last radiant.

Doctor Orcutt, who was also treating Brackett Omensetter's frost-eaten feet and fingers, had suggested to Mr. Huffley that he might pay a call of charity upon "that place of desolation," but Mr. Huffley reported that two wild girls had twice flung stones through the woods at him.

Furber chuckled.

Really, he said. Stones, eh? Were they real or virtual?

They didn't hit me but they hurt my feelings.

Ah, well, they were spiritual, then, the worst kind. It was one of that sort that brought darkness to Goliath.

In Furber's opinion the new man had small management of words, little imagination, no gift for preaching, and a narrow chest, but from his bed, Furber heard a boisterous choir, and the lusty voice of his replacement leading. This determined him to slip what he called Henry Pimber's hanging money in one of Mr. Huffley's bright new offertory envelopes before he left.

Other Recent American Novels You'll Want to Read in SIGNET Editions

THE LOCKWOOD CONCERN   by John O'Hara
A national bestseller, the century-spanning saga of a family in pursuit of money, power, status, and sex, set in the "O'Hara" country of eastern Pennsylvania.
(#Q2876—95¢)

HURRY SUNDOWN   by K. B. Gilden
The sensational bestselling novel in which a group of intensely human characters become involved in every kind of conflict when the rival forces of tradition and progress make a battlefield of their Southern community.
(#W2860—$1.50)

WANDERERS EASTWARD, WANDERERS WEST
      by Kathleen Winsor
Ranging across the continent, this is a shocking novel of bold men and women, from the rugged mining camps of Montana to the ruthless business of Wall Street, the people who shaped America. By the author of *Forever Amber*.
(#Y2822—$1.25)

YOUNGBLOOD HAWKE   by Herman Wouk
The massive bestseller about a young novelist from the Kentucky hills—a man of great talent who rockets to success and piles up and loses fortunes in a dazzling career. By the author of *The Caine Mutiny* and *Marjorie Morningstar*.
(#Y2325—$1.25)

FLOOD   by Robert Penn Warren
Old crimes and forgotten indiscretions haunt the citizens of a Tennessee town on the brink of disaster.
(#Q2611—95¢)

THE LIBERATION OF LORD BYRON JONES
      by Jesse Hill Ford
The powerful bestselling novel portraying the drama behind racial conflict in a small Southern town. "A remarkable achievement"—*New York Times*.
(#Q3043—95¢)

SHIP OF FOOLS   by Katherine Anne Porter
The big bestseller by one of America's most distinguished literary figures, in which an ocean voyage becomes a microcosm of life itself. (#Q2333—95¢)

THE BLUE GUITAR   by Alex Austin
A strange novel about a love affair between a girl and her blind brother, and of the woman who turns their life into a nightmare of torment. (#P2710—60¢)

SIGNET Short Stories You'll Enjoy Reading

SELECTED STORIES OF JEAN STAFFORD
Sixteen stories, ranging from Colorado to Germany, from the world of the child to that of the adult, by a writer hailed by critics as one of the best in America.
(#T2830—75¢)

BUBBLE GUM AND KIPLING by Tom Mayer
Stories about a young man of the American Southwest, some of which have appeared in *Harper's, The New Yorker,* and *Story Magazine.* (#P2769—60¢)

THE GRASS HARP and A TREE OF NIGHT AND OTHER STORIES by Truman Capote
Two brilliant books in one: an enchanting novel of small town people rebelling against their humdrum life, plus a compelling short-story collection. (#T2918—75¢)

SHORT FRIDAY AND OTHER STORIES
by Isaac Bashevis Singer
Remarkable tales, translated from the Yiddish, in which demons, witches and angels turn up in everyday life, whether it is lived in a Polish village or in Brooklyn.
(#T2770—75¢)

ROMAN TALES by Alberto Moravia
Stories of the exuberant life in the back streets of Rome, by Italy's greatest living writer. (#S1612—35¢)

CAST A COLD EYE by Mary McCarthy
Sharply etched short stories by one of America's finest satirists, author of *The Group.* The book also includes a short novel, *The Oasis,* which has been long out of print.
(#T2380—75¢)

THE LONELINESS OF THE LONG-DISTANCE RUNNER
by Alan Sillitoe
Stories of tough, defiant, and humorous men from the lowest depths of England's grimy industrial cities. By the author of *Saturday Night and Sunday Morning.*
(#P2629—60¢)

THE BEST READING AT REASONABLE PRICES

signet 🥚 paperbacks

SIGNET BOOKS *Leading bestsellers, ranging from fine novels, plays, and short stories to the best entertainment in the fields of mysteries, westerns, popular biography and autobiography, as well as timely non-fiction and humor. Among Signet's outstanding authors are winners of the Nobel and Pulitzer Prizes, the National Book Award, the Anisfield-Wolf award, and many other honors.*

SIGNET SCIENCE LIBRARY *Basic introductions to the various fields of science—astronomy, physics, biology, anthropology, mathematics, and others—for the general reader who wants to keep up with today's scientific miracles. Among the authors are Willy Ley, Irving Adler, Isaac Asimov, and Rachel Carson.*

SIGNET REFERENCE *A dazzling array of dictionaries, thesauri, self-taught languages, and other practical handbooks for the home library.*

SIGNET CLASSICS *The most praised new imprint in paperbound publishing, presenting masterworks by writers of the calibre of Mark Twain, Sinclair Lewis, Dickens, Hardy, Hawthorne, Thoreau, Conrad, Tolstoy, Chekhov, Voltaire, George Orwell, and many, many others, beautifully printed and bound, with handsome covers. Each volume includes commentary by a noted scholar or critic, and a selected bibliography.*